Protectors of the Guardians

Ashlynn Carter

Copyright © 2024 by Ashlynn Carter

All rights reserved.

No part of this publication may be reproduced, distributed, or transmitted in any form or by any means, including photocopying, recording, or other electronic or mechanical methods, without the prior written permission of the publisher, except as permitted by U.S. copyright law. For permission requests, contact Ashlynn Carter at ashlynn.carter@proton.me.

The story, all names, characters, and incidents portrayed in this production are fictitious. No identification with actual persons (living or deceased), places, buildings, and products is intended or should be inferred.

Book Cover by Ashlynn Carter

First edition 2024

Part One

Chapter 1

Mason followed close behind his parents as they moved through the streets. Oliver walked beside him. Even though there were four years between them, the two brothers were close. Oliver often watched over Mason when they came to the village. Now that Mason was ten, he was sometimes allowed to go to the river to fish with his best friend Clay while their parents were shopping.

A man's loud voice pulled his and Oliver's attention to the fountain that marked the center of the village. There was a large crowd that was forming there. The man was standing on the wide top of the fountain wall. He was pacing as he waved his hands through the air. His shouts were met with murmurs of agreement.

"Father, can I take Mason to see what is going on over there?" Oliver asked as he continued to study the growing crowd.

Lord Caverton glanced over at the fountain before turning to his sons. "Oliver, if things become too heated, you are to come find me and your mother. And Mason, you stay close to Oliver. This errand won't last long, so do not go down to the river."

"Yes, sir." Oliver and Mason said in unison.

Mason was a little disappointed he wouldn't be able to meet up with Clay. But his curiosity about the man and crowd took some of the sting away. He and Oliver hurried down the walkway, eager to figure out what was going on. Just as they reached the corner, Mason bumped into a woman in a white dress.

"Pardon me, my lady." Mason bowed as he apologized. When he straightened, he noticed a girl holding tightly to the woman's hand. She looked about his age and was dressed in a white gown as well. She was pressing herself so close to the woman that she was nearly hidden within the fabric of the woman's skirts.

The woman smiled down at him. "I should be the one apologizing to you. I fear I was not watching where I was going." She gave a curtsey before glancing down at the girl. "Come along, my sweet. We must hurry if we are to be back in time to assist with dinner preparations. And we are very sorry for bumping into you two gentlemen." She once again curtsied before stepping around Mason and Oliver. "Anna, everything will be completely fine. You do not need to fear others. We are safe here." She said in hushed tones, but Mason still heard.

He wondered why the girl would be frightened as he followed close behind Oliver. His experiences had taught him that people were generally nice and often helped each other. Especially those around the village. They looked out for one another. It didn't matter what your station was in life. If someone needed assistance, there was always someone there to help.

They pushed their way through the mass of people until they could see the speaker. He was short with a large bald spot on the back of his head. His face was red as he gave his impassioned speech.

"They will destroy us all!" The man swept his hand through the air as he glared out over the crowd. "The White Witches may look innocent but that is what makes them so dangerous. They lure you into a false sense of calm, only to kill our families and friends that have the ability to shift. Some of these witches can even control your thoughts with a single touch. I implore you; we need to rid Arlania of their hatred and violence!"

"We have never heard of any shifter being killed in the area." A man called from the back of the crowd.

"They have killed many from my village south of their castle. They may not have attacked this village yet, but it is only a matter of time. They kill adults and take children to use in their rituals. Twelve children from my village have gone missing this year alone."

"Come on, Mason." Oliver whispered as he grabbed his brother's arm. "We should let father know."

They ducked low as they wormed their way back through the crowd. More and more people were gathering. Many of the men looked angry. Mason was scared. His father was a shifter. Would the White Witches come for him? As they ran across the road to the store, Mason caught sight of the woman he had run into earlier. He pulled Oliver to a stop as he watched several men surround her and her daughter.

"You have no right to be touching my daughter." The woman snapped at one of the men.

"I doubt she is your daughter, witch." A man growled. "How do we know that you didn't steal her away from her family."

"She looks completely terrified." Another said.

"She is terrified because you tried to take her away from her mother." The woman glared at the men cornering her.

"Oliver, what's going on?" Mason asked in alarm.

"That woman lives at the White Castle. I think they think she is one of the witches." Oliver said quietly.

Mason swallowed hard. The girl's gaze met his and he could almost feel her fear. Her eyes were a startling light blue. He had never seen anyone with eyes the same color as hers. Tears streaked her cheeks as she cowered behind the woman. The group of men tightened their ranks, and Mason could no longer see the girl or woman clearly. Only flashes of white could be seen between the men. Suddenly a scream filled the air.

"Run, Anna!" The woman yelled. Her voice was filled with fear and pain.

Shouts and calls for someone to stop preceded Oliver grabbing Mason's arm and pulling him into an alleyway. Mason followed his brother, even though he was confused and scared. At the end of the alley, they spotted a flash of white before it disappeared around the corner of a building. Oliver slowed their pace as they approached.

The back of this building was against the forest. Mason spotted the girl. She was crouched in the foliage. She was shaking and pale. Her dark brown hair fell in curls around her shoulders. Her eyes were filled with fear.

"It's okay. We can help you." Oliver whispered as he glanced over at the alleyway. "Come with us and we can hide you." He pleaded.

The girl looked between them but didn't make a move to get up. Men's voices caused Mason to jump. He moved to her side and grabbed her hand. "They will find you if you stay here." He whispered. He could feel her trembling.

The girl got to her feet as she clung to his hand. Oliver didn't waste any time as he started to run toward another alleyway. Mason followed his brother while holding tightly to the girl. They paused at the entrance to the street. Oliver peeked around the corner before stepping out onto the walkway. He slipped into the first shop and held the door for Mason and Anna.

Their parents were talking with the storekeeper on the other side of the shop. Oliver pointed to the table of ribbons. Mason looked over at it. It was small with a white tablecloth that reached down to the floor. He looked back at Oliver who gave him a nod.

A shout from outside had Mason pulling the girl with him as he crawled under the table. He fixed the tablecloth so that they were both hidden. The girl continued to shake beside him, so he put his arm around her in an effort to comfort her. She whimpered when the shop door banged open, and several angry men entered.

"Lord Caverton!" One called.

"Mr. Jetson." Lord Caverton sighed. "I have told you that there is no reason for us to be concerned about the occupants of the White Castle."

"There is reason to be concerned. They have kidnapped a young girl. We tried to get her back, but the witch refused to hand the girl over!" The man yelled.

"What?" Lord Caverton asked in surprise. "Where is the woman and child?"

"Father, can I speak to you for a minute?" Oliver asked quickly.

"Oliver, I must see to this."

"Please. It is important."

There was a brief pause before Lord Caverton spoke. "I will be right there, Mr. Jetson." The shop door slammed shut and then footsteps approached Mason's hiding place. The girl curled more into his side as her shaking increased. "What is it, Oliver?" Lord Caverton whispered.

"Father, the man at the fountain was yelling about White Witches killing shifters and taking children. Then when Mason and I were coming to find you, we saw several men surround a woman in white. They said she kidnapped a girl, but she claimed the girl was her daughter." Oliver said quickly.

"Where is your brother?"

"He is with the girl." Oliver's voice barely reached Mason. "They hurt the woman, father. She told the girl to run."

"Where are they?" There was a small pause. "Faith, stay here with Oliver. I need to see what is going on." Footsteps retreated.

Mason rubbed the girl's arm as they waited. She was tense as she continued to shake. Time passed slowly as he held the girl. Her fear was palpable. Mason's legs started to cramp from sitting for so long. Her head settled more against him, and he looked down at her. Her eyes were closed, and she was no longer shaking. Mason listened as Oliver and their mother talked quietly nearby. The door to the shop opened and he tensed.

Seconds later, the tablecloth lifted and his father's face appeared in the opening. His face was grim as he motioned for Mason to come out. He looked down at the girl who was staring at his father in fear. "Stay here." He whispered in her ear before crawling out.

"The girl too." Lord Caverton said.

"She is scared." Mason told his father.

His father glanced at the table as he thought. "But she trusts you, Mason. I need you to ask her a few questions." Lord Caverton told him what to ask her and then he walked to the other side of the store.

Mason climbed back under the table. The girl watched him warily. "What is your name?"

"Julianna." The girl whispered.

"I heard the woman call you Anna." Mason said.

"My mom calls me Anna for short, is that okay with you?" Anna snapped.

"So, she is your mother?" The girl nodded and pulled her knees to her chest. "Where do you live?"

"The castle on the hill." Anna looked at Mason with pleading eyes. "Where is my mom? Can we go home now?"

"I think my father knows. Come on, we can ask him." Mason started to climb out, but Anna scooted farther back as she shook her head. "I will stay with you. And my mom is here too." Mason watched her with concern.

Someone knelt down next to Mason. He looked up to see his mother. "Are you all right, dear?" she asked Anna. Anna scrambled to Mason's side and clung to him. She tried to use his body to shield herself.

"Mother, where is Anna's mom?" Mason asked, putting an arm around Anna.

"Your father knows." Faith answered softly. "Anna, would you be okay with accompanying me to speak with my husband, Lord Caverton?" Anna shook her head as she pressed herself more into Mason.

The only way they were going to know where Anna's mother was would be by asking his father. He didn't want to leave her alone, so he got to his feet and grabbed Anna's hand. She pressed herself close to him. It was almost like she was trying to disappear into him. He gave his mother a nod before following her to where Oliver and his father waited.

"Allen, this is Anna. She wants her mother." Lady Caverton said softly.

Lord Caverton crouched down, and Anna flinched before ducking behind Mason. "Hello, Anna. I'm glad that my boys were able to help you earlier." Anna didn't respond. Mason watched his father hesitate before speaking again. "Would you come out from behind Mason so I can talk with you?" Anna shook her head and squeezed Mason's hand tighter. After several minutes of no one moving, Lord Caverton sighed. "Anna, your mother can't come to you."

Anna tensed and she did not seem to breathe for several long moments. "Did father find us?" she asked quietly.

"Who is your father?" Lady Caverton asked.

"Faith, now is not the time." Lord Caverton said. "Would you be okay with us taking you back to the castle?"

Anna nodded as tears once again coursed down her cheeks. Mason followed his family outside while still holding tightly to Anna. She was shaking and he was worried about her. Who was her father and why was she afraid of him? Mason stopped near the horses and waited for Oliver to mount Granger, their buckskin gelding. They had ridden double when coming into the village today.

"You are next, Anna." Lord Caverton reached for her. She screamed and dropped to the ground, curling into a ball. Mason knelt down next to her and touched her arm lightly. Her arms were over her head as if trying to protect herself. "Mason, see if you can get her to let me help her onto the horse."

"Yes, sir." Mason replied before turning to Anna. "Anna," he whispered. "My father only wants to help you onto Granger. He is a gentle horse. There is no need to fear."

"Lord Caverton, you knew where the girl was the whole time?" Mr. Jetson came stomping up.

Lord Caverton moved to stand between Mason and the angry man. "I am taking her to her home."

"We don't know where that is." Mr. Jetson snapped. "She would be better off coming with us to the orphanage until her parents can be found."

Anna uncurled herself before throwing her arms around Mason's waist as she watched Mr. Jetson. "You still don't get it, do you?" Lord Caverton said through clenched teeth. "The fear in that child is not because she was kidnapped. She is terrified of men and all she wants is her mother. You have made that impossible. I have already informed the magistrate of your crime, Jetson. If I were you, I would turn yourself in before things get ugly."

"Mason, help Anna onto the fence and get her on Granger." Lady Caverton quietly instructed.

"You would turn an innocent child over to those witches?" Mr. Jetson roared. "We didn't save her from the witch only for you to give her over to the whole lot of them."

Mr. Jetson became irate. He tried to move closer to Anna, but Lord Caverton shifted into his wolf form. His wolf had thick brown fur and blue eyes. Lord Caverton growled at Mr. Jetson, keeping him away from the kids. Mason quickly helped Anna climb the fence. Anna shook her head when Mason told her to climb onto the horse behind Oliver.

"Anna, it's okay." Oliver gave her an encouraging smile.

Mason could see the worry in his brother's eyes. "I will get on behind you, Anna. I just need you to get on first and hold on to Ollie."

After a brief hesitation, Anna put her leg over Granger's back. Oliver reached behind him to help hold her in place. His father growled and snapped at Mr. Jetson when the man tried to make a run for the horse. Mason quickly got on behind Anna. He put his arms around her and grabbed onto Oliver's shirt.

"Boys, head out toward the castle trail. Your father and I will follow you shortly." Lady Caverton whispered.

Oliver kicked Granger into a trot and Anna gasped. Her grip on Mason's arms was painful, but he didn't say anything. After they were a mile down the road, Oliver slowed Granger to a walk. He steered them into the trees and took a parallel path to the road. None of them spoke, even after they reached the fork that branched up toward the castle.

They waited in the trees for almost an hour before they heard the sound of a wagon on the road heading in their direction. Oliver backed Granger farther into the trees to keep them hidden. The wagon stopped and Mason held his breath. Anna had gone still as well.

"Oliver?" Their father called.

Oliver let out a tense breath. "We are here." He called back, nudging Granger forward. In seconds, they emerged onto the road. Their parents were sitting on the bench of a wagon that was pulled by two horses.

"Good job, boys. How is Anna?"

"Scared." Mason answered.

"Let's get her home." Lord Caverton flicked the reins.

The horses pulling the wagon began walking. Oliver pulled up alongside them. Everyone remained quiet as they travelled. Mason didn't know much about the occupants of the castle, but it was well known that they didn't like uninvited visitors. As they drew close enough to see the gates of the courtyard, three women stepped out into the road, blocking their path.

"Can we help you?" The one in the middle asked.

"Would it be possible to speak with your leader?" Lord Caverton asked.

The woman in the center whispered to the girl on her right. The girl then ran into the castle grounds. "What business do you have with us?" she asked.

"We have come with tragic news and to deliver something to you."

"Very well. We shall wait for the Matriarch." The woman said. The harnesses on the horses were the only sounds for several minutes. Mason let go of Oliver's shirt and put his arm around Anna's waist as they waited. Her grip on his arm tightened a little as she leaned back against him. A woman with long white-blonde hair came walking quickly towards them from the castle.

"Good afternoon. My name is Miranda, you asked to speak to me?" Several more women emerged from the castle. They were all tense as they studied the Cavertons.

"Miranda." Anna called softly.

"Anna!" Miranda gasped. "Where is your mother?"

Anna started to cry, and Mason pulled her tighter against him as he hugged her. "My lady, might I have a word with you, out of earshot of the children?" Lord Caverton asked. He climbed down from the wagon before turning and helping his wife down. They walked over to Miranda and began a quiet conversation. Miranda covered her mouth after several minutes, and her eyes moved to the wagon.

"And Anna, was she injured?" Miranda asked as she began walking toward Granger. They were positioned near the rear of the wagon.

"She was terrified and only allowed our youngest son, Mason, to touch her." Lady Caverton answered.

Miranda reached up and Anna practically dove into the woman's arms, nearly knocking Mason off of Granger. Mason slid off the horse and stumbled forward a step when he hit the ground. Anna was sobbing against the woman. He wanted to go to her but held himself back. She kept trying to talk, and Mason was only able to catch a few words here and there. Mommy. Bad men. Knife.

"Thank you for bringing back our Anna and Bridget. We will return your wagon to you, Lord Caverton." Miranda held tightly to Anna with tears in her eyes.

"There is no need for that. I purchased the wagon solely for this purpose. You are free to keep it and the horses." Lord Caverton lowered his voice. "I didn't tell her. I figured she would take it better from you considering how she reacted when she first saw me."

"Thank you, sir." Miranda whispered. "You have done so much for Bridget and Anna. Is there a way we can repay you?"

"Just take care of the girl and try to stay away from Woodbury village. There is much unrest, and it is no longer safe for you and your people. I will make sure that Mr. Jetson is brought to justice for his crime." Lord Caverton gave a quick nod before helping his wife onto her horse that was tied to the back of the wagon. He untied the reins and handed them to her.

Mason looked away from his parents and back to Anna. She was staring at him over her shoulder as she was led away. Anna lifted her hand and gave him a small wave. He waved back. Mason was lifted and set on the back of Granger. Once he was settled, Lord Caverton untied his own horse and mounted it. Mason didn't want to leave, but Oliver guided their horse back down the mountain road.

"Father, why was Anna so scared of you?" Mason asked once they reached the fork.

"Mason, do you remember that dog in the village last year that was afraid of men and boys?" Mason nodded. "Do you remember what happened to him?"

"He went to mother, and she took him to a friend's house in the country."

"Do you remember why he was scared?" Lady Caverton asked.

"Because some boys hurt him." Mason furrowed his brow. "Did some man hurt Anna?"

"That is what I am thinking." Lord Caverton said quietly.

"Do you think it was her father?" Oliver asked. "She seemed concerned that he had found them."

"We will probably never know the answer to that question." Lady Caverton sighed. "Boys, the women that live at the castle like their solitude. You are to leave them be. Your father has also warned them about the rumors circulating. It would be dangerous for them to come to Woodbury again."

Mason thought about what his parents had said. It didn't make sense. He was taught to respect and protect girls and women. Why would a man or a father hurt his child and wife? His father adored his mother. He knew that when he grew up, he would treat his own wife the same way. Were the women at the castle really witches? Did they give Anna over to people who would hurt her? Why would someone make up something like that? There had to be some truth to it, right?

Chapter 2

Anna woke up from another nightmare drenched in sweat. They occurred almost every night since that fateful day four years ago. Nothing she or Miranda did, helped her escape the moment she watched as a man stabbed a knife into her mother's chest. She had told Anna to run as she used her Guardian's Gift to slow down time just long enough for Anna to make an escape.

Then there were the boys that had helped her. The Caverton brothers. Miranda said that their father had done a great service in bringing Anna and her mother's body back to the castle. Every year on the anniversary of that day, Lord and Lady Caverton would drop off a bouquet of flowers and supplies for all the Guardians. Not that they knew the occupants of the castle were Guardians.

Anna splashed cold water on her face as she tried to shake the memory of her mother's death. They had come to the castle to try to escape. To be free and safe. But that was short lived. They had only been there for two weeks. Her mother offered to go to the village to get some fabric to make Anna some more dresses.

Deciding to forgo breakfast, Anna made her way to the west wing. The library was located there. She went to her favorite spot, an alcove tucked out of sight to most of the room, and sat with her book. Anna had found a way to cope with her fear and loss through her studies. Miranda had taken her under her wing, teaching her everything she could.

They were currently studying the differences between the cultures in Valencia, Arlania, and Freynia. She loved learning, but she hated having to go over anything to do with Freynia. The books Miranda had given her to read were not accurate as to how the country really was. According to them, Freynia was a big trade country that specialized in fighting and steelwork. They created everything from swords, shields, and guns to jewelry, plates, and toys. They were a harsh people because the land was harsh, but they thrived in trade.

Anna knew the truth. The people of Freynia were barbarians who thrived on killing one another. They lived in Clans. She and her mother had been part of the Crossford Clan. Her father was one of the higher-ranking Clan members. As such, he had a certain image to uphold. He had frequently said "a woman without bruises had a soft husband." And there was no room for soft men in Freynia.

Women were seen as possessions. No better than a good sword or a bag of food. The dogs were treated better than most of the women. Men were in charge of everything, including the education of the girls. Her mother had said it was to make sure the women weren't poisoning their minds with thoughts that contradicted what their purpose in life was. Ever since she could remember, Anna was instructed on her role in the world. She was to please her husband in any way he saw fit and to produce sons.

From the age of five, she was told what was expected of her when she turned sixteen and married Mr. Hawkshaw. Her skin crawled at the thought. Mr. Hawkshaw was more than thirty years her senior. Being the second daughter born, she was completely worthless. The only thing that stopped her father from killing her as a baby was the fact that her eyes were a unique shade of blue. Mr. Hawkshaw had seen her and had made an offer for her. Before she was a week old, Anna was promised in marriage.

It had taken her mother eight years of planning before she was finally able to take Anna and run. They fled to the country south of them called Arlania. Six months on the road had led them to a tavern where they overheard a conversation about a castle of women. They left that night. A week later, they were standing before Miranda.

Anna shook her head. She just needed to get through these lessons so she could move on to the next topic. She took a deep breath and let it out slowly. Maybe she should tell Miranda that she was from Freynia, so they could skip it.

"Miranda, you aren't listening to me." Sasha hissed as they stepped into the library.

"I have been listening, Sasha, and the answer is, no." Miranda said calmly.

"Where is your precious little Anna?" Sashas sneered.

"She is either sleeping or eating breakfast I imagine." Miranda sighed. "Why do you have to talk about her in such a way?"

"She is not a Guardian, Miranda. She doesn't belong here. The only reason she was allowed to be here in the first place was because her mother was a Guardian."

"She is not a Guardian, yet." Miranda stated. "You did not receive your gift until you were twenty-seven years old, Sasha. What makes you think she won't get her gift in the next several years?"

"It doesn't matter. The Guardian's Castle is a sanctuary for Guardians, not orphans. Why not send her to the Cavertons? They seem interested in her."

"They bring flowers for her mother's grave each year. That does not mean they want to take her in. It doesn't matter anyway because her home is here, Sasha. I will not hear another word on this matter."

"Do not touch me, sister." Sasha snapped. "Why don't you put your gift to good use and influence some man to marry you? Maybe then you will keep our sacred knowledge within the family instead of imparting it onto some stray."

"That is enough, Sasha. I am the Matriarch. I decide who to share certain knowledge with." Miranda sounded irritated.

"You really need to find a man. You could even bring him back here." Sasha huffed.

"That wouldn't be a good idea." Anna said without lifting her head. She wasn't trying to eavesdrop, but it was inevitable when she was stuck within earshot.

"Of course, you are here." Sasha snarled. "And why would Miranda finding a man be a bad idea, precious Anna?"

"Prophecy twelve says that the day a man is brought within the Guardian's walls, will be a day of death and destruction." Anna glanced up.

"Well, aren't you just full of knowledge?" Sasha glared at her.

"Sasha, that is enough. You are the one who asked." Miranda reprimanded. "Anna has a mind for learning."

"You are enabling her. She is plenty old enough to be sent out into the world now. I know of someone who could use an extra maid." Sasha folded her arms over her chest. Her long nails tapping in agitation.

"Anna's home is here. We are not sending her off. If that is the only thing you needed to speak to me about, I think our business is concluded."

Sasha huffed as she whirled around and stomped from the room. Anna hid her anxiety by turning her attention back to her book. She was so grateful to Miranda for keeping her here. She had a deep-seated fear of men, thanks to growing up in Crossford and watching several men kill her mother. She didn't know what she would do if she had to leave.

"You should have made your presence known when we walked in." Miranda scolded gently.

Anna closed her book and looked at Miranda. "I was here first. How was I supposed to know that your conversation was meant to be private? This is the library after all, and not a private office."

Miranda sighed as she sat next to Anna. "You are a very smart girl, Anna. You know when a conversation is meant to be private. You have a habit of trying to blend into the background to avoid people." Anna pulled her knees to her chest and wrapped her arms around them. "I don't know your story before coming here, but I can only imagine the loss of your mother only added to your desire to be invisible."

"I had the dream again." Anna whispered. She had the dream every night but maybe bringing it up would change the subject from her past.

Miranda was quiet for several minutes. "We have a Guardian that came to us two months ago. Her gift allows her to erase part of someone's memory." Miranda rotated to face Anna more fully. "I have been debating on bringing this up to you for several weeks."

"You are suggesting I remove the memory of my mom?" Anna asked in surprise.

"No, dear. Just her death. If you choose to do this, I recommend writing out every last detail of that day. That way you have the written documentation of the event in case you want to revisit it, but the memory would no longer plague you."

Anna bit her lip as she thought about it. Miranda stood and moved to the nearest table and sat. She gestured for Anna to join her, and their lessons began.

* * *

Anna spent the next three days writing out everything she could remember about the week before and after her mother died. She was not sure how much of her memory she would lose. She didn't want to forget anything about her mother. Especially how her mother was on that day.

Her mother had seemed so much more optimistic than she usually was. Like she was less burdened. Finding the Guardian's had been a huge relief. Since she had a second daughter, her life was to end on the day that Anna was married off to Mr. Hawkshaw. All Anna remembered of her father was his physical abuse, lessons about her future, and cruel words. He kept her other siblings away from them. It had broken her mother's heart to be taken from her two sons and daughter. Anna had never even met them, as far as she could remember.

But the day she died, she seemed to have decided to embrace life again. She had even told Anna several times while in the village that there was no reason to fear. They were safe. Oh, how wrong she had been. Men in Arlania were just as quick to anger as the men of Freynia. They did nothing unless they got something in return.

Anna stood from her writing desk and picked up the journal she had written everything in. She moved to the corner of her room and pulled up a lose stone that she and her mother had pried up when they first arrived. She placed the journal among her other treasures. The locket her mother had worn, The Crossford Clan symbol that was sown into all the garments of the girls to brand them, and the few coins they had were in there.

After sealing away her past, Anna left her room to find Miranda. It didn't take her long. She was in the library preparing for a council meeting. Anna stepped silently into the room. She hesitated for a moment before clearing her throat. She was so nervous, but it was time. She needed to rid herself of the nightmares.

"Miranda, I am ready to see Ginger." Anna's voice came out a little louder than a whisper.

Miranda turned to face her. "Are you sure? Have you written down your memories?"

"I have. And yes, I think it will be good for me in the long run." Anna wrapped her arms around herself as her nervousness increased.

"Very well." Miranda gracefully walked toward the door and led the way down the corridor. A few minutes later, they reached some of the private living quarters. She knocked on a door at the end of the hall and waited. When the door finally opened, Miranda smiled. "Might we have a few moments of your time, Ginger?"

"Of course." A tall, thin woman stepped from the room. Her hair was fiery red, and her face was covered in freckles. "What can I do for you."

"This is Anna, the girl I told you about." Miranda gestured to Anna, who was standing against the wall with her head bowed. "She is needing your assistance."

"I see." Ginger studied Anna. She wore a worried expression. "It might be best if we go to her bedchamber."

The trio made their way to Anna's room. Once there, Miranda closed the door before turning to face Ginger. "Anna needs your help in pulling a memory."

"What kind of memory? I need to know details so that I might extract the right one." Ginger gave Anna a reassuring smile.

"The day my mother was killed in front of me." Anna whispered. Ginger glanced at Miranda, who gave her a nod. Anna proceeded to tell Ginger about the day and event.

"I must tell you, my gift does not allow me to just lift a memory of that magnitude from someone. I have to go through your mind to find the right one. Once I do, I will need to erase the full day. If I just do the singular event, you will have shadow memories. Your mind creates its own version of what happened in order to fill the unexplained empty gap. At times, it is worse than what originally happened. If I do a full day, there is less of a discrepancy and your mind accepts the loss."

Anna nodded in understanding. She was instructed to lay down. She took several deep breaths as Ginger settled on the ground near her head. The redhead placed her hands on Anna's temples. Miranda grabbed her hand as Ginger told her to relax.

Suddenly, Anna was transported back to Crossford. She was forced to stand near the wall as she watched her father beat her mother when she was barely old enough to walk. Then she was five years old and was overheard telling a boy to leave another boy alone. Her mother was knocked unconscious so that her father could finish beating Anna. It was a fast, agonizing replay of her life. She was taken from one horrible moment to another. Finally, she was at the day she had seen every night for four years. Time seemed to slow to real time as they approached the village.

She watched as if trapped in her dreams again as the day unfolded. When she finally cried herself to sleep on Miranda's couch, the day started over. This time it seemed to fade to blackness as the day progressed. She could no longer remember what had happened a moment ago. This time when she fell asleep with Miranda, she felt like something was missing.

Someone shook her shoulder. Anna's eyes flew open, and she looked around. She thought for sure she would be in the small cabin in Crossford. She was in her room in the basement of the castle. Miranda had a look of concern, while Ginger stared at her in disbelief.

"How are you feeling, Anna?" Miranda asked.

Anna blinked a few times. "I have a slight headache, but I think I am okay."

"I had no idea you came from Freynia." Ginger stated.

Anna froze as she stared wide-eyed at the woman. "That...I...No one is supposed to know." Anna grew anxious.

Miranda looked between the two of them before laying her hand on Ginger's shoulder. "Whatever you saw in Anna's mind should be erased from your own, don't you think?" She suggested. "After all, a person's mind is a private place."

Anna watched in amazement as Ginger raised her hands to the sides of her own face and closed her eyes. After several minutes, her hands lowered, and she blinked rapidly. "Is that all you needed to discuss with me, Miranda? I mean, if Anna does want to have her memory erased, I would be more than happy to help."

"No, I think we have all the information we need. Thank you, Ginger. You are free to go." Miranda stood and walked Ginger to the door. "Get some rest today, Anna. We can pick up our studies in the morning."

Anna stared at her closed door for several minutes. She had never once seen Miranda use her gift on anyone, but she was grateful. Her past and her memories of Freynia were things she was not wanting to share with anyone right now. She laid down and thought of her mother. Their life in Freynia and their desperate escape. Her mother was gone now. She knew that, but she couldn't remember how she had passed. Anna furrowed her brow as she tried to remember but it was no use. She would need to talk with Miranda about that later.

Chapter 3

The day was overcast with a slight breeze. The grey clouds hung low in the air, giving the day a depressing feel, matching the atmosphere of those gathered in the cemetery. It rained most of the night. Luckily, the storm seemed to have stalled its deluge.

Mason stood across from Oliver. His eyes stung as he helped slowly lower the casket into the ground. Mason swallowed hard when the casket reached the bottom of the grave. He dropped the end of the rope. He just stood there, unable to pull his eyes from the pine box.

A hand settled on his shoulder, and he glanced over at Oliver as he stood beside him. They both turned their attention back to the grave as the preacher began the service. Nothing can prepare you for such a loss. Especially one so tragic.

Mason had gone fishing with Clay three days ago. The next day, word came that Clay was found along the road near the White Castle. They had planned on going hunting that day. Clay had been on the way to Mason's house when he died. Authorities had no idea how he had ended up there. According to the doctor, Clay had drowned, but there was no body of water anywhere near him and he was completely dry. What made the death even more unusual to Mason was the fact that Clay was a great swimmer. He couldn't understand how he could have drowned.

Mason shook his head. He felt the loss of his best friend deeply. He clenched his jaw to keep his emotions in check. He could get through this.

The service ended, yet Mason couldn't bring himself to move away from the grave. Most of the people began to leave. A hushed conversation to his left caught his attention.

"I am telling you, Carol; it was the witches that killed our son." Mr. Harold, Clay's father, said angrily.

"We don't know that." Mrs. Harold wiped the tears from her cheeks. "There is no way for us to know for certain if it was them."

"Lord Carson was warning us about the witches and their ability to control elements." Mr. Harold's face was going red.

Mason had heard Lord Carson and several other men talking about the residence of White Castle. For years, they have been warning the people of Woodbury about the witches. Mason had listened to a lot of their speeches. They had a point. If the women had the abilities that the men claimed, he could see how they could be dangerous. Mason had lived near the castle all his life and still didn't know anything about those who called it home.

"They drowned our son. Yet no one is doing anything about it." Mr. Harold stomped off, leaving his crying wife alone.

Mason moved to her side. "Mrs. Harold, I am so sorry for your loss." he said quietly.

"Mason, I'm so glad to see you here." She gave him a wobbly smile. "I know you two were very close."

"Yes, Ma'am." Mason looked down at the ground. "Is what Mr. Harold said true? Did the witches kill Clay?"

Mrs. Harold sighed. "There is no evidence that would suggest such a thing."

"There is also no other plausible way for your son to have drowned miles away from any body of water and he was near their castle." A man moved closer to them.

"Mason, it is time to go!" His father called from the coach.

Mason expressed his condolences one more time before walking towards his father. He climbed into the coach and sat on the rear facing bench next to Oliver. He stared out the window as he thought about what Mr. Harold and the man had said. He hated the thought that the women of the castle could have killed his best friend. An image of a scared girl with light blue eyes came to his mind. He wondered if Anna was safe. Was she living with murderers? Was she going to become one herself?

They made it home, and Mason went directly to his room. He didn't want to talk to anyone at the moment. If his parents knew his thoughts, he would no doubt have to sit through a lecture about taking rumors with a grain of salt. And how the residents of the castle have never shown any level of aggression.

He knew all of this. He tended to believe more in their innocence than not. But there was still a small part of him that questioned and wondered if they could have killed Clay. There was no other explanation. The witches had to have played a part in his friend's death. He just needed to figure out what he could do about it.

*   *   *

It had been two years since Clay Harold's death, but he was still talked about frequently. His death was still a mystery. Oliver and Mason stood in the shadows of the bakery as they watched the crowd continue to grow near the fountain.

"This is getting out of hand, Mason." Oliver shook his head. "Lord Carson is stirring up more and more trouble. Nothing good will come of this."

"To be fair, he does have a few good points." Mason shrugged as he listened to Lord Carson as he called for justice. "If the women at the castle do have the abilities he claims they do, they could be quite dangerous."

"Mason, father and I have the ability to shift. Does that make us inherently aggressive and dangerous?" Oliver turned to face Mason with a lifted brow.

"Of course not." Mason scoffed. His father and brother were some of the nicest men he knew. They were continuously serving others and dedicated their lives to making Arlania a better place. Oliver was even moving to the Capital in the next few weeks to start school to be a lawyer.

"Why do you say that? We shift into predators. We have the potential to easily kill humans." Mason just stared at his brother. "There are numerous cases of Shifters attacking other Shifters and humans. Some are even killed. Father has prosecuted the aggressors."

"But..."

"So why would these women be considered dangerous for having abilities?"

Mason looked back across the town square. Oliver had a point. "I guess you could be right. But what about Clay? How did he really die?"

"We will probably never know the truth. Dad said that Clay had a large bump on the back of his head, which many people seem to forget." Oliver pushed away from the wall. "I'm not discounting the possibility that one of the women of the White Castle killed him but that is only one possibility."

Mason nodded as he followed his brother to the livery stables. They mounted their horses and road back home. As they were passing the fork that led to White Castle, Mason slowed Granger to a walk. "I will meet you at home. I have something I need to do."

"Leave the castle alone. Mother and Father would not like it if you disturbed them."

"I know. I wasn't planning on going up there." Mason rolled his eyes.

"Be careful, Mason." Oliver kicked his mount into a gallop and continued down the road.

Mason watched until his brother was out of sight before dismounting Granger and leading him into the forest. He found a sturdy branch and tied him to it. He backtracked to the spot where Clay's body had been found. Mason sat on a large boulder as he stared at the ground. Why was Lord Carson and the other men he associated with saying the women at the castle were witches and murderers if they weren't? Why was Clay killed and by whom?

His head snapped up when he heard a stick break in the forest. He watched as Lord Carson, three men and a woman walked from the trees. They paused when they saw Mason sitting there.

"Hello, young man." The woman smiled at him. Her voice was high pitched and somewhat nasally.

Mason slid off the rock and dipped into a quick bow. "Good afternoon, my Lady. And to you, Lord Carson. Sirs." Mason bowed again.

"Young Mr. Caverton, it is a pleasant surprise to see you today." Lord Carson smiled.

"Not many people like to tarry so close to the castle." The woman glanced around.

"I am on my way home. I figured I would stop and pay my respects to Clay."

"Clayton Harold?" Lord Carson asked. Mason nodded. "You knew him then?"

"Yes, my Lord. We were close. He was actually on his way to my house when..." Mason cleared his throat and looked down.

"I see." Lord Carson said thoughtfully. "I am sorry for your loss."

"Thank you, sir."

"What are your thoughts on the tragedy?" The woman asked.

"Ma'am?" Mason looked up in confusion.

"I am sorry. I failed to make introductions. Mr. Caverton, this is my wife, Lady Sasha Carson. My Dear, this is the youngest of the Cavertons, Mason."

"Pleased to meet you, Mr. Caverton." Lady Carson dipped into a curtsey. Mason bowed in return. "Do you have any thoughts on what happened to your friend?"

"His death was a tragedy, my Lady. He was my best friend. Clay was frequently at my house and his absence has been felt." Mason swallowed past the lump in his throat.

"What do you think should be done about the witches that killed him?" Lady Carson asked.

Mason glanced at Lord Carson before returning his attention to Lady Carson. "I think whoever is responsible for his death should be brought to justice."

"What would be the justice?" One of the men asked.

"I am no judge." Mason shook his head.

"I have a hard time believing that you don't have an opinion on what the witches should face for killing young Mr. Harold." A man said.

"You believe the witches killed him?" Mason asked.

"There is no one else who could have done it." Lord Carson stated.

"Mr. Caverton, the women of White Castle are witches." Lady Carson said firmly. "I have met several of them in the past. One has even manipulated my mind through touch. I have seen what they are capable of. They seek power by eliminating shifters and creating chaos."

Mason stared at the woman in surprise. She looked so sincere, and he did not see any sign that she was lying. He didn't know what to do or say. He swallowed hard as he glanced at the castle. Anna was up there. Was she safe?

"I have heard rumors that they use children for rituals," Stated Lady Carson.

"What kind of rituals?" Mason asked. His only thoughts were for the safety of the girl he had helped take to the witches six years ago.

Mason felt sick as he listened to Lady Carson. How could someone make up such disturbing things? After hearing how the witches acquire their powers, Mason headed home. He was eager to put distance between himself and the castle. The Carson's had told him that he was too old to be a target, the witches favored victims that were ten and younger. That knowledge didn't help.

His thoughts kept turning back to Anna. She had been a few years younger than him when they took her there. She was the right age for their victims. Lady Carson had said that some of the girls who were captured by the witches were raised in their ways. They would eventually get to participate in a ritual that would give them a unique power.

When he got home, he went straight to his room. He needed time to process this new information. He wanted to talk to his father and Oliver about it, but he knew that they would tell him to take it with a grain of salt. But they didn't see the sincerity in Lady Carson's eyes or hear the conviction in her voice. The details were so horrifying that it would be hard to make it up. It had to be true.

Chapter 4

Anna hugged Laura as she prepared to leave. She and her mother had chosen to move away from the Guardian's Castle in wake of all the rumors in the surrounding villages. Anna couldn't blame them, especially after Laura's encounter a few years ago.

Laura had gone out into the forest to collect Echinacea. A sickness had swept through a lot of the Guardians. Sickness rarely came to the castle, but when it did, it hit those afflicted with it hard. As it was, their supplies were low. She had been gone much longer than she was supposed to be. When she returned, she was crying and very upset. It took days before Laura had ventured from her room.

She told Anna that she met a boy while collecting plants. He had seemed nice enough at first, but then he insisted that she accompany him back to Woodbury Village. When she refused, he grabbed her and tried to force her to go with him. She had to use her gift to knock him out. She felt bad for hitting him with a rock, so she moved him to the fork on the main road.

Laura checked to make sure he was still alive, and in a place where he would be easily seen by anyone passing by. She then hid in the trees to rest. Lifting the boy with her mind had drained her energy. She also said she wanted to make sure that someone found him. Hours later, a group of riders came down the road.

Several men and two women dismounted when they saw the boy. A man checked the boy's pulse, and the group talked quietly for a while before one of the women moved to the boy's side. She had a hood covering her face. Laura was glad someone had come to take the boy back to the village.

The woman pulled a pouch from her side and unscrewed the lid. With a movement of her hand, she lifted water from the pouch into the air. Laura had been surprised that the woman was a Guardian. She watched in horror as the woman moved the water into the boy's nose. After several minutes, the woman checked the boy's pulse again before getting to her feet.

"That should help the rumors." The woman laughed before getting back on her horse. The group rode away quickly. Laura ran to the boy, but he had no pulse. She ran back to the castle to get help.

Laura had never been the same. The knowledge that there were Guardians out there that were killing people was upsetting. Miranda usually did not keep things from the others, but no one else knew that a Guardian had killed the boy from the village. The only reason Anna knew was because Laura had told her.

Anna waved goodbye to her friend as she and her mother rode through the gates. "All will be well, Anna." Miranda said from beside her.

"I will miss her." Anna whispered.

"We all will. But I respect their decision to find sanctuary elsewhere." Miranda put a hand on Anna's shoulder.

"Miranda, is it all right if I go to my room instead of having our lessons today?" Anna looked over at Miranda.

"Of course, my dear."

Anna went directly to her room. She changed into her nightclothes and climbed into bed. She wasn't feeling very well. As the night wore on, she felt like she was getting warmer and warmer. She groaned as she tossed and turned. It felt like she was in a furnace. The excruciating heat continued for what felt like an eternity. She screamed in pain before everything faded to black.

A cool rag was placed on her forehead. Anna groaned as she rolled to her side. "Anna?" Miranda said in a soft voice.

"I am sorry. Am I late for our lessons?" Anna asked trying to open her eyes. She felt heavy and it was hard for her to move.

"Lessons can wait. How are you feeling, Little One?" Miranda asked.

Anna was finally able to open her eyes, and she looked up at Miranda. "I feel as if I wrestled several grizzly bears and am now holding up a mountain."

Miranda laughed. "Sounds about right. Do you feel up to sitting and eating something?"

Anna nodded and Miranda assisted her into a sitting position. Miranda then passed her a bowl of broth. She sipped at the soup acutely aware that Miranda was watching her. "Why do I feel this way?" Anna finally asked.

Miranda's smile widened. "You had the Guardian's Fever, Anna. You have been unconscious for two days." Anna's mouth fell open. Her mind frantically searched for any memory of what happened after saying goodbye to Laura. "The day after Linda and Laura left, you never came to the library. I came to check on you and found you unconscious and burning with fever."

"What is my Gift?" Anna asked excitedly. She had been waiting for this day since she had first learned about Guardians.

"That is for you to discover." Miranda laughed. "Now, finish your soup. If you are feeling up to it, later today we can start learning about Guardian abilities."

Anna quickly finished her food and got dressed. She was feeling much better after the warm soup. She had been looking forward to learning more about the Guardian abilities and how each of them worked.

When she entered the library, Sasha and Miranda were in another heated discussion. Anna had gotten used to Sasha yelling at Miranda. The arguments were mostly about Anna's continued residency within the castle and Miranda teaching Anna about Guardians. She had overheard a few arguments about Sasha's desire to use an artifact to control shifters to keep the peace.

"Miranda, we cannot keep living in the shadows. It is our turn in the sun. Humans have become more fearful of Shifters. We shouldn't have to keep stepping in to save man's stupidity. It won't be long before war breaks out between humans and the beasts."

"That is what we are here for, Sasha. We bridge the gap." Miranda said in exasperation. Anna stepped back out into the hall to wait for Sasha to leave. She didn't want to be lectured for eavesdropping again.

"Why? Why do we need to?" Sasha threw her arms out to the side. "Both humans and Shifters alike are calling for our blood. We cannot even leave the castle without fear of being attacked."

"The rumors will fizzle out. They always do. Over the generations, we have periods of peace, and we have periods of unrest," Miranda stated. Anna kept quiet as she listened. Both Sasha and Miranda were talking loud enough for her to hear them easily.

"They are calling for blood, Miranda! What will it take for you to see that we cannot just sit here? We need to take action."

"Sasha, Guardians keep the peace. We will not force others to bend to our will."

"Says the Guardian who can control another's thoughts." Sasha scoffed.

"I do not have the ability to control another's thoughts." Miranda sighed. "I can only put in a suggestion. They are free to choose to follow the thought I put into them or not."

"But if we used the Stone..."

"That will not happen. One, Mother had us swear to protect it, not use it. Two, the prophecy claims that only a certain pair can use it. I will not break my word to Mother, Sasha. The Stone will remain where it is."

"And where is that?" Sasha asked.

"You know that I will take that information to the grave." Miranda's voice was firm.

"You and Mother never could see the potential that the Guardians have. We could have everlasting peace within Arlania if we just used the Stone to keep the Shifters in line."

"You are not calling for peace, Sasha. You are asking for me to enslave Shifters." Miranda snapped. "I will not do that."

"You are a fool, Miranda. You are going to get every one of those living here killed. Their blood is on your hands, dear sister." Sasha sneered.

Anna heard someone approaching the door. She ran down the hall and slid behind a large tapestry of the castle as seen from Woodbury Village. Holding her breath, she waited until the footsteps faded before she peeked out. The hall was completely empty. Anna took a deep breath and let it out slowly as she headed for the library.

Miranda stared out the window. Anna could still feel the tension in the room. She cleared her throat, causing Miranda to turn to face her. "Anna, right on time. Shall we begin?" Miranda went to a bookshelf and pulled down several volumes. "We will start with these." Anna smiled at Miranda.

She reached for the top volume as a warm feeling spread through her body. Her vision slowly began to fade, starting at the edges. She almost felt like she was leaving her body as the library disappeared and she was standing in a dark room.

A man stood at the front while at least thirty men sat at tables around the room. Tension filled the space. It was almost suffocating. The man at the front began to pace.

"Now is the time, men! Now is the time to take action." The man stated. "We cannot stand by and keep letting this happen. We have already had losses. We need to stop this before more death plagues us."

"What of the king? Shouldn't he be informed of the situation here?" A young man asked.

"We have sent word to the Capital. We are waiting to hear what he has to say." The man at the front said in irritation.

"I don't understand what you will have us do if the king has not ruled on this matter. If we take the action you are suggesting, we would be considered criminals." Another man said. He was standing next to the young man that had first asked about the king.

The room started to fade, and Anna gasped when the library came back into view. She blinked a few times as she lifted her head off of the table and looked around in confusion. What had she just seen?

Miranda sat across from her. She was studying Anna with her hands folded and resting on the table. "What was that?" Anna asked in confusion.

"What was what?" Miranda asked calmly.

"The room full of men. What were they talking about?" Anna asked.

"Anna, I didn't see anything. You reached for the book, then your eyes began to glow light blue before they became vacant as you slumped forward. You remained like that for nearly five minutes." Miranda continued to watch her with a thoughtful expression on her face.

"How is that possible?" Anna asked.

Miranda reached for the book in front of Anna. She flipped through the pages until she came to the one she wanted. Anna accepted the book back from Miranda. She started reading where she was instructed to. "Visions?" Anna looked up in surprise. "It says here that a seer hasn't been documented for three generations."

"That is correct. It has been a long time since a Guardian has been given such a rare and powerful gift." Miranda stood up and beckoned Anna to follow. "I want to show you something."

Anna closed the book and followed Miranda through several rows of shelves. They passed a few of the tapestries before stopping in front of Anna's favorite picture. It had a woman with reddish-brown hair and amber colored eyes. She was elegant and beautiful. Her hand rested on the head of an enormous black wolf.

"Close your eyes, Anna." Miranda instructed. Anna complied, and a moment later she felt the air change slightly. "Follow me." Miranda said quietly.

Anna opened her eyes to see a doorway where the picture had been. She quickly followed Miranda inside a small room. The door closed quietly behind her. There was a small desk with two chairs in the center of the limited space. A small bookcase was on the back wall that held several old books. Anna's brow furrowed when she noticed that there was no window. She looked around and saw multiple rocks positioned around the room. They were glowing, giving off enough light for one to read comfortably.

"This is my private library." Miranda said. "Any book within these walls, stays within these walls. Any knowledge gained here will not be discussed anywhere else. Do you understand, Anna?"

Anna turned her gaze to Miranda. "Yes, I understand." She looked around the room again. "What is it that we will be learning in here?"

"We will be learning about the artifacts entrusted to the Guardians to protect, as well as a deeper history of the first Guardian, Mira and her mate."

"Artifacts?" Anna asked as she took a seat at the table. "Mate."

"We have three items, only one is within the castle. The Guardian's Alpha Stone, the Guardian's Amulet, and the Locket of Estell. But before we get into that, let's head back into the main library and finish learning about Guardians' abilities."

Anna nodded her head, eager to get started. She turned to leave, but Miranda touched her arm to stop her. She dropped her hand from Anna before speaking. "With your rare gift, I feel we should keep your gift between us for the time being."

"Why?" Anna asked in surprise. Why would she need to keep her gift hidden?

"There is the prophecy about a seer. We do not want others to get it in their head that you are the one in the prophecy. Granted, you could be, but there is also a big possibility that you are not. And Sasha is in one of her moods again. There is no telling what she will do if she discovers that you are a seer." Miranda gave Anna a small smile. "You are very much a treasure, Little One. Keeping the fact that you have received your Gift a secret, is for your safety."

Chapter 5

Anna knelt on the floor as she looked at her mother's necklace. She ran her fingers over the sparrow that was etched into the center of the circular locket. She had never been permitted to look inside. Her mother had forbidden it. On her wedding day, the locket would be passed down to her. Even though it had been ten years since her mother's death, Anna had never looked inside.

A knock on the door pulled her from her thoughts. "Just a moment." She called, as she dropped the necklace into the hole and quickly put the stone back in place. She pulled open the door to find Ginger standing there.

"Anna, we have a problem." The woman said anxiously.

"What is it?" Anna asked in alarm.

"It's Heidi. She was chopping wood, and the axe slipped." Ginger wrung her hands in agitation. "No one knows what to do. With Miranda gone, I didn't know who else might know of something that might help."

The two of them ran through the hall until they reached the infirmary. Anna's stomach twisted when she saw all the blood. Heidi was sweaty and crying as she lay on a bed. Blood was everywhere. Mia looked frazzled as she pressed rags around the blade of the axe, which was several inches into Heidi's leg.

Anna pushed the panic down. These women needed guidance, and with Miranda gone to visit a friend in the northern region, there was no one to turn to.

"I wish I could loan you my Gift." Mia cried.

"You can." Anna said excitedly. She had read about healers in one of Miranda's secret books. They healed quickly and they also had the potential to heal others.

"What are you talking about?" Mia looked at Anna as if she had grown horns. "I only have accelerated healing."

"No, you can heal her, Mia. I have read…"

"Of course you would think you know better." Vanessa snapped. "What do you know? You are a young human. You wouldn't understand how Guardian Gifts work."

"If Mia doesn't do what I say, Heidi is going to bleed out and die. There is no medicinal herb that can heal her in time. We don't even have access to a doctor who can perform surgery." Anna said angrily. She knew she was right about this. She couldn't tell them about the secret library or the books within, but she could help Mia harness her full ability.

"I trust...Anna." Heidi's pained voice weakly said from the bed. All eyes turned to her. "She is right. I am losing blood too quickly. Mia is the only one who can save me."

Mia's fearful eyes turned to Anna. She gave her a small nod. "What do I do?" Mia whispered as her face paled.

"We will need to have someone remove the axe while you are healing her." Anna said, moving closer to the bed. Vanessa grudgingly agreed to do it. "Mia, you need to touch Heidi near the wound. Clear your mind and concentrate on the injury. Your gift should guide you from there."

"What kind of lesson is that?" Vanessa snapped.

"The kind that will assist her in her task." Anna glared at the woman. "We don't have time for a longer lesson."

Mia put a shaky hand on Heidi's leg. She closed her eyes and took a deep breath. Anna watched in fascination as a green light began to glow from Mia's hand. The blood pouring from the wound gradually slowed. At Anna's command, Vanessa yanked the axe from Heidi's leg, causing her to scream. The bleeding increased for a few minutes before it stopped altogether. It took a total of twenty minutes for Mia to completely heal the wound. When she was finished, her eye lids fluttered, and she swayed.

Vanessa caught her before she fell and helped her to another bed. "What have you done to her, Anna?"

Anna wiped Heidi's brow with a cool rag before she started to clean up the blood. "It takes energy to heal others. With such a deep wound, I imagine it took quite a bit. Mia will be fine once she gets some rest."

Anna wasn't concerned about Mia. The book had said her natural ability to heal would be enough to keep the healer from harm as they used their gift on others. She ignored Vanessa's barbs as she continued to clean up Heidi and the infirmary.

She finished setting the room to rights and checked on Mia and Heidi one more time before heading back to the library. She grabbed the book Miranda had assigned her to study in her absence. Anna tucked herself into her favorite alcove and began reading about Valencia's packs, Alphas, and fated mates.

* * *

Anna woke with a start. She needed to talk with Miranda. She didn't bother to dress before running out of her room. When she finally reached Miranda's bedroom on the fourth floor, she was out of breath. She banged on the door until it opened.

"It happened again." Anna panted out.

"Come in." Miranda ushered her into the room before closing the door. "What did you see?"

"It was Sasha!" Anna cried. "She was talking with several men as they discussed the Stone. They are coming to claim it."

"When?" Miranda immediately became tense.

"This afternoon." Anna rubbed her arm anxiously. "They are getting others to join them. They said they were going to put an end to the witches once and for all. Miranda, Sasha was leading them. Why would she be doing this?" Anna asked.

"Anna, all will work out. You will see." Miranda gave her a small smile. "Right now, I need you to go get dressed. Make sure you grab your cloak. I am calling for a Gathering."

Anna's heart began to race. She swallowed hard before hurrying out of Miranda's chambers. How could this be happening again? She was losing her home for a second time. She pushed open her bedroom door and slammed it behind her. After dressing, Anna dropped to her knees next to the hidden compartment.

She pulled out her mother's locket and fastened it around her neck, tucking it into her dress. She shoved the little bit of money she had and her journal into her pocket but decided to leave the Crossford Brand. She didn't want any more reminders of her life back in Freynia with her father.

Anna gave her room one more cursory glance as she fastened her cloak. She swallowed hard before stepping out into the hall. Instead of turning to her right to head for the stairs that led up to the ground floor, she went left. Being in the basement had many advantages. Anna had asked to stay down here after her mother's death. She felt safer with the isolation.

The hall turned to the right and widened out. The walls were lined with statues of various animals. When she reached the bear, she stopped. She wiggled behind the statue and pressed the fourth claw on his back paw. A portion of the wall swung in. Anna quickly entered the narrow passage. She closed the door, blanketing herself in darkness.

With a hand on the wall, Anna took small steps as she walked forward. The floor gently angled downward and curved several times. There were dozens of tunnels that webbed out throughout the mountain where the castle was built. Miranda had a map in the hidden library of all the secret passages. Anna had spent hours studying it and had explored each route more than once.

Voices and a soft glow ahead alerted her that she was nearing the others. Anna stepped into the crowded room. She moved along the wall until she was on the opposite side of the room from where she had entered. All the others had their hoods up, so she followed suit.

Anna had only been in this room twice before when she was younger. She hadn't realized how low the rock ceiling was. If she reached up, she could place her hand flat against it. The walls were very rough, as if the room had been chiseled out of the mountain. Several lanterns were placed around the room. There was a stone table in the center where Miranda usually stood.

Almost everyone was accounted for. They were all whispering among themselves. The usually soft murmur of voices was magnified by the acoustics of the room. No one seemed to know what was going on, but tension still filled the room.

Not long after Anna arrived, Miranda walked in with her hood pulled back. Her long silvery hair hung straight down around her shoulders. As she moved through the room, the Guardians parted for her and a hush fell over everyone. The tension grew as Miranda surveyed the crowd.

"Most, if not all, of you have probably heard the rumors about Sasha." Miranda finally said. Sasha left the castle without telling anyone. Rumors started that she had found a man and had run off with him. According to some, it wasn't the first time. Sasha would disappear for years at a time. When she came back, she usually had a child with her. "I have called you all here to put those rumors to rest. Sasha has indeed fallen in love with a human. This news is normally cause for joy and celebrating; however, in this situation it is cause for concern."

"Miranda?" Someone called from the back. Miranda turned to face her, giving her a nod to continue. "How is Sasha finding love with a human cause for concern? Many of us have married humans in the past."

"Yes, Sasha's choice in partner is not the issue. The issue has come from Sasha telling her husband about the Guardians...and the amulet."

Miranda rolled her shoulders back, standing taller. Anna could see how much it pained her that her sister was betraying them.

"What are we to do?" Several cried out anxiously.

"All Guardians and Shifters are in danger. Our seekers have discovered that Sasha and her husband are on their way here with the purpose of possessing the amulet," Miranda stated. She had told the other Guardians that she had allies in Arlania that were called seekers, when in reality, it was Anna she was talking about. Fear began to take root in the women as the severity of the situation started to sink in. "We need to appoint a protector for the amulet." The room was completely silent. Everyone knew about the amulet but not its location or how much actual power it held. "And I nominate Anna."

It was as if no one breathed. Anna stared at Miranda in surprise. Anna was the youngest Guardian here by at least fifteen years. She had no real experiences outside of the Guardian's Castle. She would be the worst one to take up this responsibility. The woman closest to her grabbed her arm and shoved her forward. Several more joined the first, and before Anna could protest, she was standing directly in front of Miranda. Her hood had slipped off in the process, allowing her chocolate-brown hair to fall across her face.

"She is but a child." Someone called.

"Why her?" Another asked.

"Pick someone else!" Anna recognized Vanessa's voice.

Miranda raised her hand to silence the protests from the twenty women. "Yes, Anna is young, but she has a gift no one else has." All eyes focused on Anna. None of them knew Anna even had a Gift. "She can see potential threats. This gift is what we need in order to keep the amulet out of the wrong hands." Out of the corner of her eye, Anna saw several nodding in agreement. Miranda turned her attention to Anna. "Will you protect the amulet from those who seek to do harm with it?"

Anna swallowed her rising panic. How would she be able to fulfill this responsibility? She read books and memorized maps. She couldn't do this. Anna looked around at her fellow Guardians before her gaze settled back on Miranda's smiling face. Why was Miranda choosing her? She only received her Gift two years ago, and she had yet to understand it. There was so little information about seers.

Despite her fear and uncertainty, she found herself giving Miranda a small nod. "With my life, I will protect the amulet." Anna had meant to tell her to pick someone else. Why had those words come from her?

Anna barely heard the cheers of the other Guardians over the pounding of her own heart. Miranda instructed everyone to leave the castle as fast as possible and integrate into the normal population. Anna still couldn't understand how she ended up here. A hand on her shoulder pulled her out of her thoughts.

Miranda gave her a smile. The room was now empty. Anna watched as Miranda gestured towards the round table in the center of the room. When they were standing in front of it, the Matriarch made a motion with her hand and the top of the table lifted into the air. Anna gasped and took a step back. Inside the base lay a small box. It was covered in dust and cobwebs. The worn lid had delicately carved animals along the border.

Miranda lifted the box out of the base of the table. "This is the Guardian's Amulet. It has the power to control Shifters. In order to possess the powers of the amulet, one has to be in this room, so it is imperative that you keep it out of here."

Anna knew all about the amulet. She had spent six months reading and learning about the three artifacts of the Guardians. The information was mixed together, making it hard to know what each artifact did. From what they could interpret, the Guardian's Stone was here in the castle, while the Guardian's Amulet was in Valencia. The Locket of Estell was given as a gift to someone and was currently lost. No one knew where it had ended up.

"I wish we had more time, but Sasha will be here any minute. When it is safe, go to my private library and get the book that explains all about the amulet." Miranda slid the lid off the box. Inside the box lay a round metal ball. It was no bigger than a marble. All around it were 's' shaped slits allowing a glimpse of a blue stone that was inside. A silver chain was strung through it so that it could be worn as a necklace.

As Anna lifted the chain from the box, the light from the lanterns hit the stone, making it appear to be glowing. Reverently, she placed the necklace around her neck. She tucked it into her dress, just like she had with her mother's locket.

"Take it, child, and go." Miranda said urgently. "Get far away from here, and make sure no one can use the amulet for evil."

Anna ran from the room. She took the south passage before turning east. She came to the staircase that led up to the kitchen. It was the closest exit to the gate, and she wanted to get away quickly. At the top of the stairs, she slowed down. Something inside her screamed for caution.

She slipped through the door and entered the pantry. Making her way through shelves, she took several deep breaths to slow her racing heart. A noise in the kitchen caused her to stop. She peeked through the crack of the door. Several men were dumping gasoline all over the place. Anna froze in fear.

The only way these people could have gasoline was if they had traded with Freynia. Freynia was the only country that produced that specific fuel. They used it to power their machines to help mine ore in the mountains. Anna watched as the men finished dumping their last barrel. They ran out the side door that she had hoped to escape through. The door was partially open, and she hurried to it.

When she peeked outside, she covered her mouth to hold in her scream. Miranda was on her knees in front of a cloaked woman and a man. Their backs were towards her. She didn't recognize them. Miranda's voice was strong as she refused to tell the couple where the amulet was. It was like déjà vu. The woman took a dagger and stabbed it into Miranda's chest.

"Fire!" A man yelled. Adrenaline shot through Anna's veins. She needed to get out of the castle before someone saw her. The library would be her best bet. There was a passage that wound down into the mountain and ended at a door that opened into the forest. She needed to get to the west wing.

She peered into the hallway to make sure no one else was there. Two men were walking down the hall, heading east. Taking a chance, Anna slipped through the door and ran down the hall in the opposite direction. Smoke was beginning to fill the air. She grabbed the side of her cloak and raised it to her mouth and nose. Coughing, she slowed her pace.

"Let go of me!" Hiedi screamed.

Anna slipped behind the nearest tapestry. She was shaking as she listened to her friend being dragged down the hall. When she could no longer hear anyone, Anna continued. She had to hide several more times using potted plants and statues, as men moved around the castle. The smoke was becoming so thick that it was hard for her to see through it.

She managed to reach the library as she heard more voices and women screaming. She quickly closed the door as she fought her tears. She could do nothing to save the others, and Miranda had entrusted her with the amulet. She could only press forward.

She coughed as she hurried to the tapestry that hid the passageway. Anna couldn't help glancing around and getting one last look at the only real home she had known. This was going to be the last time she would see her beloved library. She pulled back the edge of the tapestry but hesitated. The bookshelf just to the right of it caught her eye.

Anna grabbed three books off the middle shelf. These were going to be the next ones she was going to be studying. A crash down the hall had Anna turning back to the tapestry. She quickly located a small rock on the lower right and pressed it. A door swung in, and she hurried inside the passageway. She pressed an equally small rock, and the door closed, shrouding her in darkness.

There was a torch, but Anna didn't waste time lighting it. She had been inside this tunnel before, so she put her hand on the wall and ran. The path sloped downward in a spiral, leading her deeper and deeper into the mountain.

After what felt like ages, Anna finally came to a solid wall. The dark and her shaking hands didn't aid in her attempt to get out quickly. She finally found the release. Her panic had been building since she saw the men within the castle kitchen, and she was near her breaking point. A blast of fresh air hit her face as the door opened. Relief that she had clean air to breathe had her taking several steps out into the open. Her coughing increased with each gasping breath she took.

Just when she thought she could continue, something slammed into her, causing her to fall to the ground. Panic seized her when she realized that it was someone, not something, that had tackled her. Images of her father knocking her to the ground before beating her, and Miranda being stabbed filled her mind.

Anna scrambled to try to get away, but whoever tackled her was too heavy. She managed to roll so she could at least see who it was that had caught her. It was a man. He was younger than most she had seen within the castle walls. He had light brown hair that fell into his eyes. He couldn't have been much older than she was. He glared down at her as he pinned her down. She couldn't stop the tears that fell from her eyes. She was beyond terrified.

The man froze has he studied her. Slowly he got to his feet. He reached down and grabbed her wrists, pulling her up to stand in front of him. Anna attempted to push him away. She needed to get away. "Please." She cried. "Please, don't hurt me." She begged.

The young man's hold on her only tightened as she continued to struggle against him. Anna knew that he was going to take her back to the castle and kill her. Or worse, send her back to her father and Mr. Hawkshaw. Given the choice, she would rather die. Desperate to get away, Anna tried to kick her attacker.

He yanked her towards him. She turned to run, but he wrapped a strong arm around her middle while his other covered her mouth. She screamed, even though she knew that was the worst thing she could do, but she wasn't thinking rationally at the moment. Her only thought was...escape.

"Shh. It's okay. I'm not going to hurt you." He whispered harshly as he tried to keep her quiet. He dragged her further into the trees. "We need to get you away from here before someone sees you."

Anna stopped fighting and the young man's hand covering her mouth loosened. She reached up and grabbed it, yanking it away from her. She started coughing again. Her throat burned and her chest felt tight. Once her coughing fit ended, the man grabbed hold of her hand and led her deeper into the forest. Anna grudgingly followed, tripping over rocks and roots.

She wasn't sure she should trust him, but at this point, she didn't see any other options. Several minutes later, they came to a stop. Anna doubled over coughing again. The man's hand rested on her back as if trying to lend her comfort. The contact only added to her rising anxiety. She glanced at him. He was looking around as if searching for something.

He grabbed her hand again and pulled her towards an enormous tree. It was so big that six men couldn't touch hands if they stood around it. Anna tugged her hand from the man's as she whirled around to face him. She was tired, her throat and chest hurt, and she was so scared. "If you are going to kill me, just do it." She snapped at him.

His hand flew over her mouth again. She tried to back away but for every step she took back, he took a matching one forward. Anna's back hit the tree. She was trapped. The young man leaned close to her; his warm breath tickled her skin.

"I am trying to save your life. I need you to climb into the tree trunk and stay there until I come back for you. Do not make a sound or try to leave. They are looking for any runaways. When I come back, I have some questions I need you to answer." The man's voice was calm.

Anna searched her mind for anyway out of this. Tears coursed down her cheeks. The man leaned back to look at her. He slowly removed his hand from her mouth and gently wiped the tears from her cheeks. She flinched at his touch. Every man that had touched her, hurt her. She squeezed her eyes closed, bracing for the pain but it never came. The young man was tugging at the bark beside where she stood. She gasped when he pulled open a makeshift door. There was a small hole carved out of the trunk just large enough for someone small to hide in.

Anna looked at the young man who gestured toward the hole. Reluctantly, she crawled inside. She had to draw her knees up to her chest in order to fit. She looked back at her attacker/rescuer. He was crouched in front of the opening. He pushed her dress and cloak farther into the trunk with her. Their eyes met and they studied each other for a long moment.

    Men's shouts snapped them out of their stalemate. The voices sounded like they were drawing closer. Anna's fear grew. What had she been thinking, allowing this man to lead her out here and trapping her? He quickly covered the opening with the thick bark and Anna found herself, once again, in darkness.

Chapter 6

Mason stood to his full height. He quickly made his way to the creek several yards away from the large tree. The voices continued to grow louder as he slowly walked along the creek. He was looking around as if he were keeping an eye out for anything suspicious.

"There you are, Mason." An older gentleman called as several men came into view.

"Yes, sir. Just looking down this way for anyone who may have run off." Mason smiled. These men were from Woodbury Village. He was glad he had hidden the girl away before they showed up.

"Lady Sasha believes we have all key people from the castle. We are to gather back in the courtyard." Mr. Jeffery said. Mason nodded and followed them back to the castle.

As he walked back, Mason's mind went over the events of the last several weeks. Lord Carson had brought more men to their village. They came with news about the men's villages just south of Woodbury. The witches had attacked them. Many of their Shifter families were targeted. Mason volunteered to join the army being assembled to stop any more deaths.

Lord Carson's wife, Lady Sasha, spoke at one of their meetings. She informed the volunteers that all the witches were women. They liked to kill adult Shifters and slowly ate the children they captured as part of their rituals. Most of the information wasn't new to Mason. He had been hearing about the witches for most of his life. His best friend's death was even rumored to have been caused by the witches. The people of Woodbury were growing more and more restless. So, when these new men showed up, it only added fuel to their suspicions of the residence of White Castle.

There were no problems in recruiting men for an army to put a stop to the violence and free this area of Arlania of such deplorable people. Mason and Oliver had been some of the first. Everyone in their family was a Shifter. He joined to protect them from becoming targets.

However, he didn't feel right attacking the women if the king wasn't in favor of such actions. When he questioned why the royal army wasn't present for the capture of so many prisoners, he was assigned to patrol the forest on the west side of the castle. Something didn't feel quite right. He pushed those thoughts aside. The witches needed to be dealt with. Besides Clay, there have been four more mysterious drownings over the past two years. He needed to help put an end to this.

Mason looked up and saw that black smoke was starting to fill the sky, and he shook his head. Lord and Lady Carson warned that the witches would set fire to portions of the castle in order to deter anyone from venturing too far onto the grounds. His thoughts turned to the woman. She had burst from the side of the mountain. She was coughing and gasping for air. She must have gotten too close to the flames her people had set.

He had been surprised to see her emerge out of solid rock. When her coughing stopped, it had snapped him out of his shock, and he acted. He tackled her to the ground so she couldn't get away. She rolled and he came face-to-face with the terror filled light blue eyes of a young woman. She was shaking with fear. Tears streamed down her cheeks, and he felt completely at a loss.

He had thought he would find emotionless, hate filled women, not a completely terrified young lady around his own age. Her soft plea for him not to hurt her stabbed guilt into his heart. He had been the cause of her distress, and he didn't like it. For some reason, he had a strong need to protect her. It had been overwhelming. So, he took her to the tree he and Oliver had played in as kids.

Hiding her would satisfy this need to keep her safe and he could get answers from her. He wanted to know exactly what the White Witches were up to. His father always said to get both sides of the story before drawing a conclusion. And that is what Mason planned on doing. If the girl was exactly what everyone said she was, then he would take her to the king himself.

They approached the gate, and Mason forced his thoughts away from the girl in the tree. Smoke hung thick in the air, and he coughed. He looked around. His brow furrowed in confusion as he studied the castle. The bottom windows were boarded up and most of the second floor was on fire. What had happened here?

The men from the village were gathering near a well. There were close to fifty of them. Lady Sasha's men doubled the number of volunteers. They positioned themselves loosely around the volunteers. An uneasy feeling came over Mason. Lord Carson moved to the front of the group as he escorted his wife, Lady Sasha.

"Today has been a success." Cheers broke out throughout the ranks. "We have captured the witches and the leader of them has been terminated. Their threat to us, and all of Arlania, will be eliminated tonight."

Many of the men cheered while others were confused. Mason looked around him. Mr. Jeffery looked angry as he talked with one of the men that had come with the Carsons. The man nodded and led Mr. Jeffery away. Two more men followed after them. They walked around the side of the castle. Several minutes passed before the three men returned without Mr. Jeffery.

Mason's heart rate increased. What had they done to the old man? And what did Sasha mean by 'terminated'? This was not what they were told was going to happen. All the witches were supposed to be captured and taken to the king to be judged for their crimes.

Lady Sasha gave an order to two men near her. They lit torches and advanced towards a door. Another man opened the door a crack as the other two men shoved their torches through the narrow opening. Mason watched in horror as flames became visible through the slits in the boards that covered the windows. Women's screams and cries of pain and fear filled the air.

Mason felt sick. This wasn't what was supposed to happen. This wasn't the justice they were promised. Several men from the volunteer army tried to run forward but were stopped. They were threatened that if they tried to get to the castle, they would be joining the witches in the flame-engulfed room. Mason clenched his jaw as he watched helplessly. Time seemed to tick by at an agonizingly slow pace. He prayed the women would have quick deaths. He couldn't even imagine what they were going through.

The blue sky continued to fill with black smoke. It didn't take long for the cries for help to die, and Mason felt relieved. Those poor women. No matter their crimes, they did not deserve to be burned alive.

Mason helped clean up some of the debris around the courtyard. He was afraid that if he tried to leave immediately, they would kill him too. Hours later, Lady Sasha released the volunteers to spread the 'good news' that the witches were no longer a threat to the community.

Mason would not be boasting about his experiences here, and he doubted that many of the men from Woodbury would be either. Mass murder was not something one gloated about. He was ashamed to have even played a minor role here. He was grateful he had managed to hide the girl.

Mason traveled back to Woodbury with the others. No one spoke and a heaviness filled the air around them. Once in the village, Mason went to the

Finn's Corner Store and purchased a satchel, a brown dress he guessed was roughly her size, and some food. He left Granger at the livery stable for the time being.

He took the long way around as he walked back to the tree. He didn't want to chance anyone following him. He was alert as he walked around the base of the cliffs. The girl had been carrying books when he tackled her. He needed to retrieve them before anyone else saw them.

*   *   *

Anna's legs had long since fallen asleep. She had been there for hours. Where was the young man? The thick bark made it impossible to hear anything on the other side of it. Only slivers of light penetrated the dark cramped space. Her silent tears cut tracks down her dirty face as she continued to wait.

Her shock was fading, replaced by deep sadness, hurt, and exhaustion. Miranda had been more of a mother to her than her mother had the chance to be. While they were in Crossford, her mother was limited in what she was able to do for Anna. The six months they had together outside of her father's influence had been amazing but far too short. Miranda had taken her under her wing after her mother's tragic death.

Anna had watched as Miranda was killed, and the only home she really had was set on fire. It was at this very moment, being burned to the ground. Shaking her head, Anna tried to clear the images from her mind. She needed to get away from this place. She needed to get as far away as possible.

She was tempted to shove the 'door' open and run before the young man returned. The only thing stopping her was the fact that she didn't know what was happening on the other side. Men could be combing through the forest, searching for her or the others and she wouldn't know it. It was better to wait for him to return. He said he had questions for her. That would buy her time to escape.

With her next course of action settled on, images from her past flooded her mind. She was trapped in a similar prison that her father had shoved her into. Her mother had tried to stop him and was slammed so hard into the wall that she immediately crumbled to the floor. He was teaching her to hold her tongue. A loose tongued girl was a dead girl.

She began to shake uncontrollably as the already tight space seemed to shrink around her. She started to pull in gasping breaths as her panic began to build. The burning and scratching in her throat grew, and she started coughing again. She needed air. She needed air now.

Just when she had decided to push the door open, it slid away. Anna threw herself from her hiding place as she took in gasping breaths and coughed.

"Are you all right, Miss?" Strong arms grabbed her shoulders, and his deep voice was filled with worry.

Anna looked up and she was met with the brown eyes of the young man that had brought her to the tree. He looked a bit paler than before, and worry was etched on his face. Her legs weren't working as she tried to scoot away from him. She tried to reason with him. "Please. Please, let me go. I've done nothing wrong." Her voice was soft and somewhat scratchy from all her coughing. Her whole body was shaking.

The man took off his coat and draped it around her shoulders. Anna couldn't understand why he was acting like this. No man was ever this soft. "I promise you, Miss, I will not hurt you. We need to get out of this area. Do you think you can walk?" His gaze raked over her as if trying to assess her physical abilities. His nose scrunched as he stared at her dress. "I have clothes for you to change into. Your white clothes will draw too much attention, and I would rather us be invisible if possible." Anna couldn't argue with that. Her white dress painted her as a target. "I will be just over on the other side of that bush. If you need anything, just yell out, but please change quickly. We really need to leave before the army decides to double-check the forest for survivors."

Anna waited for the man to disappear. She dug through the bag he had left next to her. She drew out the dress and changed as quickly as her shaking limbs would allow. She transferred her money and journal into the pocket of her new dress. Anna hesitated before stuffing her white dress and cloak into the tree and replacing the bark door. Anna found a thick woolen cloak as well and put it on. The clothes were much heavier than her white dress and cloak, but it would help keep her warm.

Anna glance to where she had seen the man disappear. She hesitated. Should she go to the man or make a run for it? She hadn't left the castle in ten years, and before that, she was locked in a two-bedroom cabin under the thumb of her father. She didn't know the area or where she should go. As much as she hated the idea of having to stay with him, she didn't see that she had much of a choice.

Taking a deep breath to calm her nerves, Anna attempted to walk to the man. Her shaky legs had other plans and gave out under her weight. She let out a soft cry as her knee hit a rock. The man was at her side in an instant.

"Being cramped in that tree combined with the shock you are no doubt feeling, is making it hard for your limbs to function. If I could, I would set up camp here and allow you to recuperate for a while before we head out, but we really must be going. Will you allow me to carry you for a while?" Anna tensed. He seemed to understand her anxiety. "Once you feel up to walking, you can continue on your own two feet." She looked down at her shaking hands. There was no way she could walk out of here right now.

The need to get away from here resurfaced and she nodded her head. He effortlessly scooped her up into his arms and began moving quickly through the woods. He glanced down at her before turning his attention back to looking where he was putting his feet. "By the way, my name is Mason."

Anna felt the need to say something to him, but she didn't want to give him her name. "Well, Mason. Thank you for not killing me." Anna said.

Mason chuckled softly and she could feel it through his chest. Silence once again fell between them. Anna was incredibly tense. The only time a man had carried her was after her father beat her so badly that she couldn't walk. Her mother had said her oldest brother had carried her home and dumped her on the doorstep. She had been six years old.

An hour passed with Mason's footsteps and the sound of the forest being the only things breaking the silence between them. Anna was ready to burst. She wanted to know what was going to become of her. Mason claimed he wouldn't hurt her, but her mother had taught her that men were not to be trusted. Her own experiences had also taught her not to trust men.

"Can I ask you something?" Her nerves got the better of her and she couldn't stop herself from asking, even though she might be beaten for speaking.

Mason's steps slowed and he set her down gently. He kept his arm around her waist as she wobbled slightly. "I will answer any of your questions if you answer mine." He met her gaze. "Why don't we take turns asking questions? Ladies first." He gave her a smile of encouragement.

Anna squinted as she studied the man in front of her. She couldn't figure out his motives. She couldn't promise to answer him, but she could try to be as honest as possible. "Okay." she said softly. "Why did you not kill me when you first saw me? I saw the hate in your eyes."

Mason took a deep breath and slowly let it out. "You were not exactly what I had assumed we were there to fight. Instead of evil witches, I found you. You looked completely terrified and innocent. I couldn't, not without knowing for sure if you did what we were told you did." He searched her face, looking for the answers he sought. "What is your name?"

Anna blinked in surprise. She thought for sure he would start questioning her about whatever crime she was supposedly guilty of. "Are you sure that is the question you want to ask?"

"It is. And since you asked a second question, I will add to my first. What is your name and how old are you?" he said confidently. Anna moved away from him. She was so confused as to what he was trying to do. His hand fell from her waist as she took a step back. Mason grabbed her hand, preventing her from moving too far away from him. "Please. I just want to help. What we were told doesn't sit right with me after seeing what they did."

Anna watched Mason. He looked sincere. There was a part of her that wanted to trust him. "My name is Anna, and I am eighteen years old."

Mason smiled at her as he squeezed her hand. There was a spark of recognition and relief in his eyes. "See that wasn't so hard, and to show you I mean no ill will, I will let you know a little secret." He took a step closer and Anna's heart rate increased at the proximity. His demeanor had changed the moment she told him her name. Why did she get the impression he knew her? "I am twenty years old." He said in a whisper with a small smile. Was he toying with her?

Her guard instantly rose. "Why are you helping me, Mason?" She asked. She was not in the mood for games.

"I am not sure how to answer that." He ran his free hand through his hair. "When I first saw you coming out of that door, I was ready to avenge the innocent lives you witches destroyed. But after I knocked you to the ground, by the way I am sincerely sorry for that, I felt the need to protect you. I don't know how to describe it." He dropped his gaze to the ground. "I know nothing about you save your name, your age, and what we were told about you; yet I-I need to make sure you are safe."

He looked back up and Anna could tell he was trying to find the right words. He was telling her the truth, but she still couldn't wrap her head around it. A man protecting her went against everything she grew up experiencing. An owl hooted and Anna jumped.

"We should probably keep going. Are you able to walk, Anna?" Mason asked. She nodded in response.

He held her hand firmly as he led her through the trees and out onto a road. He hesitated as he looked both ways. To the right was his parents' home, but it was far too close to the castle for his peace of mind. He would need to take her to Woodbury and get his horse. After that, they could ride a few towns away before stopping for the night.

After walking for a few miles, Anna moved closer to him. He wasn't sure she even realized that she had. "What did they say about me?" Anna's voice was barely louder than a whisper.

Mason told her about the rumors circulating concerning the women in white that lived at the castle. They were rumored to have magical powers that they used to hurt Shifters. He explained how the surrounding villages were nervous about the mysterious deaths over the years. A woman and man had asked for aid in ridding Arlania of the witches that ate children and killed Shifters.

Anna felt the blood drain from her face the longer Mason talked. She stopped walking and faced him. "W-we would never kill a Shifter unless in self-defense. And eating children? That is...that is utterly...disturbing." Anna couldn't believe someone would say such horrible things about the Guardians. Granted, no one knew they were Guardians, but still, they never did anything violent unless they were first attacked. Now her home and family were gone because of the lies of some sick individuals. She couldn't stop the sobs that racked her body. She covered her mouth with her hand as she tried to hold them back.

Mason pulled her to his chest. He held her tight until her sobs quieted. He leaned back just enough to see her face. "I am so sorry that I believe such horrible lies, Anna. I should have looked more into the things Sasha said. Her accusations went along with many of the rumors I have been hearing all my life, but I still should have never gone along with it until I confirmed the rumors."

"Sasha?" Anna squeaked as her whole body tensed.

"Yes." Mason said slowly.

"We need to leave. Now." Without saying another word, Anna turned away from him and practically ran down the dirt road.

Mason hurried after her. He grabbed her arm and pulled her to a stop. She was out of breath, and she was shaking again. She jerked away from him. "Anna, what is the matter? You look more frightened now than when I tackled you to the ground." What had gotten into her?

"Help me get out of here and I will explain everything." Her eyes were glancing around as if she expected the devil himself to pop out from behind a bush.

He considered his options. He could give her money and send her on her way. Or he could go with her and make sure she remained safe. If he went with her, he would finally get some answers as to why Sasha did what she had done at the castle. He knew he couldn't leave Anna to fend for herself with Sasha nearby. He nodded his agreement.

Anna was tense as they continued walking. Mason allowed his fingers to brush against hers, wanting to provide her comfort but she seemed uncomfortable with him. He couldn't blame her. Not only was he part of the mob that had attacked her home, but she was afraid of men, from what he remembered. It was a wonder she had trusted him as much as she had.

Mason was surprised when she grabbed his hand tightly. He gave her a gentle squeeze in return. Deep down he knew he wasn't going to leave her side. He was determined to protect her from those who had targeted her and her people. She had trusted him when they were kids, and he hoped to earn that trust back.

Chapter 7

Anna didn't know why she grabbed Mason's hand. All she knew was for some reason, she felt safe with him. It was completely ridiculous for her to feel safe. He had been ready to send her to her death just a few hours ago. It didn't make sense. She pulled her hand from his and wrapped her arms around herself.

Mason didn't say anything as they walked in silence. Suddenly, he grabbed her and pulled her to the side of the road. Anna's heart began to race as he shoved her to the ground. The wind was knocked from her lungs, momentarily stunning her. In the next moment, his body was on hers. She whimpered as she tried to shove him off her.

His hand covered her mouth again and tears fell from her eyes. "Anna, it's okay." She shook her head as she continued to fight against him. "There are horses coming. Please, hold still."

Anna froze. Her heart felt like it was going to beat out of her chest. She couldn't hear anything. Mason moved his hand from her mouth to her cheek. She was just about to ask what exactly he had heard when she heard it too. Anna tensed as the sound of horse's hooves and men's voices drew closer. Mason's thumb stroked her cheek gently.

"It's dark enough they won't see us." Mason's lips brushed her ear as he whispered.

Anna gripped Mason's shirt as she buried her face in his neck. He held the back of her head as he continued to whisper to her, telling her that everything was going to be okay. It felt like hours passed before Mason lifted his head. He looked around. He let out a tense breath as he looked down at her.

"Are you all right?" He kept his voice soft. "I didn't hurt you when I pushed you to the ground, did I?"

The moonless night made it impossible to see the details of Mason's face. "I don't think so." Anna finally whispered.

"Let's get you back on your feet." Mason stood and offered his hand to assist her. Anna allowed him to pull her up, but she took a step back as soon as she found her footing. "Come on. We have a little farther to walk before we get to my horse. Then we will ride to an inn."

Anna nodded and followed several steps behind him as he walked. Mason felt weird with her walking behind him. He slowed his pace so she could catch up, but she slowed as well. After another five minutes Mason stopped.

"Why are we stopping?" Anna asked softly.

"Why are you walking behind me?" Mason turned to face her.

Her eyes widened and she glanced around nervously. "Um…I'm sorry. Did I do something wrong?"

"Anna," Mason furrowed his brow. "Why would you assume you did something wrong? I was just wondering why you were walking behind me instead of in front or beside me."

Her brows pinched together as if the question confused her. "I am five paces behind you. Isn't that where I am supposed to be?"

Mason studied her for a long moment. She had her arms wrapped around her middle as if to comfort or shield herself. When he took a step towards her, he saw her flinch. "Anna, I don't know where you got that idea. It is weird for me to walk with you behind me. Would you feel comfortable walking beside me?"

He could feel her uncertainty. "Is this a trick? I am far too exhausted to want to play your games."

"No tricks or games." Mason grabbed hold of her hand. "Why do I get the feeling that you feel I am above you in station?" He began walking again.

"Aren't you?" Anna looked at him.

"Okay, so I am the son of a Lord, and as far as I know, you are not a titled lady, but I feel your views would still be the same even if I were a farm boy."

Anna shrugged but didn't say anything for a long time. "I don't understand you." He finally heard her say.

"I'm pretty easy to figure out." Mason chuckled. "I am a twenty-year-old man with a lot of learning to do. I make mistakes, but I work hard to correct my wrongs. I often find myself getting into hot water with my mother over antics she says I am too old for." Mason smiled at Anna. "See, not to difficult." Anna shook her head but said nothing. He wished he could help relieve some of her anxiety, even for a little while.

The lights of Woodbury came into view. Mason pulled Anna into the woods to keep her out of sight of the townspeople. He didn't want to take her into the town. They were at the back of the store near a large shed. The Finn's Store was relatively close to the livery stables. He was going to have to leave her here until he got back with Granger.

"Anna, I need you to stay here." Mason whispered. Her hand in his tightened. He cupped her face, and he felt her cheeks wet from tears. "I will be right back with my horse. I don't want to risk anyone in town seeing you."

"Okay." She breathed out. She was shaking again.

"I will only be gone for a few minutes." Mason stood and jogged into the trees.

Anna took a deep breath and let it out slowly. She was okay. She was fine. Mason would be back in a few minutes, and they could get out of this area. All would work out.

Mason had been gone for nearly thirty minutes when she heard male voices. She doubted he would be talking so loudly. This wasn't good. Whoever it was, was moving closer. Anna frantically looked around for a place to hide but found none.

"What do we have here?" A man slurred. Anna's head snapped in his direction.

"It looks like we've got ourselves our victory trophy." The second man laughed before taking another swig from the bottle in his hand.

Anna slowly got to her feet. She was not going to just let them take her. She had to protect the Amulet. The men chuckled as they advanced toward her. The closer they got, the bigger they seemed to get. Fear caused her limbs to freeze. The first man grabbed her and yanked her into his arms. He was so much bigger than she was.

Fear coursed through her, and she attempted to get away from him. His hand tightened painfully around her upper arm. She tried to keep quiet, but a small cry escaped from her lips.

"Let go of her." Mason's voice washed over her. He sounded angry.

"Wait your turn." The second man sneered.

Mason swung a fist into the man's face, causing him to stumble back and fall against the side of the shed. He slid to the ground and didn't get back up. "I said let her go."

"Who do you think you are?" The man holding her swayed. She took advantage of his lack of balance and shoved with all her might. He stumbled to the side, releasing her as he attempted to stay on his feet. Anna ran straight to Mason. He caught her to him and held her tight. "Get back here!" The man bellowed.

"Anna, get on the horse." Mason whispered.

"I don't know how. I have never ridden before." Anna held onto him tighter.

Mason released her as he stepped protectively between her and the drunk. The man rushed at them but tripped over his own feet and fell face first into the dirt. He tried to get up but stumbled and fell again.

"Come on, Anna." Mason put an arm around her. He didn't even look back as they walked away. He guided her toward a horse that was tied near the shed. Anna's steps faltered as they got closer to the beast. "And you have ridden before."

"No, I have not. I think I would remember getting on something that big." Anna shook her head.

Mason stood behind her and put his hands on her waist. "I know you have ridden a horse before. In fact, it was even on Granger." He lifted her and she squeaked in surprise. He set her on the horse's back, his hands staying on her waist.

She gripped his wrists tightly as she glared at his smiling face. "How could I have ridden your horse if I have never even met you before?"

Mason cocked his head to the side as he studied her. After a minute, he shook his head. "Would you like to sit in front or in back?"

"I-I don't know." Anna's grip on Mason tightened as she looked down at the horse. "Can't we just walk?"

"I am hoping to get you several towns away from here before we find a place to stay for the night. Walking would be an unnecessary risk."

"What if I fall?" Granger moved to the side a few steps, causing her to gasp in surprise. Anna's anxiousness was making the gelding nervous.

"I won't let you fall, Anna." Mason said calmly. "Scoot closer to his head and I will ride behind you so that you won't fall." Mason waited until Anna was stable before releasing her. Her eyes widened in fear as she stared at him. He quickly swung up behind her, putting his arms around her waist and grabbing the reins in one hand.

"Mason, I don't like this. What if he throws us?" Anna's voice had risen along with her anxiety.

"Granger has never thrown anyone. We will be completely fine, Anna. I promise." Mason gently said. He nudged Granger forward and the gelding began to walk down the road. "You weren't this scared last time."

"What are you talking about? There was no last time." Anna snapped as she held tightly to his arm.

"I would have thought that day would have been ingrained into your very person." He didn't think she could become anymore tense, but she did.

"You are referring to the day my mother died." Anna breathed out. "But...that...no." She shook her head.

"Anna,"

"Mason...Mason..." she said his name slowly as if trying to remember something. She straightened up and looked at him with wide eyes. "Caverton? You are Mason Caverton!"

"I am." Mason inclined his head in a makeshift bow.

"I think I do remember reading about a horse." Anna scrunched her nose in concentration.

"Reading? Wouldn't you just remember?" Mason asked.

"I can't remember that day." Anna turned to look out into the forest.

"I have heard that trauma can cause memory loss." Mason said quietly.

"It wasn't the trauma." Anna shivered and laid her head on his shoulder. She was quiet for a long time before she spoke again. "I will show you when we are safe." Her voice became softer as she grew heavy.

Mason was thoroughly confused. What had caused her gap in memory of such a monumental day in her life? The death of his mother would be a day he would never forget if he had lost her the same way Anna had lost hers. He adjusted his hold on her so that she would be more secure. He allowed her to sleep as they rode.

He needed to figure out how he was going to keep both their reputations intact, while getting her somewhere safe. He had no idea where he should even take her. She let out a soft sigh as she adjusted her head against his chest. He still needed to sort through the rumors, who Sasha was, and what Anna had to say about Sasha and the rumors.

Hours ticked by as he worked through what he should do. They skirted three towns, and the night was growing cold. They were getting close to Haydenville. It was a small village with a tiny inn. He prayed they had a room. He was exhausted and he knew Anna was too.

"Anna, I need you to wake up." Mason said as he pulled Granger to a stop. Anna didn't stir. "Anna, wake up." He said a little louder as he touched her face.

She jolted awake, nearly sending both of them off of Granger's back. She gasped as she clung to him. "Mason." she said anxiously.

"It's okay. Everything is fine." He tried to soothe her panic. "I'm sorry. I didn't mean to scare you."

"Where are we?" She asked looking around.

"We are almost to Haydenville. I am going to get off and lead Granger the rest of the way. While we are here, you are my sister, Julie. I am hopefully going to get two rooms at the inn."

"What will you have me do?" Anna sat up and looked at him with guarded eyes.

"You are going to sit on Granger, and when we get to the inn, you are going to eat, get a nice warm bath, and get some sleep. We will talk tomorrow about everything."

"You want me to ride alone?" Anna shook her head. "You can ride, and I will walk."

"Absolutely not. My mother would hang me out to dry if I ever allowed such a thing." Mason dismounted and looked up at Anna. "Just grab a fistful of his mane."

"You grab onto his hair? That is so mean." Anna looked horrified at the thought. Mason laughed. "It's not funny, Mr. Caverton. Animals have feelings too."

"It doesn't hurt him, Anna. Just hold on so we can get you in a bed and you can rest." Mason smiled as he moved the reins over Granger's head and started walking. He glanced back when he heard Anna gasp.

Mason was ridiculous. She was not going to grab Granger's hair, even if the horse made her nervous. She could never hurt anything. She couldn't even kill spiders. Miranda was the one that would take care of them when Anna found one in her room.

The first buildings of the town came into view and Anna swallowed hard. She pulled her hood up over her head. Was it safe to be in a town? Would someone recognize her and send her back to her father? Anna shook her head. She was overreacting. There was no reason to fear. She had never been here before. Anna forced herself to relax.

Mason didn't stop until they walked into the courtyard of a small inn. He passed the reins over to a boy that came running up to them. Anna let out a shaky breath when Mason finally helped her back to solid ground. He threaded her hand through his arm before walking towards the main building.

She ducked her head as they entered. Mason walked with confidence as he approached the front desk. "Good evening. I need two rooms please."

"Two rooms?" The innkeeper asked.

Anna glanced up and saw the man looking between her and Mason. "Yes." Mason said slowly, as if he were confused. "My sister and I would prefer separate rooms."

"Sister?" The innkeeper continued to study them.

"Do you have the rooms or not?" Mason asked in irritation.

"Yes, sir." The innkeeper shook his head. "My apologies, I had assumed..."

"We are both exhausted." Mason cut the man off. The innkeeper nodded quickly as he began walking up the stairs. "This way." They were led to the far end of the hallway. The innkeeper opened up two doors that were across from one another. "Is there anything else I can get you?"

"We both could use something to eat." Mason gave her a gentle nudge toward one of the rooms. "Julie, would you like a bath tonight or in the morning?"

Anna bit her lip as she glanced between Mason and the innkeeper. "I...I...I am feeling quite tired."

"I will have my wife get you a bath in the morning then and I will send a maid up with your meals."

"Thank you." Mason nodded to the man and watched him leave. "How are you doing?" he asked quietly from her doorway.

"Are you sure it is safe to stay here?" Anna wrung her hands as she glanced around. She missed her basement room. Having the window in her room made her nervous. It was another entry point.

"We will be fine for the night." Mason said softly.

"Does the other room have a window?" Anna asked.

Mason's brows furrowed. "All bedrooms I have been in have windows."

Anna nodded. "Okay."

"Is everything all right?" Mason unfolded his arms as his eyes filled with concern.

"No, Mason. Things are definitely not all right." Anna snapped. "I just watch the woman that raised me get stabbed in the chest and my home set on fire." She hissed as she stepped to the door. "Good night." She slammed the door and locked it.

She walked over to the far corner and sat down. The room was too big. She felt vulnerable. Anna drew her knees up to her chest and hugged them as her tears began to fall. It wasn't long before a knock sounded at the door, causing Anna to jump. She curled more into a ball. More knocks came, but she didn't answer.

She could hear muffled voices in the hall before a key slid into the lock. "No, I will take it into her. She is probably asleep." Mason said. The door clicked but Anna didn't look up. She could hear him moving around the room. A hand lightly touched her arm, and her head snapped up. "Your dinner is on the bedside table when you are hungry. Try to get some rest." Mason gave her a look full of pain. "And I am sorry for today. I wish I could reverse time and fix everything. I really do." He stood and left the room.

Anna ran to the door and locked it. She leaned back against it and wiped her cheeks. She didn't like the fact that someone had a key to her room. She slid down the door until she was sitting on the floor. Memories of her father coming into her and her mother's room in the middle of the night played in her mind. She had taken the punch that was intended for her mother. Her mom shoved her out of the bed and Anna hid under it. She could still hear her mother's muffled cries and the sound of his fist hitting her repeatedly.

Chapter 8

Anna woke when someone knocked on her door. She had fallen asleep on the floor in front of the door. Another knock and she was scrambling to her feet. Slowly, she unlocked the door and peeked out. Mason stood there with several male servants.

"They are here to get your bath ready. If you would like, you can wait in my room." Mason told her.

"Umm...yes, thank you." Anna pulled the door open all the way and stepped to Mason's side. He gestured her inside the other room as he turned to the men that were waiting. He instructed them to let him know when the bath was ready.

Anna moved to the fireplace and sat down on the floor. She rubbed her eyes as she yawned. She had not slept well at all. It surprised her that she could still have nightmares about her father when it had been ten years since he had been in her life.

"How did you sleep?" Mason asked as he sat on the end of the bed.

She shrugged before pulling her journal out of her pocket. Anna tried to ignore Mason as she flipped through the book until she got to the start of that horrible day. She could still feel his eyes on her when she got to the part where she climbed the fence, and Mason helped her onto Granger's back behind Oliver.

"You were right." Anna glanced up. "I have ridden on Granger before."

"Why do you say that? I mean, I knew you had, but you seemed adamant that you hadn't."

"It says it here in my book." Anna lifted it a little before lowering it back into her lap.

"What is that book?" Mason asked curiously.

"It is my memory of that day. Every last detail, every last feeling, is recorded in here." Anna looked up and met Mason's gaze. "That day haunted me. Every time I tried to sleep; I would relive it all. My fear, hearing my mother's cry of pain, the terror, the sense of loss." Anna closed her eyes and shook her head. Her voice dropped to a whisper when she spoke again. "For four years, I would wake up screaming. Then Ginger came to the castle. Miranda suggested that I write down everything I could remember about that day. Reading through the memory would allow me to know what happened without it plaguing me."

"I don't understand." Mason said.

Anna opened her eyes, and a tear slipped down her cheek. "Ginger was able to remove memories. I asked her to erase that day from my mind. It had gotten to the point that I was afraid to go to sleep at night. Nothing Miranda or I did helped. I was trapped in an endless cycle of that day." Anna looked back down at her book. "I was scared enough before we even arrived at Woodbury. Mother insisted I needed another dress. Nowhere felt safe. She kept telling me it was all going to be fine. Finding the castle was such a blessing for us. It was our safe haven. I didn't understand why she would want to leave, even for fabric."

Mason sat on the floor next to her, and she glanced over at him. "For the first year after I had the memory erased, I was afraid to read what I wrote. I was worried it would trigger the memories and the cycle would start again. Ginger reassured me that it wouldn't because the memories were no longer there to stir up. I have read this every day for the last five years. It contains the week before and after her death as well as that day."

"Anna," Mason breathed out as he put his arm around her shoulders. "I'm so sorry." He held her close. Anna laid her head on his shoulder as her tears fell.

"Mason," Anna finally said after her tears dried. "I'm so tired." Her eyes began to droop.

"Did you sleep at all?" Mason asked as he rubbed her arm.

"I don't think..." A knock on the door cut off her answer.

Mason got to his feet and moved to answer it. One of the male servants stood in the hall. He informed him that the bath was ready, before he bowed and left. Without another word to Mason, she slipped into her room and locked the door.

Mason stared at the closed door for a long moment. He went back into his room. Their recent conversation replayed in his head. Her book held her memory of that day. He was still confused as to how she had that memory erased from her mind. Were they really witches then? Had that rumor actually been true?

He paced his room until a light knock sounded on his door. Anna stood there. Her wet hair was pulled into a braid that fell over her shoulder. She was carrying a platter of food. He stepped back and she tentative moved into the room. Mason closed the door and crossed to the window. He folded his arms over his chest as he stared out at the alley below.

"Mason?" Anna asked tentatively. "Did I do something wrong?" she asked nervously.

"No."

There was a long pause before she spoke again. "You are upset about something." She stated.

He let out a heavy sigh. "I am trying to figure out how a person was able to remove another's memory, Anna. That is not normal."

"I can explain. Would you like me to do it now or while we break our fast?" Anna placed the platter on a side table before looking back at him.

He uncrossed his arms and walked across the room. After they both had plates of food and had eaten several bites, Mason cleared his throat. He was hoping she would catch his hint and start talking.

"I am sure you are aware that there are Humans and Shifters in the world." She began. Mason raised a brow, and she smiled. "You will need to have patience if you are wanting answers."

"Continue, Miss Julianna."

"There is a third race. They are known to only a few and are called Guardians. They are extremely rare. Instead of having the ability to shift into an animal, they are given a Gift. Just like a Shifter's animal form is unique to that individual, so is a Guardian's Gift. Some have the ability to control elements. Others can speak with animals or have advanced healing. Guardians are all female and the gene can be either passed down or spontaneously appear."

"So, witches?"

"No. We don't do magic or create potions." Anna rolled her eyes, causing Mason to smile. "Throughout Arlania's history, there have been conflicts between Shifters and Humans. Guardians were there every time, smoothing the discord amongst them. We are peacemakers. That is our whole purpose. The castle was a sanctuary for Guardians. We could learn about our abilities and practice using them without others becoming afraid of us."

"When does one get a Gift?" Mason asked, taking a bite of his toast.

"Unlike Shifters who have their first shift at eighteen, Guardians don't have an age when their Gift manifest itself. It could come at any point in their lifetime. Miranda said she got her gift as a baby, though it took a few years for them to realize what it was, and Adeline got her Gift when she was seventy-two. Adeline was such a wonder." Anna smiled as she became more animated.

"I remember when she came to the castle last year. She could shape shift. Imagine being able to shift into any animal or object you wanted. She only used her ability to try to scare Miranda, but somehow, Miranda was always able to remain unfazed. She would tell Adeline that she needed to not fuel the mischief of the younger generation."

"Where there many of the younger generation?" Mason asked.

Anna shook her head. "I was the youngest by far after Laura left. That was before Adeline."

"Why did Laura leave if the castle was a sanctuary?"

"Laura was gentle and kind. She could help things grow." Anna's smile slipped from her lips. "But she wasn't the same after a boy named Clayton Harold was killed. She took his death really hard and blamed herself. Two years later, she and her mother left because of the rumors circulating. They only made Laura's guilt worse."

Mason put his plate down. His eyes became intense as he watched her. "Why would she blame herself for Clay's death?" He tried to keep his voice calm, while his whole body tensed.

Anna watched him for a moment. She could feel how important this information was to him. "She watched him get killed." Anna said quietly. She told him about Laura's meeting with Clay and how she had to defend herself. She told him of Laura's desire to make sure Clay made it back home safely and the riders that found him. She described the fear her friend had faced when she realized that he was dead.

Mason stood and began to pace. "You are telling me that a Guardian, did in fact, kill Clay?"

"Not one that lived at the castle. We never figured out who she was. Miranda had many contacts and reached out to them to try to locate the woman, but no one had any information. We had no one living at the castle who could control water." Anna said as she slowly got to her feet. She could feel his rising anger and she was scared he would turn it on her.

She inched toward the door, not wanting him to see her moving. He ran his hand through his hair several times as he continued to pace. She reached the door and grabbed the handle. He turned to face where she had been sitting at the table. His head snapped in her direction.

Anna flung open the door and ran. She slowed only when she reached the crowded entry hall. She managed to reach the door as she heard Mason ask someone if they had seen her. Once outside, Anna started running again. She had almost reached the alleyway when a hand grabbed her arm and spun her around.

Mason stood there looking confused and worried. "Please. I promise it wasn't us that killed him." Anna quietly said. Her eyes began to burn with unshed tears as her body began to shake.

"Did you think I was mad at you?" He studied her face. Anna couldn't speak. "Anna," Mason breathed out as he cupped her face, brushing away a tear with his thumb. "I am mad that those who were trying to rally Woodbury into attacking the castle were using Clay's death to fuel the townspeople's fears."

Anna squeezed her eyes shut as she took a deep breath, trying to calm her anxiety. A high-pitched nasally voice floated on the wind and her eyes flew open. She glanced around, her eyes quickly finding who had spoken. She was dressed in a burgundy dress, hanging onto a man's arm as they pointed at something in a shop window.

"M-mason." Anna stuttered out as her gaze returned to his.

"Anna, what's wrong?" He whispered. "You've lost all your color." Anna pointed a shaky hand at Sasha. Mason swore when he saw her. He wrapped his arm around Anna and practically carried her into the alleyway. He pressed her up against the wall as he stepped close. His face was inches from hers. He raised his hand to cup her face. "We will stay here for a few minutes before we head back to the inn." He whispered.

Mason could still feel Anna trembling. She was terrified of Sasha. He had to bite his tongue to keep from asking. There would be plenty of time later to figure out why Anna was so afraid of the woman.

"Mason?" Oliver's voice sounded from right behind him. Mason tensed. "Mason, what are you doing?"

"Oliver, what are you doing over here? It is time to be on our way." Mason's mother said, her voice was moving closer. He heard her gasp. "Mason?"

There wasn't anything he could do now. Mason straightened and turned to face his family. He moved his body to the side to try to shield Anna as best he could. "Hello, Mother. Oliver. Fancy seeing you here."

"Mason Caverton." His mother snapped in a quiet voice as she glanced around. "What on earth are you doing in Haydenville?"

"The coach is ready, Faith. Shall we be off?" His father's eyes widened when he saw Mason. "Son?"

A tense silence filled the space. "Who is your friend, Mason?" Oliver asked after several tense moments.

"Allen, your son was just kissing that girl." His mother stated.

"I wasn't kissing her." Mason corrected.

"Sure looked like it." Oliver commented.

Mason ran a hand down his face. He had intentionally made it look that way to hide Anna. People tended to look away when they saw public displays of affection. He glanced over his shoulder. Anna had pulled her hood over her head, and she was looking at the ground. Her face was completely hidden.

"We didn't raise you to go around kissing young ladies." His mother continued. "You have ruined her, Mason."

"Now, Faith," His father touched his wife's arm as his eyes remained fixed on Mason. "Why don't we take this conversation to a more private location. I suggest the coach."

Mason felt Anna tense behind him. "Father, this isn't what it appears to be."

"Mason, escort the young lady to the coach." His father's expression was hard. Mason knew that there would be no arguing with him.

He turned to Anna and gently grabbed her hand. Their eyes met briefly, and he gave her a small smile. He threaded her hand through his arm, and he walked out of the alleyway. He spotted the family's coach and quickly moved to it. He assisted Anna inside before turning to Oliver.

"Ollie, would you be so kind as to collect my things from my room? And collect Granger?" Mason sent his brother a glare.

"Of course. But don't start without me. I can't wait to hear what is going on." Oliver smirked at him before heading for the inn.

"Get inside." His father said evenly.

Mason sighed and climbed in. Anna had pressed herself into the far corner. Her face was still pale, and her shaking had gotten worse. "Is it okay if I sit by you?" She nodded, and the moment he sat down, she grabbed hold of his arm. "Everything will be all right." He whispered.

"I don't...I'm not good in small spaces with strange..." Anna's grip tightened.

"Men?" Mason finished for her. "I know. You were the same ten years ago. My father and brother are better men than I am. You will be safe."

The door opened and his mother took the seat across from them, followed by his father. "As soon as Oliver is done collecting Granger, we will be on our way." His father said.

The air in the coach became thick with tension as they waited. Ten minutes ticked by slowly before Oliver hopped into the coach. He took the seat next to Mason, forcing him to move closer to Anna. She moved so that his shoulder partially blocked her from his parents.

The coach began moving. Only after they were out of the village did his mother speak. "Dear, what is your name?" She asked Anna.

Anna buried her face more into his shoulder. "Mother, I promise, nothing untoward has happened." Mason said.

"Mason, your mother was asking the young lady a question. You will hold your tongue and give her the proper respect she deserves." His father snapped.

"Yes, sir." Mason mumbled.

"What were you thinking?" His father continued. "We did not raise you to treat a woman with such little respect."

"A simple kiss in public can completely ruin a girl's reputation and future. You had her up against the wall in an alley." His mother added.

"Rumors were already circulating." Oliver said. "I overheard several people in the inn talking about the girl who managed to seduce one of the Cavertons."

His father's face was turning red with anger. "We will contact her family, and then you two will be married."

"What?" Mason sat up straighter. Anna gasped and pulled away from him.

"Your actions have consequences, Mason." His Mother glared at him, before looking at Anna. "Who are your parents, dear?"

Anna covered her face as she began to cry. He wanted to comfort her, but he knew she wouldn't allow it at this point. He had promised her that she would be safe. Now his family was forcing them into marriage.

"I am sorry my son has forced this on you." His mother's voice softened. "Who can we send word to?"

Anna shook her head. "I have no one." Her voice was so soft, Mason wasn't sure his parents heard.

His father's face turned a deeper shade of red as he glared at Mason. He signaled the driver, and as soon as the coach stopped, he was out of the coach. Anna jumped when the door slammed shut. She kept her face in her hands as her body shook. His mother had tears rolling down her cheeks. Mason glanced at Oliver, who lifted a brow in question.

Mason took a deep breath and let it out slowly as he looked at his clasped hands. This was not how he imagined today going. He still had no idea why Anna had run from him, then Sasha was there. The sudden appearance of his family had ruined any chance of getting Anna further away from White Castle.

Mason's father reentered the coach, and they started moving again. He put his arms around his wife as he whispered in her ear. She nodded before laying her head on his shoulder. Mason hung his head and leaned his forearms on his knees. He needed to speak with Anna without his family around. He needed to apologize for messing up, again.

The coach stopped an hour later. His father instructed everyone to get out. Mason tensed when he saw they were in front of a church. Anna moved to his side. She let out a quiet whimper as she began to shake. He glanced at her. Her head was down with her hood up over her head. He couldn't see her face. Her hands were clasped tightly in front of her. She was utterly terrified. What had Mason done?

Chapter 9

Anna could feel the tension rolling off of Mason as they stood at the back of the chapel while Lord Caverton spoke with the preacher at the front. She didn't understand why his family was forcing them to marry. She didn't care what others thought of her. She just wanted to get as far away from the castle and Sasha as she could.

Lord Caverton nodded, shook hands with the preacher, and made his way back to them. "He has agreed to do the marriage."

"She needs a new dress, Allen." Lady Caverton whispered. "She shouldn't have to get married in that." Anna squeezed her eyes closed. She didn't want to get married in the first place. "Shall we go shopping and see what we can find?" Anna knew she was talking to her.

Anna shook her head and took a step back. She definitely didn't want to go shopping. A hand touched her arm softly and she glanced up enough to know it was Mason. "I have your other dress." He whispered.

Her head snapped up. "I put it in the tree. How do you have it?" She asked, so only he could hear her.

He gave her a small smile. "I went back for it before getting Granger. That is why it took me so long."

"Even though this isn't necessarily how you pictured your wedding day, no bride should have to wear..." Lady Caverton's voice trailed off as if trying to come up with the right words. Anna knew the dress was ugly and obviously too big for her. It was necessary though. Her white dress would have stood out and gotten them caught.

"No offense my soon-to-be dear sister, but that dress is quite hideous and does nothing to flatter you. Though I can't say much since we haven't seen your face yet either." Oliver chimed in.

"Oliver." Mason warned.

"She doesn't want to go shopping, Faith. The girl obviously is terrified. Let's get this done so she can settle in. You can get her new dresses when we get home." Lord Caverton stated.

Anna took an involuntary step back. Lord Caverton's anger triggered her anxiety, and she felt the need to run, to hide. Her feet remained glued to the floor, however. What would he do if she did try to run? An image of her father standing over her just before his boot struck her stomach sending her sliding across the floor came to mind. She swallowed hard and ducked her head even more. She couldn't risk running and making Lord Caverton even more mad.

"She has another dress." Mason told the others.

Mason pressed the satchel into her hands. "Oh good." Lady Caverton breathed. She grabbed Anna's arm and pulled her from the chapel and down a hallway. They came to a door and stopped. "Would you like some help changing?" Anna shook her head. "I will be right here when you get out, then. Take your time. Allen can just be patient."

Anna slipped into the room. Despite Lady Caverton telling her to take her time, she changed as fast as she could. She wasn't about to anger the three men waiting on them. She took out her braid and combed through her hair as best she could with her fingers, before opening the door.

She felt completely exposed without a hood on. The lighter fabric of this dress made the building feel much cooler than before. As they walked back to the chapel, Anna kept her head down. Her father's voice kept sounding in her ear.

"You are to never raise your eyes higher than a man's knees unless directly told to do so." He yelled at her. "The day you marry, you belong to your husband. He is in charge of your every move. You will do as instructed without hesitation. Do you understand, you worthless thing?"

Anna was snapped out of her memories when someone grabbed her hands. She flinched slightly but didn't pull away. "What is your full name, young lady?" A man to her left asked.

"Julianna Winters." She grudgingly answered.

The man began speaking, and she realized she was at the front of the church and the ceremony had begun. Mason ran his thumbs over the back of her trembling hands. It was calming, but at the same time, it was terrifying.

"I do." Mason said quietly as his hands tightened on hers.

Anna fought the tears that stung her eyes. She needed to think positive. Her mother and Miranda always told her to look for the good in a situation. She bit her lip as she racked her brain for something. At least Mason was only two years older than she was, instead of being old enough to be her grandfather like Mr. Hawkshaw. Mason was very attractive too. So, there was that. But looks could be deceiving. Sasha was as beautiful as she was mean.

A throat cleared and she jumped. Mason squeezed her hand, and she chanced a glance at him. His head nodded ever so slightly. She dropped her gaze again. "Miss?"

"I do." She whispered, and a tear fell down her cheek.

"I now pronounce you husband and wife. You may now kiss your bride." The man stepped back.

Mason took a deep breath before taking a small step closer to her. Anna tensed when he used his finger to lift her chin. He searched her face for a moment before leaning down and softly kissing the corner of her mouth. It was so soft that Anna barely felt it.

"Mr. Caverton, she is your bride. You can do better than that." The preacher chuckled.

Mason slid his hand to the back of her neck. She was sure he could feel her racing heart. Anna closed her eyes and waited. She felt him move a little closer. His warm breath danced over her lips right before his lips gently pressed to hers. He pulled back, but she kept her eyes closed. That kiss had been nothing like she had expected.

When her father kissed her mother, he often left bruises, or her lips would be bleeding from the force of it. She felt Mason kiss her forehead and she opened her eyes. He gave her a small smile before taking a step back. He kept a firm hold on her hand as he turned to his family.

Lady Caverton rushed to Anna and pulled her into a hug. Anna froze, unsure of what she should do. "Mother, could you help Anna get changed?" Mason asked.

"Into what? That hideous gown she was wearing before?" Lady Caverton stepped back. "This dress suits her far better."

"I understand that, Mother, but she needs to change." Mason said tiredly.

"At the moment, I prefer the brown dress, my lady." Anna said softly. She could tell all eyes turned to her, even though her gaze was fixed on the ground. She pulled her hand from Mason's and retraced her steps to the room where she had changed.

She squeaked in surprise when she stepped back out of the room and saw Mason leaning against the wall. She quickly dropped her gaze. "Anna, I am truly sorry for this. I never meant for this to happen." She nodded her head and waited. "Mother is insisting we walk over to the inn to have lunch before we continue travelling."

"I understand." Anna whispered.

"Anna, look at me." Mason pushed off the wall and Anna slowly lifted her eyes to meet his. His gaze was searching as he studied her. "You are more afraid of me now than when you thought I was going to kill you." He said quietly.

She blinked back tears and dropped her gaze to his chest. "I'm sorry." Her voice trembled.

"You have nothing to be sorry for, Anna." Mason grabbed her hand. "I was the idiot whose actions caused this to happen. You are not at fault."

"Come on, Mason!" Oliver yelled down the corridor, causing Anna to jump as his voice echoed off the stone. "I'm starving."

They walked to where Oliver waited restlessly. Anna tried to drop back behind the Caverton brothers, but Mason tightened his hold on her. She didn't fight it. She was at his mercy now.

Lord Caverton had procured a private parlor for the family. The atmosphere was tense despite Oliver's frequent jokes. Anna pushed around the small amount of food on her plate. She was so anxious that any thought of food was making her stomach twist uncomfortably.

"Father, you have to admit it is quite ironic that Mason would end up married to Julianna." Oliver broke the silence.

"Why would I find it ironic, Oliver. Your brother has trapped the poor girl into a life with him."

"Don't you recognize her? If her dress didn't give it away, those gorgeous blue eyes sure would." Oliver chuckled. Anna squeezed her eyes closed. She had forgotten how distinct her eyes were while living with the Guardians. And why would any of them recognize her?

"How could I see her eyes when she is always staring at the floor?" Lord Caverton snapped. Anna tensed as she felt the full force of his angry gaze.

"Father, please try to calm down." Mason said.

"Calm down! You are telling me to calm down? Mason, I have half a mind to disown you for what you have done." Lord Caverton slammed his fist on the table, causing Anna to scream. She covered her mouth to cut it off before she got in any more trouble. Her trembling grew as she fought her tears.

Mason and Oliver were on their feet immediately. Mason had positioned himself between her and his father. Oliver stood next to him. "Father, Mason is right. You need to calm down." Oliver said firmly.

"Anna, are you okay?" Mason knelt down in front of her. The tears broke free and coursed down her cheeks. "It's okay, Anna. No matter how angry the old man gets, he would never hurt you."

Anna shook her head as she covered her face with her hands. Mason sat down next to her and put his arms around her. He guided her head to his chest as she continued to shake.

"Anna?" Lady Caverton said in surprise.

"Yes, Mother. Anna. You know, Mason's Anna? The one that we took to the castle after her mother was…" Oliver cleared his throat. "That Anna."

"She wasn't my Anna." Mason said.

"You kept asking after her and went every year with Mother and Father to deliver the flowers in hopes of seeing her again." Oliver said. "That's how we all have referred to her over the years."

"How is it that I am more mature than you are when you are four years older than I am?" Mason asked.

"I am sorry for scaring you, Anna." Lord Caverton said gently.

"How did you end up in that alley?" Lady Caverton asked.

Mason explained about the meetings he had been attending where they had multiple people speaking about the horrors they had experienced due to the witches. He mentioned how he asked about the king's involvement and was assured the monarch was in favor of the plan.

"How did the raid go anyway?" Oliver asked. "I am disappointed I missed it."

"You both were involved in this?" Lord Caverton asked in surprise.

"They killed Clay. And you should have heard Lady Sasha speaking about her narrow escape." Oliver said excitedly. "She ran when she witnessed her first ritual for another woman to receive her powers. They carved open a young girl and ate her still beating heart."

Anna shot to her feet and ran for the ash bucket near the fireplace. She threw up everything she had in her stomach. When she finally had nothing left, she sat on the floor and hugged her knees to her chest. A hand touched her shoulder. She raised her head to meet Mason's worried gaze.

"That is what Sasha was saying about us? You only said that we ate kids, not…that." Anna waved her hand in Oliver's direction. "Why would she say that? Why would she claim we did such disturbing things? Miranda was her sister. She was one of us. She was Miranda's second, until two years ago when she left. I don't understand." Anna closed her eyes and shook her head. "I don't under…"

Then it hit her. The arguments between Miranda and Sasha. The Amulet. Sasha wanted the Amulet because Miranda refused to use it to elevate the Guardians. "Anna?" Mason said softly.

"I should go." Anna struggled to her feet. "I shouldn't be here."

"Are you saying you know Lady Sasha?" Oliver asked.

"She helped raise me." Anna shook her head. "Well, kind of. Miranda raised me and Sasha tried to get Miranda to send me away." She took a few steps towards the door. "I really need to leave." Anna kept her eyes on the ground, so she didn't see that Oliver had moved to block her exit until she bumped into him. She took several steps back in surprise.

"You can't just leave, Anna. You are married to that knucklehead, remember?" Oliver gestured to someone behind her, but her eyes remained on his for a few seconds. He was right. She was married to Mason. He was in control of her future.

"I would still like to know how the two of you ended up kissing in the alley." Lady Caverton stated.

"We weren't kissing." Mason sighed. "We attacked the castle, and I asked about the king's men. I was assigned to patrol the side of the cliff that borders the river. Anna came out a secret door in the rock. I wanted answers, so I hid her away instead of turning her over to the others." Mason paused for a long time. "Father, they told us all that the witches would be sent to the king to be judged. They threatened us if we tried to stop them. With Anna hidden away, I could not risk getting killed. I had to get back to her."

"What happened, Mason?" Lord Caverton asked.

Anna turned and watched Mason. He was pale and had a haunted look in his eyes. She could feel his guilt and pain. He squeezed his eyes shut. "They trapped them in a room and set it on fire. When we finally realized what was happening, their screams...I was at the back but several of the men from Woodbury tried to get to the door. They were stopped. We were told that if we intervened, we would join them."

Anna covered her mouth as she sank to her knees. Not only was Miranda dead, but all the others were too. Sasha manipulated the people of Woodbury into doing her will. For what? An artifact that held the power to control Shifters. She betrayed her family for power.

Arms wrapped around her in a gentle hug. "Why don't we get going? Caverton Estates will be much more comfortable than an inn to process all that has been said." Lady Caverton said softly.

Anna didn't move or say anything. She couldn't seem to get her body moving. She closed her eyes as she willed the pain and loss to go away. She was lifted off the ground. The smell of pine filled her senses, and she knew it was Mason that carried her. She curled into a ball against the side of the coach. No one spoke, and Anna found herself falling asleep.

Chapter 10

Mason kept glancing over at Anna. She was curled into a tight ball as she rested against the side of the coach. He leaned back and let out a sigh. When he looked across the coach, his family was watching him. He was glad that Oliver had sat with their parents. It allowed Anna to have more room. But he hated that all of them were staring at him.

"I was taking her away from the castle to keep her safe." Mason couldn't stand the silence anymore. "She is understandably upset about yesterday. We were just about to continue north when she saw Sasha across the street. I didn't know how else to keep her out of sight."

"So, you kissed her?" Oliver said in disbelief.

"I didn't kiss her." Mason glared at his brother. "People get uncomfortable with displays of affection. I was hoping if it looked like we were…kissing, Lady Sasha and Lord Carson would just pass by without looking at her." He looked over at Anna. "I was trying to protect her."

"You didn't kiss her?" Oliver asked.

"Of course I didn't. Father would flog me if I took advantage of a woman like that." Mason crossed his arms over his chest.

"You did seem awkward at the altar." Oliver laughed.

"Leave your brother alone, Oliver." Lady Caverton scolded. "The girl was obviously terrified. Mason probably didn't want to upset her further."

Mason turned his attention to watching the scenery out the window. His cheeks felt hot as he remembered kissing Anna. He could hear Oliver snickering, but he ignored him.

The rest of the three-hour journey was done in silence. Anna didn't stir when they came to a stop in front of Caverton Estates. Mason waited for his family to exit the coach before turning to Anna. He gently brushed the hair out of her face. She had dried tear tracks on her cheeks.

"Anna." he said softly. "Anna, it's time to get up."

She blinked slowly as she sat up. She looked around and then stiffened. "Where are we?" she asked anxiously.

"Caverton Estates. One of my family's holdings." Mason got out and turned to offer his hand to her. Anna pulled her hood over her head. She hesitated before putting her hand in his. He didn't release her hand as they walked inside. The entry hall was spacious but felt crowded with his parents waiting just inside.

"You must be tired, Anna. You and Mason will be in the north wing." Lady Caverton smiled.

Anna kept her gaze on the floor. Mason leaned close to her. "Go ahead upstairs. Take the right hallway. Your room will be the last door on the right. I will be up in a little while to check on you."

She glanced at him quickly before heading up the stairs. Mason watched until she disappeared. Something felt off with her. She had become completely different as soon as his parents showed up. He needed to get this confrontation with his family over with so he could make sure that she was okay. He followed his parents into his father's study.

* * *

Anna entered the last room on the right. She paused in the doorway as she surveyed the room. It was large with two big windows that brought in a lot of natural light. The décor was decidedly masculine. She took several steps inside but stopped. Her eyes landed on the bed, and she stared at it in apprehension.

All the lessons her father had her sit through flashed in her mind and her hands started to shake. She was scared of what was going to happen. Her father had spared no detail in describing what her husband was going to do to her. A noise at the door had her spinning around. Mason stood in the doorway.

How long had she been standing there? She could still remember the feel of her father's hand on her face the last time she didn't do what he asked her to do. Fear of both being punished and of what was to come filled her as she spun back around. She unclasped her cloak and tried to undo the back of her dress as quickly as possible. She was supposed to already be in the bed.

Mason saw the fear in Anna's eyes before she turned away from him and tried to undo the back of her dress. He quickly crossed the room and grabbed her hands, stopping her frantic movements. He turned her to face him. "Anna, what are you doing?" he asked in concern and confusion.

"I'm sorry. I know I am supposed to already be in the bed." Her voice trembled.

Mason kept a tight hold of her hands as he studied her. She refused to look at him as her whole body shook in fear. "Will you sit with me for a moment?" he asked gently. When she gave a small nod, he guided her to the settee at the side of the room. Instead of sitting with her, he crouched in front of her. "Is that what you thought I meant when I said for you to come up here?"

"We are married. I know my role." Anna's soft voice barely reached him.

"I am aware that we are married, Anna. Just so we are on the same page, what do you think your role is?" Mason said slowly.

"I am to..." She swallowed hard and her chin trembled. "Keep you happy anyway you see fit and to produce sons." Anna squeaked out. She kept her gaze down, focusing on their clasped hands.

"Is that what they taught you at the castle?" Mason asked in surprise.

"No. That is what my father instructed me to do." Anna swallowed hard. "A woman's worth is dependent on how many sons she can give her husband and how much she can satisfy him." She tried to pull her hands away, but his grip tightened. "As your wife, I am to do whatever you tell me to do. I am to allow you to do whatever you want to me."

Mason was quiet for a while. He gave her hand a gentle squeeze. "I was raised differently." He finally said, and Anna glanced up at him. He was studying her with his brows furrowed. "I was taught that women and girls are meant to be protected and respected. You are my partner, Anna. My equal. It is my job to keep you safe from anything and everything that might hurt you physically or mentally. As your husband, I will provide for you and cherish you. As my wife, it is your responsibility to tell me when I am being an idiot."

Anna blinked in surprise. "I don't understand."

"I tend to make really stupid decisions. For example, assisting people in attacking a castle full of women when I didn't fully know the situation, or hiding in alleyways." Mason gave her a small smile.

Anna shook her head. "We are married..."

"Anna, we will not be doing anything that you are not comfortable with or ready for. Don't you think we should get to know one another a little more before we take that step?" Mason rubbed his thumbs on the back of her hands as she stared at him. He could see her trying to process his words.

"So, you aren't going to..."

"We are going to take things slow, Anna. Now, do you need anything before I head to my room?"

"Your room?" Anna glanced around at the bedroom they were in.

Mason smiled. As he stood, he pressed a kiss to her forehead. "I figured you would be more comfortable in your own room. I will be next door. I only stopped in to see if you needed anything before I went to bed."

Anna blinked up at the confusing man that was now her husband. She had never thought that this was how her wedding day would go. Her father had drilled it into her what was going to happen. When she was only seven, Mr. Hawkshaw had even told her what he expected of her once they were wed. Yet Mason was saying goodnight and sleeping in a different room.

Anna ducked her head and covered her face with her hands. She was still shaking as she tried to calm herself. "Anna, look at me." Mason's voice was soft, and Anna lifted her gaze to meet his.

He extended his hand to her, and she hesitantly took it. Once she was on her feet, Mason put his arms around her. She leaned against him as she breathed deeply. The smell of pine filled her lungs, helping her relax. She had no idea that that specific scent was so calming. She took half a step closer to him as she rested more against him.

Mason held Anna for several minutes. She seemed calmer than she had been when he first came into the room. What kind of father conditioned his daughter to be a slave to her husband? He tightened his arms around her. He vowed that he would do everything in his power to earn her trust and erase her father's influence on her.

"Mason?" Anna's voice was soft.

"Yes, Anna?"

"I'm scared."

Mason pressed a kiss to her brow. He couldn't stop himself. He was finding that he really liked kissing his wife. Though he would keep it to her cheek and forehead until she was more comfortable with him. "What are you scared of?"

"I don't know what is happening. I don't know why you aren't doing what I have been taught all my life would happen. I don't know why Sasha killed everyone. I don't understand anything."

Mason pulled back so he could study her face. "Your father was wrong for teaching you what I think he taught you." He said as he cupped her face. "You and I are partners, Anna. Equals." He smoothed her hair back from her face. "I never intended for us to end up married. I was only trying to protect you from Sasha. But since that is how the chips have fallen, I plan on fulfilling my husbandly duties to the best of my ability. You are my wife, my number one responsibility. Your needs come before my own."

"I still don't understand." Anna shook her head. "Every man I have ever known has been like my father. My father often said 'a woman without bruises has a soft husband. And men like that are worthless.' That is one of the reasons my mom and I left. She didn't want me to end up with Mr. Hawkshaw. Father had shoved us both into a cabin away from the rest of the clan and only came by to hurt Mother and teach me my lessons." She walked away from Mason as she wrapped her arms around herself.

"Who is Mr. Hawkshaw?" Mason asked.

"He is the man my father sold me to when I was born. He kept telling me that I should be grateful that someone wanted me, because if Hawkshaw hadn't spoken up, I would have been drowned." Anna took a deep breath and let it out slowly. "He was my grandfather's friend when they were growing up. Mother couldn't stand the thought of me being traded to him when I turned sixteen, so she planned our escape for eight years. Then we ran. The castle was supposed to be safe. We were trying to get away from the violence."

"Then your mother was killed." Mason's voice sounded from just behind her, and she jumped.

"Miranda took me to the library and gave me a book. She said when I was done with it, we could discuss it. I refused to even look at the book. Father often forced me to read books. Every last one gave me nightmares." Anna didn't turn around.

"What about the books gave you nightmares?"

"They were dictionaries of a sort. I had to memorize them before I turned eight. There would be a word followed by a detailed description of what I was supposed to do when my husband said the word." Anna shivered. "My father and Mr. Hawkshaw planned out my whole life. Once sixteen, I would be chained up in his room. His previous four wives had died from what he put them through before they turned twenty."

Mason turned Anna to face him. He could see the fear in her eyes. "I know it will not be easy, but I need you to forget everything those men taught and told you, Anna. Forget what you read in those books. Forget it all."

"You don't think I have tried?" Anna yelled before she slapped her hand over her mouth. She took a step back. "I'm sorry. I didn't mean to yell. I-I..." Panic filled her features.

"Anna, you have every right to be upset. The way your father raised you. The death of your mother. Yesterday's events. My treatment of you. Sasha. Any of it is too much for someone to have to bear. Yell. Scream. Break something. I don't care. Everyone needs to release pent-up emotions at some time in their lives." Mason's eyes moved to the side and a smile spread on his face. "Are you feeling up for a walk? I want to show you something." Anna bit her lip as she looked down. Mason lifted her chin gently. "It is okay if your answer is, no."

"Where are you wanting to go?" Anna asked.

"I want to show you where I like to go when I want to be alone and think." Mason extended his hand to her and waited.

Anna stared at his hand for a moment before putting hers in it. His smile grew as he walked towards the door. He peeked out into the hall before pulling Anna after him. He couldn't wait to see her reaction to his favorite place. He heard Oliver talking with someone and he quickly moved into the nearest room. He raised his finger to his lips to tell Anna to be quiet as he listened to his brother and his father walk by.

When the coast was clear, Mason opened the door and continued towards the stairs. Anna's grip on him tightened and he glanced at her. Her other hand was on her chest, and she was wheezing. He slowed to a walk and Anna started coughing. It was a loud barking cough and looked and sounded painful. "Are you all right?" Mason asked.

"I think so." She whispered. "Can we walk though?"

"Of course we can." Mason said. "We can send for a doctor, if you would like."

Anna shook her head. "I'm okay. I don't need a doctor."

Mason nodded as they walked across the lawn to the hedge garden. They wove through the shrubs and flowers until they reached the path that led into the trees. Mason guided Anna off the path after several minutes and came to a stop at the edge of a stream. "Would you like me to carry you across?" Anna smiled as she lifted the bottom of her skirts and stepped into the cool water. Did Mason think she was afraid of getting wet? "Where are your shoes?" Mason asked once he was standing next to her on the opposite shore.

"Shoes?" Anna scrunched her nose. "I have never worn shoes." Women in Crossford weren't permitted to. It deterred them from running away. The climate was so cold that you could lose a foot if you weren't careful. While living in the castle, she never saw a need for them. The grounds were always clear of anything that was harmful and the stones inside were smooth.

"Hmm." Mason said, taking her hand again. She followed him through the woods.

Anna took a deep breath of the fresh air and coughed. Her lungs still burned from all the smoke that she breathed in while making her escape from the castle. They came to another hedge. She glanced at Mason and his smile was huge. She could feel his excitement building as they approached a break in the hedge.

Mason paused at the opening and turned to watch Anna as she came around the corner. She gasped when she saw the gazebo. He had built it a year ago. He had turned a bench into a swing that he had hung inside it. The gardener had planted several different kinds of flowers in the small clearing. Within the hedge walls, it felt as if one was stepping into a different world. His mother had said it reminded her of a fairy garden she had read about in a book when she was a little girl.

He led Anna to the swing, and she sat down. "May I?" Mason asked as he gestured to the empty spot next to her. Anna nodded and he sat with a sigh. He put his arm along the back of the bench and closed his eyes. It felt good to just sit in the quiet.

His parents had lectured him about how he was to treat Anna now that they were married. It was irritating that they thought he was going to mistreat her in any way. They had acted as if he hadn't been taught all his life to respect his future wife.

"Thank you for bringing me here." Anna said, breaking into his thoughts.

Mason looked over at her. She pulled her feet up under her as she leaned against him. "You're welcome, Anna. It's a good place to think."

They fell into a comfortable silence. Anna laid her head on his shoulder as she let out a long breath. "Mason?"

"Yes, Anna?" Mason said softly.

"What is going to happen now?" She still sounded anxious.

Mason moved his arm from the back of the bench and put it around her shoulders. "We stay here as long as you would like. Then we head back to the house where I will send dinner up to your room so you can avoid my family for a little while longer."

"Not exactly what I was meaning." she muttered.

Mason smiled. "Tomorrow, I am sure my mother will demand some of our time. Oliver will no doubt tease me some more. Father will most likely pull me aside for another lecture."

"Mason," Irritation crept into Anna's voice, and he chuckled.

"Do you have any suggestions on what we should do tomorrow then?" Mason said as seriously as he could.

Anna sat up and glared at him. "I am serious, Mr. Caverton. My life went up in smoke and I have no idea what my future looks like. And I am terrified."

Mason sobered. She was right. Her life was a complete mess right now. "I'm sorry, Anna. I shouldn't be teasing you right now." She let out a huff before settling back against him. "I'm not entirely sure what will happen." He was quiet for several minutes. "I need to talk with my father tomorrow. I think I should ask him for my inheritance. I want to get you as far away from this area of Arlania as I can."

"I don't understand." Anna said.

"I am to inherit a house and a title. I am hoping to take you to Caverton Manor. It's a bit smaller than this place but should do us well." Mason sighed. "I really don't know what will happen, Anna. All I know is that I will be there to protect you. No matter where we end up."

Anna didn't say anything, and Mason set the seat rocking. She leaned more against him. Mason repositioned a little so that Anna would be more comfortable. After a few minutes, her head slid a little and he guessed she had fallen asleep. She had been through a lot the past few days and he wasn't surprised that she was exhausted. She seemed more at ease out here. Mason decided to let her sleep for a while before attempting to take her back to her room.

Chapter 11

Mason was stepping out of his room just as Anna was closing her own door. "Good morning." Mason greeted her. She jumped a little as she dropped her gaze to the floor. He hated that she was scared of him. He reminded himself that she had every right to be. After all, he had attacked her only a few days ago.

"Good morning." She answered softly.

"Can I walk with you down to the breakfast room?" Anna nodded without looking at him. They began walking down the hall together. "What are your plans after the meal?"

Anna glanced at him. "Whatever you wish me to do."

Mason stopped walking and she did the same. "I am not your dictator, Anna. I told you last night that we are equals." She kept her face down. Mason hooked his finger under her chin and raised it so he could see her eyes. "You are a beautiful, strong, capable woman. I have no doubt in my mind that you are far smarter than I am. If anyone of us is going to be the boss, it is going to be you."

Anna ducked her head as she started coughing. Mason put his hand on her back. When her coughing finally ended, she was wheezing. Mason studied her closely. She was a little pale with dark circles under her eyes.

"Anna, I think you should go lay down. I am going to send for the doctor." Mason was worried.

"No, please." Anna whispered as her eyes widened. "I don't need a doctor."

"I have never heard anyone cough like that before. You are having a hard time breathing." Mason touched her arm.

Anna shook her head again. "It is nothing."

He couldn't understand why she didn't want to see a doctor. He put his arms around her, and she leaned against him as she coughed again. "I can't let you stay like this." Mason whispered. He cradled her head as she struggled to catch her breath.

"I will be fine." she said quietly.

"I will send down for breakfast." Anna started to protest, but he cut her off. "You can hardly breathe, Anna. What happened to you?"

Anna took a step back and he released her. Her eyes were guarded as she watched him. "The fires." Anna said slowly. "They used hay and other fuels to cause the fire to spread quickly. The only way out was through the worst of it. I tried to use my cloak to cover my nose and mouth. The smoke was so thick at times that I couldn't see very far in front of me."

Mason ran a hand down his face. "I am sending for the doctor. Too much smoke can be dangerous, Anna."

"You just said I was the boss." Anna crossed her arms over her chest. "I will not see a doctor. You can yell at me, beat me, starve me, but I will not see one."

He stared at her in surprise. She had never been so defiant before. She was usually submissive. "For starters, I would never do any of that to you. And you can be the boss on everything but this. You need a doctor."

Anna turned around and walked back to her room. She slammed the door, and he heard the lock snap into place. He knocked on the door in irritation. "Anna, open up!" He called. She didn't respond and he growled in frustration. The blasted woman couldn't breathe properly yet refused to get help.

He stormed down the hall, determined to send for the doctor. He couldn't sit back and watch her struggle to breathe. He sent a servant to fetch the doctor before making his way to the breakfast room. He didn't look at anyone at the table as he went to the sideboard and filled up a plate. He stomped to the door and asked a maid that was passing by to take it up to Anna's room.

"Is everything alright, Mason?" His mother asked.

"No, it is not." He said stiffly as he tried to rein in his rising worry and frustration.

Anna paused at the doorway to the breakfast room when she heard Mason speaking. She had been surprised when she ran into a maid with a plate of food. The young girl said Mason had asked her to take it up to Anna. She didn't understand. He was angry with her, yet he was making a plate of food for her.

"Trouble in paradise already?" Oliver laughed.

"She can't hardly breathe with all the smoke she inhaled from the fires, yet she doesn't want to see a doctor." Mason growled out.

"What are you going to do?" Lord Caverton asked. "You know how dangerous smoke inhalation can be."

"Mr. Gregory died a week after the Smith's barn caught on fire last year." Lady Caverton added. She sounded worried. "You ended up with a fever."

"I know." Mason sighed. "I sent for the doctor. I need to know she is okay."

Anna moved back down the hall until she found the door Mason had used last night. She walked through the hedge garden and out into the woods. She didn't need a doctor. She only needed to find a few plants so she could make tea. Instead of going to the gazebo, she turned in the other direction. She kept her steps slow as she observed the plants around her.

She had been out for a good hour before she spotted one of the plants she was looking for. "There you are." Anna smiled as she knelt on the ground. Hyssop was the main one she had wanted to find. She gathered a large amount of leaves before getting to her feet.

Anna looked around again. Hours ticked by as she slowly made her way through the forest. She didn't want to venture too far away from the Caverton's home. She didn't know the area well and didn't want to get lost. Anna made it back to the gazebo with only Hyssop to show for her efforts.

She moved to the bench and sat. Her chest felt tight, and she needed to rest for a little while before going to the kitchen to make her tea. After a few minutes, she felt like she could continue. She slipped inside the house unnoticed and went directly to the kitchen. She had explored the house during the night, once she was sure everyone was asleep.

"Oh," the startled cook gasped when Anna walked into the kitchen. "Can I help you?"

"Would you be all right with me making myself some tea?" Anna asked. Some women were very strict about their space. Jacklyn had not allowed many into her domain. The woman hesitated before slowly nodding. Anna gave her a smile before walking over to the cookfire.

Anna carried the tray with the teapot and cup up the stairs. She kept her head down as she passed several servants as they hurried by. She hesitated at her door. If Mason had sent for the doctor, they would come looking for her in her room. Where would be the last place they would look for her? She glanced at Mason's door.

She knocked, and when no response came, she opened the door. Anna scanned the room to make sure he wasn't there before stepping inside and closing the door. She walked over to the window seat and set the tray down. She poured herself a cup, added some honey, and took a sip. The warm liquid soothed her aching throat. She took a deep breath of the sweet smell.

She glanced around the room as she continued to sip her tea. The satchel they had with them was on the floor next to a chair in the corner. Anna set her cup down and walked over to it. She picked it up and brought it back to the window seat.

The first thing she pulled out was her white dress and cloak. They smelled like smoke, and she coughed. Anna reached back in the bag and gasped when she saw her books. Tears filled her eyes as she hugged them to her chest. When had Mason collected her books? She had forgotten about them.

Anna ran her hand over the cover of the history book. It was the complete record of the Guardians. She had read the book once a year since coming to the castle. This was the first book Miranda had given her to read after her mother's death. She set it aside. The book of prophecies, written by the first Guardian, Mira. It was one of Anna's favorites. She was fascinated by them.

She stared at the last book for a long moment. Fated Mates. Anna leaned back to get more comfortable. She picked her cup back up and took another sip of her tea. She opened the book and began reading.

The light began to fade, making it harder to see the words on the page. Anna set her book aside and looked around for a candle or lantern. She found one on the side table. She lit it and moved it closer to the window.

Her stomach growled but she ignored it. There was no way she wanted to risk coming across Mason and the doctor. No way. Anna had seen a doctor before, after her father broke her arm. He had attempted to reset the bones but broke it in a second spot instead. Her mother had corrected his error after he had left. That had been a tamer experience than the one with her mother. She had watched the Clan's doctor torture her mother, while claiming to be helping her.

The door opened suddenly, and she froze. "Mason, you need to take a deep breath or something. You and Mother both aren't making it any easier to find her."

"Yeah well, you can just..." Mason stopped talking when he saw her sitting there. "Anna?"

"Thank you for finding my books." She said before turning back to the book. Her heart was hammering but she tried to remain calm.

"Where have you been?" Mason snapped and she flinched.

"I made myself some tea while avoiding you." Anna slammed her mouth closed. Why had she said that?

"The doctor left hours ago since we couldn't find you." His voice rose in volume.

"I told you no, Mason. I meant it. I will not see any doctor. Not now, not ever." Anna got to her feet, gathered her books, and headed for the door. "Since the doctor is not here, I will be going back to my room now."

Mason grabbed her arm, stopping her. She struggled to keep her fear in check, but she couldn't stop the tremor in her hands. "I am trying to help you."

"Then do us both a favor and leave the doctor out of this." Anna glared at the ground.

"You are impossible." Mason growled as he paced away from her.

Anna went to leave but noticed Oliver standing by the door. He was watching her. She took a step back. She felt trapped. "Why don't you like doctors?" he asked calmly, as he leaned against the doorframe.

She glanced over at Mason before turning her attention back to Oliver. "I don't trust them." she said quietly.

"Is it because they are male?" Oliver pressed. She didn't answer, so he continued. "Did one fail to cure a friend? Use leeches?"

Anna cut off his continued questions. "I watched him torture my mother while claiming to be healing her. He tried to burn the demons from her. He told my father that if she stayed under the water long enough, she might bear him another son before her execution. He almost drowned her. He broke my arm on purpose while trying to set the break I received from my father." She said angrily. "Would you like me to give you more examples of why I do not trust doctors? I have more."

Oliver stood up straight and she took another step back. She really needed to curb her tongue. She was no longer living with the Guardians. Miranda had told her to use her voice, to say what was on her mind. Now that she was no longer in a safe place, she really needed to relearn to hold her tongue.

"Why didn't you tell me?" Mason asked softly as he slowly walked towards her.

Anna looked down at the floor as she hugged her books to her chest. Her body was shaking. She knew that Mason had noticed when he stopped moving toward her. "I'm sorry." she said quickly. "I shouldn't have...I'm so sorry, I should have..." She stammered out.

"Anna, if I had known your history, I would have never insisted on the doctor." Mason said in a slightly calmer voice. "But we are still faced with the same problem." Anna glanced up at him. "You are wheezing and coughing. I will not just sit by and do nothing."

"Would a midwife know what to do?" Oliver asked.

"I'm not sure but it is worth a try." Mason headed for the door.

"I don't need a midwife." Anna said quickly. Both men stopped and faced her. "Anna,"

"I am capable of treating this myself." Anna cut him off.

"What do you mean?" Oliver asked.

"The tea." She gestured to the teapot on the window seat.

"What about the tea?" Mason asked as he crossed his arms over his chest.

"It is an herbal tea we used to help with throat and lung afflictions." Anna moved to the tea tray and lifted the teapot. It was empty now.

"When did you have tea brought up? We have been looking for you all day. No one claims to have seen you." Mason asked.

"Oh, I went out to collect the herb I needed before making the tea myself."

"Why didn't you tell anyone where you were going?" Mason sounded irritated again.

"That would defeat the purpose of not wanting to see you, now wouldn't it?" Anna froze. There was a second of complete silence before Oliver started laughing.

"Oh, I like her." Oliver continued to laugh. "Quick as a whip. We just need to get her to stop holding back on us."

Anna turned to face them and ducked her head as embarrassment colored her cheeks. "Have you eaten anything yet today, Anna?" Mason asked. She shook her head. Mason sighed and extended his hand to her. "Come on. Let's find some food for you."

She clutched her books to her chest as she stepped to his side. "I don't want to be a bother."

"Give me the books, Anna." Mason said gently. She took a step back. "I will put them in your room before we head downstairs." She looked down at her books before lifting her gaze to Mason. She finally relented and carefully passed them over to him.

The three of them moved out into the hall and Mason walked into her room. She was alone in the hall with Oliver. Her anxiety rose and she took a few steps towards her room. She ran into Mason as he stepped back out into the hall. "Ready?" Mason asked, looking between her and Oliver.

Anna latched onto Mason's arm and stepped behind him. "I think I will let Father and Mother know that Anna has been found." Oliver said and quickly walked down the hall. "Mason, we need to talk later."

They stood still until Oliver disappeared. "Would you like to eat in the library or the sitting room?" Mason asked her.

"The library." Anna said quickly.

*   *   *

Anna gasped as they walked into the library. Mason turned to see her eyes widen in awe as she stepped farther into the room. He let her hand slip from his. She quickly moved to the nearest shelf and reverently ran her fingers along the spines of the books as she slowly walked along the shelves. Mason watched the complete transformation in her demeanor.

He had never seen her so relaxed. "Do you like it?" He couldn't help asking.

She turned to face him. Her smile lit up her whole face. "I love it." She turned back to the bookshelf. "Are all these novels?"

"Umm…What do you mean?" Mason asked as he moved closer.

"Are there any books on science, philosophy, mathematics, history?" she continued to walk along the shelves.

"To be honest, I have no idea what all is in here."

"You do not like to read?"

"On the contrary, I love to read. I just do not have much time for it."

"What exactly do the Caverton's do?" Anna glanced at him.

"My father and Oliver are lawyers." Mason clasped his hands behind his back as he looked at the bookshelves.

"But not you?" Anna turned to face him.

"I tried." Mason gave her a smile. "It wasn't for me."

"Hmm. That still doesn't tell me what you do."

Mason's smile grew. "I help manage the Caverton holdings. Father pays me to keep things running smoothly. I recently got married, though."

"Is that so?" Anna's eyes sparkled with humor. Mason couldn't take his eyes off her. She was absolutely enchanting when fear wasn't crushing her.

"Mmhmm. She has been monopolizing my time for the last few days." Mason said with a serious expression.

"How so?" she asked as she pulled a book from the shelf. She was enjoying Mason's banter. Anna had never had a conversation where she was speaking about herself as if she were someone else. And Mason's smile caused her heart to trip over itself.

"She has been through something completely traumatizing and I worry about her. Both physically and emotionally. And because I worry about her, she sent be into a panic today when she disappeared for the entire day." Mason watched Anna carefully.

She glanced at him before turning and walking towards the other side of the library where the couches were. "She sounds like she is more trouble than she is worth for you."

Anna sat on the couch and Mason took the seat next to her. She had started to withdraw into herself again. Mason grabbed her hand and pressed a kiss to her knuckles. "You are worth it, Anna." He leaned back but kept a hold of her hand.

"I am not, though." Anna looked at him. "I am the second daughter. I am the reason my mother was to be executed."

"I am a second son. What does that have to do with anything? And what is this about your mother?" Mason sat up straight.

"Sons are not the same as daughters." Anna shook her head. "A second daughter marks her mother for death. Father told me she was to die as part of the wedding ceremony. It was to be my gift from him."

"Anna," Mason whispered, and she blinked a few times. Her eyes were wet with unshed tears. "Where are you from?" She took a shuttering breath. "Who is your father?" He was really trying to keep his anger in check.

"Mason, can we talk about something else?" Anna's eyes turned pleading.

Mason wasn't happy about not getting answers. He had a feeling that finding out where she came from was key to understanding Anna better. "We can talk about anything you wish to talk about."

"Would you be upset if I read?" Anna asked anxiously.

"Of course not. I brought you here because I noticed how much you treasured your books." He let go of her hand so she could hold her book.

"Thank you, Mason." She said as she laid her head against his shoulder.

Mason lifted his arm and put it around Anna's shoulders. She tensed but he didn't move. After a few minutes, she began to relax. He took a deep breath as he leaned his head back. Citrus. He smelled citrus. He sighed as he closed his eyes.

"Mason?" Anna said softly.

"Hmm?"

"I am getting tired."

Mason opened his eyes and looked down at Anna. She was watching him. "Did you get something to eat? I'm sorry I fell asleep before getting you food."

"Lady Caverton brought me something earlier." Anna's cheeks turned pink as she looked down.

"Good. Now let's get you to bed." Mason stood as he stretched. Anna slowly got to her feet. She started to head back to the bookcase. "You can take the book with you if you want to."

Anna smiled at him. "Really?" He nodded with a laugh. "I can take this to my room?"

"All these books are at your disposal. Father has a few law books in the study as well." Mason looked at the hundreds of books on the shelves.

"Thank you!" Anna threw her arms around his neck, and he froze, surprised by the gesture. He slowly returned the hug. Suddenly, she tensed and took a quick step back. "I'm sorry. I didn't..."

"You are welcome, Anna." Mason smiled at her. "But you are correct. It is getting late, and we should both get some rest."

Mason was about to enter his room after Anna was safely in hers. Oliver came down the hall with a serious expression on his normally smiling face. "A moment, Mason."

"Come in." They both entered his room, and Oliver closed the door after them. "What is it, brother?"

"I don't think you should leave Anna alone with father or me." Oliver said.

"Why? Neither one of you would hurt her. I trust you both." Mason furrowed his brow, confused at his brother's comment.

"You may trust us, but she does not. You didn't see the fear in her eyes when you walked into her room. The moment you left her alone with me, she was shaking and practically ran." Oliver gestured to the closed door. "She was completely terrified."

"She was fine when the three of us were in here." Mason shook his head.

"I think she knows she is safe with you. You are her security right now, Mason. Watch her tomorrow. You will see what I saw." Oliver opened the door and left.

Mason ran a hand down his face. Anna did seem more anxious and closed off with his family, but he figured it was being in a group of unfamiliar people. Oliver could be right that it was him and father that were setting her off. He will test the theory tomorrow. If Oliver was right, Mason would make sure that Anna was never left in a situation that triggered her anxiety.

Chapter 12

Mason sat at his father's desk. He was attempting to get some work done, but he could not seem to focus. Glancing over at the couch, he watched Anna for a minute. She was sitting with her legs pulled up under her as she read a book. Her brows were pinched together, and she was biting her lip as she concentrated.

His mind wandered back to last month. Oliver had been correct when it came to Anna's anxiety. He walked into the breakfast room the next morning to see Anna standing at the sideboard. His parents were sitting at the table speaking quietly with worried expressions on their faces. Anna was shaking. He could see it in the plate she was holding.

He walked up to her and put a hand on her back. She had stiffened at the contact until she realized it was him. Her breathing had been erratic, and she clung to him. Oliver saw what was happening and quietly got their parents to leave. It had taken thirty minutes for Mason to help calm Anna's anxiety attack.

Mason shook his head to clear his mind. He reread the report on Caverton Manor. He really needed to focus. He found his eyes and mind drifting back to the woman across the room. They had fallen into a comfortable routine during the last month. He would walk her down to breakfast before they both came to the study. Anna would read while he worked. She didn't want to be alone, and if he was being honest with himself, he wanted to keep her close. After dinner, they retired to the library where he would sit with his arm around her as she read some more.

With his family gone to the capital, Anna had come out of her shell a little more over the last two weeks. She had a quick wit and was gentle and kind. He found his feelings for her were growing more and more each day.

"Why are you staring at me like that?" Anna's voice snapped him out of his thoughts, and he blinked several times.

"I wasn't staring, I was just thinking." Mason refocused on the paper in front of him.

"You thinking? That is a dangerous thing." Anna commented. He couldn't see her face, but he could hear a smile in her voice.

"Are you saying I have terrible ideas?" Mason sat back and watched her. He was trying to keep his own smile from surfacing.

"I have never said such a thing. You were the one who said you made stupid decisions." She glanced at him.

"When did I say that?" Mason couldn't remember saying anything like that.

"Are you calling me a liar, Mason?" Anna put her hand to her chest.

Mason stood and moved to the couch. She sat up and he took a seat. "I am not saying that, my dear Anna. I am just saying I do not recall saying I make stupid decisions."

"You said your decision to attack the castle and hiding in an alleyway were stupid decisions." Anna raised a brow.

"I can concede on the castle, but hiding in that alley hasn't turned out too bad. I mean, I have definitely been less bored."

A knock on the door stopped Anna's response. Mason stood and walked to the door before opening it. "Lord and Lady Caverton, and your brother have returned home."

"Thank you. Tell them we will meet them for dinner." Mason closed the door and turned back to Anna. Her eyes were wide, and she was tense. "Come here." Mason said gently.

Anna ran to Mason and put her arms around him. She knew it was illogical to be afraid of Lord Caverton and Oliver, but she was. Oliver had made it a personal mission of his to make her laugh. She was trying to trust them, but all her experiences told her to protect herself. She didn't know why she trusted Mason. It confused her why she was so comfortable with him.

"I'm sorry." She whispered.

Mason held her tight as he kissed the top of her head. "Everything will be just fine. If you feel at all like you need to leave, you can. They will understand." Mason said softly as he rubbed her back in a slow circle. "I will be by your side all night." She nodded, and he kissed her head again before releasing her. He grabbed her hand as they exited the study.

Everyone was waiting at the table when they walked in. Anna moved closer to Mason, and he squeezed her hand. She was relieved when Mason slid his seat closer to hers and took her hand in his again. She listened as the family discussed Lord Caverton's progress on his case against those that attacked the castle. The night ticked by at a slow pace as she fought her fears.

Anna sighed in relief when Mason stopped in front of her bedroom door. Dinner had been exhausting for her. No matter how many times she told herself to relax, she couldn't seem to. A headache started halfway through the meal and all she wanted to do was go to bed.

"You did well, Anna." Mason cupped her cheek as he studied her face. "I know it wasn't easy for you." Anna closed her eyes and took a deep breath. It hadn't been easy.

She felt Mason take a step closer. He kissed her cheek and Anna's eyes popped open. He smiled down at her. Her heart skipped a beat before speeding to catch up. He had only kissed her hand or the top of her head before. Well, besides when they had kissed at the altar.

"Good-night, Anna." Mason took a step back before opening the bedroom door for her.

Anna gave herself a mental shake. "Good-night, Mason." She walked into her room and closed the door. She let out a tense breath. She didn't know how, but Mason was managing to slip through her walls. She wasn't sure how she felt about it.

*   *   *

Anna walked through the halls of the Caverton home. She still felt like a stranger. Lady Caverton had ordered several new dresses for her. She had gone out of her way to make her feel welcome. But she still felt like she didn't belong, even after six months.

Anna stepped into the sitting room where she had been summoned. Her blood froze in her veins when she saw the two men sitting on the couch talking with Lord and Lady Caverton. A third man stood behind the couch and was watching her. Mason and Oliver were pacing near the window.

"There she is." Mr. Hawkshaw smiled as his eyes traveled over her. "My dear, you have grown up to be quite a fetching creature."

"Get over here, girl." Her father snapped.

Anna's feet moved before her mind even knew what she was doing. She ran straight to Mason. He held her tight as she shook in fear. "It is going to be alright, Anna."

"I demand you release my fiancé immediately." Mr. Hawkshaw roared, and Anna clung to Mason.

"She is my wife." Mason growled.

"Gentlemen, please." Lady Caverton said firmly. "We can discuss this civilly."

"Lord Caverton, I would much rather discuss this where the women can't interject." Anna's father sneered.

"This is my home, and you will treat my wife with respect." Lord Caverton said, with barely restrained anger.

"Before things get too out of hand," the third man spoke up. "I will cut straight to the point. I am Mr. Morrison; I am representing Captain Winters and Mr. Hawkshaw in this matter."

"What matter is there to discuss?" Oliver asked.

"Captain Winters is calling into question the legality of Mr. Mason Caverton's marriage to Miss Julianna Winters." Mr. Morrison stated.

Anna tensed. This couldn't be happening. How had they found her? It had been ten years. Why couldn't they just leave her alone.

Anna blinked and she was standing in a bedroom she didn't recognize. Someone stood behind her. They grabbed her arms roughly as they leaned forward. "I won't make the same mistake he did. You will be mine." Mr. Hawkshaws hot breath on her neck sent a shiver of fear and disgust down her back as he leaned closer to her. "I have been dreaming of this day ever since I first saw you."

Anna screamed as she bolted upright. She frantically looked around. She was in a dark room with moonlight streaming through the window. Her heart was pounding painfully, and she was shaking. It had felt so real.

The jiggling of the door handle had Anna jumping. She pulled her knees up and hugged them to her chest. It couldn't be one of them at her door. It couldn't be. It was just a dream. Someone pounded on the door and her tears started.

"It was just a dream." She whispered, trying to calm herself as she gently rocked.

"Anna!" Mason's voice called, but she blocked it out.

She needed to get a hold of herself before she faced him. Over the last two months, Mason had become extremely protective of her. They had spent hours together talking about all sorts of things. She had told him about her studies with Miranda and living at the castle. She had grown quite comfortable with him. In fact, if he wasn't with her, she had a hard time being in the same room as Oliver and Lord Caverton. He had become her source of comfort.

The feel of Mr. Hawkshaws breath on her neck came back to her and she shivered. "It was just a dream. It was just a dream." She told herself again.

Someone touched her and she dove off the side of the bed. She scrambled to the wall and pressed her back to it. Her breathing became ragged. Thoughts of the old man touching her caused her to panic.

"Anna, look at me." Mason said.

Anna put a shaky hand to her forehead. "It was only a dream." She said again.

"Look at me." Mason's voice was soft but firm. Anna looked up and met Mason's gaze. "That's it. Anna, take a slow deep breath for me."

"T-they were here. They are coming for me. T-they take me." Anna was shaking as if she were swimming in a frozen lake.

"Who?"

"My father." Anna cried. "Mr. Hawkshaw."

Mason picked her up off the floor and carried her to the settee. "It was only a nightmare, Anna. You are safe."

Anna curled into Mason's side. She wasn't sure it was just a nightmare. It had felt too real. What if it was a vision? A warning of what was to come. "M-mason,"

"Shh." Mason whispered as he held her tighter. "Take a moment to come out of the nightmare. We can talk about it when you are more settled."

Anna nodded and took a deep breath. Pine. She closed her eyes and focused on her breathing. Mason's fingers started to softly run up and down her arm. Slowly she began to relax. Mason continued to remain silent as he held her.

It took a good hour for Anna to feel calm enough to sit up. She looked at Mason. He tucked some loose hair behind her ear and gently wiped the tears off her cheeks. "They are coming for me, Mason, and they succeed. I end up having to go with them."

"You are my wife, Anna." Mason stated.

"I know that. They know that. They challenged it. I don't know how, but they won. They won." Anna stood and paced away from him. He didn't understand.

"It was just a nightmare, Anna. Everything is..."

"No!" Anna cut him off. "I never told you what my Gift is."

"I thought you said Sasha tried to kick you out of the castle because you didn't have a Gift?" Mason stood as well.

"I got my Gift after she left." Anna turned to face him. "I have visions. Sometimes they come as dreams." Mason's brows rose. "I don't get them often, but they are so lifelike. It is like I am there, living through it. That's how this dream was, Mason. I can still feel his hands on me and his breath on my neck."

Mason stood still as he watched her. "You are saying you can see the future?"

"That is how I knew an army was coming to the castle. I saw Sasha talking to a room full of men. Someone asked about the king's support. I saw them coming. If I hadn't, we would have all been in the dining hall for breakfast, instead of trying to flee." Anna ran her hand through her hair. "My father is coming, Mason, whether you believe me or not."

Mason ran a hand down his face. "It's not that I don't believe you, I am just trying to process everything." He grabbed her hand. "I will talk with Oliver and my father. They can look into how your father could possibly contest our marriage."

"Thank you." Anna breathed a sigh of relief.

"Try to get some rest. We will get this sorted out in the morning." Mason said. He kissed her forehead and headed for the door.

"Mason!" Fear of being left alone had Anna calling out to him before she could stop herself.

"What is it?" Mason turned to her.

"Never mind." She shook her head. She was fine. They weren't coming tonight.

"No, not never mind." Mason said. "I know you well enough to know you don't raise your voice like that. What's wrong?"

Anna let out a tense breath. "I don't want to be alone." She whispered.

Mason didn't move for a long moment and Anna shook her head. He probably thought her silly. "What would you like to do, Anna? You need to sleep. Tomorrow is going to be rough as we try to figure this out."

"I know." Anna sighed. "But I don't know if I can go back to sleep. Maybe I will go to the library."

"Do you trust me?" Mason asked hesitantly.

"That depends. Are you going to tell me to eat something you say is amazing, when in fact it is terrible?" Anna asked. Mason walked over to her and grabbed her hand again. He led her to the bed, and she swallowed nervously. "What are you doing?"

"We are going to get some sleep." Mason said.

"In the same bed?" Anna breathed out.

"Just sleeping, Anna. Nothing more." Mason's voice was gentle.

Mason waited for her to say something. She looked between him and the bed several times as she bit her lip in indecision. She was tired, but she wasn't going to be able to relax after that dream. "I will not be able to sleep after what I saw." Anna said as she looked back at him.

"I am asking you to trust me."

Anna sighed. "I do trust you." she finally said.

"In you go." Mason said as he lifted the blanket. Anna hesitantly climbed onto the bed and Mason put the blanket over her. "Would you like me to get a different blanket for myself, or are you comfortable sharing?"

"What are you comfortable with?" Anna asked.

"I asked you, Anna. The decision is yours."

Anna pulled the blankets more around her. "I am fine with either."

"You are impossible." Mason grumbled as he walked around to the other side of the bed. He lifted the blanket and laid down. Her back was to him, but she knew he was on the far side of the mattress, giving her space. "And for the record, chocolate is amazing. You are the only person on earth that doesn't like it."

Anna bit her lip to keep from laughing. Mason repositioned and caused the mattress to move. Silence filled the room as she tried not to freak out. She was sharing a bed with a man. She reminded herself that Mason was her husband. It is perfectly acceptable for her to be sleeping in the same bed as him. Her father's voice echoed in her mind, telling her what she was supposed to do. Her anxiety started to build again.

An arm went over her waist, and she tensed. "Nothing bad is going to happen, Anna. Just breathe." Mason whispered.

"How are you so calm?" Anna asked.

"Maybe because I don't have a psychotic man's voice in my head telling me a bunch of lies." Mason said. "I would prefer it if you heard my voice instead of his."

"As would I." Anna mumbled.

Mason removed his arm from her waist as he rolled onto his back. "Try to sleep."

Anna was too anxious about her vision and Mason in her bed to sleep. She listened to his breathing deepen before he started to snore softly. The night wore on and Anna still couldn't fall asleep. Every time she closed her eyes, she saw her father sitting in the Caverton's home. She let out a tense breath as she sat up. She carefully got out of the bed and moved to the window seat. She stared up at the moon and took a deep breath.

"The whole reason I am still in here is so you can get some sleep." Mason said from the bed. Anna jumped, not expecting to hear his voice.

"Every time I close my eyes, I can see them sitting in the drawing room and hear their voices as they demand I go with them." Anna pulled her eyes from the moon and looked at Mason.

"Come back to bed, Anna." Mason sat up. Anna grudgingly crawled back under the covers. Mason put his arms around her. "Everything will be okay. We will figure it out." He said quietly.

She nodded but didn't say anything. It didn't take long for Mason to fall back asleep. His arms remained around her. Anna wasn't comfortable so she rolled to her other side. He slipped his arm under her neck and drew her closer. She tensed at first, but eventually she found herself relaxing. Her eyelids grew heavy, and she snuggled more against Mason.

Chapter 13

Mason was growing more and more irritated as he paced his father's office. "For the hundredth time, yes. Anna's father is going to try to reverse the marriage."

"How do you know this?" Oliver asked.

"I just do." Mason said. Anna had begged him not to say anything about her Gift. He had no idea how hard it was going to be to convince his father and brother to look into this without being able to explain that detail of the situation. "Look, I just need to know if there is any possible way he would be able to dissolve my marriage."

"Off the top of my head, there is only one way someone could do that, but I will look into it more when I go to the capital in two days." Lord Caverton leaned back in his chair. "Your mother will be accompanying us again. Will you and Anna be okay here, or would you like to come with us?"

"I can ask Anna what she would rather do. I have a feeling she would prefer to stay here where there are less people." Mason rubbed his eyes.

"What spurred on these thoughts about her father?" Oliver asked curiously. "You have been married for two months after all."

"Anna has been having nightmares, and to put her mind at ease, I figured I would look into it." Mason looked at his brother. "She is terrified she will end up back under his thumb."

"She is a Caverton. No one will be hurting our girl." Lord Caverton said with finality. "We will get as much information as we can on the subject to prove to Anna that she is safely out of his reach."

"Thank you." Mason said before exiting the office. He needed to find Anna and let her know what was going on. It didn't take long, she was in the library tucked away on her favorite couch. "Anna."

"Did they know what loophole my father was trying to use?" Anna sat up as she wrung her hands.

Mason took a seat and grabbed her hand. "They don't know. They are leaving for the capital within the next few days. Father said he will research it while he is there."

"They will be here in four months, Mason." She stood and paced away. "What if they can't find anything? We will not be able to stop them. Mr. Hawkshaw..."

"Julianna Caverton." Mason gently grabbed her arms, stopping her anxious pacing. He tilted her head up so she was forced to look him in the eyes. "You are my wife. I am not letting any man touch you or take you from me. Do you understand me?" he said firmly.

"But they do, Mason. They do take me. They take me all the way back to Freynia." Tears ran down her cheeks.

"Freynia? The trade country north of Arlania?" Mason's brows furrowed.

Anna wrapped her arms around Mason's waist and buried her face in his chest. He put his hand on the back of her head as he held her. After several minutes, she got the courage to speak. "Freynia is not a trade country. I mean, they trade so they can look like a peaceful people, but that is not what they specialize in."

Mason leaned back so he could see her face. "Anna, what are you saying?"

Anna took a step back and then another. "They kill people. They make weapons. They put boys through training that if it doesn't kill them, it changes them into monsters. The women are just tools. The dogs are treated better than they are." Anna closed her eyes as she fought the tears. "My father...he is the second in command of the Assassin's Guild. He trains boys to be sold to other countries to be spies and to kill." Anna froze.

That is why they wanted her. She knew too much. They weren't just going to let her go. They were going to kill her.

"What? How does no one know about this?" Mason ran his hand through his hair.

"The governments do." Anna whispered. "An Alpha from Valencia came to Crossford to purchase someone to come to Arlania. I was in the other room waiting for my lesson with Father and I overheard them." She looked at Mason. "Father became angry when he saw me. I don't remember what happened. Mother said that my older brother dumped me on the cottage steps. She hid me for three days."

"But it has been ten years since you and your mother left." Mason said. "How would they know you were even alive, let alone where you are?"

"Who knew you were from Freynia?" Oliver asked, causing Anna to jump.

Mason put his arm around her, and she leaned against him. "No one. I did not even tell Miranda. No one could have known. We had nothing from home, nothing to tie us to..." Anna put her hand to her mouth.

"What is it, Anna?" Mason said softly.

"The brand." Anna looked up at Mason. "Someone found the brand."

"What brand?" Oliver asked.

"They brand all the girls' clothing until they are married off, then they receive the brand of the clan they are traded to." Anna looked between Oliver and Mason. "Mother's brand was on the back of her neck. She always wore her hair down, and we were only at the castle for ten days before she was killed." Mason pulled her closer. "But Mother cut the brand off my dress when we left. She kept it and hid it in our room in the castle."

"Why would she keep it?" Oliver moved further into the room.

"You don't understand what they do to you." Anna wrapped her arms around herself. "From the time a girl is three, she is told her worth depends on her husband's opinion of her. She has limited contact with her mother so the father can condition her mind. Lessons are beat into you if you do not learn quickly enough. The boys are encouraged to take out their anger on you."

Mason and Oliver watched her with wide eyes. "I was lucky. As a second daughter, Mother was considered dead the moment I was born. Mr. Hawkshaw saw my eyes when my father was taking me to the lake. He liked them and a contract was made. Mother and I were isolated from the rest of the clan. As early as I can remember, my father and Mr. Hawkshaw have been preparing me for my life with him." Anna closed her eyes and shook her head. "She almost took us back before we found Miranda. It's hard to get their voices out of your head telling you that you are worthless. That you are nothing without them. I only had eight years under their influence. I can't imagine the hold my mother felt after twenty-eight years."

Anna opened her eyes. Mason was right in front of her. He cupped her cheek as he searched her face. "You aren't going back, Anna."

"You have to realize that there is a very big possibility that I will." Anna whispered.

"No!" Mason said firmly. He dropped his hand from her face. "It won't happen."

"Mason..." Anna whispered.

"I agree with Mason, Anna." Oliver cut her off. "You are a part of this family. The man you call your father and Mr. Hawkshaw will have to go through us in order to get to you."

Anna couldn't believe how protective Oliver was of her. She expected it from Mason but not Oliver. She stepped up to Mason and put her arms around him again. He kissed the top of her head. "We will figure this out before they get here, Anna."

"I trust you." Anna turned more into him. "Thank you both."

"There is no need to thank me. You are my sister, Anna, and I love you." Oliver smiled at her. "Get some sleep tonight."

Anna laughed, causing Oliver's mouth to drop. Sleep would not be easy. She was far too worked up to sleep at this point. She was planning on reading her book.

"Was that a laugh?" Oliver asked in surprise.

"I think it was." Mason chuckled.

"Sleep will be impossible. It's funny that you think I will be able to." Anna shrugged.

Mason and Oliver laughed. "I'm glad we have a few things straightened out, but I came here for a different reason."

"Go on, Ollie." Mason tightened his arms around her.

"We are leaving in the morning. There are some storms coming and Father wants to leave before they hit." Oliver said. "I will see you two in the morning." He turned and left the room.

"Ollie is right, we need to get some sleep." He let her go and she immediately felt the loss. "If storms are on their way, I need to check on a few things before they come."

"You are leaving?" Anna asked as they walked through the halls on their way to the north wing.

"I will leave after my parents and Ollie depart for the Capital. I will be back by dinner." They reached her room, and Mason kissed her forehead again. "Good night, Anna."

Anna hesitated when Mason opened her door for her. She didn't like the idea of Mason leaving. Not only would he be gone, but she would be all alone.

"Anna, if you are going to have a hard time sleeping, I can..." Mason started to say.

"Good-night, Mason." Anna felt her cheeks heat.

Mason's smile grew. "Are you sure?"

"I am sure. You snore." Anna stepped into her room and closed the door slowly.

Mason had a crooked grin on his face and her heart tripped. She closed the door and slowly locked it. She was tempted to change her mind. Last night was the first time she had slept so peacefully. She was usually up before the sun fully rose in the sky, but Mason had to wake her up. She couldn't give in tonight. She needed to figure a few things out before morning.

She spent the night thinking over everything the Cavertons had done or said in the two months she had been with them. They had done nothing but care for her. Lord Caverton and Oliver seemed to understand that she suffered from panic attacks when around men and gave her space. If they saw her in a room by herself, they never entered. Lady Caverton was so gentle and kind. She never pushed Anna to join her for visits with the neighbors, even though she always invited her.

Anna closed her eyes as she remembered her vision. Every single one of the Cavertons had been worried about her. They tried to protect her. If she continued to keep them at a distance, she would be like she was in her vision. She would always feel alone.

She couldn't keep pushing people away. She needed to step out of her comfort zone and shove her fears aside. She needed to start making an effort to trust those who were sacrificing so much for her. Mason's parents and brother have been going to the capital to try to bring charges against Sasha and Lord Carson.

Anna dressed in a light blue gown. Lady Caverton had said it was her favorite of all the ones she had made for Anna. Anna had yet to wear it. She felt like it made her stand out more than she wanted to. Today was a new day and a new start. She couldn't hide anymore. Her father was coming, it was time to make the most of her life before it was taken from her.

She ran a brush through her hair before pulling it up off her neck. She let out a tense breath as she looked at herself in the mirror. She had never worn her hair up before. Mr. Hawkshaw had branded her when she was five years old. Mother burned the brand off after they escaped. Now there was a large circular scar at the base of her neck.

A knock sounded at her door. She stood and wiped her hands nervously on the soft material of her dress. As she opened the door, she started regretting her brief surge of courage. She kept her eyes on the floor as she stepped out into the hall. She closed her door without glancing at Mason.

"Anna," he sounded breathless. He cleared his throat. "Are you ready for breakfast?"

Anna nodded and began walking. Mason fell into step beside her. He normally asked her about her night, but he remained silent. She was starting to feel like she had made a terrible decision to wear this gown. She walked into the breakfast room with Mason right behind her.

"Anna!" Lady Caverton gasped. "You look stunning. I knew that dress would look amazing on you."

"Thank you, Lady Caverton." Anna said quietly as she glanced at the woman. Oliver and Lord Caverton were sitting next to her. Oliver's mouth was hanging open while Lord Caverton smiled at her.

Anna quickly grabbed a plate and dished up a small amount of food. Her nerves had her stomach in knots. Instead of sitting as close to the door and as far from the Caverton's as she could, she took a seat near the center. She was only four seats away from Oliver. Her hands started to shake but she pushed past her rising fear.

Mason sat between her and Oliver. She gave him a grateful smile. He reached over and grabbed her hand. He did this every time they ate with his family. He squeezed her fingers gently and she looked up at him. He leaned close to her.

"You do not need to force yourself to be so close to them if you are not ready." He whispered.

Anna tilted her head and her cheek brushed his. The scent of pine hit her nose, and she closed her eyes briefly. She loved that smell, and it relaxed her a little. Mason kissed her cheek before sitting up. He studied her for a moment before turning to his plate.

She focused on her food while trying to block out the frequent glances in her direction. She was close to finishing when Lady Caverton gasped. "My dear, what is that on your neck?" Lady Caverton asked suddenly.

Anna looked up as she swallowed hard. Mason sat back and looked at her. Anger filled his eyes when his gaze returned to hers. "Umm…" Anna looked at her plate. "It is only a scar. It happened a long time ago." She reached up to pull her hair out of its pins to hide it.

Mason grabbed her hand to stop her and kissed her knuckles. "When do you plan on leaving, Father?" He looked to Lord Caverton.

"As soon as breakfast is over. The luggage has already been loaded." Lord Caverton said before taking a drink of water.

"We should probably hurry. The storm is already building on the horizon." Oliver got to his feet.

"Are you ready, Faith?" Lord Caverton asked as he stood.

Anna waited for them to leave before standing as well. Mason tightened his hold on her hand as he pulled her back from leaving. She looked at him in confusion. "I thought you said you were to be marked after you were married."

"No, I said girls were branded when they knew which clan they would end up in." Anna bit her lip as she looked down. "I was branded at five. The youngest in Crossford history." She raised her shoulder as she tried to pull her hand from his.

"That doesn't look like a normal brand, Anna."

"Mother burned the brand when we left. She didn't want me to be sent back if anyone saw and recognized it."

Mason stepped closer to her, but before he could say anything, Oliver walked back into the room. "Mason, Mother and Father are waiting to say good-bye so we can leave. You can have your beautiful wife to yourself once we are gone."

Anna's cheeks heated and she ducked her head. "We will be right there." Mason said.

"Come on, kiss her and let's go." Oliver grinned.

Oliver had teased Mason often, but he had never told him to kiss her. She felt like her face was on fire. Having someone watch as Mason kissed her was not an appealing prospect. She needed a moment to compose herself before she said her good-byes to the family. She managed to pull her hand from Mason's while he glared at his brother. She walked quickly to the door. Oliver took a step to the side to allow her space.

"You two can kiss each other." She said over her shoulder as she left the room. She was able to duck into a small alcove before the brothers made it to the hall.

"Anna seems different." Oliver said. "That dress is very flattering. Her eyes seemed bluer somehow. I knew she was pretty from the first time we met her, but she is exceptionally so today. Don't you think?"

"Oliver, Anna is my wife. Do not wax on about how beautiful you think she is." Mason said angrily. "I am well aware she is attractive."

"You know I only think of her as a sister. I am only making sure you realize how incredibly blessed you are, little brother." Oliver chuckled. "Were you about to kiss her? You looked like you were going to? Did I interrupt?"

"You are an idiot, Ollie." Mason snapped at him.

"I will take that as a yes." Oliver laughed.

They walked past and Anna let out a long breath. She shook her head. She bit her lip to keep from smiling. Was Mason going to kiss her? She tilted her head back and looked at the ceiling. After several minutes, she felt ready to go outside.

When she stepped out onto the porch, she immediately noticed Oliver, Mason, and Lady Caverton talking off to the right. Lord Caverton was just finishing up speaking with the driver. Anna glanced at Mason. Her first instinct was to go to him, but she fought it. She needed to start trusting his family.

Anna slowly walked over to Lord Caverton. He turned to face her and froze. "Thank you, Lord Caverton." she said quietly. "For everything. I know you all have had to walk on eggshells around me, and I am sorry for that."

"Anna," Lord Caverton said gently. Anna embraced him. She felt him take a sharp breath in before he slowly returned the hug. She felt the sting of tears as Lord Caverton sniffled. He put a hand on the back of her head as he held her close. "You are not a bother, my dear girl. You are a gem. I am so glad you are a part of this family."

After several minutes, Lord Caverton took a step back. He wiped his eyes as he smiled at her. Anna hadn't expected the feeling of security she felt as Lord Caverton hugged her. When they turned, everyone was watching them in shock.

"What have you done to Father?" Oliver asked as he looked between her and Lord Caverton. "I don't think I have ever seen him cry before."

"Ollie, leave the girl alone." Lady Caverton swatted his shoulder.

"I am thoroughly confused right now." Oliver continued to stare at her.

Mason moved to her side and put an arm around her waist. "Are you all right?" he whispered.

Anna nodded as she stepped away from him. He watched her carefully. She stepped up to Oliver. She looked down at her shaking hands. "Can I hug you now?" he asked hesitantly.

She answered by putting her arms around his waist. He gave a small laugh of surprise as he returned her embrace. "Thank you, Oliver. For everything."

"There you go making me turn into Father." He sniffled. He took several deep breaths and let them out slowly before he stepped back. "How does Mason always have his arms around you and not turn into a watering pot?"

"Don't tease my girl, Oliver." Lord Caverton said firmly.

"Your girl? I thought she was Mason's?" Oliver's lips twitched as he tried to keep a straight face.

"She is my daughter."

"I am your son." Oliver laughed.

"Daughters take priority over my sons, Oliver. You know this. Your mother comes first and then my daughters. So, when you find a woman to marry, her wellbeing will trump yours and Mason's. Just like Anna's does."

"Okay, okay. I get it." Oliver held his hands up. "Anna is your favorite child."

Anna looked at Lord Caverton. He had a smile on his face as he turned to her. "She absolutely is." He winked at her, and she smiled. "Mason, take care of my girl. Faith, Oliver, it is time to go."

The trio said good-bye and climbed inside the coach. Mason laced his fingers through hers as they watched the coach disappear. He led her back inside before saying anything.

"How are you doing?" Mason asked.

"To be honest, tired." Anna sighed. Facing her fears by reaching out to Lord Caverton and Oliver had taken a lot out of her.

"You didn't need to do that with Oliver and Father." He tucked a loose hair behind her ear. "They understand. They love you."

Anna gave him a small smile. "I need to stop letting my fears stop me from living. My father will be here in a few short months. I don't want my whole life to be lived afraid of my own shadow. My room was in the basement of the castle because I couldn't handle being around others. The basement felt safe."

"You are one of the strongest women I have ever known." Mason kissed her forehead. "Why don't we get you up to bed and I will see you this evening after I make sure all the tenants are prepared for the storm."

"Mason," Anna swallowed down her fear of being left alone.

"It will only be a few hours. I will come to your room when I get back to check on you." Mason said.

Anna allowed Mason to guide her upstairs. She dreaded the moment he was going to leave. Mason opened the door to her room, and she hesitated. She glanced up and he cupped her face. He took half a step closer. Her heart rate accelerated as his head slowly dipped towards hers. He stopped just shy of his lips touching hers.

"Anna, the decision is yours." He whispered.

All it would take for their lips to touch would be for her to raise the slightest bit on her toes. She moved her face to the side and pressed a long kiss to his cheek. She stepped back and he looked completely shocked. "Be safe today, Mason." Anna walked into her room and closed the door.

Chapter 14

They were on their fourth day of storms. So far, they had not been too bad. Anna spent the majority of the time in her room. Mason was gone all day helping tenants and other people in Woodbury mending fences, fixing roofs, and looking for lost livestock. Every night he came home exhausted, but he stayed with her in the library until she was ready to go to bed.

Anna hadn't been sleeping well. Every night had brought a vision of her father and Mr. Hawkshaw coming for her. Each one was a little different but ended the same. She was taken by Mr. Hawkshaw. On top of that, storms brought memories of the fighting between the clans. Normal rainstorms weren't the problem, it was the thunder and lightning that reminded her of the explosions.

She had heard some thunder in the distance, and she was growing anxious. She paced her room for what seemed like the hundredth time. Mason had yet to come home, which only added to her worry.

She couldn't take staying in her room any longer. She needed to get lost in a book. Anna walked quickly down the hall and down the stairs. As she reached the bottom step, the front door opened. Two men and a wolf came in. Anna tensed, prepared to run back upstairs. None of them had noticed her yet, and she was afraid to move too quickly.

The wolf shook out its fur as the men took their overcoats off. Anna took a slow step up. What was a Shifter doing here and who were these men? She took a second step up. The wolf's head turned and stopped when it saw her. Their gazes locked. It took a step towards her, and she took a matching step back.

One of the men noticed her. "My Lady, it is good to meet you." He started walking towards her.

Before she could react, the wolf moved between her and the man. It let out a low growl and the man raised his hands as he walked backwards. The two men quickly went into the sitting room, leaving her and the wolf alone. She was just about to run when the wolf shifted.

Mason stood at the bottom of the stairs. Anna jumped from a few steps up, throwing her arms around his neck, causing him to stumble back a step. "You scared me." She snapped at him.

"I'm so sorry, Anna." He tightened his arms around her. "I didn't expect you to be down here."

A loud clap of thunder hit, and Anna tensed. Her hands slid down his chest as she tucked herself more against him. "I am soaked from the rain, Anna. You are going to get all wet." She shook her head. "Yes, you are." He chuckled. "I am going to take you back upstairs while I meet with Mr. Stevens and Mr. Finn, then we can eat. How does that sound?"

"Alright." Anna stepped back and turned for the stairs. Mason slid his hand into hers as they walked. "Why didn't you tell me you were a Shifter?" She asked.

"I never really thought about it. Father and Oliver are as well. Father is a wolf and Oliver is a fox." Mason shrugged. "I really didn't mean to scare you."

"I was scared because two men and a Shifter walked into the house, and I was completely alone." Anna glared at him.

Mason stopped at her door. "Again. I am sorry." He kissed her forehead. "Now that I know you are safe and sound in your room, I need to get back to my meeting. You should also change into something dry."

Anna nodded and entered her room. She was once again by herself with no new book. Sighing, she quickly changed into a dry dress. She grabbed the book on top of the stack she kept on the side table before climbing into bed. Who knew how long the meeting was going to take. She needed to keep herself too busy to think about the thunder drawing closer.

She began rereading her book on fated mates. Several pages in, Anna covered her mouth as her eyes widened. Her mind started to race. Mason was a Shifter. That fact gave new meaning to what she was reading. She flipped to the front of the book and started again. Fated mates felt safe and protected with one another. They also were protective of the other. Fated mates had a distinct scent that the other could smell. The scent was unique to the person and brought comfort to them. The longer they were together, the stronger their bond. Some bonds would become so strong, the pair could feel each other's emotions.

This explained why she felt safe and comfortable with Mason, even after he had attacked her. Why he smelt like pine all the time. His protectiveness and desire to keep her safe, despite first thinking she was a witch. His ability to calm her. All of it. How had she not seen it before? She shook her head. Probably because he never said he was a Shifter.

Her mind was racing so much that she couldn't read any more. Anna returned the book to the table before laying back down. She liked Mason. She really did. She hated to be parted from him. Her favorite part of the day had quickly become their time together in the library. He would hold her while she was curled up beside him. She loved the feelings of being safe, protected, and cared for, that being in his arms gave her.

The way he looked at her sometimes sent butterflies through her stomach and her heart racing. Anna covered her head with her blanket. She could admit to herself that she more than liked Mason. She was in real danger of him stealing her heart. She bit her lip and shook her head. She needed to be careful. He might not like her the same way she liked him. She needed to protect herself until she knew how he felt about her.

*   *   *

Anna heard the click of the door. She tensed, but didn't move. Who was in her room? She closed her eyes and pretended to be asleep. This had saved her from her father's wrath before.

"Oh, Anna." Mason said quietly. "I am so sorry I took so long." She heard him move closer to the bed. He softly brushed the hair out of her face. He pressed a long kiss to her forehead. "Sweet dreams, Anna."

Mason left the room as quietly as he had come. Anna sighed as she stared up at the ceiling. She should have sat up. She hadn't spent any time with Mason all day. Well, really, for the past several days. She missed him.

When were the storms going to end? She wanted sleep and she wanted her days to return to their normal routine. She sighed as she rolled to her side. She was being ridiculous. She had breakfast every morning with Mason and they ate dinner together in the evenings when he got back. It wasn't like she didn't see him. Sleep, she needed sleep.

The rumble of thunder jolted her awake. Another sounded and Anna scrambled out of bed. She ran to the window just as a flash of lightning lit the sky. Immediately a crash of thunder sounded. Anna ran for the door. She stopped outside Mason's room. She ran her hands on her nightgown. Her heart was racing. What was she doing? She couldn't go in there. She bit her lip in indecision.

Another clap of thunder had her knocking softly as she turned the knob slowly. She peeked inside but didn't immediately see Mason. She closed the door behind her before moving further into the room. Mason was lying on the bed. Her steps faltered again.

"Mason?" She whispered. What if he was awake? She listened carefully. His breathing remained even.

Mason lay still. What was Anna doing? He could tell she was anxious about something, and he didn't want to scare her. Thunder rolled and he heard her move to the other side of the bed. She hesitated before carefully climbing under the covers. She let out a tense breath.

"Please, stay asleep." she said quietly.

He waited to see what she would do. She lay there shaking and he grew worried. He slowly reached for her. Anna tensed when his arm went around her.

"Mason?" Anna asked anxiously.

Mason held still. He kept his breathing slow and even. He wasn't about to tell her he was awake. She needed him close but was afraid of the closeness as well. Mason had no idea why she was afraid, but he would be here for her.

Anna let out another tense breath as she relaxed. Mason pulled her more against him. After a few more minutes, she relaxed even more. Her breathing evened out and Mason sighed. She had fallen asleep. He kissed her neck before closing his eyes. He wished they could sleep like this every night.

He had wanted to hold her like this ever since that first night after her vision. While he held Anna, Mason quickly realized that he was completely in love with her. The thought of her father and Mr. Hawkshaw taking her away from him was terrifying. He would do anything to keep her safe.

Mason took a deep breath and sighed. Citrus. He loved the smell of citrus. Anna turned in his arms and buried her face in his chest. He kissed her forehead and closed his eyes.

Anna blinked her eyes open and tensed. She was using Mason's chest as a pillow. His arms were wrapped around her. The sun was just starting to lighten the sky. Anna's heart began to pound in her chest. She needed to get out of here before Mason woke up.

She slowly got out of bed and tiptoed to the door. She glanced back as she opened it. He was still asleep. She breathed a sigh of relief when she made it back to her own room. She quickly got dressed and sat on her bed to wait. If their schedule held true, Mason would be knocking on her door in about an hour.

Anna stood at the window as she watched dark clouds build on the horizon. Another storm. Another day where she would be all alone. A knock came on her door. She was no longer looking forward to the day.

"Come in." Anna called without taking her eyes off the storm clouds.

"Is everything all right?" Mason asked from the doorway.

Anna's shoulders slumped. "I don't know." She was tired. Stressing over her father's inevitable appearance, facing her fears about the Caverton's, the storms, realizing that Mason was her mate. It was all taking its toll on her.

Mason's arms came around her as he stood behind her. "What is on your mind?" he asked softly.

She closed her eyes and leaned back against him. "I don't want to go back." she finally said.

Mason took a deep breath. "I will never let that happen, Anna. I will fight with everything I am to keep you here where you are safe." He kissed her neck. A shiver ran down her spine at the unfamiliar sensation. It wasn't unpleasant but completely unexpected. "Shall we go down for breakfast, or would you like to eat it up here in the room?"

"If you are planning on leaving, can we eat up here?" Anna asked without moving.

"I am staying home today."

Anna turned around to face him. "But the storm..." she said confused.

"Everyone should be fine for today. I need to catch up on some things here. Would you like to join me for a boring day in the study?" Mason smiled down at her.

She was so relieved she wasn't going to have to be alone today. She leaned against Mason and closed her eyes. This was what she needed. She needed him.

"Hey," Mason tightened his arms around her. "Did something happen while I was gone during the last few days?"

Anna sighed and nodded her head. "I have had a few more visions."

Mason tensed. "What visions?"

Anna stepped away from him. "I'm hungry. I am going down to breakfast." She really didn't want to talk about the visions right now. She made it to the hall before Mason caught up to her. He grabbed her hand and tried to pull her to a stop, but she shook her head as she slipped out of his hold. "Not now. I want to eat before I lose my appetite."

"Anna," Mason didn't sound happy that she didn't want to talk about it. He sighed as he threaded his fingers through hers. "Would you like to eat in the library this morning?" he finally asked.

Anna turned around and hugged him. Mason held her tight. "Thank you for giving me time." she said quietly. She took a step back and gave him a half smile. "The library sounds perfect."

He gave her a forced smile. "Let's get you fed."

They entered the library with plates in their hands. Mason was slightly in front of her as they walked towards their couch. Warmth spread through her body and her heart rate sped up. She stopped walking as her vision began to fade.

"Mason," Her voice sounded as if it were far away. She felt herself slipping to the ground as the library faded.

She was standing in the doorway of the sitting room. Her father and Mr. Hawkshaw were sitting across from Lord and Lady Caverton. Her father demanded she come to him. Instead of running to Mason, she held her ground. She didn't move.

"No." she said, even though she was shaking.

"Excuse me!?" Her father roared as he got to his feet.

Mr. Hawkshaw rose as well. She didn't expect the old man to move so quickly. In a blink, he was in front of her. He backhanded her, and she stumbled into the wall. There were several growls and men shouting. Anna looked up to see two wolves stalking toward her father while Oliver had Mr. Hawkshaw pinned against the wall.

"Stop!" the officer yelled. "If you cannot contest what Winters and Hawkshaw are claiming, Julianna will be going with them."

Anna blinked and she was standing in a snow-covered field. She held the hand of a little girl. The girl looked up at her with light blue eyes. "I don't understand, Mommy. I thought we were leaving."

"We cannot leave right now. It is far too cold for us to leave. It would be dangerous if we did." Anna picked her daughter up and kissed her cheek. "I love you, my darling."

The field began to fade. Anna blinked several times. Suddenly Mason's face came into view. She blinked again and took a deep breath and let it out slowly. She closed her eyes.

"Anna?" Mason said anxiously.

"I...I am okay." Anna opened her eyes again.

Mason held her closer as he buried his face in her neck. "I thought you died." He leaned back and kissed her forehead as he rocked her. "What happened? Your eyes glowed blue and then went blank."

Anna sat up and realized she was sitting in Mason's lap. "It was a vision." She whispered. She leaned against him, and he kissed her head.

"Does it always look like that, like you died?"

"Miranda explained it the same way you did. So, I guess it does." Anna snuggled closer to Mason, needing to feel his comfort. The vision had been different this time. Her father came for her. She was told she was going to go with him. She had a daughter, and they were planning on leaving somewhere. Silent tears rolled down her cheeks.

"What did you see?" Mason asked after several minutes. He continued to hold her protectively.

"It was the same as all the others. Father and Mr. Hawkshaw came. I have to go with them." Anna stood. She wiped her cheeks and took a deep breath. A daughter. She was going to have a daughter. But when? She shook her head. She didn't want to know. She didn't want to have a daughter and subject her to the life she had before running away with her mother.

"Anna, are you all right?" Mason asked. "I know the contents of the vision are not..."

"Mason, I am terrified." Anna cut him off. "Every time I go with them. Little things change but the ending is always the same."

She left the library and walked outside. She didn't stop until she reached the gazebo. She put her head in her hands as she sat. Anna was tempted to run. It would be better if she just disappeared. The Caverton's didn't need her father coming into their home and causing chaos. Would she make it very far? Her father was good at what he did. He would eventually find her. No matter where she went, he would come.

The swing swung as someone sat next to her. She sat up and looked at Mason. She laid her head on his chest as he put his arms around her. "The future isn't set in stone, Anna. Every decision we make affects it. Each of the little differences in your vision is probably due to the decisions you have been making." Mason set the bench swinging. "I still stand with what I have been saying from the beginning; you are my wife, and I am not letting you go."

"I am not worth so much trouble. I wouldn't blame you if you cut me loose." Anna sat up to put distance between her and Mason.

Mason grabbed her face and turned her to face him. He gently stroked her cheek with his thumb. "You will always be worth the fight." He kissed the corner of her mouth before kissing the tip of her nose. "I will never cut you loose. Anna, I need you to trust me. I need you to get these thoughts out of your head."

Anna closed her eyes as she tried to block out the vision. Mason rested his forehead against hers. She breathed in his pine scent. Anna pulled her legs under her and laid her head back on Mason's chest. They sat there in the quiet for a long time.

He was right about the future not being set in stone. It is always changing. Maybe he was right. Maybe there was still a chance that her father would not take her away.

Chapter 15

Anna stood at her window watching rain run down the glass. She was fighting her fears as the thunder rumbled outside. Mason had barely gone to his room after working late. She took a deep breath to steady her nerves. She needed to wait a little longer.

The storms were wearing on her. She was hardly sleeping and constantly tense. Living at the castle, the stormy season had not been this taxing. The walls were so thick that she barely heard anything, and if she did, she would spend her days in the basement where no sound reached her.

For two weeks the storms had been off and on. She had snuck into Mason's room three other times. Tonight would mark the fourth. A clap of thunder caused her to jump. There were no breaks between the flashes of lightning and the thunder. She was at the end of her rope of control.

She quickly made her way to Mason's room. As always, she softly knocked before opening the door. She slipped inside and turned to carefully close the door behind her. When she turned back around, Mason was sitting in a chair with no shirt on and his boot half off. A single candle sat on the table at his side, casting a small amount of light.

Anna froze. They stared at each other for a long moment before a clap of thunder pulled her from her shock at seeing Mason still up. "I'm so sorry." Anna kept her eyes on Mason as she tried to turn the knob behind her with shaking hands.

Mason got to his feet and quickly walked over to her. "Is everything all right?" Thunder seemed to shake the windows and Anna squeezed her eyes closed. "The storm? You are upset about the storm?"

Anna hung her head as she leaned back against the door. "It reminds me of the explosions and the fighting." She whispered.

Mason didn't say anything. He grabbed her hand and led her to the bed. Her eyes widened as she looked up at him. "Lay down. I will finish changing and be right back."

"But…" Anna's cheeks heated.

"You have not been yourself for the last few days. You look tired, and I know for a fact you won't be able to sleep in your room with the storm raging outside. You sleep better in here anyway." Mason raised the blankets and waited.

"You knew!" Anna gasped. Her face felt like it was on fire. She couldn't even look at him.

"Anna, it's late and we are both tired." He nudged her towards the bed.

Anna glared at him. He had known the whole time she was sneaking in here, and never said anything. She huffed before climbing onto the bed. Mason's lips twitched as he fought his smile. She rolled on her side, facing away from him. She was so frustrated with him and completely embarrassed.

A few minutes later, Mason laid down beside her. He sighed and Anna rolled to face him. "Why didn't you say anything?"

Mason looked at her. "You were terrified of something and seemed to need to be in here. You didn't want me to know you were coming in. I wasn't about to say something and take away your sense of safety. Plus, you knock before opening the door."

Anna rolled so she was on her back. She was so embarrassed, but at the same time, she was relieved he knew. She was struggling to know how to act around him with him not knowing that she slept in his room. Mason let out a long breath and she glanced at him. His hands were behind his head and his eyes were closed.

"Thank you for letting me sleep here tonight." she said quietly.

He slowly turned to look at her and their gazes met. "Anna, you are welcome to sleep here any time you want. Having you sleep here tonight is purely selfish on my part, I sleep better with you nearby."

Anna bit her lip. It was probably the mate bond that allowed them to sleep better when they were close to each other. "Good-night, Mason." She turned to face the other wall.

She tensed when she felt him scoot closer to her. "Anna?" She looked at him over her shoulder. "You know I would never hurt you, don't you?" he asked.

Anna rolled again to face him. "Of course I do." She furrowed her brow in confusion. Why would he ask that?

"If I ever do anything you are uncomfortable with, just tell me to stop and I will. No matter what it is." Mason said, and she could tell he desperately wanted her to understand that he never wanted to hurt her.

"I know." She answered. Anna tilted her chin up to get more comfortable on the pillow at the same time Mason leaned forward.

His lips pressed to hers and she felt him tense. He barely pulled back. "That was not your forehead." he said in disbelief.

"No, it was not." Anna was trying hard not to laugh at his sudden nervousness. She had wanted him to kiss her for weeks now.

"Anna, I am..." He started to apologize.

She didn't want to hear an apology for kissing her, so she pressed her lips to his to cut him off. Mason froze for only a second before returning her kiss. His hand tangled in her hair. Mason pulled back and rested his forehead against hers.

"Anna, we shouldn't. Not while we are in bed." Mason whispered.

She reached up and put her hand on his jaw. Mason took a deep breath and let it out slowly. Anna fully trusted Mason. She loved him. Her heart beat faster at the realization. She loved Mason Caverton. She wanted to kiss him. She wanted him to hold her. She kissed him again.

Mason groaned as he pulled back yet again. This woman was driving him mad. She had no idea what she was doing to him. He tried to tell her again that they shouldn't be kissing in bed, but she pressed her lips against his again. He kissed her back before sitting up. This was a bad idea. He should never have told her to stay.

"Anna, we shouldn't...I can't...I won't..." He ran a hand down his face. No matter how much he wanted to, he had to put her first.

"Did I do something wrong?" Anna asked.

Mason looked down at her as she lay with her hair fanned out on his pillow. She was an enchantress. A beautiful, wonderful, sweet, enchantress. "You have done nothing wrong." He laid back down. "I am just losing my self-control. We should keep kissing for when we are not in my room." He kissed her forehead.

Anna studied his face for a long moment. She could see the inner battle he was having. She tentatively reached up and ran her fingers through his hair. He closed his eyes and let out a tense breath. "I understand." She whispered.

Mason looked into her eyes. She didn't seem nervous or upset. She smiled shyly at him and his heart skipped a beat. He slowly lowered his head towards hers again. She didn't flinch or move away from him. She returned his kiss without hesitation.

* * *

Anna stared at the wall as she listened to Mason's soft snores. She had trusted him despite her father's voice in her head telling her what was going to happen, causing her to be anxious. She curled into a ball as she tried to make sense of what happened compared to what she had expected to happen.

Mason put his arm around her and kissed her shoulder. "Are you okay?" he asked hesitantly.

"I just don't understand." She whispered.

"What don't you understand?" His voice sounded nervous.

"You didn't use chains or knives. They said they would carve into me." Anna shook her head.

Mason tensed and she could feel his anger building. "There will never be any of that. Not for any reason. Anna, that is not how a husband should ever treat his wife." He slid his arm under her neck and held her close. "Try to get some sleep."

Anna forced herself to relax. She needed to stop thinking of her father. She was here with Mason, and he was gentle, kind, and protective. She was safe with him. She would always be safe with him.

Mason woke to the sound of someone banging on the door. Anna shot up and looked around with fear in her eyes. He sat up and turned her face to look at him. "Everything will be fine." He kissed her forehead and got up. He quickly pulled his pants on before going to answer the door. He kept the door mostly closed to keep Anna from being seen. "Greg, what is it?" He asked when he saw their butler.

"Sir, a letter came for you."

"Thank you." Mason accepted the letter and closed the door. He moved back to the bed and sat on the edge of it. He leaned over and lit the candle on the bedside table. Anna scooted up to his side and he glanced at her. She was wrapped in a blanket. Worry was written all over her face.

"Who is it from?" she asked anxiously.

Mason kissed her. "I don't know yet." He turned back to the letter and broke the seal. He read the letter twice before getting to his feet. He ran his hand through his hair as he started to pace.

Anna stood and watched Mason as he got more and more upset. He stopped in front of her after several minutes. He put his arms around her before he buried his face in her neck. "What has happened?" She asked.

"Oliver has been attacked." Mason said quietly.

"What?" Anna took a step back as she looked into Mason's face. "Who would do that? Why would he be targeted?"

"Father said he was taking all of their documents to the king. He was found on the steps of the courts. He has been badly beaten and he had a lot of fluid in his lungs." Mason's jaw clenched.

Anna's hand flew over her mouth as she stared at him. That couldn't be. Not Oliver. Tears slipped onto her cheeks. "Is he...Did they...?" She couldn't bring herself to even say the word.

"He is alive but unconscious. At least when Father wrote the letter three days ago. He is asking us to go to the Capital. Mother is beside herself and Father needs help with the investigation and Mother." Mason shook his head.

"I love your family, but I cannot go to the Capital." Anna sat on the bed.

"I could be gone for months, Anna. I don't want to leave you alone for that long. It is hard enough for a few hours during the day." Mason crouched in front of her.

"I can't, Mason. All the people. I know that men from Crossford are there. It was the one place Mother said we could never go. It was not safe." Anna wiped the tears off her cheeks. She didn't want to be separated from Mason, but his family needed him, and she could not go. "When will you leave?"

Mason hung his head. "I will leave in a few hours."

"Not immediately?"

He stood up and lifted her into his arms. He climbed back onto the bed and laid her down. He settled down next to her. "No, not immediately." He blew out the candle before pulling her close. "Are you sure you won't come with me? We can keep you out of sight."

Anna rolled so she was facing Mason. She wanted to go, but she couldn't. The risk was too great. "Don't ask me to. Please. My father made frequent trips to the Capital. He has connections there. What if this is what caused my father and Mr. Hawkshaw to know where I am? What if this is what caused everything?"

Mason kissed her. "I don't like it, but I can understand your reasonings." He held her until the sun rose. Anna tensed when he moved to get up. "It's time, Anna."

Anna slowly got up. When they were both dressed, she moved toward the door, but Mason stopped her. "What is it?" she asked nervously.

"I can't leave without telling you," He was interrupted by a knock on the door. He sighed and pulled the door open.

"Your horse is ready, Sir." Greg informed him.

"Thank you, Greg. We are coming." Mason turned to her and offered his hand. She took it and they walked together out onto the front driveway. Anna's mind and heart were racing. What was Mason about to say? She pulled him to a stop, and he looked at her.

"Mason,"

"I will be back as soon as I can. Anna, I know you find peace at the gazebo, but please stay inside until I get home." Mason cut her off. He smiled at her as he cupped her face. "Anna, I love you." Anna was shocked into silence. Mason leaned down and kissed her. She still couldn't find her voice. Mason kissed her again before letting her go and mounting Granger.

Warm tears coursed down her cheeks as she watched Mason ride down the drive. "I love you, too." She whispered. She waited until she could no longer see him before walking back inside.

She couldn't believe he would tell her he loved her, and then just leave. Why didn't he say so last night? She had been taken completely off guard by his confession. She had thought his feelings were from the mate bond. She shook her head. When he got back, she was going to tell him just how unfair he was to tell her the way he had.

Chapter 16

Mason sat heavily in his chair. He tapped two letters against his leg as he thought. He had written to Anna as soon as he had arrived at his family's townhouse and had been updated on Oliver's condition. She had responded quickly saying she was glad that Oliver was in better condition than they had originally thought. Over the following weeks, her letters started taking longer to arrive. Something felt off with her.

"Penny for your thoughts." Oliver said.

Mason glanced over at the bed. "I received a letter from Anna."

"You are usually happy to hear from her. What has you looking so confused?" Oliver sat up and leaned back against the headboard.

"I think I might have screwed up." Mason shook his head. "She is afraid of thunderstorms and started sneaking into my room during the night, so she wasn't alone. In the morning, she would leave before I woke up. She hadn't wanted me to know she was in there."

"Okay…" Oliver sounded confused.

"We got father's letter. I asked her to come with me, but she refused." Mason sighed. "I asked her to come since I had no idea how long I would be here. She said her father has contacts here and she couldn't risk them recognizing her. I didn't push it, but I couldn't leave without telling her that I love her. So, I did. I said good-bye and got on Granger. I was so nervous about how she would react that I didn't stick around long enough to see it."

"Let me get this straight. You told your wife you love her, said good-bye, mounted your horse, and rode off all before she could react?" Oliver stared at him.

"Yup. Pretty much." Mason ran his hand down his face. "Her first letter expressed relief over you not being as bad off as we had assumed. Her second asked after Mother and Father. Her third said she was glad the storms weren't as frequent." He held up her letter. "Here is her fourth."

"Four letters in two months?" Oliver rubbed his chin. "How long did this one take to get here from the time you sent your last letter?"

"Each letter has come later and later. This one took two weeks." Mason didn't know what to make of it. "She wrote inquiring after everyone. She said a lot of the household has come down with an illness she was told has hit the village."

"Did she say if she was ill?"

"She said she was doing well despite what anyone else says. She told me to stay here and finish what needs to be done." He passed the note to Oliver. There was nothing personal in it anyway.

Oliver took it and read it several times. "This sounds like a letter given to an acquaintance, not your spouse. Do you think she is distancing herself again?"

"I don't know." Mason really hoped she wasn't. "As soon as you are cleared for travel, we can head home. So, hurry up will you? I have a wife to figure out." Mason tried to lighten the mood, even though he was panicking inside.

"What does that other letter say?" Oliver asked.

"It is a letter from Greg. He says that Anna has been quite ill but refuses to see a doctor. She has spent the majority of the last month in her room, only coming out occasionally to exchange books in the library."

"She will be fine, Mason. Just like the cough, she probably has a remedy she is taking." Oliver tried to soothe his worry. It wasn't working.

*   *   *

Anna was anxious as she approached Woodbury. The entire household was ill, and they needed to get more supplies for soup. Greg had tried to convince her to see a doctor, but she refused. He had not been happy.

The town was eerily quiet. There were only a handful of people around. Anna pulled her cloak tighter around herself as she hurried to Finn's Store. She quickly gathered the ingredients she would need. As she exited, she spotted an apothecary shop.

Anna hadn't been feeling well enough to hunt for herbs to help calm her nausea, headaches, and fatigue. She had been one of the first to get sick. Even though the worst of it passed within a few days, she was still not fully over it.

She decided to see if they had what she needed. A bell rang when she pushed the door open. The shop was empty except for a woman browsing shelves and a man behind the counter. The woman looked up and smiled at Anna. Anna gave her a small smile in return. She hoped the woman would not try to start up a conversation with her. She was far too tired to interact with others.

Anna scanned the shelves but didn't see what she was looking for. She sighed in disappointment before making her way to the door. She stepped out onto the walkway and began crossing the road to head home.

"Excuse me!" A woman called. Anna tensed, but didn't slow her steps. "Excuse me, My Lady."

Anna grudgingly stopped as she turned to face whoever was following her. She was surprised to see the woman from the apothecary shop. "Can I help you?" Anna asked.

"I was going to ask you the same question." The woman smiled at her. "My name is Penelope Harper. My husband and I are travelling around the country looking for a good place to settle down. In the meantime, we try to help those who need our assistance."

"I don't understand what you are getting at." Anna eyed Mrs. Harper suspiciously. She felt a little guilty for speaking to the woman so rudely, but she really wasn't feeling well.

"We are doctors. Well, I am a midwife, and he is the doctor; but we work as a team." Mrs. Harper smiled. "I don't mean to be nosey, but I couldn't help noticing you are quite pale and look a breath away from throwing up. You didn't seem to find what you were looking for in the store ."

Anna's shoulders sagged. She really wasn't doing well. "I was hoping to find something to help with the nausea. Our household has been hit hard by the sickness going around. I alone was well enough to come into town for supplies."

"I see." Mrs. Harper's lips pulled into a thin line. "Forgive me, but you really don't look well. Can I offer you a ride home? I have my supplies in the carriage. I have something that might help with your nausea."

Anna studied the woman. She wasn't much older than Anna was. She had kind eyes and a gentleness about her, despite her forwardness. Anna found herself nodding and following Mrs. Harper to a coach that wasn't far away. She was relieved that Mr. Harper wasn't inside.

"Where to?" Mrs. Harper asked as she began looking through a large black bag.

"Caverton Estates." Anna closed her eyes and leaned her head back.

They rode in silence for several minutes before Mrs. Harper spoke again. "How long have you been experiencing symptoms?"

"Several weeks. I was one of the first to fall ill. I lived a very sheltered life and was never sick before. I think I am much worse than the others because of it." Anna opened her eyes.

"That could very well be it. But I am still concerned. To be sick for several weeks is not something to ignore. What are your symptoms?" Mrs. Harper pulled out a pad of paper and pencil.

"Frequent headaches, nausea that comes and goes, and I am tired all the time. I have also had a fever." Anna grew nervous with each new question Mrs. Harper asked.

"I have a tea I like to have my patients use to help with nausea. We recently got back from Valencia. They have a fruit that when cut, the smell can calm the stomach." Mrs. Harper handed Anna a bag as they came to a stop. She glanced out the window and was relieved to see the Caverton home. "I gave you what I have on hand and written instructions. Would it be all right if I stop by in a few days to see how you are faring?"

"Umm." Anna glanced at the woman. She didn't know what to say. She seemed genuine and Anna just wanted to feel better. "That would be fine."

She slowly walked down the hall towards the kitchen with her basket of ingredients and the bag Mrs. Harper gave her. She placed the items on the worktable and began unloading the supplies. She started on the soup. When everything was in the pot over the fire, Anna turned her attention to the bag.

Anna smiled when she saw a large pouch of peppermint. That had been what she had gone into the shop for. She immediately began making some tea. The next item she pulled out was a lemon. She had read about them in the book on Valencia. The fruit was in the citrus family. Mrs. Harper's instructions said to cut it into slices. The smell might help her stomach. She could also add a slice to her water or just suck on it.

Slicing into one of the fruits, Anna inhaled deeply. She loved the smell. It made her mouth water. Curious, she cut the slice in half before popping it into her mouth. She gasped as her face puckered. She quickly spit it out. A shiver ran down her spine. That was not what she expected. It was so sour.

Anna put a smaller portion in her mouth and resisted the urge to spit it back out. After a few minutes, she got used to it and found she really enjoyed the flavor. She went back to the soup. It wasn't very flavorful, but it would get nutrients back into everyone.

She walked down the hall with the last bowl of soup she had to give out. She knocked on Greg's door and turned the knob. Taking care of the household had pushed Anna out of her bubble of fear. She had to take care of seven men and thirteen women. It had been really hard in the beginning, but they had needed her. She put her fears aside and did what needed to be done.

"How are you feeling today, Mr. Gregory?" Anna asked, setting the bowl on the small table.

"I have told you, My Lady. Everyone calls me Greg." The man said weakly.

He became ill only a few days ago. He was still burning with fever. "You also said I reminded you of your mother in the way she took care of you as a child when you were sick, and she called you Gregory." Anna smiled at him. "So, my dear Gregory, how are you feeling today?"

"Tired, exhausted, and weak." Greg sighed. "What have you brought me?"

"Nothing fancy I am afraid. It tastes terrible but will help you keep up your strength." Anna took a seat before passing him his bowl. "Shall I start where we left off?"

Greg gave her a nod and she flipped through the mystery novel she had found a few weeks back. She found her place quickly and began to read. After an hour, she put the book back on the table. The older man was not taking it very well that he could not perform his duties in his present state. They had compromised. She would visit him for an hour every day if he stayed in bed until he was well again. Apparently, Mason had tasked him with keeping an eye on her.

"I do not like how pale you still are, My Lady." Greg said as she stood.

"Put your mind at ease, Gregory." Anna patted his hand. "I saw a doctor today, and they plan on coming back in a few days to check on me." She felt a little bad for lying. But it wasn't an outright lie. Mrs. Harper said she and her husband worked as a team.

"Thank the stars." He muttered.

Anna rolled her eyes as she left. It wasn't that bad. Just a little nausea and a headache. He was worrying over nothing. After all, she was the one taking care of the household at the moment. She had even taught herself about estate ledgers and running a household. With all the Cavertons out of residence, someone had to keep things in order. She had been impressed with Mason's and Lord Caverton's thorough record keeping. Without it, she would have never been able to know where to start.

Chapter 17

Mason let out a sigh of relief when he saw the house come into view. It had been a long, stressful three months. Oliver was still regaining his strength, but he was acting like his normal self. Mother hovered over Oliver, much to Oliver's frustration. The three of them couldn't wait to get home. The three days of travel were exhausting.

The coach came to a stop and Mason jumped out. He reached back into the coach to assist his mother as he resisted the urge to race inside to find Anna. She had only written to him once in the last four weeks. Another impersonal note.

The front door opened, and Mason turned around to see Anna standing on the porch. She was a little thinner in the face and pale. He swallowed hard. Greg had been right; Anna had been very sick. He slowly walked up the steps, not sure of the reception he would receive.

Anna fought her desire to throw her arms around Mason. She had missed him so much. But she needed to keep her distance now. He couldn't know. It would change everything. She didn't know how he would react. She still did not know how to take it.

Mason approached her slowly, uncertainty written in every feature. "Welcome back." Anna said softly as she wrapped her arms around herself. She could see that Mason noted the action. She needed a distraction. Oliver stopped at Mason's side. "How are you feeling, Oliver? Near drownings aren't fun to recover from."

"No, they are not." His eyes narrowed on her. "Are you talking from experience?"

"Lady Caverton, how have you been coping?" Anna asked, desperate to change the topic. If Mason grew protective, he would want to touch her.

"I am surviving. How are you, dear? Greg reported of an illness that swept the area." Lady Caverton started inside, and Anna fell into step beside her.

"It has been rough." Anna said. "All of the staff became ill. I am sorry if things seem out of sorts. The household is barely starting to get back on its feet."

"Do not let her fool you, Lady Caverton. This angel is the only reason the house is still standing." Gregory walked down the hall. "Despite being the sickest of us all, she cooked, cleaned, and nursed us back to health. Rumor has it that she even managed the estate books." He held up a tray with a teapot, covered bowl, and cup.

"Now, don't you sound like a boasting child, Gregory." Anna clicked her tongue. "Thank you, sir. I will take that." Anna reached for the tray. With it in hand, she turned to face the Cavertons. They were all watching her with wide eyes. She curtsied. "I am sorry to be disappearing right after you have arrived, but I must take this."

She didn't wait for a response before turning and walking up the stairs. She quickly went to her room and locked the door. She knew Mason would be here any minute. Maybe he wouldn't notice. She wasn't too big. She shook her head. She was big enough that he could easily notice if he put his arms around her waist.

She put a small slice of lemon in her mouth just as the doorknob jiggled. Anna sat on the window seat and waited. The door opened a moment later, and Mason walked in. He was tense and his eyes were guarded. She swallowed hard.

"Would you like some tea?" she asked into the tense silence.

"No. I would like to know what is going on?" Mason studied her, and she squirmed under his scrutiny.

Anna sighed and put her head in her hands. This was so much more difficult than she thought it would be. She wanted to start distancing herself from the Cavertons. That way when her father took her, it would hurt less.

She heard him move the tea tray before sitting down. There was a moment when nothing happened, then Mason put his arm around her shoulders. She leaned into him, and he kissed the top of her head. Anna pulled her legs up so, hopefully, he wouldn't move his hands lower around her waist.

She had needed this. She snuggled more into him and breathed in deeply. She sighed. "A lot has happened in the last three months."

Mason ran his hands through her hair. "What has happened, Love?" He decided to test the waters with her. In three months, she had not acknowledged the fact that he had declared his love for her.

She tilted her head back and looked up at him without lifting her head off his shoulder. "The storms, the sickness, having to take care of everyone, facing fears."

Mason cupped her face as he looked into her eyes. "I'm sorry I was not here for you."

"Don't be, Mason." Anna sat up as a wave of nausea hit her. "You did what you needed to do. We all survived."

She leaned down and grabbed another lemon slice. She put it in her mouth and closed her eyes. She took several slow breaths. "Anna, what's wrong?" Mason asked anxiously. "What is that?"

"It is a lemon." Anna glanced at him and smiled. "You are welcome to try one."

"A lemon? What is a lemon?" Mason picked up a slice and smelled it.

Anna laughed. "It is a fruit." She poured herself a cup of tea. "I got it from a doctor." She took a sip of her tea as she watched him out of the corner of her eye.

Mason froze with his hand halfway to his mouth with a lemon. "A doctor gave it to you?" he asked in disbelief.

"Mmhmm." She took another sip. "I told you; a lot has happened."

"You saw a doctor?" Mason stared at her in complete shock.

Anna shrugged. "Are you going to eat that or not?" She pointedly looked down at his hand.

Mason followed Anna's gaze and remembered he held a slice of lemon. He quickly put it into his mouth. He squeezed his eyes closed as he bit into it and the juices spread throughout his mouth. Anna started laughing when his face puckered. He coughed a few times but managed to swallow the sour substance.

"What was that?" he coughed.

"A lemon. Didn't you like it?" Anna was still laughing.

"Not particularly." He shivered. "What is it for?"

Anna put her cup down and sat back. She looked completely exhausted. "Living at the castle didn't provide us much exposure to illness. In fact, it was quite rare that we were sick. Whatever swept through here affected me much worse than the others because I have never been exposed to it before. At least that is what Dr. Harper said. The lemon is to help settle my stomach so I can keep food down. As does this tea."

"Anna,"

"It is fine, Mason. It would have happened sooner or later." Anna picked up the tray and carried it to the side table. "Mason," She took a deep breath. "I don't want to sound rude or mean or..." she sighed. "The Harpers have said I need to try to get a nap during the day."

"Anna, be honest with me." Mason said as he stood. "How bad was it?"

She looked over at him. "I couldn't get out of bed for over a week. The fever was off and on for a month. I am recovering, but slowly." She gave him a smile. "Now, Mr. Caverton. You need to go get cleaned up and change out of those dirty stinky clothes. I will see you at dinner."

Mason walked over to her. "I would much rather stay with you. I have been worried about you since I left."

"I am going to sleep. I am sure you need to catch up on a lot, considering you were gone for so long. Do not worry about me." Anna needed him to leave before she begged him to stay. If he did, she wouldn't be able to hide her growing belly from him. Distance. She needed to start putting distance between them.

Mason leaned down to kiss her, moving slowly while watching her face. As much as she wanted to let him, she couldn't. She turned her head just enough for his lips to touch her cheek instead of her lips. She could feel his disappointment and she bit the inside of her cheek to keep from crying. She could do that later.

"I will see you tonight at dinner than." Mason said as he stepped back. At the door he paused, looking back at her. "What I said before I left still holds true, Anna. I love you." He walked out, closing the door behind him.

"I love you, too." Anna whispered as her tears began to fall.

* * *

Mason could not believe what he was looking at. There were pages upon pages of estate records for the last three months. They were tucked in among the pages of the record book. Anna. Greg had been right; she had been keeping up with it. He started to review the information. So far, everything was adding up. How on earth had she managed to teach herself this in only a few months. It had taken him years to learn how to do the estate records.

A knock on the door brought his head up. Oliver stood there. "Can we talk?"

"Close the door." Mason sighed as he sat back.

Oliver made his way over to the chairs in front of his desk. "What is going on with Anna?"

"That is the question I keep asking myself. She said she is still recovering from her illness. A Dr. Harper said Anna needs a lot of rest right now." Mason straightened the papers on the desk.

"But..."

"But that doesn't seem like everything. She hardly looks at me. She is tense and anxious. She fidgets whenever I am close to her." Mason looked at his brother. "When I left, my wife was comfortable with me. She would allow me to just sit with her. Now, she is distant and avoids any contact with me."

"I saw her on my way here." Oliver stated. "She was more comfortable with me when she first got here. She is no longer afraid, just...distant."

"Do you think she is pulling away from all of us? Putting up walls?" Mason studied his brother. Both sat in silence for several minutes. "Anna believes that her father will come for her in a month. You don't think she is trying to separate herself from us emotionally, do you?"

"It's a sound theory. If I thought I would be ripped from those I cared about and returned to a life of abuse, I would want to protect myself as much as possible. Including, putting up walls to keep everyone out." Oliver said thoughtfully.

"What do we do?" Mason stood and walked over to his brother.

"We do nothing. I know it will be hard for you but give her space. Allow her to set her boundaries." Oliver gave him a sympathetic look. "After she realizes she won't be taken away, she will open back up to us."

Mason let out a long breath. "It probably doesn't help that she recently went through the attack on the castle."

"Probably. We just need to be patient and understanding." Oliver leaned back. "She missed you. When she came out the front door and saw you, she looked relieved and excited before her eyes filled with pain and sadness. Then she put on her mask."

"What do I do, Ollie? She allowed me to hold her for a brief moment before she put physical, as well as emotional, distance between us." Mason was at a loss. All he wanted to do when he got home was hold his wife.

"When we go into dinner I suggest just sitting and eating. Do not hold her hand like you usually do. Bring her into the conversation, but do not focus on her or force her to participate." Oliver stood. "Let's see how that plan works out."

Oliver and Mason walked into the dining hall with serious expressions on their faces. They glanced at Anna before looking at each other. There was an unspoken conversation between the two brothers. She narrowed her eyes in suspicion as she watched them move to their seats. Oliver took the seat directly across from her and Mason sat beside her.

She put her hands on the table, afraid he would accidentally brush her stomach with his hand if he reached for hers. The meal got underway with Lady Caverton monopolizing the conversation. Anna grew more and more frustrated with Mason and herself. Mason, because he seemed to catch on that she needed space, and herself, because she wanted desperately for him to not give it to her.

Anna attempted to eat, but her stomach was in knots, and she had no appetite. She had only managed to take two bites by the time Gregory stepped into the room. He glared at her when he saw her plate. He always did this. He would push her to eat, and then she spent the majority of the night throwing up. Well, not tonight. She pushed her plate away as she stood. Oliver stopped mid-sentence as all eyes turned to her, but she didn't care.

"Don't do this tonight, Gregory." She snapped.

"Anna?" Mason quietly said her name, but she was already heading for the door.

"Sir, if I may speak freely?" Greg asked.

"Go..." Mason started to say.

"No, you may not." Anna pushed past him. She had asked the servants to speak freely while the Cavertons were not in residence. It felt weird having that social barrier. But she was glad for it tonight.

"With all due respect, My Lady, he has the right to know." Anna froze as panic began to fill her. Did Gregory know? He couldn't know. No one knew. She only figured it out a week ago. She slowly turned to face him. Mason and Oliver stood just behind him.

"What is it you think he should know, Gregory? I have already told him what the Harpers have instructed me to do." Anna crossed her arms over her chest. Gregory looked surprised.

"Greg, what is going on?" Mason asked, clearly confused.

"Sir, Lady Anna has been sick for nearly three months. The first month was the fever. Then came the vomiting. She still can't hold down more than broth, toast, and tea."

"Gregory, I didn't nurse you back to health for you to tattle on me like I am a child." Anna glared at him. "I have already told Mason all of this. Now, if you will excuse me, I am going to bed."

Anna turned and stomped away. Mason watched her go, completely shocked by the conversation he had just witnessed. Oliver let out a slow whistle. "Who was that? I don't think that is the same Anna we left here."

Greg bowed. "Sir, I apologize for over-stepping."

"You are fine, Greg. Tell me more about what has been happening here." Mason turned to the man.

Mason listened to Greg carefully. Much of what he was saying was what Anna had told him. She had apparently become quite the little fighter while caring for the staff. Greg said she had been terrified the first couple days, but then seemed to come out of her shell and take charge.

Mason had to admit that he liked this take charge, willing to fight Anna, over the scared and timid Anna. He dismissed Greg to go about his business and Mason went up to his room.

He tried to go to sleep, but even being exhausted didn't help. He lay there wide awake. After several hours, he got out of bed. He snuck over to Anna's room. He gave a soft knock before turning the handle. To his surprise, it was unlocked. He slipped inside and waited. He could see Anna in bed. She appeared to be sleeping.

He quietly walked over to the bed, but hesitated. She would be furious with him if she caught him in her room. He glanced at the door before turning back to Anna. He let out a soft growl. "I hope you are still sleeping." He whispered.

As carefully as he could, he climbed into the bed. Anna rolled and he froze. "Please don't wake up." he muttered under his breath.

She was facing him now. With the moonlight coming in through the window, he could barely make out her facial features. Her eyes were closed, and her face was relaxed. He let out a sigh of relief as he made himself more comfortable. A few minutes later, Anna moved again. This time she laid her head on his chest. She relaxed with a sigh.

Mason placed a light kiss on her forehead before closing his eyes. The exhaustion of travel and the stress of the past several months were finally catching up to him. His body began to feel heavy. He pulled Anna closer to him as his concern for her momentarily faded.

Chapter 18

Anna looked out her window with a frown. Any day now, her father would be showing up. Her anxiety increased with each passing day. The only thing keeping her sane was Mason. He had snuck into her room a few times over the past three weeks. She had pretended to be asleep, and he climbed into her bed. He held her while they slept. He would go back to his own room before she 'woke up'. Most of the time, she had been awake for at least an hour before he woke up.

She made sure she was facing him, so his arm wouldn't ever rest on her belly. She needed to tell him. It was getting harder to keep it a secret. She was terrified of what he would say or do.

In Crossford, a pregnant woman was considered sacred. It was the only time a woman was safe from the violence and abuse. All the clans respected them during that time. She was not to be touched in any way. If anyone harmed her, they faced death at the hands of the clan leaders.

She didn't want Mason to look at her like that. Like she was suddenly worth something, or more accurately, like she carried something of value. To her, this child was special no matter its gender. She was worried Mason would put a value on the child, like the men of Crossford.

A knock on her door pulled her from her thoughts. She answered the door to see Greg standing there. "Lord Caverton has arrived home. The family awaits you in the sitting room."

Anna nodded and walked down the hall. She was so lost in her own thoughts about Mason that she hardly remembered how she arrived at the sitting room. She took a deep breath and let it out slowly, preparing to face Lord Caverton again. She walked into the room but froze after several steps. She felt the blood drain from her face when she saw Lord and Lady Caverton sitting across from her father and Mr. Hawkshaw.

"There she is." Mr. Hawkshaw smirked at her. "You have grown into quite the beautiful young lady." He paused as his eyes traveled up and down her several times. "Hmm. Maybe a little too fat, but we can fix that."

Mason growled and Anna looked at him. He looked angry. Tears filled her eyes. She knew this day was coming. She closed her eyes and ducked her head. It was too painful to look at him now that the day had come for her to leave.

"Come here, girl." Her father snapped.

Anna hesitated. In her vision, she had refused and was punished for it. Slowly her feet moved forward. She stopped just out of striking distance of both Mr. Hawkshaw and her father. Silent tears rolled down her cheeks. She noticed that there were three other men standing around the room, other than Oliver and Mason.

"It is good to know that the girl is still here. It is a relief to know she is safe." One of the men said.

"What is all this about?" Lady Caverton asked.

"Lord Caverton, I would prefer to discuss this where the women aren't interjecting." Her father sneered.

"This is my home, and you will treat my wife with respect." Lord Caverton said angrily. Anna had never heard him so mad before. Not even when he had forced her and Mason to get married.

"Lord Caverton, Captain Winters has brought up concerns about his daughter's marriage to your son, Mason. He wishes to dissolve their union." Another man said. He was timid and spoke quietly but clearly.

"On what grounds?" Mason asked. Anna glanced up. He was glaring at the men across the room.

"We just went over this, Mr. Caverton. Must I explain it again?" the man said. "We have several witnesses stating that you don't even share a room with your supposed wife."

"What I do with my wife is no one's business but ours." Mason snapped. "I have already told you that your argument is invalid."

"How can we prove such a thing?" Oliver asked in exasperation.

"As her father, I can examine her." Captain Winters stood.

"You are not touching her. You will not be in the same room alone with her." Mason took a threatening step forward.

"Gentlemen, that is not a situation that is going to happen." The first man said. Anna chanced a glance at him. He was larger than the others and wore a uniform. "We will send for a doctor."

Mason ran his hands through his hair as he began to pace. Anna could feel his hopelessness and frustration. But there was nothing for it. She had told him this would happen.

"While we wait, Julianna will need to come with us to the inn."

"Why can she not stay here?" Lady Caverton asked in concern.

"She needs to be isolated from both parties until this matter can be resolved." The man began walking towards the door. "Shall we?"

Anna couldn't stay here any longer. It hurt too much to hear the pain and fear in Lady Caverton's voice, as well as seeing the looks on Oliver, Lord Caverton, and Mason's faces. At least she wouldn't be staying with her father or Mr. Hawkshaw yet.

She stepped outside and her steps slowed. The other man stepped to the side and was talking with the third man. She felt a presence behind her but didn't turn around. She hesitated next to the coach.

"Get in." Mr. Hawkshaw ordered. Anna's heart beat faster as the fear she had been trying to suppress broke free. She swallowed hard. The interior of the coach almost seemed like her own coffin. Her feet remained rooted in place.

Mr. Hawkshaw grabbed her shoulder and spun her around. His fist connected with her so fast and so hard that Anna stumbled and fell to the ground. Her mind was spinning and the world around her was unfocused. She had forgotten how painful getting punched was. There were shouts erupting all around her.

Anna flinched when someone touched her shoulder. A man she had not seen before was kneeling next to her. He looked concerned as he pressed a handkerchief to the corner of her mouth. Anna blinked several times, trying to figure out who the man was. He helped her sit up before standing and getting in Mr. Hawkshaw's face. She turned as several men were yelling and shoving each other on the steps.

"Taweret!" The man yelled as he shoved Mr. Hawkshaw against the side of the coach. All activity ceased. Anna stared at the man in surprise.

"What?" Hawkshaw sputtered.

"You are from Freynia are you not?" The man asked, looking a little less sure of himself.

"We are but..." Captain Winters started to say.

"Then this man just signed his own death warrant. If I remember right, every clan has the Taweret Law." The man kept a firm hold on Hawkshaw.

Someone knelt by Anna, and she looked over at them. "Mrs. Harper?" Anna breathed out in surprise.

"You know nothing of our laws." Mr. Hawkshaw snapped.

"I know enough. Julianna Caverton is protected by the Taweret Law." No one moved. No one breathed.

Anna slowly looked over at Mason. He was staring at her with his mouth hanging open. She squeezed her eyes closed and hung her head. Her heart started beating so fast it felt like it was going to beat out of her chest. She was struggling to draw in a breath. What was Mason going to do? Did he know what that said about her?

"Anna, are you all right?" Mrs. Harper asked in concern.

"How do you know she is with child?" Captain Winters asked with barely restrained anger.

"My name is Doctor Lucas Harper. My wife and I have been treating Mrs. Caverton for the past three months. She has been suffering from morning sickness. In fact, that is why we are here. We came to check in on her to see how she is faring." Dr. Harper said. "Now, Mrs. Caverton. Let's get you inside."

He assisted her to her feet and Mrs. Harper put her arm around her. "Lucas, she is having a panic attack." she said quickly.

Anna put a hand to her chest as she struggled to draw in a breath. He was going to be so angry with her. What would he do now? What would Lord and Lady Caverton do? And Oliver? Her father was going to kill her once the baby was born. She couldn't breathe.

"Mason." She gasped. She needed him.

Suddenly she was scooped up. She kept her eyes closed as she tried to calm herself down. Several people started shouting again but their voices faded as she was carried away from them.

Anna was put down and she opened her eyes. Mason stood in front of her with a confused and worried expression. He gently brushed the hair off her face.

"Anna, focus on me." He whispered. He guided her head to his chest, and she leaned against him. She grabbed hold of his shirt as she continued to fight for breath. "Slow breath in, slow breath out." A few minutes ticked by, and she couldn't seem to calm herself. "Do you feel me breathing?" he asked as he rubbed her back slowly. She nodded. "Good, match your breaths with mine."

Anna concentrated on Mason's chest as it rose and fell with his breathing. It took several more minutes, but she managed to slow her breathing and rapidly beating heart. Mason continued to hold her. Anna found herself relaxing against him despite her fear of what he was going to do now that he knew she was pregnant.

Someone knocked and she tensed. "Enter." Mason stated without releasing her.

"How is she?" Mrs. Harper asked.

"Calmer." Mason answered. She had never known him to answer with such short answers before. Her anxiety began to grow again as his frustration grew. She could feel it building within him.

"Anna, can I take a look at where that man struck you?" Mrs. Harper asked.

Mason moved to step back but stopped when Anna whimpered. "Don't leave me." She quietly begged so only he could hear her.

She looked up at him and he pressed a kiss to her forehead. Mrs. Harper moved to their side. Anna turned in Mason's arms to face her. His hand landed on her stomach, and she heard him let out a puff of air as if someone had punched him in the gut.

Mrs. Harper gently touched Anna's cheek. She turned her chin a little to the side as she examined her face. The woman's lips pulled into a thin line. "There will no doubt be some bruising but there will be no lasting damage." She stepped back and looked over Anna from a distance. "Other than being attacked outside. How have you been doing?"

"The tea and lemons help. But how did you…I didn't know when we first met." Anna shook her head. She felt so much calmer when Mason was with her. He kept quiet but she knew he was listening very carefully to everything being said.

"My mother was a midwife, and I was raised around pregnant women. I became a midwife because I enjoyed helping to bring new life into the world." Mrs. Harper smiled. "I didn't know for sure, but I suspected as much. When I stopped by a few days later, I was pretty confident that you were. I talked with Lucas about your symptoms, and he agreed with my assessment."

"So, Anna is okay?" Mason asked. "She and the baby?"

"The baby would not have been affected by that man striking your wife. As for Anna, she will need some rest for the next few days. That panic attack was severe, and she is no doubt exhausted." Mrs. Harper gave Anna a pat on the arm. "Get some rest, I will be back tomorrow to check on you."

Anna nodded and watched as the woman left the room. She looked around and realized they were in Mason's room. "Let's get you in bed." He said quietly. She didn't resist as he helped her under the covers. She was surprised when he pulled his boots off and climbed in beside her. He put his arms around her, settling his hand on her stomach. "Why didn't you tell me?"

Silent tears rolled down her cheeks. She closed her eyes for a brief moment. Now that he knew, she needed to just be honest with him. "I," she sniffled. "I was scared."

"Are you upset about the baby?" He asked. "Did you think I would be mad?"

She wiped her cheeks but didn't say anything. He sighed before kissing her shoulder. She closed her eyes as she curled into a ball.

*　　　*　　　*

Mason tightened his arms around Anna. He had no idea why she didn't tell him she was pregnant. He was still reeling from the news. That revelation had completely taken everyone by surprise, except for the Harpers. While everyone froze, Anna had panicked. The fear in her eyes when she looked at him was enough to snap him out of his shock.

When he reached her side, she was calling out to him. He brought her straight to his room, despite her father and Mr. Hawkshaw's protests. The constable, his father, and brother had to hold them back from following him.

Anna was having a panic attack again. He could see it in her eyes that she was scared of him, but at the same time, she hadn't wanted him to leave her.

Mason moved his hand on her stomach. There was no denying that she was pregnant. Her bump wasn't huge, but it was more rounded than she normally was. He let out a little laugh. Anna was pregnant. They were having a baby. He kissed her shoulder as he smiled.

Anna was asleep for several hours before she started to stir. She rolled to face him, and he slipped his arm under her neck. She moved her head to his chest with a sigh. Her hand settled over his heart. He put his hand over hers. She tensed.

"Anna, are you awake?" he asked quietly.

"Mason, I'm sorry." Anna started to cry.

Mason sat up, causing Anna to as well. She tried to move away from him, but he didn't let her. He was done with her pulling away from him. "Not this time, sweetheart." She looked at him with fear in her eyes. "Why are you scared of me? What did I do?"

"Nothing. You have done nothing." She wiped her cheeks and tried to scoot away from him again. He tightened his arms around her, keeping her against him. "It's what you will do."

Mason tensed. "What do you mean? What do you think I will do?"

Anna rotated to face him. Her guard was up again. "What will become of me and the baby?" she asked tentatively.

It was then that he realized what she was so scared of. Where she was from, the children were taken from their mothers. "For starters, we are going to go downstairs and get you something to eat." He kissed her forehead. "Then, I am moving back into my room. I don't care if I snore. You will just have to get used to it."

"Mason,"

"Let me finish." He cut her off. "Then we are going to discuss baby names and whether you want to stay here or if you are feeling well enough to travel to Caverton Manor before our baby is born. I am planning on asking the Harpers to stay close by, since you feel comfortable with them."

"I know you know what I am asking, Mason. Please just answer my question. I can't..." Anna's eyes flashed with irritation and concern.

"I don't know what you want me to say, Anna. We are having a baby, and we are raising this baby together." Mason looked in her eyes so she could see his sincerity.

"What if it is a girl?" Anna asked anxiously.

"I hope it is." Mason smiled. "I would adore her as much as I do her mother. The two of them would no doubt keep me on my toes as well as being the lights in my life." Mason cupped Anna's cheek. "Now, if we have a boy, I must apologize. He will probably be just like me and be a constant headache for you. I am sure my mother would be more than happy to share her wisdom in how to deal with a child like me."

"You are not taking the baby away?" He could see a guarded hope in her eyes.

"Why would I take our child away from you when you would be the best part of its life?" Anna closed her eyes as tears spilled onto her cheeks. She turned her face more into his hand. He pressed his lips to hers and she returned his kiss. Mason pulled back, but he stayed close enough that his lips brushed hers as he spoke. "Now, that is how I had hoped to be received when I got home." Mason smiled at her before kissing her again.

Anna sighed as she laid her head against Mason's chest. All her stress and anxiety over the past several months disappeared with Mason's reassurance that her baby would stay with her. He put his hand on her stomach. "I cannot believe we are having a baby." He whispered in awe.

"The thought never crossed my mind. I had been so sick that I just assumed it was from the illness going around. Then my belly started to grow. It didn't make sense that my stomach would grow when I had been struggling to keep anything down and losing weight." Anna looked up at Mason. "I was so scared."

"I know." He stroked her cheek. "How are you feeling now?"

"Like you are a complete and utter jerk." Anna sat up and glared at him. His eyes widened in surprise. "Who says they love someone for the first time, and then leaves immediately?"

"In my defense, I didn't know how you would react, and I was nervous about your response." Mason stood and paced away from her as he ran his hand through his hair. "For all I knew, you would have slapped me."

Anna stood and walked to the door. "Well, I would have told you that I loved you too." She closed the door behind her and ran down the hall before slipping into a guest room just as Mason made it into the hallway.

She smiled when he ran by. A little taste of his own medicine would do him good. She waited another moment before exiting the room. She leisurely made her way to the kitchen. She grabbed an apple before heading for the sitting room. Her steps slowed as she approached the door. She really hoped her father and Mr. Hawkshaw were not inside.

Lady Caverton sat on the couch reading a book. She looked up when Anna entered. She gestured for Anna to join her. Anna sat before looking wearily at Lady Caverton. "How are you feeling, dear?" Lady Caverton asked with a kind smile.

"I am doing better than before my father came." Anna looked down at her hands clasped in her lap. "Is he still here?"

"No. That man is being escorted back to Freynia." Lady Caverton patted Anna's hand.

"I don't understand what happened. Why were they here? I thought I was going to have to go with them." Anna looked up.

"Arlania has a law that says if a married couple does not seal their marriage physically within six months, the marriage can be dissolved by the bride's father. They claimed you and Mason had not, since they were told that you two do not share a room. The constable was going to have a doctor or midwife examine you to confirm whether or not you and Mason had been intimate." Lady Caverton set her book off to the side. "Doctor Harper confirmed that you were pregnant and that was that. Mr. Hawkshaw and your father left with Allen and the constable."

"Father, it doesn't make any sense. Why would the two turn on each other?" Mason asked in confusion as they walked into the sitting room. His eyes locked with hers. "Julianna, what kind of stunt was that?" He stormed towards her.

Anna shrugged. "Same one you pulled. Now, Lord Caverton, what is going on?"

"You aren't changing the subject." Mason grabbed her hands and pulled her to her feet. "Excuse us for a moment." He bowed to his parents before dragging her from the room. He didn't stop until they reached the study. He closed the door and pushed her up against it. "I didn't quite hear what you said before you disappeared."

"What did you hear?" Anna asked innocently. "That way I don't repeat myself."

Mason narrowed his eyes. "You said you would have told me...and then you were too quiet for me to hear."

"You heard me. Otherwise, you wouldn't be reacting like this." Anna lifted her brow in challenge.

Mason's lips were on hers in the next moment. She put her arms around his neck and drew him closer. "I love you." He murmured against her lips.

Chapter 19

A throat cleared and Anna gasped. Mason kept one arm around her while his other hand went to her belly. Holding her protectively. They turned to see Oliver lounging on the couch.

"I hate to interrupt, but you are blocking the door, and I can't get out without you two moving." Oliver got to his feet.

"Oliver, what are you doing in here?" Mason sounded irritated.

"Don't act like I came snooping." Oliver laughed. "I was in here first. You didn't look in the room before accosting your wife."

"You could have said something earlier." Mason said.

"How could I?" Oliver walked towards them. "What I thought was a simple conversation quickly turned into…"

"Oliver, do you know what is happening with my father?" Anna asked. She could feel her cheeks heating.

"Uh…no. I have been trying to look up the Taweret Law. Has something happened with Father?" Oliver looked between them.

"You won't find it in any of these books. It is an unwritten law." Anna shook her head. "Mason, can we go speak with your father about this. I need to know what has happened."

"Sure, Love." Mason kissed her one more time before opening the door.

They entered the sitting room to find Lord and Lady Caverton sitting on one of the couches. Mason led her over to the other couch. He put his arms around her, and she leaned against him. His hand once again moved to her stomach.

"Taweret Law? What is it?" Oliver asked.

"I have told you how women are normally treated in Freynia." Oliver nodded. "Adding boys to a clan is crucial because they lose so many in the battles between the clans. When a woman becomes pregnant, she is considered protected. They don't want to risk the unborn child." Anna looked down at Mason's hand on her belly. His thumb was gently rubbing the bump.

"Okay, so..." Oliver started to say.

"If a man harms a pregnant woman, he is executed before the day is done." Anna cut him off. "One of the ruling clan members is required to fulfill the punishment or lose his life as well. I have witnessed three executions while I was there."

"Your father attacked Mr. Hawkshaw before we got out of Woodbury. It was so quick. No one saw it coming." Lord Caverton shook his head. "Anna, I do not wish to upset you." He said slowly. She could see the weight he was carrying on his shoulders.

"You do not need to say it. I know. I would be surprised if you said he was still alive. Mr. Hawkshaw has lived for so long because he is a good fighter. My father was equally as good." Mason kissed her temple.

"You do not seem upset about the loss of your father." Lady Caverton observed.

"I have only had one father in my life, and he is sitting in this room." Anna smiled at Lord Caverton.

His eyes started to glisten. "Then you better start calling me such."

"You broke Father again." Oliver said, pointing his finger at Lord Caverton. Lady Caverton sent Oliver a warning look. "Now that Anna is no longer in danger, can I address something that I am still reeling from? Like seriously, I was taken completely off guard."

Anna narrowed her eyes at him. He was grinning at her, and she didn't like the mischievous look in his eyes. "What is it you wish to discuss, because I am reeling from the fact that I am still here and not with my father."

"The fact that, somehow, we all missed that." He pointed to her belly. "With Mason's hand on it, it is completely obvious."

"To be honest, I thought the Harpers were protecting you. I never expected it to be true." Lady Caverton covered her mouth.

Mason's hand rubbed her stomach as he smiled. "No, the Harpers were not lying about Anna's condition."

"I am going to be a grandpa?" Lord Caverton breathed out.

"I hope it is a girl." Oliver grinned.

"Why?" Anna asked in surprise. Mason kissed her cheek.

"The world doesn't need another Mason, for starters. That, and I can't wait to strike fear into all the boys that think they are good enough for her." Oliver was rubbing his hands together.

"It would be nice to have less male influence in the house. These three would teach a boy all sorts of mischief." Lady Caverton laughed.

Anna bit her lip. She had two visions, and each one had the same little girl in it. Her daughter, Bridget. Had today's events changed what she had seen? Warmth spread through her. This was not good. She met Oliver's gaze across the room. His eyes were wide, and he stood frozen. His scared face was the last thing she saw before everything went black.

"Mommy! When can we go see Papa?" Bridget asked.

They were standing in a snow-covered meadow holding hands. "My sweet, we can't leave just yet. We have to wait for the storm to pass before we can go. Plus, your father and Uncle Oliver need to come home first."

"Why are they taking so long?" Bridget looked at her with her brows furrowed.

"War is hard on people, Bri. The borders to Valencia and Freynia have been sealed. People are getting paranoid. People have turned on one another. Your Papa, Uncle Ollie, and father have gone to help those who are being targeted." Anna tried to explain what was happening in a way her five-year-old could understand.

"Mommy, look! Daddy is home!" Bridget pulled free of Anna's hand and ran through the snow.

She smiled when she saw Mason riding up the long drive. Instead of riding to the stables, he turned in their direction. When he was close enough, he dismounted. He scooped up their daughter and kissed her cheek. "You are far too cold, my little sparrow. How long have you kept your mother out here?"

"We have been waiting for you. Mommy said you would come today." Bridget wrapped her arms around Mason's neck.

"Dreaming about me again, My Love?" Mason smirked at Anna.

"I have, but there is one big difference." Anna smiled. "You are much cuter in my dreams than you are in person."

He slowly put Bridget down. He had a look in his eyes that she did not trust. As soon as their daughter was on the ground, he lunged for her. She screamed and ran. He was much faster than she was, and easily tackled her. There was two feet of snow on the ground, creating a cushion as they fell.

Anna was laughing as Mason pinned her down. "Cuter?" he growled before kissing her.

"Will you two please act like mature adults until we get inside? I am freezing." Oliver yelled, breaking into their moment.

"Mommy said Daddy is cuter in her dreams." Bridget brought him up to speed.

Mason helped Anna to her feet before brushing the snow off of her. "That wouldn't take much doing." Oliver loudly whispered, causing Anna to laugh.

Mason scowled at her. She wrapped her arms around his neck as she looked up at him. "I missed you, My Love." Anna said.

She gasped as the sitting room came into focus. She glanced around the room. Mason was holding her, looking completely unnerved. Oliver was pacing while Lord Caverton was comforting Lady Caverton. She blinked several times as she sat up.

"Anna?" Mason held her hand tightly, allowing her to sit up. "What did you see?"

Anna took in the room again. There was now a food tray on the side table, though nothing was missing from it. "Was I out long?"

"Thirty minutes." Oliver snapped. "You were dead for thirty minutes. Mason here didn't see the need to call for a doctor."

"I was not dead." Anna rolled her eyes. She cocked her head to the side as she thought about what she had seen. "Mason, does a sparrow mean anything to you?"

He looked confused. "No. The only thing I can think of that is sparrow related is your necklace."

Anna let go of Mason and reached up. She unclasped the necklace and looked at it. She ran her thumb over the sparrow. She slowly opened it. A folded piece of paper fell out. There was nothing else in the locket. Her hand was trembling as she picked up the piece of paper.

She unfolded it carefully. It was a letter from her mother. The tears started to fall before she started reading the hastily written note.

> My sweet Julianna,
>
> You are and will always be the reason I am alive. This locket was passed down to me by my mother. She claimed it was given to her by the man she loved. He was killed by the clan when they were caught trying to escape together.
>
> If the wearer opens the locket and turns the dial counterclockwise for one full rotation, then closes it again, they will be granted the ability to shift into a sparrow. Be warned, there is a price that comes with using the locket.
>
> I am giving it to you so that you may escape the corruption and life of the clan. Hawkshaw will destroy you if you stay. Spread your wings, my dear.

Do not allow what your father has done to you, make you lose faith in humanity. There are better people out there. Never forget where you have been, but do not dwell there. I hope you learn that love is not a fantasy and will be the thing to set you free.

Forever yours Mama

Anna couldn't believe it. Was this the Locket of Estell? It sounded like one of the artifacts she read about in the secret library. But Miranda had thought the Locket of Estell was what provided the wearer protection. Anna had read the book, and she could see how the information could have been mixed up. The book was confusing at best. If this was the Locket of Estell, she was now in possession of two of the three Guardian Artifacts.

She carefully refolded the letter. Anna looked up and was surprised to find only Mason in the room. "It was a note from my mother." she said softly.

"I figured." Mason drew her to him. "What did you see, Anna?"

Anna smiled as she snuggled more into his side. "I saw us in five or six years." Mason's hand briefly paused its movement as it travelled up and down her arm. "You tackled me into the snow."

"That does not sound like something I would do." Mason laughed.

"You did. You hugged our child then put the child on the ground and chased me." Anna sat up so she could look at him.

"Are you going to keep saying our child? Because I have a feeling you know if the child is a girl or boy." Mason lifted his brow with an eager expression on his face.

Anna leaned forward and kissed him. "You really are going to adore our daughter." She whispered against his lips. Mason let out a laugh as he kissed her. She could feel his excitement. "Oh, I have a book I need you to read." She smiled at him as she sat back.

"Is that so?" Mason grinned at her.

"The history of the Guardians. Chances are, she will be one as well."

"I can do that." Mason kissed her. "What does she look like? Please tell me she has your eyes."

"You might enjoy another book I have. It has to do with Shifters and the ones they are connected to."

"Anna." Mason's voice held a warning. "I need to know everything you know about my little girl."

Anna smiled as she laid her head against his shoulder. His excitement was causing her excitement to grow. Mason's hand went back to her belly as she described what she had seen in her vision and every detail she could remember about their daughter.

"I can't wait to meet her." Mason whispered as he pressed a kiss to Anna's temple. She pulled her legs under her as she cuddled with him. Neither could she.

Part Two

Chapter 20

The stars shone brightly in the cool night. Emmett kept his senses alert as he rode through the busy streets. He hated being in the Capital. Thousands of people constantly running around without a thought of what was going on in the world. War was breaking out on the borders of Arlania. People were dying daily, and yet, no one here seemed to know or care about it.

The trade with Freynia had completely stopped when one of the biggest Clans lost two high ranking members in Arlania. No one knew of the circumstances around it, but it had greatly affected the relationship between the two countries.

The border to Valencia was also closed. There have been more and more Shifter attacks over the last twenty years. Valencia was a country full of Shifters. In order to keep the human population safe, the king issued a command to block the border.

Now, the Arlanian people were terrified of all Shifters. Many had called for a mass execution, but the king denied the requests. For the most part, Shifters went into hiding. Emmett included. He had seen too many good people lose their lives, just because they had the ability to shift.

Four years ago, Emmett overheard a conversation about a man that had killed several people near Larkhall in his shifted form. The men speaking were planning to capture the man and take him to the king. Emmett had left for Larkhall immediately. He wanted to help stop those who fueled the fear and hatred for Shifters. He was the one to find and stop the murderer. The men had come upon him shortly after.

That is how he met Lord Mason and Lord Oliver Caverton. They invited him to join their organization known as the Hunters. The group was small, but canvased Arlania, Valencia, and Freynia. No one outside of the Hunters knew the identities of the members. The head of the organization was only known as the Pheonix. There were rumors who the other Hunters thought was the Pheonix. Some said it was someone in either Freynia or

Valencia. Others said it was the king himself. Emmett didn't know what to think.

The Caverton's townhouse came into view, and he pushed everything from his mind. He was to report on his mission to Ashford. Then he could go home and rest. It had been a long month on the road.

He jogged up the steps and quickly knocked. A minute later it opened to reveal Greg, their butler. "Good to see you, My Lord." The older man bowed.

"As it is you, Greg. I am here to speak with both Lord Cavertons." Emmett smiled. Seeing the old butler was familiar and, in a way, felt like he was coming home.

"They will meet you in the study, sir." Greg said as he led Emmett down the hall to the room he knew was the study. He had been here many times.

"Thank you, Greg." Emmett bowed and stepped into the large room.

He was only a step in when an unexpected voice stopped him. "Mother said you would be here tonight." A woman said quietly.

Emmett scanned the room and found a woman lounging on the sofa with her back towards him. She looked to be reading a book with her legs outstretched along the cushions. Her bare feet were kicked up on the arm of the couch.

He glanced around the room. They were alone. All he would have to do was take a large step back and he would be in the hall again. He definitely did not want to be caught in a room with a woman. Marriage was not in his cards right now.

"Have I told you lately how much I love you?" she asked.

Emmett swallowed. Being a titled gentleman, he was used to women trying to get his attention, but he had never had any be so bold as to be waiting for him in a room and declaring her love. He needed to leave. Now.

She sat up and turned to face him. Their eyes met and her face paled. She had the most startling blue eyes. He recognized her as Lord Mason's daughter. They had recently been introduced, but he had yet to speak to her at all in the two months he had known her. She was quiet. He didn't even remember ever hearing her speak. She usually sat in a corner of her father's office with a book. She never looked up, or spoke, or acknowledged anyone in the room. During dinners, she was the same. Silent.

"Young, you are early." Lord Caverton's voice directly behind him caused him to jump.

Emmett took a step to the side to allow Lord and Lady Caverton to enter. "Yes, sir."

"Bridget, what are you doing in here?" Lady Caverton asked. She had the same startling light blue eyes as her daughter.

"I...I..." She sat up straight as she looked between her parents and Emmett.

"Did I hear you right?" Lord Mason asked as he studied both of them in turn.

"Sir, I just arrived. Greg directed me to wait in here for you and Lord Oliver." Emmett said quickly.

Lord Mason held up his hand and Emmett snapped his mouth shut. "Bri, did you just say you loved Lord Young?"

"I thought he was Uncle Ollie." She stood up quickly. "I don't even know who he is." She gestured in his direction. "Mother said Uncle Ollie would be here this evening and I was planning on asking him..." Her voice trailed off.

"You cannot say such things so carelessly. Society has strict protocols for such displays." Lord Mason said slowly.

Emmett was about to speak but a noise behind him had him turning and looking to see who else had entered the room. Lord Oliver strolled in with a smile on his face. "What scandal have you brought to the family this time, Mason?"

"Your niece mistook Lord Young for you."

"What did you say, Bri? That I was roguishly handsome? You would die if you couldn't see me?" Lord Oliver grinned.

"No, she asked if she has told you lately how much she loved you." Lord Mason scowled.

"Oh, that is drastic. What is it that you want from me my dear niece?" Lord Oliver chuckled.

"That is not the point, Ollie." Lord Mason sighed.

"Oh, come now, brother. Both of them look completely shocked. It's not like they were kissing in an alleyway."

"We were not kissing." Lord Mason huffed in exasperation, while Lady Caverton laughed.

"Do not worry, Lord Young, Mason is just trying to teach Bri that society looks for every opportunity to gossip." Lady Caverton smiled at him. Emmett relaxed slightly. Thank goodness they weren't going to force anything.

"Gossip isn't what I am worried about, Anna. Bri could be forced into marriage for something like that." Lord Mason put his arms around his wife.

"Mason, there is no harm done. Now, Lord Young is here to give his report. Why don't we all get back to the task at hand." Lady Caverton motioned for everyone to sit.

Lord Oliver quickly took a seat on the only chair in the room while Lord and Lady Caverton took a seat on one of the two couches. Emmett inwardly groaned as he sat next to Lady Bri. It wasn't that he disliked her. She was quite beautiful, but after this most recent conversation about forced marriages, Emmett wanted space from her.

"Lord Young, what have you discovered?" Lord Oliver asked.

"I found the shifter. He is a python." Emmett cut right to the chase. "As far as I have been able to gather, he has killed two men."

"When do we send a team to capture him?" Lord Mason asked.

"We have caught him three times. The issue is how we keep him from escaping." Emmett said.

Silence filled the room as everyone thought. Emmett was frustrated with the whole situation. The man had managed to escape a locked cell without damaging the lock or walls. Emmett's guards had been knocked unconscious.

"He has been caught three times?" Lady Caverton furrowed her brow.

"Yes, My Lady. Each time he escapes without leaving any evidence on how he managed to get out, and my guards are knocked out." Emmett shook his head.

"That is because you are treating him like a man." Lady Bri commented quietly.

"What do you mean, Bri?" Lord Oliver asked.

Emmett looked at the woman beside him. Her cheeks were flushed, and her eyes were fixed on her hands that were clasped in her lap. "He is shifting. That is how he is escaping." Lady Bri glanced at him. "As a snake, he is able to slip through the bars."

"How do you suggest we capture him then?" Emmett asked. This girl had no idea what she was talking about. How were they supposed to transport a man that could slip through the bars?

"Do you catch him as a man?" Lady Bri looked at him.

"Yes." Emmett nodded.

"When he goes to escape, trap him as a snake."

"How will that help?" Emmett raised his brow.

"Well, if he is in a cage built for a snake, he will not be able to escape it. He won't even be able to shift back to a man in that small of a space." Lady Bri shrugged. "He will be far easier to transport as well."

Emmett sat back as he thought. Her suggestion had merit to it. If he could get the man to shift to his snake form and then get him into a smaller cage, he might just be able to get the man back to the Capital to be judged for his crimes.

"Do you think you can capture him again, Young?" Lord Mason asked.

"Yes, Sir." Emmett scratched his jaw as he continued to think of a plan to trap the man for a fourth time.

"When do you want to leave." Lord Oliver asked. "And are you wanting to take anyone with you?"

"I will leave first thing in the morning. I should be fine on my own. He has been pretty easy to track down and capture. Now that we have a plan to keep him that way, it should be smooth sailing." Emmett said. He had to make arrangements if he were to be gone for another few weeks.

"You are going alone?" Lady Bri stared at him in concern.

"Lord Young is one of the best we have, Bri. Do not worry, he will return. This time hopefully with a snake." Lord Oliver smiled at his niece. "Now, what is it that you are requesting of me?"

"Umm..." she glanced at Emmett. "I was hoping you could take me to the ball in a month. Father says he cannot and the sooner I attend the agreed upon ten society soirees, the sooner I can be done with this place."

"I see." Lord Oliver rubbed his jaw. Emmett glanced around at the Cavertons. "I will look into my schedule, Bri."

"Thank you, Uncle Ollie." Lady Bri stood and crossed to her uncle. She kissed his cheek before exiting the room.

"Lady Bri does not care for society?" Emmett asked in confusion. He had never met a lady that didn't enjoy the parties and the dances and the theatre.

"Bri was raised in a remote part of the country. She is not taking to the Capital." Lord Oliver said. "She is quiet and timid but smart. She cannot stand society's ignorance."

"Hmm. I cannot blame her. Society is quite blind." Emmett stood. He bowed to the Caverton's. "I have much I need to settle before I can leave tomorrow."

"Young, stop by before you leave. I will have a cage you can use." Lord Mason put his arm around his wife. Emmett bowed again and walked out.

He was just stepping out of the hallway and into the entry hall when someone collided with him. He put his arms around the person to keep whoever it was from falling. He looked down and was surprised to see Lady Bri.

"I am so sorry, My Lord." She said quickly as her cheeks turned an enchanting shade of pink.

"First a declaration of love and now you are throwing yourself into my arms. I am beginning to believe you do fancy me." Emmett smiled.

Lady Bri's eyes widened in surprise. "I...No..." She shoved off his chest. She squared her shoulders as she glared at him. "Don't flatter yourself, My Lord. You are not that cute. I simply forgot my book in my father's study."

"I will see you when I return." He winked at her, and she scoffed before walking past him. He watched her until she entered her father's study.

Emmett smiled all the way home. He had not expected his evening to go as it had. He had been truly worried about Lord Mason forcing a marriage, but when Lady Caverton had assured him that it wouldn't happen, he had found the humor in the situation. Lady Bri apparently had not. She was far too easy to tease. She had said he was cute. Well, to a degree.

He shook his head. He shouldn't care if she thought him cute. He was not in the market for a wife. He needed to focus on capturing this Shifter. Once that was done, he was leaving for Freynia. There were rumors of smugglers transporting guns and other weapons into Arlania to be used against the Shifter population. The Phoenix was concerned about the innocent being targeted.

Chapter 21

Bridget sat at the table with her mother. They were waiting for her father and uncle to finish a meeting so they could have dinner. They were already half an hour late, and Bridget was starving. The door opened behind her, and she sighed in relief. "Finally, Uncle Ollie. I am wasting away." She said as she turned around.

Laughing blue eyes met hers. Of course he was here. She felt her cheeks heat and she quickly ducked her head. Why was he always around?

"Sorry, Bri." Her uncle chuckled. "Young arrived."

"He was giving a report on the snake Shifter. I invited him to dinner." Her father kissed the top of her head as he passed. "Lord Young, take a seat."

"Thank you, sir." Lord Young took the seat across from her.

The meal was brought out. Her plate was placed in front of her, and she was glad to have something to focus on. She glanced up and her eyes met Lord Young's. He was replacing his cup on the table. She could tell he was fighting a smile, causing her to glare at him.

"Lord Young, how was your trip?" her mother asked.

"It went much better this time around. Thank you, Lady Bridget. I owe my success to your plan." He inclined his head in her direction. Her cheeks heated even more. "It is good to have a home cooked meal."

"You are always welcome, Lord Young." Her mother smiled at him. "We enjoy having you here with us."

"It is nice not eating alone." He cleared his throat. "What have you thought about the Capital, My Lady? I hear this is your first time."

"I think I prefer the country." Her mother said. "There are a lot of people. Much more than what I thought there would be. I do not do well with large groups of people."

"I can understand that. I am not a big fan of the crowds either." Lord Young nodded. "I have an estate up north where I prefer to be. Society tends to get tedious."

"I would have never thought you to dislike society." Her mother said. "You are a frequent topic of discussion at every event we have attended over the past two months."

"This sounds good." Lord Young grinned as he took a bite of his food. "What have they been saying about me?"

"Bridget, what was it that Lady Harris was saying just yesterday?" Her mother laughed. "Something about being elusive."

Bridget cleared her throat. "Um...I believe the ladies were discussing how the handsome and eligible Lord Young could have his pick of any lady, but he was elusive at best." She kept her eyes on her plate. "Miss Davenport has hopes though."

"I also heard that Miss Newton was quite upset that you did not ask her to dance." Her mother said.

Lord Young laughed. "What function was this? I have to admit that I do not know any of these ladies."

"You tend to keep to yourself and hide behind me." Uncle Oliver chuckled. "You are so anti-woman that I have heard rumors that you will never settle down."

"That is a possibility. All the women in the Capital do not hold my interest. They are all seeking a title and wealth. Connections are more important than the actual person they are trying to align themselves with. If they knew who I was, I doubt they would still be interested in me."

"I think that is a lie. You are handsome and kind, with a wonderful sense of humor." Her mother scowled at Lord Young. "Mason, Oliver. Tell him."

"I appreciate your kind words, My Lady." Lord Young looked slightly uncomfortable.

Uncle Oliver saw the shift in Lord Young's demeanor and changed the subject. Bri glanced up to see him looking at his plate. She wanted to bring back the smile that was usually on his face. This serious version of him did not seem to fit him. He participated in the conversation but was quieter.

Dinner ended and her father escorted her mother towards the drawing room. "I am heading up to bed. I will see you tomorrow, Emmett." Her uncle said before turning to the stairs.

Lord Young stared after him for a moment before glancing at her. He smiled. "May I escort you into the drawing room, My Lady?" he offered his arm.

Bridget tentatively put her hand on his arm. They walked into the drawing room to find her parents sitting together on one of the couches. Lord

Young led her to the couch facing them. Her father raised a brow at the two of them.

"Where is Oliver?" Her father asked.

"He went to bed." Bridget answered.

Her mother started whispering to her father and his attention turned to her. They were snuggled together like they usually were. Bridget turned to Lord Young. "Your trip sounds like it went well. How long did it take to track him down?"

"One day. He was bragging about his latest escape in a tavern. I have been back for three days, but I was busy getting his trial sorted out." Lord Young smiled at her. "Do you share your mother's opinion of the Capital?"

Bridget scrunched her nose. "I do. I thought I would enjoy interacting with others, but I find it makes me anxious. Smaller groups I can handle, but the big events are difficult for me. I guess I am a country girl at heart." She looked over at him. He was studying her.

"That isn't a bad thing. The country holds much more appeal than this place. I cannot stay within the Capital for more than a few weeks at a time before having to escape." His voice was low to keep their conversation between them. "What is your country estate like?"

Bridget smiled. She loved her country home. "It is beautiful." She sighed. "The house sits in a large clearing. We have a creek that cuts through the meadow. There are woods all around. It is isolated but there is a village an hour away. We have horses as well. Father taught me to ride. It is one of my favorite things."

"That sounds wonderful." His eyes had softened as he smiled at her. "What mischief have you gotten into? I do not believe for a second you are as quiet and as sweet as you seem to be."

Bridget put her hand to her chest in mock surprise. "I am nothing like my father and uncle, sir. I am very much a quiet girl."

Lord Young's eyes twinkled. "What did you do that has you so defensive? I must know, now."

"Bridget has a sharp mind and outsmarts her uncle on a regular basis." Bridget's mother laughed. Bridget sat up straight. She had forgotten she and Lord Young were not alone. "I remember one time; Oliver thought it would be a good idea to take her out in the forest and pretend to leave her behind. Bri hid in a tree and when Oliver went back for her, he could not find her. He went into a panic. She followed him home and sneaked into the library. We did not find her for four hours."

Lord Young laughed. "I knew you were trouble. It is always the quiet ones you have to look out for."

Bridget blushed. Lord Young was as bad as her uncle when it came to teasing her. "And what of you, sir? You were quiet up until a little bit ago."

"I am definitely trouble." Lord Young grinned at her.

"How so, My Lord?" Her mother was smiling.

"Lord Young is not always a jokester. He is different on missions." Her father said. "He is lethal. I am glad he is on our side."

Lord Young's smile slipped a little. He did not like talking about fighting it seemed. Bridget continued to watch him as he spoke with her parents about a number of different things. He seemed to slowly relax as the topics moved away from him and fighting. After an hour, he excused himself to head home.

Bridget went up to her room not long after. Her parents were hard to be around sometimes. They adored one another. They were not shy in showing it. Society, however, frowned upon such displays. Bridget usually did not mind, but since coming to the Capital, her mother had been struggling, and her father was always nearby. She missed her confident and strong mother.

Over the next two weeks, Lord Young was at their townhouse every few days. He spent a lot of time in meetings with her father and uncle. Her mother would invite him to stay for dinner and he always accepted. This had been the routine since they came to the Capital. The only difference was that Bridget and Lord Young spoke to one another now.

He was a tease, but he also listened and asked questions about her life before the Capital. He seemed genuinely interested in learning all he could about Caverton Manor.

Bridget was sitting in the drawing room with her mother when her father, uncle, and Lord Young walked into the room. Uncle Oliver took the seat next to her. She felt a little sad that she and Lord Young would not be able to converse as easily as if he were directly beside her. He sat in a chair off to the side.

"How was your day, gentlemen?" her mother asked.

"Lord Young has Caverton Security running smoothly, despite a few hiccups that arose this week. It would not surprise me if he said he did not sleep this entire time." Her father sighed.

"He does seem tired today." Uncle Oliver chuckled.

Bridget glanced over and Lord Young's head was back with his eyes closed. His breathing was slow and even. She smiled. He had not been in the room for more than five minutes and he was already asleep.

"Should we wake him?" her mother asked.

"Let him sleep a little more. He leaves in the morning on another mission for the Hunters." Her father said. "If he goes home now, he will most likely start packing for his trip."

"How long will he be gone this time?" her mother asked.

"That depends. It is just an information gathering mission, so he will be gone as long as it takes him to get what we need." Uncle Oliver said.

Bridget looked back over at Lord Young. He was frequently being sent away on missions, and he was in charge of Caverton Security. How did he manage to keep up with both? It had been a lot for her father and uncle, and they were working together.

"I should not be gone longer than two weeks at most." Lord Young said without opening his eyes. He had just been resting his eyes when the Cavertons thought he was asleep. "And I sleep plenty."

"You are falling asleep right now. I was ready to find some paints to color on your face." Lord Oliver laughed.

"Just resting my eyes." Emmett sat up. "I might have broken your wrist if you tried to paint my face in my sleep."

"I am quicker than you give me credit for." Lord Oliver gasped.

"I would love to go a round or two with you." Emmett grinned.

"You will not get the chance. I may still be able to hold my own against most men, you are a different story. I have seen you fight."

"I am only twenty-four. It is not like I have a load of life experience." Emmett put on a look of innocence. "I think I could learn a lot from you, Lord Oliver."

"Fat chance, boy." Lord Oliver shook his head.

Emmett laughed as he stood. "I should probably get going though. I do have several things I still need to do before I leave tomorrow." He bowed to the room. "It is always a pleasure, Lady Caverton, Lady Bridget."

Emmett left the Cavertons with a smile on his face. He found himself enjoying his time there more and more. Over the past few weeks, he found a sort of friend in Lady Bridget. She was not like most women he met. She had a good head on her shoulders and a hidden sense of humor that rarely made an appearance. He had yet to hear her laugh, but he was determined to coax one from her.

* * *

Bri hummed as she put another rose in the flower arrangement in the entryway. She stopped humming when she heard the door open and her uncle speaking. "I am glad you are here early. The sooner you leave, the sooner we can get this over with." She added a small amount of Baby's Breath as she listened. "Beautiful, isn't it?"

"Yes, Sir. Quite beautiful." Lord Young said, and she tensed.

"I was speaking about the flowers." Her uncle laughed.

"As was I." Lord Young said quickly.

Bri turned around to face the gentlemen. "Uncle Ollie, you are up rather early."

"I have a meeting with your father and Lord Young." He smiled. "I will go hunt him down. Lord Young, why don't you meet us in the study."

Lord Young nodded, and her uncle headed down the left hall towards the dining room. Bri started to turn back around but stopped when Lord Young cleared his throat.

"Your mother said you would be here today." He said with a smile. Bri lifted a brow in confusion. "Have I told you lately how much I..." Bri jumped forward and covered his mouth with her hands. She could feel his smile grow. She glared at him.

"That is not funny, sir." She whispered harshly.

Lord Young grabbed her wrists gently and pulled her hands away from his mouth. "I was only going to say I am enjoying the warmer weather we have been having."

"That is not what you were going to say, and we both know it." Bri glared at him.

"It is what I was going to say." Emmett grinned. "What did you think I was going to say?"

Bridget felt her cheeks heat at the words she had said the first night she spoke to him. "You are a pain." She whispered. He was teasing her. He was enjoying this if the dimpled smile and laughter in his eyes were anything to go by.

A knock on the door caused them both to jump. They were standing far too close to one another. Panic stole through her as her father's warning about forced marriage came back to her. Before she could do anything, Lord Young pulled her around the corner to the hall leading to the study. She was just out of sight when she heard Greg open the door.

"May I help you, Sir." Greg asked.

"I am here to see Lady Bridget." She groaned quietly when she recognized Lord Percival's voice.

The man had been relentless in his attention. He was tall, thin, and looked like a vulture. Uncle Oliver had said he was a gambler. Definitely not someone she wanted to be around.

"I take it you are not a fan of Lord Percival?" Lord Young whispered close to her ear. Bridget shook her head. "Stay here. I will get rid of him then."

"Lord Young…" Bridget tried to stop him, but he had already walked back around the corner. She heard the men greet each other and she pressed herself more against the wall.

"I did not expect to see you here, Lord Young." Lord Percival said with a hint of suspicion.

"Neither did I expect to see you." Lord Young responded. "What brings you to the Caverton residence on this fine morning?"

"I am here to see if Lady Bridget will go for a stroll with me. It is a lovely day, and I would hate for the world to be deprived of something even lovelier." Lord Percival's statement caused Bridget to shiver. He made her so uncomfortable. Walking with him anywhere would be a painful experience.

"What a coincidence, I am here to see her as well." Lord Young said in surprise.

"You? I have never seen you show interest in any woman."

"One can never predict when a beautiful woman will cross their path and put a spell on them." Lord Young said. "She quite made me speechless the first time I saw her. Her conversations are quite unparalleled." Bridget glared at the floor. The first conversation she had had with Lord Young had been mortifying.

"Gentlemen." Her father's voice entered the mix. "Right on time, Lord Young. Lord Percival, what can we do for you?"

"I am here to see your lovely daughter." Lord Percival said quickly.

"I am afraid she is not available to go out this morning." Her uncle said stiffly.

"I see. Would you let her know that I stopped by?" Lord Percival asked formally.

"We will." Her father said. The door opened and it was quiet for several seconds.

"Lord Young, are you coming?" Lord Percival sounded irritated.

"I was not planning on taking Lady Bridget out." Lord Young sounded like he was smiling.

The door clicked closed, and Bridget sighed in relief. "Where did Bri go, Lord Young?" Her uncle asked.

"Last I saw, she was heading down that hall." Lord Young said.

Bridget took a step away from the wall and came back around the corner. Her father watched her closely while her uncle and Lord Young smiled. "Thank you for sending him away, father." She moved to his side and hugged him.

He put his arms around her and kissed the top of her head. "I do not like the attention he gives you, Bri. You need to be careful when it comes to Lord Percival."

"Do you think I enjoy that man's company? A porcupine, or even Lord Young, would be better companions than he is." Bri said stepping back.

"Was that an insult or compliment, My Lady?" Lord Young smiled at her.

She glared at him. "Father, is mother in the library?"

"Yes."

Bridget didn't say another word as she climbed the stairs. She heard her uncle ask Lord Young about his interaction with Lord Percival. She could feel eyes on her all the way up the stairs. She glanced down as she walked along the balcony towards the library and her eyes met those of Lord Young's as he was walking behind her father. He winked at her. She pulled her eyes from him, and lifted her chin.

Bridget would not let him get under her skin. He was handsome to be sure. He was shorter than her father and uncle but still a head taller than she was. His dark brown hair was shorter than most of the men she had seen around town. His dark blue eyes shone with intelligence and humor. He was definitely attractive. She had thought so since she had first seen him several months ago.

*   *   *

Emmett was trying hard not to smile as he entered the study behind Lord Mason. Lady Bridget was unlike any woman he had ever met. He would have never thought she had a drop of fight in her, given how quiet and reserved she always seemed.

He took a seat on the couch and sat back. Lord Oliver was watching him closely. "I find myself confused." He finally said.

"As do I." Lord Mason crossed his arms over his chest. "What is the nature of your relationship with my daughter?"

"I have no relationship. Well, maybe friends but that would probably be stretching things." Emmett stated. His earlier amusement over her reaction to his teasing fled. "She seemed uncomfortable when she heard Lord Percival at the door. I told her to hide around the corner and I would see if I could get rid of him."

"You said you were here to see her and that she made you speechless." Lord Mason's eyes narrowed.

"Uh...yes. I will be honest, when I first saw your daughter, I was not expecting to see a young lady sitting in the corner of your office while we discussed a murderer. The first time I spoke to her was a few weeks ago, and that conversation was unexpected to say the least." Emmett shrugged. "Lord Percival seemed threatened by my presence. I figured he would leave if he thought someone else was interested in her."

It was quiet for several minutes before Lord Oliver spoke. "I believe him, Mason. Bri doesn't seem too thrilled to see him or even be near him." He chuckled. "Did you see the glares she was sending his way?"

Lord Mason ran a hand down his face as he sat heavily in a chair. "Is it ever going to get easier, Oliver?"

"Bri is growing up, Mason. She is going to leave the nest soon. That is inevitable. You need to start preparing for it because you can't hold onto her forever." Lord Oliver gave his brother a sympathetic look. "Concentrate on running off the bad ones. Anna is right about one thing."

"What is that?"

"You are not taking this well at all. Maybe it is a good thing Anna isn't up to going to the ball in two weeks. Poor Bri is likely not finding success because you are scaring everyone away." Lord Oliver grinned.

"I'm sorry to interrupt, but I really should be leaving soon." Emmett was starting to get uncomfortable listening to them talking about Lady Bridget's marriage prospects. He didn't particularly like the idea of her getting more attention.

He gave himself a mental shake while he tuned back into Lord Mason as he described the area he was going to and the information they were wanting. He listened to the instructions, committing them to memory. Twenty minutes later, the three of them were in the entry hall.

Lady Caverton and Lady Bridget were descending the stairs. Emmett swallowed hard as his gaze met Lady Bridget's. She had a small smile playing at the corners of her lips. He desperately wanted to coax the rest of the smile to appear. The ladies stopped at the base of the stairs. Lord Mason immediately walked to his wife and pulled her in for a kiss.

Emmett resisted the urge to move closer to Lady Bridget. He glanced at Lord Oliver, who was watching him. "I will send an update as soon as I have what we need. It should go quickly." Emmett said, trying to get his head back on straight despite his heart hammering in his chest.

"Travel safe and we will await word." Lord Oliver inclined his head. "Are you sure you do not want anyone to go with you this time?"

"The man is cocky. His holdings are poorly guarded. I have been inside several times." Emmett smiled. "If I need help, I will send word."

Emmett glanced over at Lady Bridget. Even though she held a neutral expression on her face, he could see the worry in her eyes. The urge to go to her again pressed on him. He took a step towards the door. He needed to get away from here before he did something completely stupid. He didn't turn back, even though he could feel her watching him. He closed the door harder than he had intended and winced. Taking a deep breath, he let it out slowly. Emmett needed to stay focused on the task at hand. When he returned, he could revisit these confusing thoughts and feelings

Chapter 22

Bridget looked out over the crowd. The women were dressed in beautiful gowns with sparkling jewels that complimented them. There had to be at least a few hundred people at this ball. She took a deep breath and let it out slowly, calming her nerves. There was no need to be nervous. Growing up at the remote Caverton Manor had made her unprepared for the sheer number of people within the Capital. It overwhelmed her.

She had already danced three times this evening and was on her fourth. That was more than she had at the ball three weeks ago. Uncle Oliver had been right. Without her father there to scare everyone off, she was getting much more attention. She did not know if she liked it or not.

Her current dance partner returned her to her uncle's side, bowed, and disappeared into the crush of people. Uncle Oliver glanced at her before turning his attention back to the man he was talking to.

"Tell me Lord Caverton, what is your stance on the king's refusal to eliminate the Shifters within Arlania?" The man asked.

"I think those that are dangerous should be dealt with accordingly." Uncle Oliver said carefully.

Bridget hated these conversations. They created divides among the people. This man was obviously in favor of killing all Shifters. Little did he know that he was speaking to one. That fact was known only within the family. The violence was growing, and to keep everyone safe, the Cavertons were keeping the fact that they were Shifters a secret.

"Uncle Oliver, I need some air." Bridget said quietly.

"Go to the balcony. Stay within sight of the doors and do not be gone long." He whispered to her.

Bridget nodded and started making her way slowly to the balcony doors on the other side of the ballroom. She scanned the faces around her. Lord Percival had sent her flowers with a note saying how he could not wait to see her here tonight. She was hoping to avoid him.

She was almost halfway around the room when she spotted Lord Percival entering the ballroom through the main doors. He scanned the room as if looking for someone. One of the perks of being only a few inches above five feet tall was that she was easily hidden by those around her. She did not trust that it would last though.

Spotting a door not too far away, Bridget made her way quickly to it. She slipped through and found herself in a darkened hallway. She bit her lip in indecision. She wasn't supposed to be here, but she didn't want to encounter Lord Percival.

Slowly she walked farther down the hall to her right, looking for a second hall or door that would connect back to the ballroom. She made it to the end with no luck. Sighing, she turned around to head back the way she had come.

She squeaked in surprise and her heart started to hammer in her chest. Lord Percival stood only a foot from her. She took a step back and his smile grew. Without warning, he slammed his hand over her mouth as he wrapped his arm around her waist.

Bridget resisted the urge to scream. That was what he probably wanted. She realized just how wrong this would look. A man and woman, alone in a dark hallway. Fear began to build inside her. She tried to push away from him, but he dragged her into a room and closed the door. He released his hold on her, and she quickly took a step away from him.

"I have been looking for you, Lady Bridget." Lord Percival's smile was predatory. Bridget didn't speak. She took another step back, keeping her eyes on the man that trapped her. "Why aren't you screaming?"

"That is what you want me to do. Screaming would bring someone. I for one, do not wish to be shackled to someone like you." Bridget snapped out.

She glanced at the door before returning her eyes to Lord Percival. He blocked her exit. He grabbed her roughly and shoved her up against the wall. Bridget bit the inside of her cheek to keep from crying out. She was not going to be trapped by him. She was going to get out of this. She prayed she could get out of this.

Suddenly, Lord Percival was yanked away from her and another man stood between her and her attacker. At first, she thought it was Uncle Ollie, but this man was several inches shorter than her uncle. Her head barely reached his shoulder. His dress coat was tailored, showing off his athletic build. She pressed herself against the wall behind her, not knowing if this new man was better or worse than Lord Percival.

"Do not touch her." The man growled out through clenched teeth. His voice was vaguely familiar, but her fear was not allowing her to think clearly.

"Lord Emmett Young." Lord Percival sneered. He cleared his throat. "You caught us. Looks like you are going to have to tell Lord Caverton about this."

"Oh, I fully plan on telling the Cavertons about this." Lord Young said angrily. Bridget whimpered. Would she be forced to marry Lord Percival? She did not want anyone to know about this. She started to shake as the full realization of what was happening started to sink in. Lord Percival was forcing her hand. "Come, Lady Bridget. Let's get you back to your uncle."

"I agree. Come, my dear. Time to let everyone know our good news." Lord Percival tried to move to her, but Lord Young stopped him.

"You will not touch Lady Bridget." Lord Young moved a little to the side to prevent Lord Percival from seeing her. "She is not without protectors, Percival. You have messed with the wrong family."

"Are you threatening me?" Lord Percival said angrily. "You can't save her from this. Society will have her ruined for even having rumors of this nature spread."

"There will be no rumors." Lord Young's voice held a warning. Bridget touched his arm lightly. He reached back and grabbed her hand, giving it a gentle squeeze before letting her go.

"Ha! There most certainly will be." Percival laughed as he moved closer. "Now, give me the girl."

"Emmett!" She called as Lord Percival tried to hit Lord Young.

Lord Young drew his fist back and punched Lord Percival so hard that she heard the crunch of the man's nose before he crumpled to the floor. She covered her mouth to keep from making a sound. Lord Young crouched down and checked the man's pulse before turning to her.

"Let's get you back to your uncle, Lady Bridget."

He stood and extended his hand to her. Bridget hesitated. She looked at Lord Percival and then back to Lord Young. She put her hand in his and let him lead her out of the room. She was still shaking as they walked. He pulled her into a dark alcove before cupping her face.

"Are you all right? Did he hurt you?" Lord Young asked with concern in his eyes.

Bridget blinked back the tears that wanted to fall. No, she was not all right. The man she had been trying to avoid for over a month tried to trap her into marriage with him. The possibility of having to marry him was still not out of the realm of possibilities of how this nightmare was going to end.

Lord Young took a step closer as he guided her head to his chest and his other arm wrapped around her. She sniffled and leaned against him. He held her until her shaking had mostly stopped. He leaned back and looked down at her.

"Bridget, I need to get you to your uncle before your absence is noted." He whispered. Bridget nodded and let out a shaky breath. "You are safe now. I promise." He peeked out into the hall before pulling her after him. He put her hand on his arm as they got to a more lit area. Bridget clung to his arm as she walked beside him. They entered the ballroom, and she immediately felt eyes on her. "Time for that dance you promised me." Lord Young said loud enough for several others to hear.

Bridget looked up at him in confusion. She thought he was going to take her to her uncle. She didn't resist as he walked to the dance floor. A waltz was just starting up. Lord Young put his arm around her waist and pulled her close. He softly counted and then they were off.

Emmet was surprised at how graceful Lady Bridget was. He could feel the eyes of most of the gathering on him. He glanced down to make sure Lady Bridget was doing all right. She was slightly pale with a worried expression on her face. "How are you doing?"

"Why is everyone staring at us?" she whispered in a shaky voice.

"That is my fault." He smiled at her. "I do not dance at functions. I have heard rumors that I lack the skill."

"But you are dancing with me." She furrowed her brow.

"Am I?" he asked.

"You are teasing again." She closed her eyes briefly. "I am not in the mood for it."

"I am sorry. You are right. I should not be teasing you right now."

"Why are you dancing with me if you do not like dancing?"

"I don't make it a habit to escort ladies into a ballroom. To take suspicion off of our arrival, I thought it best if we danced." Lord Young said.

"Our arrival?" Bridget asked in confusion.

"We do not want them thinking we were doing something we should not have been doing." Lord Young whispered.

"But we weren't." She protested.

"Well, holding you in a dark alcove isn't exactly Proper behavior." He smiled at her. Her cheeks heated, and she dropped her gaze to his chest. He was right. "How are you doing though? Truly."

Lady Bridget sighed. "I just want to go home."

The song came to an end and Emmett put her hand back on his arm. He gave her a smile as he began walking. She walked close to him as they made their way through the crowd. Several people tried to stop him, but he said he needed to get Lady Bridget back to her uncle as he promised he would.

They made it to Lord Oliver after several minutes. He positioned them so that their backs were to the wall. He wanted to be able to see if Lord Percival returned.

"I see you found Lord Young, Bridget." Lord Oliver said with a lifted brow.

Bridget gave her uncle a forced smile. "He found me, actually."

Emmett leaned close to Lord Oliver, dropping his voice so only he could hear him. "You need to take Lady Bridget home immediately. I will be a few minutes behind you to explain."

Lord Oliver's eyes snapped to Lady Bridget. She was shaking again, and Emmett wanted to put his arms back around her. He needed to get her out of here before she broke down.

"Bridget, would you be okay if we left right now? I need to speak with your father about Caverton Estates. I forgot to tell him about some of the repairs I had to do. He needs to know before we start the remodeling." Lord Oliver smiled at his niece.

"That would be fine. I am feeling tired anyway." She said so quietly that Emmett barely heard her.

Lord Oliver offered his arm and Lady Bridget let go of Emmett. She glanced back at him as her uncle guided her out of the ballroom. Emmett waited twenty minutes before he left. He was able to go back to the room to see if Lord Percival was still there. He was gone.

Emmett rode up to the Caverton residence and knocked on the door. It was getting late, and he hoped that everyone was awake. He really needed to let Lord Mason and Lord Oliver know what he had seen. The door opened and Greg gestured him in. He wore a grim expression as he led the way to the study.

The scene before him made him want to hunt down Percival, while at the same time, wanting to stay close to Lady Bridget. She was lying on the couch with her eyes closed. Lady Caverton was kneeling on the floor combing her fingers through her daughter's hair. Lord Mason and Lord Oliver were pacing. With Emmett's arrival, all activity ceased.

"What is going on, Lord Young? I have never seen Bridget like this. She cried all the way home and then cried herself to sleep." Lord Oliver said stiffly.

"Bri, sweetheart, I need you to get up. Lord Young is here." Lady Caverton said softly. Bridget's eyes fluttered open. She sat up slowly and looked around. "What happened at the ball?"

Bridget's eyes snapped to Emmett's. Fear filled them as she wrapped her arms around herself. He knew she was scared of being forced into a marriage with the cad, but Emmett was sure her family would not allow it.

"I arrived late after getting home not long before the ball began." Emmett said as he closed the door. "I heard something and happened to glance to my left. At the far end of the hallway, I saw a woman being pulled into a room by a man. I ran and quickly slipped into the room. I heard Lord Percival ask why the woman wasn't yelling. I recognized Lady Bridget's voice when she responded to him. I stepped in."

"Bri, is this true?" Lord Mason said, clearly trying to restrain his anger.

"I needed air. Uncle Ollie said to go to the balcony. I was halfway around the room when I saw Lord Percival enter. He was looking around and I knew he was looking for me. I slipped through the nearest door. I found myself in a darkened hallway. I hoped to find a way to loop back around, but it was a dead end. When I turned around, he was there. Before I could do anything, he covered my mouth and dragged me into a room." Bridget wiped her cheeks.

Lord Mason moved to Bridget's side. He put a hand on her head. "Did he hurt you?"

"He asked me why I wasn't screaming. I told him because it was what he wanted me to do." She sniffled. "Lord Young pulled Lord Percival away from me and told him to leave me alone. Lord Percival said he was going to start spreading rumors. He tried to hit Lord Young, but Lord Young stopped him. Lord Young then took me back to the ballroom. Everyone was staring at us as we entered, so we danced before he took me to Uncle Oliver."

Emmett was so relieved that she left out the part where he held her in the darkened alcove. That would not have gone over well with her family. She looked up at him with apprehension.

"Where is he now?" Lord Mason turned his attention to Emmett.

"He was unconscious when we left the room. I went back to check on him once Lady Bridget was safely gone. He wasn't there." Emmett ran his hand through his hair. "He made it clear that he was going to start rumors. He is desperate to have her."

"It's not her he necessarily wants, but her inheritance." Lady Caverton smoothed the hair out of her daughter's face.

"Just disinherit me." Lady Bridget said softly.

"I am not going to do that, Bri." Lord Mason shook his head. "Lord Percival doesn't know who he is dealing with. No matter what he says, you will not be marrying him."

"Thank you, daddy." She whispered and Emmett felt his heart strings tug a little. She looked so scared and upset by what had happened. Her chin trembled slightly as she looked at him. "And thank you, Lord Young. If you had not come in, I do not know what would have happened."

"How is your arm, Lady Bridget? Lord Percival grabbed you pretty hard." Emmett glanced at her arm.

"Show me." Lord Mason commanded as he lifted her arm carefully and his face hardened. "Anna, take Bridget upstairs."

Lady Caverton stood and helped Bridget to her feet. Bridget kept her eyes directed at the floor, but Emmett saw the tears rolling down her cheeks. It took everything in him not to reach out as she passed. He watched the ladies leave before turning back to the Lords.

"Is there anything else we need to know?" Lord Oliver asked.

"Not that I am aware of. She was pretty shaken. I got her back to you as soon as I was able to."

"After dancing with her." Lord Mason lifted a brow.

Emmett sighed before crossing the room and sitting on the couch. "I never walk into a society gathering with a woman. When I entered the ballroom with Lady Bridget, we quickly became the focus of the room. Considering she had been out of the ballroom for several minutes, I didn't want to fuel whatever rumors that Percival is going to dredge up."

"You do not dance either." Lord Mason pointed out. "I have never seen you dance before."

"I don't. But if I had been doing anything untoward with a woman, I would not be asking her to dance. It would draw way too much attention to the lady. In order to try to distract everyone's attention from the fact that I arrived with Lady Bridget, I danced with her." He ran his hand down his face. "It worked. Most of the gossip floating around was that I danced for the first time in five years."

"Thank you for protecting my little girl." Lord Mason dropped into his chair. "Oliver, I am going to kill him." Emmett had never heard Lord Mason sound so angry.

"No, you won't." Lord Oliver shook his head. "Anna would never forgive you if you did."

"She would understand. Percival's handprint is on my daughter's arm."

Oliver moved to the door and leaned out. He whispered to someone before closing the door again. "There are other ways to let Percival feel the error of his ways. Might I suggest bringing back your better half. She is probably going to be more logical at the moment."

The door opened and the ladies walked back in. "Oliver. You sent for them? I told Anna to take Bri upstairs for a reason." Lord Mason glared at his brother.

Lord Mason sat stiffly as he clenched and unclenched his fist. He was clearly not happy about this evening's events. Emmett couldn't blame him. If someone had tried to do the same to his daughter, he would be livid.

"Mason." Lady Caverton said as she wrapped her arms around his neck. He was tense for several minutes before he visibly relaxed. Emmett was a little confused as to what he was watching. Lord Mason was ready for murder a few minutes ago and now he was holding his wife so tenderly. "I am angry, too, My Love. But I need you to calm down."

"Sweetheart, he hurt our baby. I will not stand for that." Lord Mason cupped his wife's cheek. "He needs to know Bri is off limits."

"I do not disagree with you. But we can do it smartly." Lady Caverton kissed Lord Mason.

Bridget came and sat down next to him. Emmett glanced at her. She pulled her legs up under her and laid her head on the arm of the couch. She looked completely exhausted. Why was she down here? She should be up in bed.

"No, we are not killing him." Lady Caverton said with a smile in her voice. Emmett returned his gaze to the couple across the room. "Bridget, what are your thoughts?"

"I don't have any." she said softly.

"You cannot fool us, Bri. The man literally dragged you into a room to try to trap you into marriage." Lord Oliver said in exasperation. "Now would be the time to step up and speak with the intelligence we all know you have."

"Do not push her, Oliver. I will not stand for it." Lady Caverton glared at Lord Oliver.

"She is not a simpleton, Anna." Lord Oliver argued.

"No one said she was." Lady Caverton said. "You have no idea what it feels like to be in her position. To feel completely at the mercy of someone bigger and more powerful than you. To face the possibility of your future being ripped from you."

"Anna." Lord Mason pulled her back to him. "Bri is safe. You are safe." Lady Caverton burrowed more into her husband's embrace.

Bridget sat up as she watched her parents. "Mom was abused by her father and was going to be traded away to someone before she met my father." she explained quietly.

Emmett's attention refocused on the couple. He could see the fear and almost panicked look in Lady Caverton's eyes. Lord Mason was whispering in her ear as he comforted her. This situation with Lord Percival was hitting the family much harder than he first realized.

"You are right, I don't. But she can't hide from the world, Anna. She will not always have us there to solve her problems for her. I love her as if she were my own, but we need to have her start making choices." Oliver said gently.

"You want to know my opinion?" Bridget stood. "I think the best thing to do is to do nothing. He is expecting some sort of retaliation. If we carry on as if nothing happened, then he will not know what is going on. He is a pebble in my shoe. Nothing more than an annoyance. He isn't worth my time, and he certainly isn't worth all this." She waved her hand around the room. "Goodnight."

Everyone watched Bridget leave. Oliver was the first to recover. "I do not like her plan at all."

"You were the one who was insisting on hearing it." Lady Caverton rolled her eyes.

"I was hoping for something more...violent." Lord Oliver ran his hand through his hair.

"I believe I broke his nose, if that helps." Emmett commented.

Lord Mason looked at him. "We can go with Bri's plan as long as no rumors arise."

"We will have to wait and see what comes of this." Lady Caverton said. "Thank you, Lord Young. I cannot express how much we are indebted to you for stepping in and saving Bri."

"You are welcome, My Lady." Emmett stood. "It is getting late. I just wanted to make sure you were aware of everything tonight." He bowed before taking his leave.

As he was pulling on his overcoat, Lady Bridget walked into the entryway. She paused when she saw him. She looked like she was going to say something but then her eyes moved to something over his shoulder. She gave him a nod as she continued up the stairs. Emmett turned around to find Lord Mason standing there.

He expressed again how relieved he was that his daughter was safe. He told Emmett to rest for a week before coming back for the information on his next assignment. Emmett agreed before he left. As he rode home, he couldn't stop thinking about beautiful blue eyes and how it felt to have Lady Bridget in his arms.

Red hot anger burned his veins when he saw Percival pressing her into the wall. Emmett had been ready to tear the man's head off for hurting her. He had needed to hold her as much as she had needed the comfort at that moment. She was the only reason he had been able to remain calm. Dancing with her probably wasn't necessary, but he hadn't been ready to let her go just yet.

He shook his head as he climbed the stairs to his townhouse. She was a distraction. He had attended the ball to talk with a man that might have information on the smuggling going on near the Freynia border. The fact that he was just now remembering his real purpose for the evening's events just proved how much Lady Bridget Caverton was messing with his mind.

Chapter 23

Bridget was beyond upset with her father and uncle. They were taking this situation with Lord Percival too far. She clenched and unclenched her fists as she walked down the stairs. She couldn't even concentrate on reading right now. The ball had been two days ago, and the rumors Lord Percival promised were already in the papers.

Greg pulled open the front door and Lord Young stepped inside. "Good morning, Greg. How are you faring today?"

"Considering someone is targeting the family, I would say I have had better days." Greg said as he closed the door.

"Thank goodness you are here, Lord Young." Bridget said when she reached the bottom step. His head snapped in her direction. His brows rose in surprise. "Maybe you can talk some sense into my father and uncle."

"What exactly is happening?" he said slowly as he fell into step beside her. She was on her way to the drawing room to confront her father about his demands to have an armed guard with her at all times.

A knock at the front door had her stopping and looking back down the hall. Greg once again opened the door. Lord Percival's voice reached her, and she tensed. "Emmett." She whispered anxiously. He put his arm around her waist and pulled her close to him.

"Young, what are you doing?" Bridget heard her father's growl.

"Lord Percival just arrived. Lady Bridget is…not liking him being here." Lord Young said as his arm tightened around her.

Bridget squeezed her eyes closed as she tried to control her reaction to the man. He could not hurt her here. She was safe. A hand touched her face, and she flinched. Opening her eyes she looked into the worried ones of her father.

"Stay here, Bri." He kissed her forehead before storming out of the room.

"Mason, wait!" Uncle Oliver called.

"My Lord!" Lord Young said anxiously. Bridget looked around the room. Her uncle was standing in the doorway. He looked back at her and Lord Young. "You cannot leave, sir."

Bridget stepped away from Lord Young. She hadn't realized she was leaning against him. She wrapped her arms around herself and walked to the window. She turned back around to look at her uncle. "Both of you can go."

A look of pain crossed Lord Young's face. He looked between her and the door. Her uncle looked anxious as he glanced down the hall. "I need to make sure Mason isn't going to kill the man, but Bri cannot be left alone."

"I can stand in the hall at the door." Lord Young said. He moved quickly from the room and her uncle disappeared.

Bridget took slow measured breaths to keep herself calm. Just hearing Lord Percival's voice had caused her to freeze in fear. She had never had such a strong reaction before. She didn't even remember walking the rest of the way to the drawing room. Thank goodness she hadn't been alone. What would Lord Percival do if he happened upon her in the hall by herself.

She jumped when she heard several angry voices. She turned in time to see the four men walk into the room. Bridget swallowed hard as her eyes met those of Lord Percival. He smiled at her, and she took a step back.

"What is it that you want, Percival?" Her father said stiffly. Lord Young moved so that he was between her and the man she feared.

"No need to get your hackles raised." Lord Percival took a seat.

"No need!" Uncle Oliver yelled. "You have spread word that my niece and Lord Young are engaged!"

"Are they now? I have not heard such a rumor." Lord Percival grinned.

"Have not heard? It is plastered in the papers." Her father crossed his arms over his chest.

"Are you telling me that they are not engaged?" Lord Percival looked surprised. "After their display at the ball, I am surprised they are not."

"What do you want?" Bridget snapped. She was tired of his games. She didn't understand what he was playing at. He had wanted to marry her, but he was now spreading rumors she was engaged to another.

The room became quiet as all attention turned to her. Even Lord Young turned to look at her. "What makes you think I am responsible for the rumors?"

"I was the one you tried to trap, remember? I am not an idiot, sir. You are doing this for some sort of gain." Bridget stepped around Lord Young so she could see Lord Percival. His face was bruised, and his nose was swollen.

"Trap? That doesn't sound like something I would do." Lord Percival shook his head.

"Why are you here?" Bridget asked.

"I wanted to give you a heads up on another rumor I have heard a few whispers about." He grinned. "How far along are you, Lady Bridget? Since you have only been in town for a few months, I can't imagine very far."

Bridget gasped as she pressed a hand to her stomach. "Excuse me!?" Her father yelled.

"I have heard that she is with child." Lord Percival stood and walked over to the fireplace. "Broken engagements are one thing; a bastard child is another." Bridget stared at him with her mouth slightly open in shock. She would be ruined. Completely marked by society if such a rumor existed. Her eyes were glued to the man as he smirked at her. "I should be congratulating the two of you on your impending parenthood."

"What do you want, Percival?" Her father asked coldly.

"Money." Lord Percival turned to her father.

"You want me to pay you for your silence?" Her father narrowed his eyes.

"I want a monthly..." Bridget didn't want to hear it. She marched over to him and punched him in the face as hard as she could. Her uncle had taught her to throw a punch several summers ago. She never thought she would have to use the knowledge, though.

"Get out of my house." She growled out. For a long moment no one moved. The shock on Lord Percival's face was priceless. "I said, get out." She stepped aside and pointed to the door.

"You will regret this." Percival sneered.

"No, sir. You will regret this." She glared at him.

She watched until he left the room. She moved back to the window and glared out at the backyard garden. How could he spread such awful rumors about someone? Her life was going to be over in regard to her acceptance into society. Despite her anxiety in large gatherings, Bridget found she loved dressing up in fancy gowns and seeing the other women in their finery. All that was going to be taken from her.

"Bri, I know you are upset about what he said, but you shouldn't have kicked him out before we came to an understanding. We need to make sure he does not..." Her father said behind her.

She shook her head as she cut him off. "No matter what you say, how much money you give him, Lord Percival was going to start the rumors."

"We could have come to an understanding, Bri. Between your father and I, plus Lord Young, we are three of the most influential men in the Capital. Lord Percival is not as important as he thinks he is." Her uncle touched her arm.

Bridget pulled away from him. "You may be more influential but even a hint of a rumor like that will destroy my reputation. I will be tolerated because of my connections, but I will not be fully accepted."

"So, you kicked him out before we could scare him into keeping quiet?" Lord Young asked angrily.

"Sorry for the interruption." Greg said from the door. "Lady Bridget, your mother is requesting your presence in the parlor for tea."

"Let Anna know that Bri will not be there today." Her father said.

"Tell mother I will be right there." Bridget turned to her father. Greg bowed and left the room. "Mother and I can take it from here. You gentlemen can do whatever it is you do when we ladies are busy." She walked from the room with her head held high. There was no way she was going to allow Lord Percival to ruin her life.

"What did she mean, she had it covered?" Emmett asked, once Lady Bridget was gone.

"I have no idea." Lord Mason shook his head. "What are we going to do about this? Lord Percival is going to retaliate tenfold."

"How do you feel about everything?" Lord Oliver looked at Emmett.

"We could have ridden out rumors of an engagement. Talk about me being here several times a week could easily be chalked up to us being in business together." Emmett ran his hands through his hair. "This other rumor...I do not even know how to begin extinguishing it."

"You mean the rumor you are going to be a father?" Lord Oliver asked. His lips twitched at the corners.

"Yeah, that rumor." Emmett glared at the man. "Would anyone believe such a thing?"

"You two did make quite a handsome couple on the dance floor. If I didn't know any better, I would have thought you were involved." Lord Oliver smiled. "Did you even notice that all the other couple stopped to watch you two?"

"They, what?" Emmett's eyes widened in surprise.

"How could you not notice?" Lord Mason asked.

"I was trying to keep Lady Bridget from crumbling. She was shaking and upset about what had just happened. I was distracting her until I could get her to Lord Oliver." Emmett said in exasperation.

"He has a point. Bri was very upset. As soon as we were in the carriage, she started to cry." Lord Oliver nodded his head, but he was still fighting a smile.

"Oliver this is serious. My daughter is going to be facing some nasty rumors that will follow her throughout her life." Lord Mason sighed.

"I know, Mason." Lord Oliver shook his head. "I know one way we can fight the rumors."

"Which is?" Lord Mason asked.

"The two of them can marry."

Emmett's eyes widened in surprise. "Bri will not marry Percival." Lord Mason growled.

"Oh, heavens no. Not Percival." Oliver laughed. "Young."

"Me?" Emmett shook his head.

"You are rumored to be engaged to her." Oliver pointed out. "What better way to kill a rumor than to make it true?"

"What of the baby?" Lord Mason asked. Emmett looked between the two brothers as his heart began to race. They could not be serious. He couldn't marry Lady Bridget just because they were rumored to be engaged.

"Time will prove that she is not with child, Mason." Oliver said gently as he put his hand on his brother's shoulder.

Emmett shook his head as he stared at them. "I am not sure this is the best course of action." Emmett said quickly. "There has to be a different way."

"Are you not a fan of Bridget, or marriage in general?" Lord Oliver asked.

"I am not at a point in my life that marriage is a good idea. I am planning a trip to Freynia, and who knows how long I will be gone. This is ridiculous. I cannot marry anyone." Emmett was pacing as his mind was spinning. How did he end up in this situation?

*   *   *

Bridget took a deep breath before entering the parlor. She didn't bother trying to smile when she walked in and sat by her mother. Mrs. Jorgenson and her daughter Miss Cythia were there. Two of the biggest gossips Bri knew.

"Sorry I am late. The meeting with father, Lord Percival, and Lord Young ran longer than expected." Bridget glanced at her mother.

"And is everything settled?" Her mother asked with a raised brow.

"Not remotely." Bridget sighed.

"So, the rumors are true then?" Mrs. Jorgenson scooted to the edge of her seat, eager for more information. "Are you and Lord Young engaged?"

"No, we are not." Bridget shook her head.

"But we saw you two at the ball. You danced with him." Miss Cythia said.

"He is my father's business partner. Father asked Lord Young to dance with me as a favor since I have been asked so little times at the previous balls." Bridget sighed. "Quite embarrassing but it is true."

"Then why were you in a meeting with him this morning?" Mrs. Jorgenson asked.

"Lord Percival arrived and asked to speak with my father and me. Father was in a meeting with Lord Young at the time." Bridget glanced at her mother. She was watching Bri intently.

"What did Lord Percival want?" Miss Cynthia asked in a quiet voice.

"He has been trying to get Lord Caverton to agree to a marriage between Bridget and him." Her mother said in exasperation. "He has been coming around for over a month. He is quite persistent."

"This time was different. He said he was going to tell everyone I was with child if father did not pay him monthly installments. He made it sound like he was the one that said Lord Young and I were engaged." Bridget widened her eyes as if she were surprised. She looked between the women before leaning forward and whispering. "Do you think he was upset that I refused him and tried to ruin me?"

"Bridget!" her mother gasped. "That seems rather rash. Why would he be so upset?"

"I heard Lord Percival is in quite a bit of debt. He is looking for an heiress to pay off his creditors." Mrs. Jorgenson reached over and patted Bri's hand comfortingly. "You poor dear. Do not worry. We will stand with you. That man is nothing but trouble."

"I do not want to spread rumors." Bridget said quietly as she looked down at her hands. "It is just my suspicions."

"Lady Bridget, if that man has been trying to procure a marriage with you, but unable to and suddenly there are rumors starting that can ruin you...No man will look at you, he is trying to make himself your only option." Mrs. Jorgenson said.

Bridget nodded slowly. Was that his plan? To make him her only option for marriage. All the stress and frustration of the past few days caused her eyes to tear up. She blinked rapidly to try to keep from crying. The Jorgenson's only stayed for another twenty minutes before taking their leave.

All the ladies were standing in the entryway when Lord Young, her father, and Uncle Oliver walked into the room. Lord Young glanced at her father, who nodded slightly. He turned back to Bridget. He looked like he was going to say something, so she turned to the Jorgenson's. The men must have settled on a course of action despite her telling them she had it covered.

"Thank you, ladies, for being so understanding." Bridget curtsied.

"Say nothing more, Lady Bridget. Keep your chin up. Lord Percival is a snake. No one would believe such a sweet girl like you would ever do such a thing." Mrs. Jorgenson returned the curtsey.

"Remember, he is just trying to isolate you. You had more than one man looking at you last night. I doubt that is going to change anytime soon. Mr. Peterson couldn't stop raving about how beautiful you were." Miss Cynthia smiled widely.

Bridget's cheeks heated and she ducked her head. Her mother said goodbye and the hall was filled with silence. A throat cleared, and she looked up.

"What was that all about? What other young men?" Her father looked between her and her mother.

"Your daughter has a good head on her shoulders, Mason. She is also the talk of the Capital. It seems many do not believe in the engagement rumor. There is much speculation on which of the five gentlemen she danced with at the ball will claim her hand."

"I am going to go lay down. I have a headache." Bridget said softly before walking upstairs. She didn't even look back when her father called after her.

"Anna, Lord Percival said he…"

"Wanted money in exchange for keeping quiet." Lady Caverton finished for her husband. "Bri told me. Did he really threaten to say she was with child?"

"Yes." Lord Mason sighed. "But we have a plan."

"Your daughter has already put out the fire." Lady Caverton said calmly.

Emmett looked between the Cavertons in confusion. "What do you mean, My Lady? The rumor hasn't even been spread yet."

"Bri mentioned Lord Percival's interest in her and how she did not like it. She told them of her meeting with the lot of you and how Percival had demanded money in exchange for keeping quiet. The Jorgenson's believe he is trying to ruin her reputation beyond repair so that no one else will court her, leaving him as her only option." Lady Caverton moved to her husband's side.

"How is that going to stop the rumors?" Lord Oliver asked. "She just started them herself."

"She is smarter than you give her credit for, Ollie." Lady Caverton smiled. Emmett was about ready to have a heart attack. His heart was beating painfully fast. The blasted woman just sealed their fate. He had held out some hope that no rumors about a baby would arise and here she was starting them herself. "The Jorgensons are very social. They are no doubt talking to someone right now about how Lord Percival will try anything to get a woman with a sizable inheritance to marry him. He is even desperate enough to start rumors about a young lady's virtue if her family does not pay him off."

Emmett stared at Lady Caverton in surprise. Is that how Bridget had painted the situation? It was the truth. Percival was desperately seeking funds. He ran his hand down his face in relief.

"What was your plan, sweetheart?"

"Lord Young and Bridget were to marry. When no baby comes in a few months, everyone will know that Percival lied." Lord Mason shook his head.

"I am in favor of Lady Bridget's plan." Emmett said quickly.

"Have no fear, Lord Young. The only way you will be marrying my daughter is if you can convince her of your love for her." Lady Caverton kissed Lord Mason's cheek before smiling at Emmett. "Now, if you gentlemen will excuse me, I need to check on Bri. She was looking unwell during tea."

Emmett tilted his head back and let out a tense breath. She had saved them from having to marry. He was immensely grateful for that. A forced marriage rarely worked out for the best. When he eventually married, he wanted what the Cavertons' had. Love, happiness, a partner. Someone he could rely on, and in return, relied on him. His parents were constantly fighting. He would never settle for a relationship like that.

"You look relieved, Young." Oliver said with a laugh.

"No offense to Lady Bridget, but I am not ready for marriage." Emmett said.

"You are in your mid-twenties. You should be ready for marriage and a family." Lord Mason eyed him.

Emmett shook his head. "I will die a lone man if I have to. I will not put myself in a situation like my parents. Now that the crisis has been averted, can I get the information on my next assignment?"

"We are just waiting for word from the Phoenix." Lord Mason was studying Emmett closely. "We received a letter already, but it was unclear exactly what was needed."

"Let me know as soon as you can." Mason grabbed his coat from Greg and left the Cavertons.

Never had the Caverton home felt so stifling. He actually preferred their residence. His place was quiet and lifeless, but it was better than staying at the Caverton's right now. He was rarely home, so he had the bare number of servants to keep it going. His place in the country wasn't much better. His parents passed away from a sickness when he was in his teen years, and he was an only child. It was sad that as his business partners and bosses, when it came to the Hunters, the Cavertons were the closest thing to a family he had.

Chapter 24

Emmett should not be nervous. This was a long-standing meeting he had with the Cavertons every Thursday at ten o'clock. He took a deep breath and let it out slowly. This was ridiculous. He needed to stop being such a coward. He had heard the rumors about him and Bridget and the possibility of a baby. They were always followed with laughter and talk about how Lord Percival's desperation had reached a whole new level.

He knocked on the door. Greg opened it, but didn't let him in. "What can I do for you, Lord Young?" Greg asked. The man looked tired.

"Uh...I am here for my appointment with Lord Caverton." he said hesitantly. What was going on? "The same one we have every Thursday."

"I am sorry, My Lord, but the Cavertons are not open to visits today." Greg started closing the door but stopped.

"For crying out loud, Greg, let him in. His appointment with father is not a visit." Lady Bridget said, clearly irritated.

"My Lady, you should be up in bed." Greg turned his attention to Lady Bridget.

Emmett used the moment of distraction and stepped inside. He looked up to see Lady Bridget slowly walking down the stairs. She was pale with dark circles under her eyes. Her hair was in a thick braid over her shoulder, and she was wrapped in a blanket.

"Lady Bridget, is everything all right?" Emmett took a step towards her out of concern. She did not look well at all.

"Please, My Lord. Do not try to coddle me as well. I am fine." Lady Bridget said. Greg scoffed behind him. "My father is most likely in his study. I am sure you know the way."

"Uh...yes, but can I escort you to wherever it is you are wanting to go?" Emmett didn't feel comfortable leaving her alone while she looked like this. She looked ready to fall over.

"I am on my way to the drawing room to read. It is not all that far. Do not trouble yourself." Bridget shook her head as she began walking slowly.

"I will let his lordship know that you are here while you assist Lady Bridget." Greg whispered.

"I heard that, Greg. I do not need help." Bridget snapped.

"For my benefit, please allow me to walk with you." Emmett tried again. She sent him a glare before nodding slightly. Emmett hurried to her side. "How are you feeling?" he asked after a minute.

"Like I am in a furnace." Bridget sighed. "The fever started a few days ago. The worst of it is over but a small fever remains. Everyone is making a bigger deal out of this than it is worth."

They made it to the drawing room door. Lady Bridget walked inside. After a few steps, she stopped and turned to face him. Emmett did not cross the threshold. He watched her from where he stood. She cocked her head to the side before shaking it. What was she thinking?

"Fevers can be quite dangerous, My Lady." Emmett said. It was what had taken his own parents.

"Not this one." She smiled at him. "Tell me, My Lord, has there been much talk around town?"

Emmett smiled back as he leaned against the door frame. "Borders are still closed. There have been a few skirmishes with Valencia but no major casualties. Many are looking forward to a large dinner party next week. Several young men wish to meet the young lady that has managed to convince Lord Young to dance and Lord Percival to pursue her for nearly two months. Though I have heard several women correct them by saying it was a pity dance."

"Wasn't it?" Lady Bridget raised a brow in challenge.

"I do not do anything because of pity. Dancing with you was mutually beneficial. A strategic move." Emmett narrowed his eyes at her. Did she really think he only danced with her because of pity?

"Mutually beneficial? That is news to me. I understand your motivation so that I did not fall under suspicion. But what was it you got out of it?"

Emmett was tempted to confess that he was able to hold her longer but stopped himself. "I learned I still knew how to dance. It has been five or so years since I have stood up with anyone. And to my surprise, I still could."

"You more than danced." Emmett jumped at Lord Oliver's voice behind him. "You two floated."

"Lord Oliver." Emmett bowed.

"What are you doing out here, Young?"

"I came for our weekly meeting." He held up his financial book.

"I meant in the hall. Wouldn't it be more comfortable to have a conversation while sitting?" Lord Oliver walked into the drawing room. He stopped when he saw his niece wrapped in a blanket. "Shouldn't you be dressed?"

"Considering you all have shut the doors and are not allowing visitors, I thought it safe to come down and spend time reading." Bridget's cheeks turned pink as she looked down.

"Have you heard many rumors, Lord Young?" Lord Oliver turned back to him.

"A few. There is still speculation about whether Lady Bridget and I are engaged. Those that do bring up the possibility of...a baby," Emmett cleared his throat. "Laugh at how desperate Lord Percival has become."

Bridget glanced up at Lord Young as he spoke. He seemed just as uncomfortable with the baby rumor as she was. He glanced at her and their eyes met. She looked down and he stopped talking. Her uncle didn't say anything either. She looked back up and met the eyes of Lord Young. He was standing there not moving.

"Lord Young?" He didn't move. He just stood there watching her. Uncle Oliver was the same way. "Uncle Ollie!" She yelled as she moved to his side. She shook his shoulder, but he was stiff as a board.

"Bridget, what is going on?" Her mother came running down the hall. She stopped when she saw the two gentlemen.

"What is happening?" Bridget cried. They seemed so alive but at the same time they were unmoving. They weren't even blinking.

"Bri, I need you to take a deep breath. You need to calm down." Her mother stood in the hallway. She couldn't get into the room with Lord Young and Uncle Oliver standing frozen in the way.

"How can I calm down when they are frozen?" Bridget took several steps back.

"This is your Gift. You need to relax." Her mother said softly.

Bridget sat on the couch and put her face in her hands. When she awoke yesterday, her mother explained to her about Guardians. They were not sure what her Gift would be, but her mother promised to help her when she figured it out. Had she accidently killed them? No, she saw her uncle breathing. Her mother once again told her to relax. Bri took several more deep breaths.

"That is good...Anna when did you get here?" Uncle Oliver said.

Bridget's head snapped up. "Mommy." She ran to her mother and threw her arms around her. Her mom held her tightly.

"Everything will be alright, Bri." Her mother rubbed her back. "Gentlemen, would you please excuse us. Bridget and I need to talk."

"What is going on, Anna? Bri was fine a second ago." Uncle Oliver asked as he followed them down the hall.

"Bridget will be fine, Oliver." Her mother stopped at the bottom of the stairs.

"She is shaking as if she has seen a ghost." Bridget looked up to see Lord Young watching her closely. "She looks scared to death." He pointed out.

"Who looks scared to death?" Her father joined the group.

"Your daughter." Lord Young stated.

Her father looked at her and moved to her side. He wrapped both her and her mother in his arms. She pressed herself more against her mother as she continued to shake. "Have you found your Gift, sparrow?" he asked, just loud enough for them to hear.

"She has." Her mother answered. "It can be frightening at first."

"Why are Oliver and Young so upset?" Her father kissed the top of her head.

"Bri can freeze individuals. She did it by accident. They were the ones frozen, so they do not know." Her mother said.

"What is going on, Mason?" Uncle Oliver said again.

"I am sorry, daddy. I didn't know." Bridget wiped her cheeks. "I didn't mean to."

Her father looked down at her and kissed her forehead. "Get back in bed, sweetheart. You still feel feverish. I will be up in a little while to check on you and your mother."

Bridget let her mother guide her upstairs. When they reached the top landing, she looked back. All three men were watching her. Lord Young's brow was drawn down in concern. Their gazes locked and she could see confusion, worry, and frustration in his eyes.

*   *   *

Emmett continued to watch Lady Bridget until she disappeared. She was scared and confused. He could see it in her eyes. What had happened that caused her to become so scared?

"You better start talking, Mason." Lord Oliver growled.

"Not here." Lord Mason began walking. Emmett followed them to the study. He shut the door behind him before taking a seat near the brothers. "Lord Young, I am trusting you. What I am about to say will not be repeated.

If I find out that this information is out there, I will hunt you down and I will kill you. There will be no corner in this world that will be safe. Do you understand?"

Emmett looked between the Cavertons, both wore very serious expressions. Lord Mason was completely serious. He would kill Emmett if word of this got out. He rarely spoke to anyone anyway. "I understand."

Lord Mason ran his hand down his face. "Have you heard rumors of the witches near the Valencia border?"

"I have heard stories about them. The villagers were concerned about them because there were several mysterious deaths in the area." Emmett furrowed his brow. "What does that have to do with what is effecting Lady Bridget?"

"My wife, Anna, grew up among them. They were not actually witches. Just like Shifters, they had a different gene that gave them a Gift. These Gifts could be anything; like controlling or producing elements, healing others, talking with animals, or even helping things grow." Lord Mason held Emmett's gaze. "When a Gift manifests, it presents as an extremely high fever. A low fever lasts for several days following."

"Bri got her Gift." Lord Oliver said quietly. "That is why she has been feverish."

Lord Mason sighed. "Yes. We did not know what it was. Anna believes she just discovered what it is."

"She was fine, and then she was completely upset." Emmett said. "What could she have discovered?"

"You seem awfully calm about this." Lord Mason said, watching him.

Emmett smiled and shrugged. "This information isn't new to me. Well, your family's abilities are new, but not the whole Guardian thing."

Lord Mason and Lord Oliver stared at him with wide eyes. "What?" Lord Mason found his voice first.

"My...Uh...my grandmother was one. She had the ability to influence someone's thoughts through touch. My mother didn't have a Gift, but Grammy visited every few months." Emmett shrugged.

"Maybe Anna should be part of this?" Lord Mason said covering his mouth.

"Mason, what did Bri experience? Young is right. She was fine one second and the next Anna was there, and Bri was beyond scared." Lord Oliver crossed his arms over his chest.

Emmett held his breath as he watched Lord Mason. "Anna thinks she can freeze people. She accidentally froze the both of you but did not know what was happening. She kept apologizing."

Lord Oliver stood and walked to the window. "If she can't control it..."

"It is not a matter of if she can. She just needs to learn how to control it. Anna can help her with that."

"How can she help her? Does she have the same ability?" Emmett asked.

"My Anna spent most of her youth learning about various abilities and how they work. She can help Bri learn to control this."

"Until then, she will need to stay home and not have any visitors." Lord Oliver said. "It is too big of a risk. We cannot have her accidently exposing herself."

A knock sounded and all conversation stopped. Lord Mason stood and walked to the door. He cracked it before pulling the door all the way open. Bridget stood there. Emmett got to his feet but stayed where he was.

"Where is your mother?" Lord Mason asked quickly.

"She said I should stay with you until she comes downstairs." Lady Bridget said quietly.

"Is she...?" Lord Mason suddenly grew tense. Lady Bridget nodded. "Stay with your uncle." He ran from the room.

Lady Bridget watched her father for another minute before looking back in the room. She looked apprehensive. "Bri, come sit with me." Lord Oliver said as he moved to the couch.

She slowly made her way over to him. Emmett felt a pang of jealousy as he watched her uncle put his arm around her. She leaned against him and sighed. "How is your mother?"

"She is fine. Just the normal."

"And how are you?" Lord Oliver asked.

She let out a small laugh. "I have had better weeks." She glanced at Emmett. "I would have thought you left."

"Why would I leave?" Emmett asked.

"Maybe because I have done nothing but create problems for you." Bridget looked at him in bewilderment.

Emmett smiled at her. "No one should go through life without some problems."

"There is something wrong with you." Bridget shook her head.

"Life would be boring without a little trouble now and then." Emmett chuckled.

"Is that why you hunt down dangerous Shifters?" Bridget narrowed her eyes. "You feel the need to have trouble in your life?"

"A man has to do something to fill the time until he realizes there is more to life than saving it." Lord Oliver laughed. "Isn't that right, Mason?"

"A man's greatest purpose is discovered when he finds his woman." Lord Mason said.

"Or he could attack her and end up forcing her to marry him." Lady Caverton stated.

"You are never going to let me live that down, are you?" Lord Mason kissed his wife's cheek. "And you are far more trouble than any I found on my own."

"That is a lie. I am the one who keeps you out of trouble. Bridget, do not listen to any of their advice. A woman helps settle a man's restless nature. She gives him purpose." Lady Caverton smiled at her daughter.

Emmett bit the inside of his cheek to keep from smiling as a blush rose on Lady Bridget's cheeks. She looked down at her hands. "I am curious to know more about your grandmother, Young." Lord Mason said as he pulled his wife down next to him on the other couch. She curled more into his side, and he kissed her temple. Emmett wanted that in his life. He was tired of being alone. It had pretty much been just him since he was thirteen.

"She lived near the Valencia border and visited every few months." Emmett shrugged. "Not much to tell."

"You also said she could influence someone through touch." Lord Mason said.

Lady Caverton stared at him in surprise. "Miranda." She breathed out.

Emmett was shocked. He looked between everyone a few times. "How did you know her name was Miranda?" he finally asked.

"She was my mentor. The Matriarch of the Guardians. She raised me." Lady Caverton said, while studying him. "I had no idea she had a family. She never said anything."

Emmett stood and began to pace. He had overheard his grandmother mentioning living at a sanctuary for women. She had told him about her ability and that she was called a Guardian. She never said anything else about her life. She mostly spent time playing with him and soothing the discord between his parents. She died when he was three years old.

"No, no, no." Lady Bridget muttered anxiously.

He turned back to the room. Everyone was still sitting. Lady Bridget was perched on the edge of the couch as she looked at her family. He moved closer when no one tried to calm her rising panic. He stopped when he realized they were sitting as still as statues. Lady Bridget buried her face in her hands.

"Bridget?" he said softly.

"It happened again. Why is this happening?" She looked at him with tears in her eyes.

"It's okay." He took a step closer. "What did you do last time to unfreeze me and your uncle?" He tried to remain calm. He had never encountered anything like this. The Caverton's were alive and breathing, but they were as still as death. No wonder Bridget was so scared.

"I...I...Mom said to relax." She shook her head. "But I don't think I can." She stood and tried to run from the room.

Emmett caught her around the waist before she could make it to the door. She tried to push his arm away, but he held her close. "Shh. You are okay." He whispered. Bridget shook her head. "Take a deep breath for me."

"Emmett, this isn't going to work." She shook her head.

"It will work, Bri. Just breathe." He turned her to face him. She had her eyes squeezed shut. He held her hand and ran his thumb over her knuckles. He trailed his other hand slowly up her arm. "Look at me." he said softly. He cupped her face and using his thumb, brushed her tears away. "Have I told you lately..."

"You are seriously going to be teasing me right now?" She opened her eyes and glared at him.

He smiled. "You are never in the mood for teasing."

"You always try to at the worst times." Bridget shook her head. She bit her lip and uncertainty filled her eyes. "Emmett, I cannot do this. I can't unfreeze them."

"Focus on a single point." She met his gaze. "Concentrate on only that. Breathe." He held her gaze as he waited. He continued to gently stroke her cheek with his thumb. How would he know when she was able to unfreeze them? Would there be some sort of indicator? "Just breathe. Focus on that spot and take a deep breath."

A few minutes later, a throat cleared. Emmett glanced over to see the surprised faces of the Cavertons. He let out a tense breath. He slowly released Bridget and turned her around to see her family. "See? I told you that you could do it."

"How do I get this to stop?" she asked, covering her face.

"It happened again?" Lady Caverton asked as she moved to her daughter.

Emmett nodded as his hands dropped from Bridget's upper arms. Lady Caverton embraced her daughter. He took several steps away before looking at Lord Mason. A muscle worked in his jaw as he watched Emmett. Lord Oliver had a thoughtful expression on his face.

"How long?" Lord Mason asked.

"For what?" Emmett's brow furrowed.

"How long were we out?" Lord Oliver stood.

"Uh...ten or so minutes, I think." Emmett glanced at Bridget. She was clinging to her mother as Lady Caverton whispered to her.

"I was scared and tried to run, but Lord Young stopped me and told me I was capable of undoing it." Bridget sniffled. "Thank you, sir."

Emmett inclined his head. "My grandmother often told me that the key to mastering one's ability is to concentrate on a single point, letting go of everything else."

"She told me the same thing." Lady Caverton said quietly.

"Seeing as your family is...adjusting. I will leave you all so that you can settle in." Emmett made for the door.

"Young, what happened for those ten or so minutes?" Lord Mason called, and Emmett stopped. He could hear Lord Mason getting to his feet. The air around him became tense. He had no idea what happened. Lady Bridget was frequently making him do things he never thought he would; like holding a woman while comforting her.

Emmett didn't turn around. "Lady Bridget was upset. She tried to run out the door and I grabbed her before she could. I asked her what she did the first time to undo her ability. She said her mother told her to relax. She did not think she could. I turned her to face me. I asked her to concentrate on a single point and to breathe. That was all."

"Father, he is telling you the truth. Nothing else happened." Lady Bridget said softly.

Emmett slowly turned around to face the room. "Sir, I respect you. I respect your family. I respect your daughter. I value our working relationship too much to do anything to ruin that." He crossed his arms over his chest. "If you feel I have done anything to break our trust in any way, I truly am sorry.'"

"It is not that, Young." Lord Oliver said, coming to his feet.

"Then what is it?" Emmett asked in frustration.

"You have had your arms around Bri more than once." Lord Oliver stated.

"Ignore them, Lord Young. If you feel the need to leave you are free to do so, but you are welcome to stay, as always." Lady Caverton gave him a smile. Emmet bowed and turned to leave. "I will walk you out, My Lord."

Emmett stopped and waited for her to reach him. They walked several steps in silence. "Is there something you wished to speak to me about, Lady Caverton?"

She sighed heavily. "I wanted to thank you for talking Bri down. She is terrified of her Gift right now."

"Hmm. I am glad I was able to help."

"You do not sound so sure."

"I am truly glad I was able to assist Lady Bridget in undoing what happened." He took a deep breath and let it out slowly. "I apologize for my short fuse. I am just growing restless. I think I will head out of town this evening. Could you let Lord Oliver know they can reach me at the Bird's Nest?"

"You are leaving?" Lady Caverton asked in surprise.

"I can't stay in the Capital for long. I am reaching my limit of society at the moment. I am sorry if this is going to cause you any issues." Emmett bowed and took his leave.

He did not know why he was getting so worked up. He needed to get his head back on straight. He felt like a loose cannon. Emmett turned his horse to the south gate. He wasn't even going to go home first; he felt so suffocated.

Chapter 25

"You two have really overstepped." Bridget's mother stormed into the room. She put her hands on her hips as she glared at the men in the room. "He left."

"He said as much before walking out of the room." Uncle Oliver stated.

"He left the Capital, Oliver. He said he was restless and if you wanted to reach him, he would be at the Bird's Nest." Her mother snapped.

Her father sat up. "When does he leave?"

"He already did, Mason. He was helping Bri, not trying anything, and you two treated him like he was Percival."

"He looked like he was going to kiss her." Uncle Oliver pointed out.

"He was holding her face and telling her to concentrate and to breathe. As soon as he knew she reversed it, he turned her around to face us. Not once has he done anything that would warrant you calling into question his motives." Her mother took a seat away from her father. "You have taken him under your wing, Oliver. I have heard you say nothing but praises for the man. I have only known him for two months, but I have no issues with him."

"I care for the kid, Anna." Uncle Oliver said. "He is like a son to me. He is a good man."

"Then why did you treat him as if he had tried to take advantage of Bri? Is he not what he seems?"

"That isn't it. If Bri likes him and he likes her, I will wholeheartedly encourage the match. He has said he is not at a point in his life when he wants to think about a family. He is focusing on other things right now." Uncle Oliver shook his head. "He has seemed off lately, though. Distracted in a way."

"What is the Bird's Nest?" Bridget asked as she slowly walked closer to her family.

"The Bird's Nest is...a tavern of sorts." Uncle Oliver said hesitantly.

"I have never heard of it." Her father said.

"It is below the Raven's Perch."

"Why would he go there?"

"Lord Young spent a lot of his time there before we met him." Uncle Oliver said evasively.

"Oliver." her father warned.

Uncle Oliver sighed. "Young is good at hunting down dangerous Shifters because he has many contacts of...questionable ethics. When we met him four years ago, he was regularly participating in illegal fights at a place he called the Bird's Nest. He goes back every now and then to make contact with people that might have information about criminals we are hunting."

"Illegal fighting?" her mother gasped.

"There are a few locations around Arlania that host the fights. After he came to Arlania, he fell in with the wrong crowd. Joining the Hunters has calmed his more...impulsive side. However, being in the Capital makes him feel caged. If he is here too long, he needs an outlet." Her uncle explained.

"He has only been in town for a week or two." Lady Caverton stated.

Uncle Oliver ran his hand down his face. He suddenly looked tired and worried. "He will be back in a few hours. We can visit him in the morning."

Bridget watched her uncle for the rest of the night. He seemed more withdrawn and tense. Was Lord Young really participating in illegal fights? She had overheard several gentlemen at a dinner party weeks ago talking about several men that died in fights recently. Was Lord Young safe?

Morning could not come fast enough. Bridget dressed in a dark blue dress and headed downstairs. She had no idea when they were planning on visiting Lord Young, but she wanted to be ready. As she entered the breakfast room, she saw her uncle and father deep in conversation. She quietly got a plate as she listened closely.

"If he isn't at home, would he still be at the tavern?" her father asked.

"I honestly do not know. His butler said he received instructions only an hour earlier informing him that Young would be out for a while." Her uncle sighed.

"What are you planning on doing?"

"After I eat, I am heading for Raven's Perch."

"You are going to get yourself killed, Oliver. Raven's Perch is not the safest of places, especially for a titled gentleman." Her father put his fork down. "Anna said he was tense when he left. Maybe we should give him a few days."

"You can't just leave him there if it is dangerous." Bridget said, looking between them.

"He will be fine, Bri. There is a lot more to Lord Young than you know. Your father is right, we should give him a few days before we start to worry."

Bridget could not believe this. They knew how dangerous Raven's Perch was and they were going to leave Emmett there. He had saved her from Lord Percival, helped calm her when she was panicking when Percival showed back up, and talked her through unfreezing her family. How could they sit back knowing he was in danger? She couldn't sit there anymore. She did not want to hear what kind of danger he was in. It made her feel anxious.

Bridget found her mother in the library, and she sat heavily next to her. "Uncle Ollie and father are talking about Lord Young. He has not returned. His butler said he will not be back for a while."

"I do not like the sound of that." Her mother said. They sat quietly for several minutes before she spoke again. "Why don't we work on controlling your Gift."

"I can't control it. It just happens." Bridget immediately became tense.

"Sweetheart, you can control it. You can even freeze some things while keeping others active." Bridget was apprehensive as she listened to her mother.

* * *

Emmett's head was pounding. Men's raised voices reached him, and he winced. He was regretting the last few fights. He had fought one of the men before. Lincoln Trevors. Trevors was a captain in the military. He had tried to recruit Emmett for years. This time had been a wager. If Emmett lost a fight with him, he would sign up for six months of military service under Trevors.

It had been a hard fight. He had been taking on multiple fights each night for the last two weeks. He was exhausted before the fight even began.

A door slammed and he groaned. Raven's Perch really needed to invest in upgrades to the rooms. He could hear everything. He rolled onto his back, causing pain to shoot through his ribs. He grabbed them as he took slow, even breaths.

"When did he arrive?" A man's voice asked quietly.

"A man dropped him off less than an hour ago." John said. Emmett held still. How was John at Raven's Perch?

"We will take it from here. Thank you, John." Lord Oliver? Mason slowly opened his eyes, well eye. One was swollen almost completely shut. "Get some sense knocked into you this time?" Lord Oliver asked.

Emmett chuckled. "You ask me that every time."

"And you always deflect." Lord Oliver sounded irritated. "Sit up, Emmett."

Emmett grabbed his ribs as he sat up. He glanced around, taking stock of his environment. "How did I get here?"

"A man dropped you off."

"Trevors." Emmett shook his head as he muttered.

"What were you thinking, Emmett? You have been gone for two weeks. How many fights did you participate in?" Oliver growled.

"One too many." He looked up. His eyes met those of Lady Bridget. She was standing next to Oliver. He jumped to his feet and his head began to spin. Someone grabbed his arm, forcing him to sit again.

"Just sit before you fall over." Lord Mason said. "Looks like you took quite a beating."

"Yeah well, it feels like I took quite a beating." Emmett grumbled. Why would Lord Oliver bring Lady Bridget with him to Emmett's place?

"My Lord, I was instructed to give you this when you awoke." John handed him a letter.

Emmett had a feeling he knew what it was. He broke the seal and scanned the letter. He threw it on the table and ran his hand through his hair. He had a week to prepare for a six-month absence.

"Oliver, I am going to be gone for a while. I will have my solicitor stay in contact with you in regards to the running of Caverton Security." Emmett stood and walked over to his liquor cabinet. He rarely drank. He could count on one hand the number of times he consumed alcohol in the last six years.

"What are you doing?" Oliver asked, grabbing the glass from his hand. "You don't drink."

"I do today."

"What does this mean?" Lady Bridget asked. Emmett turned to look at her. She was holding his marching orders. "It says you are to meet Captain Lincoln Trevors next week for further orders."

Emmett grabbed the glass out of Oliver's hand and downed it. "It is as it appears, Lady Bridget." He couldn't look at her. "Those are my orders."

"You re-enlisted? Are you mad?" Oliver asked. Emmett had told him a little about his two years of military service.

"I lost the fight." Emmett walked to the window and looked out at the busy street.

"You better start talking before I give you another beating." Oliver stated firmly.

"Trevors enlisted me when I turned seventeen. He liked to recruit out of fight houses. He is stationed near Freynia. I served my two years and wanted out. He tried to change my mind. He was at the Nest for the last few days. He approached me again; said I had only gotten better, and he could use me. I turned him down."

"If you turned him down, how did this happen?" Lady Bridget shook the letter.

He turned around and looked at her. He leaned against the wall so he wouldn't fall over. "I lost the fight." Her eyes widened in disbelief.

"How many did you lose?" Lord Mason asked.

"Just the one."

"Trevors. Is that the man you served under for two years?" Lord Oliver asked.

"He is. I was winning but got distracted." Emmett's jaw clenched as he remembered the conversation he overheard while in the ring.

"You never lose focus in a fight." Oliver stated.

"There is a first time for everything, sir. Now if you don't mind, I have preparations that need to be made."

"Emmett, this doesn't make any sense. Why is Trevors still trying to recruit you? Why would you spend two weeks at the Nest? How in heaven's name did you lose?" Lord Oliver poured himself a drink.

"He is trying to recruit me because my skills match those we are fighting." Emmett returned to Oliver's side and poured himself another drink. He hated this part about himself.

"The only way your skills could match those in Freynia is if you come from Freynia." Lady Caverton said quietly.

"My father loved my mother, but life in Lockston was difficult for her. As soon as I was sent to training, my father saw an opportunity and took her to Arlania." He swirled the amber liquid in the glass. "I wasn't aware of their defection until my commander told me they died of an illness. I completed my training a few years later. I was first sent to Valencia. That is where I met Trevors for the first time."

"How did you end up in Arlania as a titled man?" Lord Mason asked confused.

"The Trevors owned a fighting ring where I was...encouraged to participate. Lincoln was granted a pass to see his family. He purchased me and said if I managed to live for two years, I could earn my freedom. After I got out, I found the Nest. I earned money by winning fights. A man wanted to challenge me but had no money. He offered up his title and everything that went with it." Emmett shrugged as he continued to look at his glass. "He claimed I was some long lost relative and passed the title to me. No one in society questioned it since his estate was on the verge of ruin. The man was a compulsive gambler."

"You are from Freynia." Lady Caverton said softly.

"A fact that I am not proud of." Emmett downed his glass.

"Lockston is an eastern clan, if I remember right."

"It is. One of the most dangerous clans, second only to Crossford. The two were always at war with each other. Lockston specialized in explosives and firearms, while Crossford housed the Assassin's Guild."

"A man from Freynia that does not treat women..." Lady Caverton said in disbelief, causing Emmett to laugh.

"You sound like you are familiar with Freynia's culture." Emmett studied her.

"I am from Crossford."

Emmett's eyebrows rose in surprise. He glanced at Lord Mason. There had to be an interesting story behind how she got to Arlania and ended up living with the Guardians. He shook his head. Now was not the time for stories. He needed to get ready to meet Trevors.

"We are getting off topic." Lord Oliver said. "You answered the why you are wanted, but not why you stayed away for two weeks."

Emmett sighed. Why had he stayed away for so long? Why had he felt so frustrated? If someone was frequently seen touching his daughter the way Emmett had with Bridget, he would be suspicious of the man. Even if his motives were pure. Then there was the alcove and dancing. None of that had been necessary. He had been selfish and wanted to have Bridget in his arms. What was wrong with him?

"I have a lot going on right now." Emmett finally said. "I needed to blow off steam."

"You blow off steam every few months, but never for a solid two weeks. Emmett, this isn't like you." Oliver pressed.

"Not like me." He muttered. "I have been trained since the age of three how to kill. Maybe what you know of me is not really who I am. Maybe fighting, killing, is the real me." He looked at Lord Oliver.

"That is where you are wrong, Lord Young." Lady Caverton spoke as she moved to Emmett's side. "Who you are isn't what someone molds you to be. Despite growing up in Freynia and receiving the training you have; you have spent years taking down people that are dangerous. Being a champion for those who cannot save themselves. No one was forcing you to do that."

Emmett shook his head. They didn't understand the things he had done. "Thank you for the vote of confidence, My Lady, but I fear it is misplaced."

"How did you lose to Trevors?" Lord Mason asked.

"I was distracted. The slightest of distractions can cost a fighter greatly. In this case, it was Lord Percival." Emmett rubbed the back of his neck. "He was speaking with a man about smuggling more men across the border to find a woman." Emmet turned to Lady Caverton. "A Julianna Winters. I had only heard part of her description when Trevors got the best of me."

Lady Caverton's face paled. Lord Mason was at her side in a flash. Lord Oliver was halfway there when everything froze. Emmett's gaze snapped to Bridget.

"Are you really leaving?" She asked.

"I lost the fight. As a result, I have to re-enlist for six months." Emmett glanced at her parents. Lady Bridget seemed completely calm. "You are getting better at that."

"I have had time to practice." Her attention didn't waver from him. "You shouldn't have to go."

"Bridget, the terms were set, and I failed. I have to go." Emmett smiled at her despite the heaviness of the conversation. "You almost sound worried something might happen to me."

She rolled her eyes. "Have you seen yourself in a mirror? If this is the best you can do, then yes, I am worried."

Emmett walked over to her and grabbed her hand. He immediately felt calmer. "I will be fine. I did it for two years, six months is going to be nothing."

Bridget ducked her head as she tried to step away from him. He tightened his hold on her hand so she couldn't get far. "Why were you gone for two weeks? Uncle Oliver and mother were worried about you."

"Just them? You seem irritated with me, too." Emmett pulled her a little closer.

"You are a pain, you know that?" She huffed. "I do not even know why I consider you a friend."

"You know, I do not think anyone has ever called me a pain before." Emmett grinned. He could feel the tightness of the swelling on the left side of his face. He tucked a strand of loose hair behind her ear.

Bridget glanced at her family before turning her attention back to Lord Young. "You need to go back over there before I unfreeze them." Lord Young looked over and sighed. He raised her hand to his lips before stepping back. Her heart was racing. No one had ever kissed her hand before. As soon as he was standing where he had been a few minutes ago, she unfroze her family.

Her father hugged her mother as she shook. Bridget sat on the couch and watched them. Emmett remained across the room, but she could feel his eyes on her. Someone was looking for her mother. They had suspected as much for years, but that wasn't what was troubling her. It was her feelings towards Lord Young that were really confusing her.

Bridget could not deny her attraction to him. Over the past two weeks, she had been beside herself with worry for the man. He had helped her with Lord Percival and when she froze everyone. Then he disappeared. Tears stung her eyes, but she blinked them back. He was leaving for the Freynia border. Of all the places he could be stationed, he had to be sent to one of the most violent ones.

"Mason, we need to be careful. If they are still looking for me…"

"I bought you some time, Lady Caverton." Emmett spoke up. He wasn't about to tell them that it was Bridget they were after. "The man asking about the woman challenged me after Trevors did."

"You fought after losing to Trevors?" Lord Oliver asked in surprise.

"I didn't feel I had a choice. He was asking for people willing to capture the target, since he couldn't get his men into Arlania for another month." Emmett pushed away from the wall.

"How did you buy time?" Lord Mason asked.

"He knew the risks climbing into the ring." Emmett refused to look at anyone. He did what he needed to do in order to keep Bridget safe. "I know the time and location of where his men plan on crossing. Thanks to Trevors, I will be there."

Bridget's eyes widened as she covered her mouth in surprise. Emmett killed the man. Realization dawned. "You lost the fight on purpose. You wanted to be enlisted. You weren't distracted, you intentionally did it." She was angry now.

Emmett swallowed hard as he met Bridget's glare. If looks could kill, he would be on his way to his own funeral. "I did what needed to be done. I did not want to re-enlist." Emmett said through clenched teeth.

"Why would you even gamble with re-enlisting?" Lord Oliver sat heavily in a chair. He looked completely confused.

"I have my reasons, Oliver." Emmett snapped. He was getting tense again. The desire to return to the Bird's Nest was once again coming back to him. He started to walk to the door but stopped when it opened.

John stood there with a bag in his hands. "Sir, this was just delivered."

Emmett took the bag and excused John. He dropped it on the floor and knelt next to it. He pulled it open and froze. His uniform. There was a note on top of it. He read it quickly. "John! Have Harry and Jacob bring down my trunk!" He called as he pulled the garment out. This was going to be a long six months.

Chapter 26

Today was the day. Emmett slowly climbed the front steps of the Caverton townhouse. He had not seen any of them since he had received his orders. Lady Caverton had made him promise to stop by before he left. He had waited until he was leaving the city. The thought of having to say goodbye to Bridget was not a happy one.

Greg opened the door and showed Emmett to the drawing room to wait for the family. He tugged at the collar of his uniform as his eyes scanned the room. His gaze landed on several family portraits on the mantel. He moved to them. They looked like they had been done recently. Bridget was just as beautiful as ever.

"You look quite dashing, Lord Young." Lady Caverton said from behind him. He turned to face her and bowed. "You look like a natural born soldier, though your smile seems to be missing."

"I am a soldier, My Lady. As for the smile, it is never easy leaving for war." Emmett clenched his jaw.

Lord Oliver, Lord Mason, and Bridget stepped into the room just then. Lord Oliver's lips were in a thin line and his face was grim. "Am I to assume you waited until you were leaving before stopping by?" he asked.

"Yes, sir." Emmett shifted his weight nervously from one foot to the other.

Lord Oliver crossed the room and pulled Emmett into a hug. Emmett returned the embrace. Lord Oliver was the only father figure he really knew. All his memories of his father were of him fighting with his mother. He squeezed his eyes closed. This was harder than he thought it would be.

Lord Oliver stepped back, resting his hands on Emmett's shoulders. "I fully plan on writing to you while you are gone. If I do not get anything back, I will march up there to see for myself that you are well."

"I understand, sir." Emmett swallowed.

"Safe travels, Lord Young." Lord Mason extended his hand.

Emmett shook it and gave a small smile. "For the next six months, I am Lieutenant Young."

"Lieutenant, I fully expect you to come back alive and in one piece. I do not want to look for another business partner." Lord Mason gave Emmett a pointed look.

"Yes, sir." Emmett inclined his head.

Lady Caverton crossed to him. She hugged him, taking him off guard. "You are a member of this family, Emmett. Remember that." She said softly before taking a step back and wiping her cheeks. "You will be missed."

"Yes, ma'am." Emmett swallowed past the lump in his throat. He looked at each person in the room. This was not at all how he had expected this to go. He knew it would be hard, but he felt close to tears. He had not cried since word of his grandmother's death had reached him. "I must be off." He said before bowing to the room.

Everyone walked with him to the entryway. Greg grabbed the handle and then stopped. It took a second for Emmett to realize he was frozen. He turned around and Bridget threw her arms around his neck. He held her tight as he closed his eyes. He buried his face in her neck and breathed in slowly.

"Bridget, I need to go." He whispered. Her hold on him tightened and he felt her take in a shuttering breath. His heart ached. He did not want to let her go, but knew he needed to.

"Promise me you will be careful." she said quietly without releasing him.

Emmett leaned back so he could see her eyes. He studied her for a long moment. He rested his forehead against hers and he closed his eyes. "I fully intend to make it back home." He sighed. "But you need to understand, we are at war. There will always be risks."

Bridget took a step back. She glared at him. "Of course there are risks. That is why I am..." She shook her head. "Just be careful. Uncle Oliver would hate it if you were killed."

Emmett could see the fear in her eyes. He did not want to leave with her looking so upset. "Have I told you lately how much I..." He paused and she quirked an eyebrow. "You aren't going to interrupt me this time?" He asked. The corner of her mouth twitched. "Very well. Have I told you lately how much I appreciate you and your family?"

That did it. Bridget smiled as she shook her head. Emmett winked at her as he squeezed her hand. He turned back to the door before he could give into the urge to kiss her. A moment later, Greg pulled open the door and

Emmett stepped outside. A group of women were passing. They slowed their steps and began whispering as they kept glancing at him.

"Are we going to have a wedding soon after your return?" Lord Oliver asked with a laugh.

Emmett looked back at him with a smirk. "That is unlikely. I will see you all in a few months." He bowed again before descending the stairs and mounting his horse.

He looked back up at the townhouse. The Cavertons stood watching him. Lady Caverton had tears in her eyes, while Lord Caverton had his arm around her. Lord Oliver gave him a nod before putting his arm around Bridget. Bridget was biting her lip with a look of concern.

Emmett couldn't stay any longer. If he did, he would go back inside. He kicked his horse, and he shot forward. He did not bother riding slowly through the crowded streets. The more distance he put between him and the Cavertons, the more he wanted to turn around. He needed to get his mind focused on his task.

Bridget was in danger. People from Freynia were coming for her in order to get back at her mother. He needed to stop them before they could get to her.

*   *   *

Bridget fought back tears as she watched Emmett ride down the street. She swallowed hard as her uncle guided her back inside. Her parents moved into the drawing room, but her uncle held her back.

"He will be back, Bri." Uncle Oliver whispered.

Bridget shrugged. "He said as much." She did not want anyone to know just how much Emmett's leaving was affecting her.

"You did not freeze all of us at the door, Bri. Whether you and Emmett realize it or not, you like each other." Bridget's mouth fell open in surprise. "Why did you not say something?" She whispered. Embarrassment heated her cheeks.

"He was right that there are risks involved in going to the border. I would never forgive myself if you were not able to say goodbye without an audience." Uncle Oliver hugged her before kissing the top of her head. "Let's go in and see how your parents are faring."

Bridget followed her uncle. When she walked in, her eyes immediately went to the fireplace where Emmett last stood. He had looked incredibly handsome in his uniform. Her heart had stuttered before picking up speed.

Her parents and uncle were speaking quietly. Bri walked over to the fireplace. Her family's portraits were there. She was about to turn around when she caught sight of a piece of paper under her picture. She carefully slid it out from under the frame. Her name was written across the top of it.

She glanced behind her and froze her family. She quickly tucked the envelope into her dress so no one would see it. She unfroze her family. Her heart was hammering so hard she was sure they would be able to hear it.

"I think I am going to go to the library." She said, and her mother looked over at her. She nodded and Bri quickly left.

Bridget took the letter out once she was safely inside the library. Her hands were shaking slightly as she read. Tears burned her eyes. Emmett told her she was right that he had intentionally lost the fight with Trevors. He felt he needed the support of the king's military in order to protect her and her mother.

He said the man was hired to get back at the woman responsible for his employer's father being killed, by killing the woman's daughter. He promised he would do everything he could in order to stop the men. The man responsible was supposed to be coming across the border with the group to get his revenge.

Why did he not tell them about the real threat? He had said he bought them time but that was it. They might have come up with a different way to keep everyone safe.

She stood and marched back to the drawing room. Her family was still there. "He lied to us." She seethed.

"What are you talking about?" Uncle Oliver got to his feet.

"The man isn't after mother; he is after me." She handed her uncle the letter. "His employer wants revenge because he thinks she got his father killed. My death is what he wants as restitution."

"That is why he lost." Her uncle sat as he stared at the letter. "He is protecting Anna and Bridget."

"What else does it say?" her father asked.

"Nothing. Just explaining his reasonings for leaving and warning us to stay vigilant." Uncle Oliver passed the letter over to her father.

"Hmm." Her father rubbed his chin.

"Stop reading more into it than what it was meant for." Her mother kissed her father's cheek. "He and Bridget are friends. If he had addressed it to you or Oliver, you two would have tried to stop him. He needed time to leave before you knew what it was all about."

"Why are you so calm about this?" Her father asked. Her mother shrugged before standing. Her father's eyes narrowed. "You have seen something."

"I never said that."

"No, but you are..."

"Mason, Lord Young means no harm to our daughter. He is literally risking his life in order to save hers." Her mother hugged Bridget. "He will come back. He has to."

Bridget spent the next two weeks trying to keep herself busy. Her thoughts often turned to Emmett. It was infuriating that the man consumed so much of her mind, and he wasn't even there. When he had been around, he teased her. She had seen him often for the first two months after they had arrived in the Capital. She had never talked to him though. He was usually meeting with her father and uncle to talk about business. He often watched her during the meetings. She had pretended not to notice, but she had.

He was knowledgeable and thorough in his reports. In the four years he had been acquainted with her father and uncle, he had become their most trusted man, both with the Hunters and for the family business. From what she had gathered, two years ago her father and uncle turned over the day-to-day running of Caverton Security to him. Emmett had done well and made more of a profit for the company.

Not only was he business minded, but he was also very kind and generous. He had dinner at their house several times a week. Mother had taken a liking to him. Bridget had also seen the bond between Emmett and Uncle Oliver. They laughed and joked frequently. She had found that she liked his company but had been far too shy to say anything.

Then she had mistaken him for her uncle. That had been completely embarrassing. He started teasing her. Her mishap seemed to have broken the barrier between them. They had many conversations after that. His blue eyes sparked with humor whenever he teased her. She was so relieved when he saved her from Lord Percival. Having him there had helped her feel safe. He was the only reason she had not fallen apart that night. Bridget felt like they were starting to develop a friendship.

She sighed as she mentally shook her head. He was a pain. Always teasing her and making reckless decisions. First, the fight club, and then re-enlisting. What had he been thinking? She knew her father and uncle had written to him a few times with no response. Bridget couldn't sit around waiting anymore. She stood from her favorite spot in the library and headed for her room. She was going to write her own letter and ask her uncle to send it with his next one.

*   *   *

Emmett was tired. They had another skirmish during the night. Four of his fifteen men were injured. They had managed to push back the enemy, but it had been a long fight. Everyone was exhausted. The next watch group came to relieve Emmett's men just after the fighting had stopped. He really could have used the extra manpower, but there was nothing he could have done about it. They had been cut off from the main base and were unable to send for reinforcements.

Camp came into view and Emmett dismissed his men to get cleaned up and rest. They would be back out on the line in the morning. Emmett watched as his men slowly spread out as some went toward the river and others headed for the mess hall. He followed the four injured to the medic tent. He himself needed a few stitches.

"Lieutenant Young, what can we do for you?" The young man in charge of intaking the wounded asked.

"My men get treated first." Emmett nodded toward his men.

"Sir…" the man tried to argue but Emmett glared at him. "Yes, sir." He finally said.

It took several hours for Emmett to be seen. He had a gash on his back. The one time he did not use his steel armor, he found himself fighting against someone from the Assassin's Guild. The men had a hidden dagger. Seventeen stitches later, Emmett was heading for the river to get cleaned up. He was covered in blood, dirt, and sweat. The icy river was not the most enjoyable of experiences, but it was better than nothing.

Emmett was heading back to his tent when he heard someone's hurried steps. "Lieutenant Young!" Milo, Emmett's second in command, called, and Emmett grudgingly stopped. Now that he was clean, all he wanted to do was go to sleep.

"Milo, what can I do for you?" Emmett asked once he had reached his side.

"Captain Trevors asked that I give these to you." Milo handed him a stack of letters. There were at least ten of them.

"I will see that the men receive their mail." Emmett gave the man a smile.

"I already have, sir. Those are yours."

Emmett looked down in surprise. He never got mail. "Thank you, Milo." Emmett saluted him and Milo scurried off.

Emmett waited until he was inside his tent before opening the first letter. It was from his solicitor, Mr. Jeremy. It was dated four weeks ago. He quickly scanned the contents. Just a report on the business and his own holdings. The next three were the same. Lord Mason wrote to him as well, asking after him and telling him how things were going with the Hunters.

Emmett set them aside and opened the next letter. Lord Oliver was demanding a report on how Emmett was doing. He also told him that Lady Caverton and Lady Bridget had been put under constant watch, even though they did not know it. He smiled at that. Neither lady was one to like the idea of a security guard hanging around.

He opened the last letter, and a folded piece of paper fell from it. Emmett retrieved it but set it aside to scan Lord Oliver's latest plea to hear back from Emmett. He sighed and opened the folded piece of paper. He had expected another one of Lord Oliver's demanding notes, but instead it was a message from Bridget.

A smile spread on his face as he read.

Lord Emmett,

How dare you lie to me. I can't believe you did not tell me to my face that I was in danger. Why? Did you think I would break down? Did you think I could not handle the news? You are wrong, sir. I am capable of knowing that someone is trying to kill me. You owe me an apology. And if you do not, the Freynians are the least of your problems.

Lady Bridget

Emmett laughed as he closed his eyes and laid down. This had been what he had needed. Lady Bridget's letter was a ray of sunshine in his dark world. He could see her glaring at him, like she had so many times. She was definitely angry with him. He sat up. He needed to send a few letters back home.

Emmett found someone with some extra paper and a writing utensil. He quickly wrote short notes to Mr. Jeremy, Lord Mason, and Lord Oliver. He let them know that mail was only delivered once a month, if it was safe. He would make sure to write every time the mail carrier made it up to his unit.

He took his time writing his response to Lady Bridget. He couldn't help smiling as he tucked it into Lord Oliver's envelope and sealed it. He found the young man tasked with the mail and handed over his three letters. Now that he was done with that, he returned to his tent. Thoughts of Bridget were floating around in his head as he fell asleep.

Emmett awoke to shouts of alarm. He ran from his tent to see several men grabbing weapons and heading for the border. He called for his men to gear up as he grabbed his sword. He followed the others. It wasn't long before he heard the clashing of steel and men's cries of pain. The Freynians were getting more and more violent with each failed attempt to cross the border.

He scanned the battle for his target, the main reason he was here. He did not see the Crossford Chief, so he moved to the nearest enemy who happened to be fighting with Milo. The man cried out as Emmett brought his sword down on him from behind. Milo gave him a nod before they both focused back on the fighting around them.

*   *   *

Bridget listened to her parents and uncle as she pushed her food around on her plate. It had been three weeks since she had sent her letter off with her uncle's. Still, there was no word.

"Oh, I received a letter from Emmett this afternoon." Her uncle took a drink. Her head snapped up and his eyes flicked to hers. "He said that mail only gets up to him every month or so. Sometimes it takes longer if there is a lot of fighting at the time. He also said he was doing fine. He is in command of a small unit and all of his men are doing well. He said to let everyone know that he will send updates with each mail carrier."

"My letter from him said his solicitor is sending updates to him and that the business is doing well. He said this was the first time he had received mail. It was a pleasant surprise, and he looks forward to when he can return." Her father said.

"So, he is doing well?" her mother asked eagerly.

"He sounds like it." Uncle Oliver took a bite. Bridget continued to watch him. Had Emmett written to her as well?

She gave herself a mental shake. Of course, he didn't. Why would he? It was improper for a man and woman to exchange letters before they were married. Her uncle had been kind enough to put hers inside his, so that no one would know. It was bad enough that she sent a letter. Him sending her one in return would be foolish.

Dinner continued as her family discussed Emmett and the positive nature of his letters. She ate slowly as she listened. When they were heading into the drawing room, Bridget excused herself. She was not feeling up to keeping up appearances tonight. She just wanted to be alone for a little while.

"Bri." Her uncle stopped her. He glanced at her parents, and she froze them. He looked back at her before holding up a folded piece of paper. "You two are lucky that I am willing to help you." He said as his lips twitched. "I expect a huge thank you."

"Thank you, Uncle Ollie." Bridget rose up on her toes and kissed his cheek. She quickly tucked the letter into the book she was holding. She unfroze her parents.

"Goodnight, Bri." Her uncle winked at her.

Bridget concentrated on keeping her walk at a normal pace. She could not wait to read what Emmett wrote to her. It better be an apology. She sat on her bed before pulling the letter out.

> *Lady Bridget,*
>
> *I meant no offense in keeping from you the true nature of the threat. It was not my intention to make you feel you are any less the strong woman you are. With that said, I do not apologize for keeping it from you. I would do it again and again. I could not risk you or your family trying to change what needed to be done. This is the only way to keep you safe. If that means you being angry with me, so be it.*
>
> *I am sure Lord Mason and Lord Oliver told you what I wrote to them. I must admit that I was completely taken by surprise when all of your letters came. This was the first time I have ever received letters while fighting. It is a light in the darkness around here.*
>
> *We have several skirmishes with the Freynians a week. My men are good at what they do, and we watch each other's backs. So far, we have only had minor injuries.*
>
> *But tell me about what you have been doing? How is the gossip with Lord Percival? Has he given up on trying to drag your name through the mud?*
>
> *Have I told you lately how...man this is not the same with you not here to interrupt me. The men around here don't enjoy my teasing like you do. If you are able to write again, tell me something funny.*

Emmett

Bridget reread the letter a few times. He was such a pain. He was sorry for making her feel like she was not strong, but he was not at all sorry for not telling her the full truth. A small smile curved her lips as she ran her fingers over the last part. His teasing was definitely not the same on paper.

She sighed as she laid back on the bed. She missed him. It already felt like he had been gone for ages, even though it had only been a little over a month. The next five months were going to be long.

Bridget spent the next couple of weeks trying to get as much gossip as she could. Emmett asked for gossip, and she was going to give it to him. Uncle Oliver, once again, hid her letter in his before he sent them off. How long would it be before she heard from Emmett again?

Chapter 27

Emmett was heading back to his tent after eating when Milo handed him another stack of letters. Emmett couldn't help but smile as he jogged towards his tent. He had been looking forward to this for weeks. He tossed all but Lord Oliver's to the side. He would read the others later. He was praying Bridget had written to him again.

Once again there was a letter tucked in with Lord Oliver's. He quickly unfolded it.

> Emmett,
>
> I guess I can wait until you get home to get the apology you owe me. Because you will give it to me. Your re-enlisting is just ridiculous. But we can call a truce for now.
>
> Thanks to you, I am now under house arrest. Father refuses to allow mother and me to go anywhere. I cannot even go to the drawing room without an armed escort. You will be answering for that as well.
>
> As for the rumors around town... We are still engaged, according to many. Others think that I was not worth it, and that you ran off in order to not have to tie yourself to me. Lord Percival is rumored to be hiding in the country. The men he owes money to are demanding payment.
>
> How are you and your men? Have there been many more skirmishes? What is the country like that far north? Is it as cold and harsh as I have read about? Do you ever miss the Capital?
>
> Please be smart while you are there. It would tear Uncle Ollie up if you were injured.
>
> Bridget

Emmett chuckled. Lady Bridget was definitely going to give him an earful when he got back. The thought of Lord Percival forced into hiding was amusing. He was a coward of a man. He deserved more than to be hiding away from society.

He thought about the rugged country he was in. It was beautiful in many ways, but it held many dangers, besides the enemy. Steep drop offs, rivers with fast moving currents that look calm on the surface, and even the extremely cold nights could be deadly.

Emmett wrote out his response before reading his other letters. An hour later, he walked into the captain's tent. "Sir, I have some mail that needs to be sent."

"Lieutenant, you are quite a popular man. It is a far cry from the last time." Captain Trevors sat back in his chair. He was a decent man, especially compared to his relatives in Valencia. He had helped Emmett realize there was more to life than the next person he was to kill. "Seems you have found some good friends."

"Yes, sir." Emmett handed over his three letters.

"How are your men doing?"

"They are doing well. All of them are decent fighters and have been able to hold their own on the battlefield." Emmett clasped his hands behind his back. "I have been wanting to talk with you about something."

"What is it, Lieutenant?" Captain Trevors lifted a brow in surprise. Emmett did not ask for anything.

"If anything happens to me, I want Milo to deliver my things to the Cavertons. They have taken me in, and I feel like they should be the ones to have it."

"Do you think something will happen to you?" Trevors sat up and studied Emmett closely.

"I hope not, but we are at war. The skirmishes happen several times a week and the Freynians are becoming more aggressive."

"True. I will make note in your file that you wish the Cavertons to inherit your belongings if anything were to happen to you."

"I wish for Milo to deliver them." Emmett was adamant about it. Milo had proven himself to be a great ally. He felt like he could trust him with this task, and that Milo would be aware of the emotional toll such news would bring to the Cavertons. He had seen men be callous in the way they deliver news of a loved one's death to their families.

"As you wish. Have you informed him yet of what you are tasking him with?"

"I plan to as soon as I am done here." Emmett said. Captain Trevors gave him a dismissive nod and Emmett left.

It was almost time for his unit's turn at the front. He gathered his gear and rounded up his men. As they walked, Emmett asked if Milo would be willing to deliver his things to the Cavertons if anything were to happen to him. Milo grudgingly nodded. He could understand the kid's reluctance. It wasn't a task anyone wanted.

Emmett gave his orders to his men before climbing a ridge. Tonight, he was going to start off with a bird's eye view. His rifle had a scope on it that allowed him to pick out targets at farther distances than a normal rifle. He had smuggled the scope out of Lockston a few weeks ago. Not only that, but he had also been slowly gathering the supplies needed to create explosives.

He was planning on creating a trap, so when the Freynians tried to cross the border, it would go off. He couldn't leave without first eliminating the Crossford Chief.

On a recon mission, Emmett had shifted into his falcon and listened in on several conversations within the camp of the Freynians. He had learned a few things about Chief Talon. He was obsessed with finding Julianna Winters. She apparently was his sister. The previous Crossford Chief refused to allow Talon to hunt down his sister because the death of his father was legal within their laws.

Talon had issued a challenge and killed the chief, becoming the new leader. Now Crossford was suffering under his rule. His men were afraid that if they did not follow him, they would end up in his line of fire.

Emmett looked down his scope and slowly scanned the mountain trail. This place was incredibly dangerous to try to cross. There was no clear path. The mountain was steep and slick. The rocks were loose and there were frequent rockslides.

The hoot of an owl drew Emmett's attention. Milo let out another hoot. The enemy was spotted. He scanned the rocky outcroppings, looking for any movement. A few moments later, he saw it. It looked like close to twenty men making their way through the rough terrain. Emmett lined up his sights, let out his breath, and pulled the trigger. The crack of his rifle echoed off the rocks. He quickly reloaded and fired again.

He was able to hit three men before return shots were fired. He ducked down as bullets ricocheted off the rocks near him. He waited another moment before making his way carefully down to his men. He stashed his rifle before reaching Milo's side. With so many rocks around, it was dangerous to fire his gun in the ravine. Ricocheted shots could easily kill him or his own men.

"How many are we looking at?" Milo asked, handing him his sword.

"Little less than twenty. Send Glen back for reinforcements." Emmett ordered. Glen was the youngest of his men at the age of seventeen. Emmett did his best to watch out for the kid. He often sent him to request aid when they needed it, just to get him out of danger.

Ten minutes after Glen disappeared, the fighting broke out. Emmett could tell these fighters were from Crossford. They were more aggressive, and their fighting style was more deadly. It felt like an eternity before help arrived.

Once the fighting ceased, Emmett sat at the base of a tree. He had been stabbed and was losing quite a bit of blood. Milo knelt down beside him. "Lieutenant, how about we take a look at that?"

"What about the others?" Emmett winced as Milo removed Emmett's armor and pulled up his shirt to reveal the wound.

"Glen is rounding everyone up. I'm not sure how everyone is. Sir, this looks pretty bad." Milo pressed on the wound, causing Emmett to groan. "Medic!" He yelled.

Soon there were three men surrounding Emmett. They transferred him to a stretcher, and they quickly began walking back to camp. "I want a full report, Milo." Emmett called, and Milo gave him a salute.

Emmett closed his eyes as the pain increased with each jostle of the stretcher. He let out a sigh of relief when they made it to the medical tent. He was instantly swarmed by the staff. The doctor pulled back the bandage and immediately started giving instructions. Something was stabbed into his arm. A few seconds later, everything went black.

*   *   *

Greg walked into the drawing room holding a stack of papers. "My Lady, today's mail has arrived."

"Thank you, Greg." Bridget's mother accepted the mail. Her father and uncle walked into the room and sat. "These are for you." She handed all but one letter over to them.

Uncle Oliver quickly opened his letter and scanned it while her father read his. "Emmett is doing well. He says he is looking forward to returning and getting a decent meal." He said.

"When was that letter written?" her mother asked.

"Five weeks ago." Uncle Oliver got a thoughtful expression. "He only has two months left."

"This letter was written four weeks ago." Her mother looked at everyone.

"Emmett wrote to you?" Her father asked.

"No, this is addressed to the Caverton family. It is from Captain Trevors." Her mother said looking back down at the paper she held. Bridget's stomach knotted with dread. Why would he be writing to them? Her mother cleared her throat. "I write in regard to Lieutenant Emmett Young's health. Per his request, I am reaching out to you. A skirmish broke out on his watch. He fought valiantly and saved many of his fellow soldiers. However, he was injured. He has received surgery and seems to be healing well. Lieutenant Young regained consciousness briefly. The doctors have assured me that he will make a full recovery as long as infection does not set in. If anything changes, I will be sure to inform you. Best wishes, Captain Lincoln Trevors."

Bridget covered her face as she fought back her tears. This could not be happening. She stood and left the room. Before she could reach the stairs, someone grabbed her. She looked at her uncle. "He is strong, Bri. He will be okay." He said softly. He put a folded piece of paper in her hand and gave her a sad smile.

She swallowed past the lump in her throat. She ran up to her room and pressed her back against the door. She slid to the floor. The letter in her hand felt heavy. She slowly opened it.

Bridget,

You are so generous in calling a truce. I will gladly take full credit for the armed guards. As long as you are safe, I will happily take any and all blame.

Percival is a coward. I hope his creditors catch up to him. There is not a man alive that would trade you for war. The rumors will pass. Just hang in there.

The country up here is rugged. It is densely forested with lots of rivers and ravines. We are stationed on a mountain with tons of steep drop offs and sharp rocks. It is dangerous to cross the border here because the only pass is known for crumbling, and many have fallen to their deaths.

My men are hanging in there. I have several young men in the unit. I do my best to watch out for them, but it is getting tougher. Skirmishes are breaking out more and more.

The Capital will never be home. But I do miss some of the people I have met there. After spending the last three months here, I do miss good food, a bed, and sleeping through the night.

I go out on patrol soon. Wish me luck.

Emmett

Bridget couldn't hold back her sob anymore. She pulled her knees to her chest as she continued to cry. How bad was he injured? It sounded bad. She leaned her head back. She reached up and started playing with her locket. She froze. She looked down at it.

Bri ran her finger over the sparrow that was etched into the front. Her mother had given it to her long ago. Her father called her sparrow because she always wore it. It gave the wearer the ability to shift into a sparrow.

She stood and locked her door. She was going to see the infuriating man and see for herself that he was well. Bridget opened her window and took a deep breath. She opened the locket, turned the dial and closed it again. Pain shot through her body. She squeezed her eyes closed. When she opened them again, she was on the floor.

It took her a minute to realize she was a sparrow now. Bridget stretched her wings and took flight. It was strange at first, but once she got used to it, she loved the feeling of flying. It took hours before she saw the slight flicker of light through the trees. Bridget landed on a tree branch as she studied the multiple tents below.

Despite it being the middle of the night, there were men moving around. She spotted a large tent in the middle of the camp. She flew down and slipped into the tent. Several men were sleeping in beds that lined the space. She flew a little farther in and perched on a support post.

"Milo, go to sleep man." Emmett sighed. "I am not going anywhere. I am perfectly fine."

"You had a sword stabbed into your abdomen, sir. No offense, I am surprised Captain Trevors didn't send you home." The young man Emmett called Milo, said.

"I asked him not to. I have some things I still need to do here." Emmett smiled at Milo. "Plus, you would miss me too much if I went home now."

"Sir, you are something else. You hate it here. I have seen the way you light up when the mail comes. You miss home. Why would you turn down the chance to leave?"

"I have my reasons, Milo. Look, I am tired. We have patrol tomorrow evening. Tell the men to rest up. I fully expect everyone to be at one hundred percent." Emmett dismissed the young man. Milo shook his head before leaving.

Bridget was fuming. What was wrong with Emmett? He could have come home. She waited to make sure no one else came in before flying down and shifting back to human. She moved to Emmett's side. His eyes were closed, but he tensed when she sat on the side of the bed.

"You are an idiot." She whispered.

Emmett's eyes flew open. "Bri." He breathed out as he stared at her in shock. "How did you...?"

"I have my ways of getting around." She cut him off. He sat up as he continued to stare at her with wide eyes.

"You shouldn't be here, Bri. It is far too dangerous. You need to leave."

"You could have been home?" She glared at him.

Emmett sighed as he pinched the bridge of his nose. "I came here for a reason. I will not leave until I am done." He grabbed her hand. "He is still trying to get through, Bri. I haven't been able to stop him yet."

"We can think of some other way."

"No." Emmett shook his head. "I can't risk him getting into Arlania."

"You are a pain, Emmett Young." She stood and walked several steps away.

Emmett stood and followed Bridget. He moved to stand in front of her. "It is really good to see you." He whispered as he grabbed her hand again. "Have I told you lately how much I..."

"You are still on that?" she interrupted him as her cheeks flushed. Thankfully it was dark. Emmett chuckled. "Uncle Oliver and mother were very upset when we got the letter from Captain Trevors. He said you were close to death for a while."

Emmett groaned. "He sent a letter?" He shook his head. "Is that why you are here? To check up on me?"

"The letter made it sound bad, Emmett. We got it the same time as your letters." Bridget touched his chest. "We were all concerned."

Emmett put his arms around her, and she leaned against him. He was a little sore, but the pain was not too bad. He pulled her closer, and she sniffled. Gunfire in the distance caused Emmett to tense.

"You need to leave. Now." Emmett took a step back. He wiped the tears off her cheeks. "Please. I need you safely back with your family." Bridget's eyes widened as she looked out the tent door. "Bri, look at me. The wounded will be arriving soon. You need to go. I will write in a few weeks, okay?"

Emmett desperately needed Bri back in the Capital where he knew she was safe. Bridget's eyes filled with concern. "Emmett, are you going to...?"

"Not tonight. I am required to rest until tomorrow. But you really need to go." Emmett cupped her face. He wanted so badly to keep her with him. He had missed her so much.

She put her arms around his neck and hugged him. Emmett buried his face in her neck. He swallowed hard. He pulled back and looked into her eyes. "Just two more months, Bri. I will be back." He tucked her hair behind her ear. "Please, I need you to go. I need you safe."

"Promise me you will be safe." Her voice was little more than a whisper.

"It's war, Bridget. There are risks. I will do my best, though."

"You better." She stepped away from him and grabbed her locket.

"You almost sound like you care about me?" Emmett grinned.

Bridget rolled her eyes. "I will see you in a few months." She said as she opened her locket.

She turned the dial and closed it. She gave Emmett a small smile just before the pain hit her. It was worse this time. Emmett reached for her as she fell. She closed her eyes. When she opened them, Emmett was gently lifting her off the floor with his hand.

"Well, this is unexpected." He muttered.

She chirped before flying out of the tent. Emmett shook his head. This was not how he expected the night to go. He walked to the opening of the tent and looked up into the night sky. He knew he would not be able to see the little sparrow, but he looked anyway.

He smiled as he returned to his cot. It had been so good to see and hold Bridget. He laid down. The woman was completely mad. Who flies into a war zone just to check up on someone? Bridget, that's who. He had no idea she was a Shifter. She needed to be more careful. Many of the men here would kill a Shifter if given the chance.

Emmett rubbed his face. Had it all been a dream? Had Bridget really been there? He had no proof that she was. Maybe the painkillers they gave him were stronger than he thought. He let out a heavy sigh as he listened to the sound of distant fighting. Just two more months. He only had two more months. If he was unable to stop Chief Talon, he was going to have to sign up for another six months.

That was the furthest thing from what he wanted. He realized something tonight. Though he originally thought of Bridget as a friend, that was not the case now. He missed her the most. He looked forward to her letters more than the others. In fact, he would be perfectly happy if she was the only one he received letters from.

The gossip was completely wrong. He would not have left if he had Bridget. Well, under normal circumstances he would never leave her. But this was different. Someone was trying to kill her. He could not go home until he knew she was safe.

Chapter 28

Emmett took a deep breath and let it out slowly. His side did not like him moving around so much. He pressed on it to try to find some sort of relief. It had been six weeks, but still the wound pained him more than he was going to admit to anyone.

"How are you doing?" Milo asked quietly.

"Focus on the mission." Emmett grumbled back.

"I will take that as you are hurting." Glen joined in the conversation.

Emmett clenched his jaw. Of course he was hurting. He had a sword shoved into his abdomen followed by surgery and a fight with infection. His men needed to see him as strong. He could not let them or Bridget down.

"I am fine. Now be quiet. Any noise will draw their attention." He moved from his position and slowly made his way down the line, checking on all of his men.

He wished he could shift and fly over to see if the enemy was going to be coming. He hated the distrust when it came to Shifters. This war with Freynia would be so much easier if Arlanians were free to use their Shifters to the best of their abilities.

His men were doing good. They were all wide awake and ready for the enemy. Emmett hoped tonight would be a quiet one. Hours ticked by with no issues. The sky started to lighten with the rising sun. The next unit appeared, and Emmett's men quickly made their way back to camp.

Emmett gave Milo orders to make sure everyone was fed and got some rest. Milo saluted. Emmett took the path to the river where the men bathed. He came to the deep pool. He hesitated and glanced around to make sure he was alone. He needed a few more things to finish his explosives.

Emmett jogged into the forest and shifted. He flew high and circled around a few times to make sure no one was around before heading north. He hated returning to Lockston. He had no good memories there, but it was the only place he could get what he needed.

He landed three miles from the clan. He shifted back to human and pulled his bag out of the trunk of the tree where he had stashed it . He quickly changed into his clothes, hiding his uniform in the bag and putting it back into the tree.

Emmett walked the rest of the way to the clan. It would eat up valuable time, but the people of Freynia were not Shifters. Freynians hated Shifters more than the people of Arlania. Emmett got his Shifter gene from his mother. His father had married her in Arlania while he was there on business for the Clan.

Lockston came into view, and he slowed his steps. He kept his hands where they were easily seen. There were always guards on duty. The clan was very leery of visitors. Not anyone could just walk in. One hundred feet from the gate he stopped and waited.

"My name is Emmett Nevill of Lockston." He called from where he stood. He had changed his name to his mother's maiden name after he earned his freedom. He was determined to leave this part of his past behind him. It just seemed to creep back in, no matter how much he tried to bury it.

He did not have to wait long. A man materialized out of the forest to his right. Emmett held still.

"It has been a while since I saw you last, Em." Blake smiled at him.

Emmett grinned. "I have been busy." He and Blake had gone through training together. "You are looking good."

"I am doing good. Having a wife changes a man for the better."

Emmett was taken by surprise. "You are married? Since when?"

Blake laughed. "Since three weeks ago. She is a sweet quiet girl. We get along well." They started walking toward the main gate. "What brings you back? Last I heard you were some sort of champion in Valencia." Blake nodded to several men who opened the gate for them.

"I got out of the fighting business for the most part. I do enjoy a good match here and there though." Emmett shrugged. "I came to purchase a few things."

Blake didn't say anything for several minutes as they walked through the streets of Lockston. Emmett's senses were on high alert. They always were when he was here. The last several times he had flown in and stolen materials in the middle of the night. This time he felt exposed.

"What do you need?" Blake glanced at him.

"Black powder." Emmett kept his voice low.

Blake stopped walking and stared at Emmett with a raised brow. "Black powder? What do you need Black powder for?"

"I have my reasons, Blake."

"You were always one to protect those you value. It was your downfall. It was what caused you to be sold in the first place. Who are you protecting? I know that look in your eyes." Blake lowered his voice. "What trouble are you in, Em?"

Emmett ran his hand through his hair. Blake had been his greatest ally when they were in training. They had saved each other's lives more than once. He really did not want to re-enlist, again. He would have to if he could not stop Chief Talon in the next few months.

"Can we go get something to eat? I am famished." Emmett finally said.

"Sure thing, Em. Follow me." Blake led the way out of the trade district towards some of the housing. He opened the door to a cabin halfway down the road. "Welcome to my home."

Emmett stepped inside and immediately saw a woman standing in the kitchen. She turned around at the sound of the door. Her eyes widened in surprise. "Blake, I did not expect you home yet." she said anxiously.

"I will not stand for mistreatment, Blake." Emmett muttered as he took his coat off and hung it up.

"A lot has changed in Lockston, Em. Chief Elias was challenged by his son Payton. Chief Payton put in laws to protect women after he found his wife." Blake smiled at Emmett. "Laura comes from a different clan and is weary of men."

"Understandable." Emmett nodded.

"Laura, this is my friend, Emmett. He was born here but ended up being traded to Valencia shortly after training." She moved to Blake's side, using him as a shield from Emmett. Emmett moved a little away to not be as threatening. "He is here to trade."

Blake asked Laura if she could make something for them to eat while they talked. She nodded and moved back into the kitchen. Blake gestured to the table. Emmett held his breath as he sat. He really needed to hurry this up so that he could go lay down.

"Tell me, Em. Why are you in need of that particular item?"

"Have you heard of Chief Talon of Crossford?" Emmett asked instead.

"Who hasn't? The man is unhinged. Not a soul respects him. He is ruthless and dangerous. I have heard he is looking for a woman that he feels is responsible for killing his father." Blake crossed his arms over his chest. "Have you gotten mixed up with him?"

"I have never met him in person." Emmett scratched his jaw. "Tell me about this woman he is after."

"Her name is Julianna. She is his second sister. His mother and Julianna ran away when she was a child. Their location remained unknown until Talon heard rumors of a beautiful woman with light blue eyes in Arlania. His father did some digging, and sure enough, it was her. When he went to retrieve her, Julianna was already married. Hawkshaw hit her before they knew she was with child. Her father was required by our laws to kill him. Hawkshaw put up a fight and both men died." Blake shook his head. "What is this about, Emmett?"

"Talon is not after Julianna anymore. He is going to kill her daughter." Emmett clenched his jaw.

"Ah. I see. You were hired to take out the girl." Blake said stiffly.

"No. I was not hired to kill her. I am planning on killing Talon in order to protect her and Julianna. I have been at the border stopping his attempts to cross for the last few months." Emmett was taking a risk in telling Blake this, but he needed the powder.

Blake studied him for a long time. Laura put a plate in front of Emmett, and he gave her a smile. "You are going to get yourself killed to protect two women? Why?" she asked in confusion.

"I haven't been killed yet." Emmett took a bite of the sandwich. "They are friends of mine."

"A man was beating his daughter and Emmett saw it. He nearly killed the man in order to protect the girl. The next day he was sold. He sees himself as a protector, despite how we grew up." Blake sat back in his chair. "Just friends? Come on, Emmett. Be honest with me. Are you doing this for friendship?"

Emmett set his sandwich down and stood. He paced over to the fireplace. "She is my friend, Blake." He discovered he wanted more than friendship, but at this moment, that was all they were.

"You look like you aren't happy with that." Blake laughed. "Are you just discovering your feelings for her, or does she not feel the same?"

Emmett ran his hand down his face. "We are only friends. Her father and uncle would most likely kill me if I tried anything with her." He turned back around. "I need to be getting back. Can you help me with the powder or not?"

Blake was grinning. "You are so in deep, Em. Risking your life for a woman you are only friends with."

"Stop it, Blake. I think it is romantic." Laura piped up. Emmett groaned. He was not trying to be romantic. He was only trying to keep her safe. "You should help him."

"Help him?" Blake shook his head. "He is trying to take out the leader of the Assassin's Guild. That is suicide."

"I am not asking you to risk your life, Blake. I would never ask that of you. All I need is black powder." Emmett gave his friend a pleading look. "Enough to destroy Devil's Staircase."

"You are planning on blowing up one of the only two ways into Arlania?" Blake's eyes opened wide. "You are mad."

"The two countries are at war. It will be seen as a tactical move, not an assassination." Emmett countered.

"Are you sure you are Emmett Nevill, my best friend? Because that Emmett would never have thought of such a dangerous and reckless plan." Blake yelled.

"I can't lose her!" Emmett snapped. The room went quiet. Emmett hung his head. "I can't lose her." He repeated, this time quieter. "If you are unable to help me, I will find a different way to kill Chief Talon."

"You are in love with her. You said you were just friends." Blake accused.

"We are friends. And yes, I am in love with the blasted woman. She is nothing but trouble." Emmett shook his head. He needed to be getting back to the base. He had been gone for hours. "Look, Blake. I need to leave before my absence is noted."

"I can help you with the powder." Blake shook his head. "I will give you enough to take out the Arlanian side of Devil's Staircase. I will rig the Freynian side to blow when yours does. You will need to be ready in four weeks, Em. A small army is moving this way from Crossford. Roughly a hundred or so men."

"And you think they are going to cross?" Emmett's mind was racing.

"Chief Talon is leading them. He has not bothered with the other clans in months. His sole focus has been getting into Arlania."

"Thank you, Blake." Emmett embraced his friend. "I cannot express my gratitude." Blake gave him a smile. "It was nice meeting you, Laura." He bowed and she smiled at him.

"Good luck, sir. I wish you the best." she said quietly.

Blake walked with Emmett to the trade district. They purchased the powder before they headed for the gate. Blake had promised to help him smuggle the large amount of powder into Arlania over the next few days. Once out of sight of Lockston, Emmett ran for his tree, and quickly changed into his uniform. He shifted and flew back to the river. He perched in a tree as he scanned the woods. Feeling confident that no one was around, he landed and shifted back to human.

Emmett stripped before entering the water. It was frigid at best. He held his breath and sat down, leaving only his head above the water. He concentrated on breathing slowly until his body became numb. He dunked his head quickly. His hair was getting longer. It now fell into his eyes. There was a man that cut the other soldier's hair, but Emmett just hadn't gotten around to it.

He finished bathing and reentered camp. He managed to slip into his tent unseen. Hopefully, no one had come looking for him during the last three hours.

Chapter 29

Bridget felt calmer after going to see Emmett. She was not happy that he was continuing to put his life at risk, but she had to admit he looked better than she thought he would. He did not even seem to be in pain. Bridget smiled when she remembered his shocked expression when he had seen her standing there.

"Lady Bridget, what is so amusing?" Miss Davenport asked.

Bri had to resist the urge to glare at the woman. She had been going on and on about how much more desirable Lord Young was now that he was a soldier. "I was just remembering a previous conversation." She ducked her head.

"Do tell? I love a good story." Miss Davenport pressed.

"I prefer not to." Bridget gave the woman a forced smile.

"Miss Davenport, have you met many of the recently arrived men in the last month? Bridget and I have not been to many functions since the Randell Ball." Bridget's mother said with a smile.

"Oh, yes. However, none of them compared to Lord Young." Miss Davenport fanned herself. "He is quite handsome. Though he could use some work when it comes to manners and conversation."

Bridget's mother tensed. "Lord Young?"

"Yes. He does not seem to be capable of having a conversation. Every time I have tried, he only gives one- or two-word responses. He has even walked away from me and several other ladies while someone was speaking to him." The other ladies murmured their agreement.

Bridget was starting to regret coming to this lady's tea. Her mother had talked her into it. They had been cooped up in the house for months now and they both needed to get out. Father had reluctantly allowed them to go. Their armed guards were waiting outside the house for them.

"Perhaps he was not interested in you, Miss Davenport." Miss Cynthia smiled. "After all, he was frequently at the Caverton's. Maybe they know more of his character."

"Is he always that beastly then, Lady Caverton?" Miss Davenport raised her brow. Bridget swore every lady present leaned forward, eager to hear more about Lord Young.

"I have not seen him act anything but the gentleman he is." Her mother's lips were tight. She was getting upset with these women. "He works closely with my husband and brother-in-law. He dines with us when their business runs late into the evening. He is lighthearted and can hold a conversation quite well. Isn't that right, Bridget?"

"He is quite the chatterbox when he wants to be." Bridget smiled at her mother. "Do you recall that night he kept going on and on about the constellations?"

Her mother laughed. "Your uncle finally cut him off after nearly two hours."

"Father told him to come back only if he could talk about something else." Bridget smiled.

"Lord Young? Constellations?" Miss Davenport's eyes flashed with irritation before her expression smoothed. "I dare say Lord Caverton must have a lot of patience to listen to someone speaking about stars for two hours."

"Oh, Lord Young wasn't speaking with Lord Caverton." Her mother smiled. "He was talking with Bridget. I do not know who knew more about the topic. Each equally participated."

Bridget felt her cheeks heat. She had forgotten they were not alone. Her parents and Uncle Oliver had just listened until the hour grew late. She missed him terribly. She gave herself a mental shake. She could think about Emmett later. Right now, she had to get through this gathering.

"Are the rumors true then?" Miss Cynthia asked. "I saw the way he looked at you shortly after the ball."

"I do not know what you mean." Bridget furrowed her brow. She did not recall him looking at her in any particular way.

"Like he wanted to shield you from Lord Percival and the vicious rumors he was trying to spread about you." Miss Cynthia smiled. "If only a man looked at me like that." She sighed.

"I...I do not recall such a look. And the rumors of an engagement are just that, rumors." Bridget shook her head.

Her mother changed the subject, steering the women into conversations that did not involve Emmett or Bridget. After another thirty minutes of avoiding stares and Miss Davenport's continued attempts to bring Emmett back up, Bridget climbed into the carriage.

The drive home was quiet. Neither she nor her mother talked. The front door opened as they ascended the front steps. Her father was pacing the entryway.

"Anna." Her father hurried over to her mother's side. "Where have you been?"

"Tea? You were okay with it this morning." Her mother said, confused.

"I wasn't expecting you to be gone all afternoon." He shook his head.

"While you two figure this out, I am going to go read until dinner." Bridget hurried up the stairs and headed for the library.

She wanted solitude in order to think over her visit with Emmett. He was completely shocked to see her, that was for sure. He had teased her. Again. The moment he put his arms around her, her tears threatened to fall. She struggled to keep them in, but she wasn't able to. Anna felt cocooned in his embrace, completely safe and protected.

Then the gunshots sounded, her blood had run cold. Emmett's only concern was the fact that she was there. He did not seem stressed or fazed by the gunshots. She had been so scared that he would run off to fight. His assurance that he wasn't at the moment, did little to calm her fears.

There was a moment when he wiped her tears that she had thought he might kiss her. Bridget chewed her bottom lip. Would she have let him? She sighed as she cracked her book open. She knew she would have.

Lord Emmett Young was a pain, impulsive, and teased her relentlessly. But he was also kind, protective, and she cared deeply for him. The past five months had been complete torture. She missed him and worried about him constantly. When her mother read the letter from Captain Trevors, she felt like her heart was shattering.

Bridget hated that it took so long to hear updates on Emmett's wellbeing. Going four or five weeks between hearing from him was driving her mad. Throw in the gossiping women of the Capital, and Bridget was ready to go home to Caverton Manor. She could not believe that the rumors about her and Emmett were still circulating.

Today had been difficult. Her heart hurt when she told everyone that she and Emmett were not engaged. When the rumor started right after the ball, Bridget had been embarrassed and uncomfortable with the very idea. Now, it just reminded her of how much she missed Emmett.

"Bridget? Are you in here?" Uncle Oliver called.

"I am over here." She said from her favorite chair.

"I thought you might be." He took a seat next to her. "I wanted to talk with you about something."

"Okay." She closed the book she had not even begun to read.

"Emmett." Her uncle said quietly.

Bridget swallowed hard. "What about him?" It had only been a few weeks since her flight up to see him. Had something happened?

"He said something a few weeks ago in his letter to me that I cannot seem to get out of my mind." Uncle Oliver ran his hand down his face. "He wrote that if he cannot finish what he set out to do, he will be re-enlisting for another six months."

Bridget gasped. "He wouldn't dare."

"I am worried he would. He seems determined to keep you safe." Her uncle studied her.

"I would never forgive him if he did. Re-enlisting is completely uncalled for. If he has not been able to do what he wanted during the last few months, than he needs to come back and rethink his options." Bridget stood and glared at her uncle. "He cannot do this." She stormed out of the library and went straight to her room.

What was he thinking? Why would he even consider such an option? She opened her locket and turned the dial. The man was going to get an earful. She whimpered as the pain slammed into her. Each time she used it, the pain got worse. Her mother did say there was a price for using it. Could the pain be the price?

It did not matter. Right now, she needed to speak with Emmett. She flew back to the camp. The sun was just setting and there was a lot of activity. A group of ten or so men were emerging from the trees.

Bridget perched on a tree limb as she watched the men below. Several went directly to a large tent on the south end of the camp. Others went to a path that branched southeast. Two men stood with their backs facing her, near a group of smaller tents.

She flew closer to get a better look at them. Emmett and Milo. Her heart sped up. He was looking much better than a few weeks ago. She had not noticed just how long his hair had grown when they were in the dark medical tent. He was covered in dirt and sweat. He was unshaven, giving him an untamed look.

Milo saluted before walking away. Emmett watched him go and she could see how tired he looked. He ducked his head as he stepped into the nearest tent.

Bridget flew through the opening before the door was dropped into place. She landed on the pillow. She heard Emmett curse, and she turned to look at him.

"You are insane!" He whispered harshly. "What on earth are you doing here?" He held up his hand. "Scratch that. Do not shift until I have you somewhere more private."

He reached out and picked her up. He was gentle, even though he looked livid. He put her in his coat pocket as he muttered to himself. She could not make out what he was saying, but she had a pretty good idea he was talking about her.

It was dark in the pocket, but she could feel he was walking quickly. "Milo."

"Lieutenant? Is everything okay?" Milo sounded confused.

"Just a little out of sorts tonight. Have all the men returned to camp?" Emmett practically growled.

"Uh...I believe so. The river is getting colder, and no one likes to spend too much time in it." Milo said slowly. "Are you planning on sitting in it again? Is your side still bothering you?"

"I was planning on soaking to get rid of the pain on my left side." Emmett's voice had a hint of amusement in it. Bridget glared at the tiny bit of light at the top of the pocket. She was on his left side. "Stop looking at me like that. I will be fine by morning."

"I will make sure you get some time."

"Thank you, Milo." Emmett began walking again. It felt like forever before he allowed her back out of his pocket. "All right, we need to talk." He was definitely angry with her.

She was okay with that because she was furious with him. She flew several feet away before shifting back to human. She balled her hands into fists as she faced him. "I would rather punch you in the face than talk." She huffed.

Emmett's brows rose in surprise. "What have I done to earn your ire, besides what we have already discussed? You are the one flying into a warzone."

Bridget turned her back to him and walked away. Her anger was growing. Could he really not see how ridiculous his plan was? Did he really not know why she was so upset with him? She heard Emmett sigh before he grabbed her hand, pulling her to a stop.

"Bri, what has you so upset?" His voice was softer, though he remained tense.

She tried to pull her hand from his, but he didn't let her. He tried to cup her face. She slapped his hand away. "You are an idiot. A pain." She seethed.

"Bridget..." He started to say, but she smacked his chest.

"Let go of me, Emmett." She attempted to pull away from him again. He put his other arm around her waist and drew her up against him. "I said let go." Bridget dropped her eyes to his chest as tears burned them.

"Not until you tell me why you are so mad at me." Emmett said softly.

"Re-enlistment, Emmett." She hit his chest. "Why on earth would you even consider doing something so idiotic?" She hit him again. "I can't believe you would even think about doing it." She smacked him again.

Emmett took several steps back. Before she knew what he was doing, she was engulfed by freezing water. She gasped as she threw her arms around Emmett's neck. Her head and shoulders were the only things above the surface. "Loosen your grip, Bri. I can't breathe." Emmett whispered.

"I can't swim." She whimpered.

"Bri, I have you. Nothing is going to happen to you." Emmett chuckled.

"This isn't funny." She hissed, but she did loosen her hold around his neck.

"It is a little." Emmett tucked her hair behind her ear.

She scowled at him. "I am still angry with you."

Emmett smiled at her. "I figured as much. Who told you I was re-enlisting?"

"Uncle Oliver said you wrote him saying that you would if you could not finish what you wanted to do." She shivered.

"That is the plan if I cannot finish this." Emmett sighed. "I can't go back until this is done, Bri."

"You can." Bridget argued. "We can figure something else out." She buried her face in his neck as she shivered again.

Emmett began walking. Bridget's arms tightened around him. She allowed him to carry her to shore. He slowly lowered her feet to the ground. "I have to." He whispered. Bridget shook her head. "It is the only way."

"The only way to what?" She leaned back and glared at him.

He cupped her face. "To keep you safe, Bridget. He is coming to kill you."

"You are trying to protect me?" She snapped. "How about this?" She pushed against his chest. "You re-enlist, and I go directly to Crossford."

Emmett tensed. "Don't even joke about doing something like that."

Bridget used his moment of surprise and stepped out of his arms. "I'm not joking, Emmett. I will do it." She started to walk away. "Food for thought." She said over her shoulder.

Emmett did not let her get far. He pulled her back against him. "You are not handing yourself over to them." He whispered angrily in her ear.

His arms were tightly around her waist holding her against him. Her back was against his chest. She turned to face him. His jaw was clenched, and his expression was hard.

"Then you know what you have to do." Bridget raised her brow.

Emmett growled in frustration. "You are a pain. Seriously, Bri. If you go to Crossford, they will kill you. If they make it through the border, they will kill you. What part of that do you not get?"

"I understand what is at stake. But there has to be a different option to stop it."

Emmett sighed as he rested his forehead against hers. "Bri…"

"Lieutenant?" Milo called out. Bridget pressed herself more into Emmett. "Sir, are you all right?"

"I am fine, Milo. What do you need?" Emmett asked.

"You didn't seem yourself when you left camp. I just wanted to make sure you were not suffering from another infection or something." Milo said in concern.

"Milo, I am better than I have been in months." Emmett kissed the top of Bridget's head. She looked up at him. "I want you to go back to camp. I will be back in a little bit."

"If you are the same woman from the medic tent, thank you for giving this crazy guy a purpose." Milo chuckled. "But a warzone is not safe for you to keep visiting him."

Bridget giggled when Emmett groaned. "Go away, Milo." Emmett looked over his shoulder. "I need to talk some sense into her before sending her home where she belongs."

"Talk? I am eighteen, sir. I know that married couples kiss and stuff." Milo laughed.

"Milo, thank you for watching Emmett's back, but we aren't married. We are friends and I am trying to convince him to stop being an idiot." Bridget smiled as she laid her head on Emmett's shoulder.

"Might I suggest something?" Milo asked.

"Milo…" Emmett warned.

"Just marry her already, sir. Both of you will be much happier. Captain Trevors can even do it."

"I am not going to marry her in a warzone." Emmett could not believe what Milo was suggesting.

"Suit yourself." Milo said before turning and walking back towards camp.

Bridget bit her lip to keep from smiling. Emmett's hand moved to the back of her head as he continued to hold her. She shivered again. "I cannot believe you dragged me into that water."

"It got you to stop hitting me." Emmett sighed. "What am I going to do with you?" he asked.

"Milo's idea wasn't too bad." She muttered quietly to herself.

Emmett froze and she realized he had heard her. Bridget's cheeks flushed with embarrassment. She closed her eyes, wishing she could reverse time instead of freezing it. She hadn't meant for him to hear her. She was too afraid to move, not sure what he was going to do.

"We are in a warzone, Bri. Not to mention your family would kill me when they found out." Emmett finally said. "We can't just walk into camp and ask Captain Trevors to marry us. You aren't even supposed to be here."

A stick snapped and Emmett pushed Bridget behind him as he scanned the trees. There was movement to the south, but he could not make out what it was. This was not good. He should have kept Milo close by just in case something like this happened.

Chapter 30

Bridget clung to the back of Emmett's shirt. The noise had come from the opposite direction Milo had gone, so chances were it was not someone from the camp. A fox suddenly appeared followed by a wolf. Her heart lodged in her throat.

"Oh, no." she muttered. Her father was going to kill her. She stepped out from behind Emmett, but he pulled her back.

"What are you doing?" he asked her, not taking his eyes off the wolf and fox. They were slowly approaching. "I am not thrilled that you came here in the first place, and I will not let you put yourself in any more danger."

"Emmett…" Bri whispered.

"No, you are going to stay behind me until I know it is safe, and then you are going home." He snapped.

Her father shifted first, followed by her uncle. They both had stoney expressions as they glared at Emmett. Bridget felt him tense beside her. This was not good, not good at all.

"Father…" Bridget tried to explain, but he held up his hand stopping her. "Before you start yelling at me, you should know that the military camp isn't too far away." She pushed on as she stepped back around Emmett.

"What were you thinking, Bri?" Her father said, far too calmly. "Oliver followed you to your room and saw you shift before flying out your window. This is not a safe place for a young lady to be."

"I am sorry to have caused you to worry." Bridget said quietly as she looked at the ground. "I was coming back home ."

"You were coming back." Her father said with barely restrained anger. "You should never have gone in the first place. How many times have you done this?"

Bridget glanced at Emmett. He gave her a look of concern. "Um…once before, right after Captain Trevor's letter."

Her father threw up his hands before pacing away. "Bri, do you realize what this could do to you?" Oliver asked.

"It can't be worse than some of the other rumors about me." She said before clamping her mouth shut. Her father whirled back around with fire in his eyes.

Emmett stepped in front of her. "Sir, I asked her to come." Bridget's eyes widened in surprise. What was he trying to do, get himself killed?

"How long do you think we have been here?" Oliver laughed in disbelief.

Emmett swallowed hard. He had no idea how this encounter was going to play out. Her father had every right to string him up and leave him to die. He had been holding Bridget for quite some time before Milo showed up.

"You seemed pretty angry that she was here for a man that invited her." Lord Mason stated. "The only thing I am confused on is why neither one of you flat out turned down the suggestion of the young man that was here earlier?"

Emmett glanced at Bridget. This wasn't exactly how he thought this would go. "Lieutenant!" Milo yelled. He was running towards them. "They are calling up our unit." He stayed just out of sight.

Emmett swore. He put his arm around Bridget and dragged her over to her father. He shoved her to him. "Get her out of here." He ordered before turning around to head back to camp.

"Emmett!" She cried.

Bridget broke free of her father's hold. She ran to Emmett, reaching him just as he turned around. He held her tight while she clung to him. She felt a hand on her back and knew it was either her father or uncle. She shook her head.

Emmett leaned back and looked down at her. "You have to go, Bridget. I need to know you are safe and as far away from here as possible." He smoothed her hair back from her face.

"Sir." Milo said anxiously.

Emmett kissed her cheek. "I will come back for you." He whispered. "Lord Mason, please keep her safe. Oh, she has a locket that I think she uses to shift. Make sure she doesn't use it again."

Bridget smacked him before he kissed her forehead. He gave her a gentle but firm push backwards. Arms wrapped around her, keeping her in place as Emmett started to jog away.

"I will never forgive you if you don't." She called after him.

He turned around and smiled at her. "I have something to live for. I won't be screwing that up." He winked at her before disappearing into the trees.

Bridget felt like she couldn't breathe. She turned and buried her face in her father's chest as she began to cry. His arms tightened around her. The sound of distant gunfire sounded as she squeezed her eyes closed.

"We need to move. The fighting sounds closer." Uncle Oliver said quietly.

Bri numbly let her father lead her south. She knew they could travel faster if they all shifted, but there were risks in that. Her father and uncle were predators, and on top of that, Shifters were hunted more than the animals themselves. She could not believe Emmett told them about her necklace. He just ruined any chance she had of coming back to see him. But she figured that was his plan to begin with.

They had been walking for nearly thirty minutes. The sounds of fighting had faded not long ago. Suddenly her father stopped walking, his body tense. She looked at him. He was scanning the woods around him. Her uncle looked tense as well. More so than they had when they started.

A man came running into the small clearing they were crossing. When he spotted them, he stopped. He seemed to be studying them. Her father slowly moved her behind him as her uncle moved to stand next to him.

The man approached cautiously. "I am sorry to have scared you. I am seeking shelter. Might I stay in your barn for the night?" he asked, looking over his shoulder.

"I am afraid we cannot offer you lodging." Uncle Oliver said calmly. "We are mere travelers. We ourselves are looking for a place to stay for the night."

"You travel with a woman and do not have shelter?" The man sounded skeptical.

"My daughter is none of your concern." Her father stated firmly.

"Easy friend, I mean no harm. I was just inquiring." The man moved a little closer. "Could you tell me which way the nearest town is?"

"An hour's walk east of here." Her uncle said.

"I am heading south." The man was close enough now that she could see his facial features. He had scars marring his flesh. "Looks like that is the same way you are headed." He scratched his jaw. "We can travel together."

"I do not think that is wise. And we are headed west." Her father became more tense.

The man smiled, his scars causing his skin to pinch in an odd way. He looked almost demonic. "I wasn't asking."

He lunged for her father, and she ran for the trees. She quickly hid behind one and watched the fight. Her uncle was the first to go down. The stranger's fighting skills were definitely superior. In less than five minutes, both her father and uncle lay motionless on the ground. The man looked in her direction and she froze in fear. He started moving towards her and she ran.

Bridget did not make it very far. The man caught her easily, turning her to face him. His grip on her arms was painful to begin with but when their eyes met, his grip tightened, causing her to cry out.

*   *   *

Emmett made it back to camp just as his men were lining up. He grabbed his gear and rifle and turned to them. "I know you all are tired, but our fellow soldiers need our help. Move out." He ordered.

Milo fell into step beside him. "Where is...?" he asked quietly.

"Hopefully safely away from here." Emmett gave Milo a look that told him to leave it alone. "I need you to spread the word for all Arlanians to stay off Devil's Staircase."

"Yes, sir." Milo jogged ahead, quickly spreading what Emmett said.

They reached the battle in minutes. Close to fifty men were fighting among the rocks and trees. It was easy to see that the Freynians outnumbered the Arlanians three to one. This had to be the army Blake had talked about.

A man ran out of the trees, swinging his sword. Emmett pulled his up just in time to block the strike from connecting with his head. He parried a few more strikes before delivering one of his own. The man fell and Emmett moved on. He needed to get to a vantage point to see when the rest of the army was coming through. Once they were, he would blow up the pass.

Emmett was struggling to get to where he needed to be. For each man he killed, two more would appear. His frustration was mounting. He needed to blow the pass soon. Milo was at his back as they faced off with three men. Everyone stopped for a second when a scream of pain echoed off the walls.

"Sir, was that a woman?" Milo asked after parrying a strike.

"I think so." Emmett's heart rate increased as panic grew. He lunged forward and stabbed the man in front of him. Emmett had a sickening feeling that the scream had come from Bridget. He needed to find her. He did not waste any more time. He aggressively attacked the other two men, eliminating them quickly. Another scream echoed.

"You need to go." Milo looked worried. "We can handle this."

Emmett nodded and ran in the direction he thought the screams were coming from. The echoes made it impossible to know for sure. He dodged small groups of men fighting, fully focusing on reaching the owner of the screams.

A flash of blue in the rocks drew his notice. Bridget had been wearing a light blue dress. The moonlight gave him enough light as he jumped over rocks and slipped through narrow openings. He needed her to scream again, so he would know if he was going in the right direction. He was ready to yell in frustration, but he remained quiet and kept going.

"I said let go of me!" Bridget yelled.

"Shut up, girl." A man snapped. "Keep fighting and I might just push you over the edge right here, instead of making you an example."

Emmett veered to his left and stopped. They were almost to the start of Devil's Staircase. The man was taking her back to Freynia. He could not let that happen. Emmett grabbed a large rock and threw it so it hit near the man's head. He spun around to face Emmett.

"Looks like your screams brought company." The man backhanded Bridget across the face. She fell against the boulder next to her.

Emmett was seeing red. "Let her go." He warned.

"Do you have any idea who I am? Do you have any idea how many men you are going to lose tonight?" The man looked amused.

"Chief Talon of Crossford, I will only tell you this one more time. Release her." Emmett took a step closer as he readjusted his grip on his sword. The man was well over six feet tall. He was huge compared to Emmett.

Talon laughed. "You think you can save her? That is rich." He continued to laugh as he grabbed Bridget by the throat. Her eyes flicked to Emmett. Fear shone in them as she scratched the back of Talon's hands in her attempt to make him let go. "That is the problem with Arlanians. They think a woman is worth more than she actually is."

Emmett took out his dagger and threw it. The blade embedded in Talon's wrist, just below Bridget's hands. Talon released her and she gasped for air. She stumbled in Emmett's direction, and he ran to her. She started crying when she got to him.

"Are you okay?" He whispered. He kept his eyes on Talon. "Bridget, are you hurt?" he said again when she didn't respond.

"He...he killed father and Uncle Ollie." She cried.

"I need you to shift and fly to the camp. Wait for me there." Emmett kissed the top of her head before moving her behind him. Talon was recovering.

"It hurts every time I do. I do not know if I can." Emmett could feel her shaking as she grabbed the back of his shirt.

"There are too many fights going on between here and the camp. I need you to do this, Bri. I need you out of harm's way." Emmett said desperately.

Her hands released the back of his shirt. A moment later, she gasped and whimpered. Her head rested on his back for a split second before she was gone. Emmett heard a small chirp, but his eyes remained fixed on the threat.

"What have you done with her?" Talon demanded when he realized Bridget was no longer with Emmett. "She is mine. You will not take this away from me!" He roared.

Emmett got in his fighting stance. "You are not taking her."

Talon drew his own sword. He slowly advanced toward Emmett. Hatred burned in his eyes. Normally, Emmett would have moved back so that his enemy did not have the high ground, but he needed to keep him on the pass. He could not let him back on Arlanian soil.

Talon brought his sword down and Emmett blocked it. He spun and tried to slash Emmett's side. Again, Emmett blocked. The strength behind Talon's attack was surprising. The clang of their swords rang off the cliffs.

Sweat dripped from Emmett's face as he pushed Talon back slowly. They had been exchanging blows for a while and Emmett was starting to tire. Talon was like a machine. Each strike that Emmett blocked reverberated down his sword and through his arms. He did not know how much longer he would be able to keep this up.

The hoot of an owl reached his ears. Milo. The army was coming. They needed to set off the explosives now if they had any hope of stopping the army. The only problem was that Emmet was in the blast range. He grunted as he slammed into Talon, taking them both to the ground.

"Do it, Milo!" he yelled. He punched Talon in the face.

Talon rolled them. He slammed his fist so hard into Emmett's head that Emmett was seeing stars. Before Emmett could get his senses back, an elbow slammed into his face. He took several more hard blows before he was able to roll them again.

"I said, now!" He yelled again, just before he took a fist to the stomach.

An explosion shook the mountain. Talon stopped his attack, and Emmett kicked him off of him. Another explosion. Emmett scrambled to his feet and tried to run back down the trail, but he was tackled from behind. Talon sat on him and grabbed his throat.

Emmett tried to break his hold, but Talon only squeezed harder. Emmett glanced around, trying to find something that could help. A large rock was to his right. He reached for it. His fingertips barely grazed the rock. Emmett grabbed Talon's wrists and pushed hard. He was able to get enough air in that he wasn't going to pass out. Another explosion caused the ground to shake. He made another attempt for the rock. This time he was able to grasp it firmly in his hand.

He slammed it into the side of Talon's head. Talon fell to the side and Emmett rolled to his feet. There was no way Emmett was going to make it off the mountain in time. He started to shift just as the final explosion went off.

Chapter 31

Bridget flew into the tent Emmett had been in earlier. She shifted back to human. Her shoulder was killing her, but she ignored it. There were bigger problems at the moment. She chewed her nails as she paced. How long was this going to take? Would Emmett be okay? What of her father and uncle? She needed to see if they were alive.

Bridget hesitated before leaving the tent. Emmett had told her to wait for him here. But he did not know the full situation. He could not blame her for checking on her family. She squared her shoulders and walked out of the tent.

The camp was oddly quiet. The past two times she had been here, there were men around. Now there was no one. The sounds of fighting were still going strong. Bridget did not know what to do. Her shoulder stung and she looked down.

Her abductor had stabbed her right shoulder when she attempted to run away. That was when she had screamed. He had hit her and yelled at her to be quiet before dragging her towards a mountain pass. The sight of the blood had her head spinning. She put the back of her hand to her forehead as she closed her eyes.

"What the...?" She heard a man say. Bridget looked over to see a man in white hospital clothes standing near a large tent. "Who are you and how did you get here?" He looked confused and a little irritated.

"Lieutenant Young..." she felt weak. "He sent me..."

"Ma'am? Are you alright?" The man moved in her direction, but she blacked out before he reached her.

"I don't know, sir. She was standing in the middle of camp and then she fainted." A man said quietly.

Bridget slowly blinked her eyes open. She was in the medical tent. Two men stood a short distance away. They had their heads close together as they discussed her.

"And she was injured?" The second man asked.

"Yes, sir. She has a stab wound in her right shoulder. It was quite deep."

"Do we know how she was injured or how she ended up at our camp?"

"All she said was Lieutenant Young's name and said he sent her here."

They looked over at her and Bridget sat up. She winced at the pain in her shoulder. She glanced at it to see a thick bandage poking out of a large dark grey shirt. Where was her dress? The men moved closer, and she returned her attention to them.

"We are in the middle of a battle, so I am going to cut right to the chase. Who are you? What are you doing here? And how did you get injured?" The second man asked.

"Um…My name is Lady Bridget Caverton." Bridget did not want to get Emmett into any trouble by mentioning her visits. "I was taken by a man. He attacked my father and uncle a few miles south of here. He was trying to take me to Freynia. He was the one that stabbed me."

"And Lieutenant Young?" He asked, narrowing his eyes.

"He saw the man trying to take me on a mountain pass. He saved me and said to wait for him here." Bridget glanced at the door. "How long have I been here?"

"Ma'am, I found you about half an hour ago. I stitched up your wound immediately."

An explosion caused her to jump. Both men ran for the tent opening. Bridget followed them, thankful that she had on a pair of men's trousers as well as the shirt. She had to hold the waist to keep them up. She stopped just outside when she saw black smoke billowing into the air near where the fighting was taking place. Another explosion rocked the camp. What was happening? Where was Emmett?

"No." Bridget breathed out. She tried to run to where the smoke was coming from. The second man grabbed her, holding her back. "Let me go!" She yelled, desperately trying to get away.

"If Young sent you here, it was for a reason." The man shook her shoulders. "If you go running into danger, you will be a distraction."

Bridget stopped struggling as she looked from the man to the smoke. He was right. She would just be a distraction. Emmett had said a single distraction could be the thing to cause a fighter to lose. Tears course down her cheeks. She watched in horror as eight more explosions went off in succession.

Men started to emerge from the trees assisting the injured a few minutes later. The first man called out for his team. They met the injured and helped them to the tent. The second man guided Bridget to a different tent.

"I know you want to see if Lieutenant Young has returned, but I am going to need you to stay here. My medical staff needs to be able to attend the wounded without an extra body to try to navigate around." The man said.

"Sir, I...I cannot just stay here." Bridget argued.

"Captain Trevors." He bowed quickly. "And yes, you can and you will. You are injured and do not know our routines for workflow. You will only be in the way."

Bridget grudgingly nodded her head. She sat on the chair and gingerly touched her injured shoulder. Captain Trevors watched her for a long moment before leaving. Now that she was alone, she allowed herself to cry. To feel the fear and pain of the last hour. The loss of her father and uncle, the unknown state of Emmett. She allowed herself to feel all of it.

Eventually her tears and the chaos of the battle's aftermath ceased. The sun was peaking over the nearby mountains. Yet no one had come for her. Bridget was restless. She needed to get some sort of information before she went insane.

Bridget peeked her head out of the tent. Not very many people were around. She walked toward the medic tent and slipped inside without anyone noticing her. She looked around for the captain, but did not see him. She debated whether she should go look for him or go back to Emmett's tent.

A groan of pain in a nearby bed caused her to look over. A young man was laying there. His face was contorted with pain. Bridget moved to his side and put a hand on his arm. He looked so young. Maybe a few years younger than her own twenty years. There was a bowl of water on a table next to the bed with a cloth in it. She wrung it out before dabbing the soldier's forehead.

"What is your name, soldier?" she asked quietly.

"Glen, ma'am." He grunted out.

"Would you like a drink of water, Glen?" He nodded and she assisted him in getting a small drink.

"Thank you, ma'am." He winced.

"Where are you hurt?" Bridget once again wiped his brow.

"Just a stab wound. Doc said I would make a full recovery, but that doesn't make it hurt any less."

"What a coincidence." Bridget smiled at him when he looked at her. "I was stabbed too. Mine is in my shoulder. And I agree. The pain is not at all comfortable."

"Mine is in the leg." Glen's eyes dropped to her shoulder. "How did you get stabbed? And no offense, but I do not recall a woman being in camp."

Bridget laughed. "I arrived yesterday. Some crazy man thought he could take me to Freynia and stabbed me when I tried to escape." She put the cloth back in the bowl. "I will let you rest, Glen. I will be back to check on you later." She patted his hand and stood.

"Thank you, Ma'am. For speaking with me. It was a pleasure to meet you." Glen gave her a bright smile.

She smiled back as she headed for the door. She looked back. Every bed was full. Men were groaning in pain and the atmosphere felt heavy. She glanced back at Glen. He still had a small smile on his face, even though his eyes were closed. He seemed more at peace.

Bridget could do nothing but wait for word of Emmett. If she could brighten these men's day, even a little while she was here, she should do so. She moved to the bed across from Glen's. The man looked to be asleep, so she moved on.

She stopped and spoke with every man that was awake. They all seemed in slightly better spirits as she headed for the door. She walked outside and looked north. A few of the men had told her that they had been fighting when the mountain just started exploding. Three of the men were there for injuries caused by flying debris from the explosions.

"My Lady!" A man called. She turned in his direction. "My name is Milo Peterson. I have been looking for you."

"I was visiting with the wounded. What can I do for you, sir?" She held her arm. It was really starting to pain her.

"First, we will get you something for the pain you are in. Then, I have a few questions for you."

Bridget nodded and followed Milo back to the medical tent. He gave the doctor there an earful about not giving her anything for the pain. When she was given something, Milo led her back outside.

"What did you need to ask me?" Bridget asked.

"Ah, yes. We have two men that claim to be looking for a woman. They say she was kidnapped."

"May I see them?" Bridget didn't want to get her hopes up, but she was failing. "Please." Milo looked torn before finally nodding. He led her to a tent that had armed guards standing at the door. She stepped inside and immediately saw Captain Trevors. He was standing with his back to her. In front of him were two men. They were kneeling with two more guards holding blades to the back of their necks. Their hands looked to be tied behind their backs.

"We have told you. We were attacked by a man. He took my daughter. We came here seeking assistance in finding her." Her father said.

"Daddy!" Bridget ran forward and dropped to her knees in front of him.

"Bridget." He sighed in relief as she leaned into him. He kissed the top of her head. "Are you hurt?" He asked with emotion heavy in his voice. "Please tell me you are not hurt."

"Release them." Captain Trevors barked out. As soon as her father's hands were cut loose from the ropes binding them, he wrapped her in a tight embrace. She gasped as pain shot through her shoulder. Her father released her and leaned back to see her face. "Lady Bridget had a stab wound to her shoulder when we found her in our camp last night."

"Bri." Her father hugged her again, this time more gently.

"I know I do not hold a candle to your father, but do I get a hug?" Uncle Oliver asked. Bridget smiled and she hugged him as well. "How is Emmett?"

Bridget looked at Captain Trevors. She wanted to know the same thing. He seemed to realize they were all waiting for him to say something. "Uh...As of right now, Lieutenant Young is unaccounted for."

Her uncle pulled her head to his chest, and she turned more into him. Emmett was missing. "It will be okay, Bri." He whispered.

"I need some air." Bridget rushed out of the tent.

She ran to Emmett's tent and put the flap down. She needed privacy. She needed Emmett. Bridget lay down on the cot and closed her eyes. She took a deep breath and choked back a sob. The bed smelled like him. She curled into a ball and cried herself to sleep.

*   *   *

Three days. It had been three long days and still no sign of Emmett. He wasn't the only one missing, there were a total of five. The men that were not injured took turns sleeping, being on guard duty, and searching for the missing men. Bridget spent her time visiting with the wounded. Captain Trevors had been gracious and allowed her and her uncle to stay. Her father returned home to let her mother know what was going on.

Bridget was just walking back to the medical tent after getting some lunch. She promised Glen that she would play cards with him. She did not know how she would. Her arm was in a sling and her pain was constant. She hid it from everyone, not wanting to be a burden. It was bad enough that she had fainted on the second day at the camp.

One of the missing men was brought in on a stretcher. She had run into the surgical suite, which was just a curtained off portion of the medical tent. There was so much blood. Bridget did not even get to see the man's face before she fainted.

It had been embarrassing to wake up in Emmett's tent with her uncle sitting close by. He explained to her that she had lost consciousness after seeing the blood. Trevors made two rules that day. She was not allowed to leave the camp for any reason, and she was not allowed in the medical tent if someone was being treated.

"Lady Bridget!" Milo yelled, stopping her just shy of entering the medical tent. "You are not allowed in there at the moment. I would be happy to keep you company until you are cleared to enter again."

"Has another been found?" Bridget asked as she looked back at the tent.

"Uh…three, actually, but only one survivor. He is being evaluated now." Milo said nervously.

He wouldn't look at her. He had never acted like this before. "Who has been found, Milo? And do not try to lie to me." She narrowed her eyes.

"The two deceased were from my unit, Jason and Raul." He gestured back to the tent that the meals were served in. "Shall we grab something to eat?"

"I just ate." She said stiffly. "Who is inside?" She was shaking. Milo's nervousness was making her think that Emmett was inside. "He is, isn't he?" She looked back at the tent flap. "Emmett is in there."

"My Lady, please. He was in really rough shape. We thought he was dead at first." Milo looked pleadingly at her. "His leg was crushed under a pile of rocks. He might lose it."

Milo grabbed her arm to hold her back, but she knew she would be sent home if she entered. There was no way she would go home now. "Will he live?" she asked quietly.

"I am not sure." Milo sighed. "Come now. Let's go wait in the mess tent."

Bridget reluctantly followed Milo. Each step made her heart hurt more and more. All she wanted to do was see Emmett. She sat quietly and ran her finger along the grain of the wood table. Milo brought her a cup and set it down in front of her. He then sat down across from her. Time seemed to tick by at a snail's pace. Milo remained, though he had taken up tapping his heel.

"You do not need to babysit me." Bridget sighed. "I am going to lay down." She had missed her dose of pain medicine, and she was hurting.

"I have my orders." Milo stood and followed her out.

Bridget only made it two steps outside when someone called her name. She stopped and turned toward the camp doctor. "How are you feeling, My Lady?" His attitude toward her had changed quickly when he realized she was a titled woman. He no longer treated her like an irritant. He was almost smothering.

"I am alive, sir. That is all I could hope for." She gave him a small smile. It was all she could muster at the moment.

"You are in pain. I can see it in your eyes. Come on, it is time you took your medicine."

"She is not allowed in the medical tent right now." Milo piped up.

"I am fine. I will just go lay down for a while." She turned to go, but the doctor grabbed her arm.

"All the blood has been cleaned up. You need to stay on top of the pain, My Lady, or it will become much worse and harder to get it under control."

"All right." she said tiredly.

The doctor pulled her to the medical tent, with Milo tagging along. She kept her eyes on the floor. Now that she was within reach, she did not know if she wanted to see how badly Emmett was hurt. He led her to a chair at the back of the tent next to a bed. If she remembered right, the man that had occupied this bed had returned to duty.

She sighed and put her head in her hand. Milo touched her shoulder lightly. She looked up and he handed her first the pain pills and then a cup of water. "Thank you, Milo." She closed her eyes and held her arm closer to her body. Maybe tomorrow she would be able to see Emmett.

"Have I told you lately how much..."

"Emmett!" she gasped as she jumped to her feet. He was lying in the bed with a smile on his lips. His face was bruised and swollen with several cuts. He looked much like he had after coming back from the Bird's Nest. She sat back down as she continued to stare at him in surprise. He reached over and cupped her face. She closed her eyes, fighting her tears.

"Bri." he said softly. She opened her eyes and looked at him. "Come here."

She glanced around and saw that both the doctor and Milo had disappeared. She sat on the side of his bed. "I am so mad at you right now." She glared at him as a tear slid down her cheek.

"I know." He tried to reposition himself and pain filled his expression. "Can you save my lecture for another time? I feel terrible." He closed his eyes. She gently brushed his hair off his forehead.

He moved his hand to her waist. He began to relax as she slowly combed her hand through his hair. Bridget only stopped when his hand fell away from her, and she knew he was sleeping. She carefully got off the bed before moving the chair closer. Her pain medicine was starting to kick in. They always made her sleepy.

She grabbed Emmett's hand and laid her head on the mattress. She closed her eyes as she listened to his even breathing. She felt so drained, on top of the medication she had taken.

Chapter 32

The pain in his leg had Emmett jolting awake. He could not get comfortable. He tried to sit up, but something tightened on his hand. He looked over to find Bridget. She was asleep sitting in a chair with her head on the bed and her hand in his. That could not be comfortable.

Emmett slowly moved his hand out from underneath hers and placed it on her head. She did not even stir. He ran his fingers through her hair, but still, she did not move. Emmett grew worried as he studied her. No one slept that deeply.

"Her pain medicine makes her sleep." Milo said quietly. Emmett glanced at his friend who was sitting in a chair at the foot of the bed. "You should be sleeping, sir."

"Sleeping is not in the cards for me right now. And what pain medicine? Why does she need pain medicine?" Emmett kept his voice quiet, though he felt like lashing out at something. He focused on brushing her hair with his fingers.

"She was stabbed, sir." Milo sat back in his chair. "She said she tried to get away, but the man stabbed her shoulder." Milo glanced at Bridget. "She had a rough day. Doc lost track of time and did not give her the meds for several hours."

"How did he lose track of time? I asked you to look after her. How did you not know?" Emmett was fuming. The thought of Talon stabbing Bridget, and her in pain, was triggering him.

"We brought you back to camp and captain had his rules, so I took her to the mess hall. She didn't say anything. She just sat quietly for five hours until she said she was going to go lay down." Milo said defensively.

"What rules?"

"She is not allowed in the medical tent when a patient is being evaluated." Seeing Emmett's confused expression, Milo continued. "She has a little thing about blood. She passes out when she sees it. Gave Doc a heart attack when she went down the first time."

"Blood?" Emmett was surprised. "Really?"

"Don't laugh at me, Emmett." Bridget said without lifting her head. Her words were a little slurred.

"I am not laughing, Bri. I am just surprised. You did not seem to have a problem when you saw me after my two weeks in the ring." Emmett continued running his fingers through the silky strands.

"I was as surprised as Doc was." She blinked her eyes open and looked at him. A small smile curved her lips. "Plus, you only had swelling and bruising that time."

"You know, you would be more comfortable on a bed." Emmett traced the lines of her face.

"I'm too tired to walk back to the tent." She closed her eyes.

"I think there is room up here with me." Emmett grinned when her eyes shot open.

"I will have to draw the line there, sir." Milo chuckled. "Maybe if you two were hitched…"

"Go get Captain Trevors." Emmett winked at Bridget. Her cheeks heated as she slowly sat up.

"You have got to be kidding?" Milo laughed in disbelief. "Your bride is drugged and can barely keep her eyes open. You are in so much pain you can't sleep. Her father would have to approve of the match, and everyone is off on various tasks."

"Uncle Oliver is around here somewhere. Maybe he could give his permission." Bridget smiled.

Emmett laughed. "Have I told you lately how much I love you?"

Bridget's eyes narrowed. "I do not believe you have ever said you loved me."

"Bridget Caverton, I love you." Emmett groaned when he tried to move his leg the smallest amount. He breathed deeply for several minutes. When he looked back at Bridget, she was watching him in concern. "Will you marry me, Bri?"

"Hey, she is going to marry me!" Someone called from the other side of the medical tent.

Bridget started laughing. "So many eligible men. How am I going to choose?"

Emmett scowled at her as he grabbed her hand. He tugged her close enough that he was able to cup her face. He pressed his lips to hers before she could react. "You are a pain." He whispered before kissing her again.

"Are you kissing her?" Glen called. "I can't see from where I am."

Bridget sat back with her cheeks a deep red. "Do not tell me that was your first kiss, Lady Bridget." Milo laughed.

"I...Well...No...I mean..." Bridget covered her face.

"The only answer you better be saying is 'yes'." Emmett narrowed his eyes as he studied her.

Several men chuckled, which caused Bridget to glare at Emmett. This was all his fault. "I am going to find my uncle." She stood to go but Emmett grabbed her hand. She looked at him and he looked almost panicked. "Is something wrong?"

"Several things." He said. "First, my blasted leg is killing me. The woman I fully intend to marry has yet to give me her answer. She is also reluctant to say whether she has kissed other men. And..."

"Okay. Okay. Okay." Bridget sighed. "I get you are not the happiest. Milo, find Doc to get Emmett something for the pain. I need to speak with my uncle." She tried to move toward the door, but Emmett's hand tightened on hers.

"You are not going anywhere. I need you where I can see you." Emmett said firmly.

"You are being a little..." Bridget paused as she tried to think of the right word.

"Possessive?" Milo asked.

"No." Bridget shook her head. She studied Emmett for a minute. "Not possessive."

"A man that almost lost the woman he loves." Milo suggested.

"Maybe." She tried to hide her smile.

"You two are so funny." Emmett grumbled. "Bri, please. I watched as Talon dragged you around and hit you. I heard your screams. I can't be away from you right now."

Bridget sat down next to him. He put his hand on her waist. He let her pull her hand from his. She gently touched his face. He closed his eyes and took a deep breath. Bridget kissed him softly. "How can I ask for my uncle's permission if I cannot go find him?" she asked as she sat up.

"Where is Lord Oliver and Captain Trevors!" Emmett yelled.

Bridget covered his mouth with her good hand. "You are the pain." She tried not to laugh. "Why are you yelling? I can go find Uncle Oliver."

Emmett grinned at her. "I told you; you are not leaving my side. Someone else can fetch him for us. Now, you still haven't answered if that was your first kiss."

"Was it yours?" She questioned back with a raised brow.

"You two are kissing now?" Her uncle said behind her, causing her to jump. "I thought you said it would be unlikely to have a wedding when you got back."

"It was unlikely." Emmett shrugged. "I thought you were talking about the women on the street."

"I was present when you two were saying goodbye." Uncle Oliver said with a smirk. "The rumors about you two are barely starting to die down. This..." He gestured to them. "Is only going to start them up again."

"About that...Lord Oliver, I want to ask your permission to marry Bridget. Today if possible." Emmett groaned as he sat up.

Bridget put her hand on his chest as she began to protest. He ignored her as he breathed through the pain. She laid her head on his chest, and he put his arm around her waist.

"Bridget, come here." Uncle Oliver said firmly. Bridget grudgingly stood and moved to her uncle's side. He leaned down and whispered in her ear. "Your father has already given his blessing. He said if you didn't come home as Bridget Young, he would kill Emmett. Your mother sent a bag for you. It is in the tent. Go see what she sent."

"But..." Bridget tried to protest, but her uncle gave her a hard look.

"I told you to go to the tent, Bri. I will be there in ten minutes." Uncle Oliver gave Bridget a gentle shove toward the tent opening.

She glanced back at Emmett. He had been almost desperate for her to stay with him, and now she was being sent away. She did not want to leave him if it was going to stress him out. Milo moved to her side. He put a hand on her back, guiding her outside.

The sooner she looked in the bag, the sooner she could get back to Emmett. She closed the flap before finding the bag her uncle had mentioned. She reached inside and pulled out a beautiful white dress with gold embroidery along the hem and neckline. A letter fell out, and she quickly picked it up.

Her name was written across the front of it. She sat on the cot and opened the letter. Her mother expressed her love and excitement for this big step in Bridget's life. She went on about Emmett's wonderful nature and his goodness. She could not wait to see the both of them when they came back to the Capital.

The last half of the letter was from her father. He expressed his love and hesitant agreement for her to marry Emmett. He said that Oliver would be standing in his stead since he was unable to be there.

Bridget smiled, setting the letter on the cot next to her. She looked at the dress with excitement but then her smile slipped. She could not get dressed in this gown with only one hand. This was not going to feel very good. She slipped her sling off her arm and took several deep breaths before undressing.

Her brow was wet with sweat, and she was shaking by the time she managed to get the last button done up on the dress. The action of reaching behind her and over her head had caused so much pain in her shoulder. She sat heavily on the cot. She was hurting and she was tired.

"Bri?" Uncle Oliver asked from the other side of the tent flap. "Are you ready? Captain Trevors has agreed to officiate."

"I think so." she said softly. She stood, wobbling slightly.

"You look as beautiful as your mother did on her wedding day." He smiled at her with tears in his eyes when she stepped from the tent. She gave him a small smile.

He put his hand on her back, and they slowly walked toward the medical tent. Bridget barely noticed the lack of people moving around. Her sole focus at the moment, was breathing through the pain. Before she knew it, they were standing next to Emmett's bed. She turned to him. He was watching her with his brows drawn down in confusion. He mouthed 'freeze them'.

"Bri, what's wrong?" He asked anxiously when she sat next to him after freezing everyone.

His arm went around her back and she leaned against him. His other hand came up to her face as he held her. "Emmett, my shoulder keeps spasming."

"When do you need your next dose of pain meds?" He kissed her forehead.

"Not for another hour or so." She sat back up. "I am sorry I am complaining, you have it much worse than I do."

Emmett pressed his lips to hers. When he pulled back, he rested his forehead against hers. "Never apologize for telling me when you are in pain, Bri. Your wellbeing is what matters most to me." He kissed the tip of her nose. "Now, my love. Let's hurry up and get married so we can both take a nap."

Bridget laughed and Emmett grinned. "I don't trust you to be alone. Who knows what dumb thing you will do, and I am not sleeping in here."

"They are moving me to my tent. Doc said he would come over and check on me throughout the day." Emmett chuckled. "Unfreeze them so we can get you something for the pain."

Bridget stood and moved back to where she was before freezing everyone. Emmett continued to watch her. Her uncle kissed her cheek and paused. "Doc, Bridget doesn't look like she is feeling good." He took a step back.

Doc rushed over and looked at her. "My Lady, I am going to take a look at the wound." Bridget nodded and he pulled down the collar of her dress just enough to peel back the bandage. "Have you been moving this arm around?" he asked after a moment.

"Um…some, when absolutely necessary." Not a single person moved as they stared at her.

"What is absolutely necessary for you to do? There is a whole camp of men that could do any task for you." Her uncle glared at her.

She glared back at him as she sat down next to Emmett again. "There are things that I will not have anyone in this camp help me with. You are right, this is a camp full of men, Uncle Ollie. I am a woman."

Doc's face turned red with embarrassment. "All right, I get what you are saying. There is something I can give you that will help with the pain you are obviously in. It will put you to sleep though."

"More than the normal?" she asked.

"The other just makes you groggy and tired. This will knock you out. I suggest waiting until you are ready to lay down for a while."

"Very well." She sighed.

"In that case, shall we?" Captain Trevors smiled at her.

Bridget looked at Emmett. He was smiling, but he looked worried. He gave the captain a nod and he began. With the ceremony finished, Emmett kissed her, and when she tried to pull back, he didn't let her. She laughed, causing him to smile against her lips. She laid her head on his shoulder when he finally released her and closed her eyes.

"Oliver, can you help Bri to the other tent? Doc, I want you to go with them. She needs some sort of relief." Emmett ordered. When she looked at him with a scowl, he kissed her. "Milo and Captain Trevors are going to be helping me. I will be right behind you."

Bridget stood and immediately sat back down. She was so lightheaded. She felt hands on hers. She looked up to see her uncle looking at her in concern. He assisted her to her feet before putting an arm around her. He guided her slowly out of the tent. Instead of going to Emmett's tent like she had hoped, he took her to the mess tent.

"You need to eat something before you can take anything for the pain." He explained.

"I do not think I can right now." She said as he helped her sit.

All she managed to eat was a bite or two. Her stomach was upset because of the pain she was in. She was relieved when her uncle gave up trying to get her to eat and they made it to Emmett's tent. He told her the doctor would be by in a few minutes and left her standing there. Bridget stepped in and stopped. Emmett was lying on the cot already.

"I was wondering where you ran off to?" Emmett smiled at her. His hair was damp, and his face was pale.

"Uncle Oliver tried to force me to eat." She sat on the cot. It was really small. She had no idea how Emmett expected them both to sleep on it. "I think your plan is flawed."

"How so?" He sat up with a groan.

"I do not see how both of us are going to fit on the cot."

"There is enough room. Just come and lay down. They said Doc would be by in a little bit." Emmett kissed her temple.

"I need to change out of my mother's dress first." Bridget sighed. She was already hurting. The thought of having to undo the buttons again was daunting. Emmett started on the buttons, and she tensed. "What are you doing?"

"I am guessing the reason you are hurting so much is because you reached back here to get dressed earlier." Emmett said softly. "I have two good hands. There is no need for you to hurt yourself more."

Bridget held still as Emmett made quick work of the buttons. "Thank you." She whispered when he was done. She felt Emmett lay down and she glanced back at him. His eyes were closed, and his jaw was clenched. She stood and walked to where her blue dress was.

"Your uncle sent someone for a different dress, so you do not have to wear that ruined one or my clothes anymore." Emmett grunted as he tried to reposition himself.

Bridget easily found the new dress and changed. She watched Emmett for several minutes, debating if she should disturb him. He was finally not moving restlessly. The thought of her uncle and the doctor coming in with her back completely undone had her moving back to the bed. "Emmett?"

"Hmm?" He glanced at her.

"Could you help me?" she asked softly.

Emmett sat back up and her guilt increased as the pain he was feeling was evident on his face. She carefully sat down, and he quickly buttoned the dress. He laid back down before giving her a pointed look.

"There isn't room. I can go somewhere else." She protested when he grabbed her hand.

"No, you are not. Bri, lay down. I promise there is plenty of room." Bridget hesitantly lay down on her side facing him. She put her head on his chest and let out a small sigh. "See, plenty of room." Emmett kissed the top of her head.

Bridget had to admit she was comfortable, besides the pain in her shoulder. Emmett stroked her hair while holding her close. A throat cleared and Emmett told the person to enter.

"How are the two of you?" Doc asked quietly.

"We are both in a bit of pain." Emmett answered.

"I bet. Sir, your leg was broken in three different locations, from what we could tell. I reset it, but with the amount of damage, you are lucky I did not have to remove it. As soon as you are stable, you will be moved to a hospital in the Capital."

"I am lucky. Now, can you get Bridget what she needs and then I could use something." Emmett said. She could hear in his voice how much pain he was experiencing. "We can talk about my injuries and recovery after we get some rest."

"Yes, sir." Doc said.

Bridget attempted to sit up, but Emmett kept her down. "Just relax, sweetheart."

"But I cannot swallow laying down." Bridget protested.

"You will not need to swallow anything." Doc said. "It is an injection."

Bridget tensed. She had never had an injection before. Doc put his hand on her arm and then there was a pinch. A burning sensation spread from that spot. She turned her face more into Emmett. He kissed her head. Doc released her. A minute later she heard the tent flap fall back into place.

She lifted her head and looked around. "I thought Doc was going to give you something for the pain." She looked at Emmett.

"He did. I am use to receiving injections. You apparently are not." He smiled at her.

"I have never had one before." she admitted.

Emmett tucked her hair behind her ear. He kissed her slowly. "I love you, Bri." He whispered against her lips.

"I love you, too." Bridget rubbed her nose against his.

"Get some sleep. You should feel better when you wake up." Bridget put her head back on Emmett's chest. She was starting to feel heavy. "I have needed this." He muttered.

"Mmm." Bridget smiled. "You have needed some strong pain medicine?"

"Bridget, go to sleep." Emmett chuckled. Bridget snuggled closer to him and sighed. She listened to the steady rhythm of his heart.

Chapter 33

Emmett resisted the need to reposition. Bridget was sleeping soundly, and he did not want to risk waking her up. He had been awake for hours, the pain not allowing him to sleep at all. The tent flap was pulled back briefly before falling back into place. Emmett did not bother to look to see who it was.

"I cannot believe you were willing to give her up in order to stop the Freynians." Milo said quietly.

"I was willing to do what I had to do in order to protect her, Milo." Emmett said in irritation. "The only reason I re-enlisted in the first place was because one of the Freynian Chiefs was trying to kill her."

"You set those charges. You knew where they were located, yet you told me to set them off. You could have killed yourself." Milo began pacing.

"The man trying to kill Bridget is named Talon. He is ruthless and would stop at nothing to get her. He nearly succeeded in getting her back to Freynia. I was fighting with him on the pass."

"I saw." Milo growled. "Why did you not kill him yourself? Why the explosives?"

"He had the upper hand, Milo. I was not going to last much longer against him. Not to mention his hundred men that were going to be coming through the pass. I had to keep Bridget safe. At all costs, I needed her safe."

"It amazes me you even survived. I saw you jump off the cliff and then..." Milo stopped. "I saw you go down after being hit by flying debris. I knew roughly where you landed. It took me two days to dig you out and another for the men to lift the rock off you. I was ready to have Doc amputate your leg there in the ravine so we could move you out of there."

"I am grateful to have my leg, but a part of me wishes it had been taken. The pain is constant and excruciating." Emmett placed his hand on Bridget's head. Having her with him was, in its own way, a balm for his pain. He did not want her out of his sight. Not until Talon's death was confirmed.

"Doc says you will be lucky if you can ever walk again. He thinks you will be in a wheelchair the rest of your life."

Emmett sighed. "That bad?"

"That is just what I have heard him say to the others. Lieutenant, you were literally blown up. If losing the use of your leg is the only issue you have to face, then I think you came out on top." Milo shook his head.

"When will they ship me out?" Emmett asked.

"That depends. You were brought to camp less than twenty-four hours ago. The bone was sticking out through the skin, and you had multiple breaks. Doc is worried about internal bleeding, and he wants to make sure an infection does not set in. It is a two-day journey by road, and you cannot be in danger of dying along the way."

"Dying would be a big problem for me." Emmett sighed. "Milo, other than the stab wound, how has she been?"

"Mostly fine, I think. She has been quiet unless speaking with the wounded. She spends most of her days cheering up the men. Glen has become attached to her."

"Glen?" Emmett said in surprise.

"He is like a little brother." Bridget mumbled.

"I'm sorry if I woke you." Emmett softened his voice. "How are you feeling?"

Bridget moved her head so she could see him. Her eyes blinked slowly, and she looked half asleep. "I hurt a little, but I am too tired to care." She closed her eyes again.

"I will go find Doc." Milo said as he left.

Emmett kissed her forehead, and she smiled. Her eyes slowly opened again. "How are you so awake? Didn't you get the same stuff I did?"

"I did." Emmett chuckled.

"Mmm." she closed her eyes again and snuggled closer.

Emmett smiled. He could not even describe how happy he was that they were married now, and that he was able to keep her close. The last five months had been hard not seeing her. He had not realized how much he needed her.

"Emmett?" Bri whispered.

"Yes?"

"I do not want to get up." She sighed.

"I am glad we are on the same page." Emmett smiled. "I do not want you to get up either." He hugged her closer. "I quite like having you in my arms."

She laughed softly. "But I do need to get up."

"I do not think so. We are both where we need to be."

"Emmett." Bridget looked back at him as she tensed. "One, I would much rather be home right now instead of in a tent. Two, you need to get back to the Capital so you can get the medical help you need. Three, I am starving. Four..."

Emmett kissed her until she relaxed. "Wherever you are is where I am supposed to be." He stroked her cheek with his thumb.

"Have I told you lately how much I love you?" she smiled.

"I don't think you have." Emmett grinned. Bridget kissed him and then sat up. "Hey! Where are you going?" He winced as he sat up.

"I told you I needed to get up. I will be back in a little bit." Bridget opened the flap of the tent.

"Bri..." Emmett started to protest.

"I will be back, Emmett. Give me a few minutes." She smiled at him and left the tent.

She heard him grumbling as she walked away. She quickly made her way to the bathroom before heading back. She paused when several men came into the camp with a stretcher. They passed her and she saw the man's face. He was covered in dirt and blood, but she recognized him. She grew lightheaded as her heart raced. She heard someone call to her just as her vision faded to black.

Emmett was not happy. His blasted leg was proving to be more of a hinderance than he thought. He did not like the idea of Bridget walking around without someone protecting her. She had been gone for close to ten minutes and he was growing restless. He should send Milo to find her.

"Bri." Lord Oliver said cheerfully. "Bri!" He yelled.

Emmett attempted to get up, but the searing pain in his leg caused him to cry out. He rolled to his side, fighting the sudden urge to vomit. The tent opened and Lord Oliver walked in carrying Bridget. She was white as a sheet and limp.

"What happened?" Emmett asked through clenched teeth as pain continued to spasm through his leg.

"A stretcher was brought into camp, and I think she saw the man on it." Lord Oliver laid Bridget next to Emmett. He put his arm around her as he placed his forehead against her cheek. "What happened to you? You look close to passing out as well."

It took Emmett another moment before he was able to answer. "I tried to move my leg." He said through the pain.

Lord Oliver stuck his head out the door and spoke to someone. He looked back at Emmett with a look of concern. "I sent for Doc."

Emmett nodded and closed his eyes as he concentrated on his breathing. Doc came running and examined Emmett's leg. His lips pulled into a thin line. He whispered to Lord Oliver as he headed for the door of the tent. Doc left but Lord Oliver stayed. He looked more worried now than before.

"Give it to me straight, Oliver." Emmett said.

Lord Oliver ran his hand down his face. "The risks of keeping you here until your pain is more manageable and he knows no infection has set in, is no longer an option. He is getting arrangements made for you to leave immediately."

Emmett gave a small nod. Bridget began to stir. "Stay still, sweetheart. You are going to bump my leg." Emmett whispered.

Bridget turned her head so she could see him. He was pale with sweat beading on his forehead. Pain pulled at his features. She reached up and ran her hand down the side of his face. He was incredibly tense. "I saw him." She whispered.

"Who?" Emmett's brows drew together in confusion.

"The man that took me."

"Where?" Emmett's voice had a hard edge to it.

"On the stretcher. He was...he was..." she closed her eyes as a shiver ran down her spine.

"The blood." Emmett sighed and kissed her forehead. "Lord Oliver, can you go check on him? I need to know if he is still a threat or not."

"I can answer that for you." Milo stepped into the tent. "He is not a threat." He gave Emmett a nod. "You ready to go, sir?"

"As ready as I will ever be." Emmett was dreading this. He was still dealing with his attempt to barely move his leg.

"Ready for what?" Bridget asked as she carefully sat up. She laced her fingers through Emmett's as she pulled it around her middle.

"Doc is sending you guys to the Capital." Milo gave her a tight smile.

Bridget tensed. She thought it was too dangerous to move Emmett. He wasn't stable enough. What had happened to make him change his mind? She swallowed before looking back at Emmett. He was in much more pain than he was when she left a few minutes ago. Doc came back in as he was issuing orders to several men who were carrying a stretcher.

Her uncle took her outside to wait for the men to load Emmett. She heard his muffled cries of pain as Uncle Oliver pulled her over to a covered wagon. Two other men were inside. The men carrying Emmett arrived within a few minutes. Emmett looked grey. His eyes were closed and he was tense.

She watched anxiously as he was loaded into the wagon. "You are next, My Lady." Milo offered her his hand and she quickly took it. She was eager to check on Emmett. "Doc sedated him, but he was still in a lot of pain."

Bridget nodded and moved to Emmett's side. He was all the way at the back. Uncle Oliver climbed up as well with a bag over his shoulder. She smoothed Emmett's hair off his forehead as the wagon began to move. She needed to feel him close right now. This move was dangerous, and she did not understand why Doc was pushing for it now.

*   *   *

They had been in the Capital for a month. The trip had been incredibly tough for Emmett. Every bump in the road caused him immense pain. After waking up, he had moved himself into a sitting position and held her. He had kept her in his arms for the full two-day journey.

When they arrived, he was the first one unloaded. Bridget had not been allowed in. They had talked about keeping their marriage a secret for now and she was regretting it. Her uncle had told her that no one, family or not, was allowed to see Emmett. A month later, she was beyond stressed. All she knew was that he had required immediate surgery, and he made it through it okay. Her parents tried to keep her busy, but her mind never strayed from Emmett.

Tonight, Bridget was going to a ball she did not want to go to. Her parents talked her into it against her better judgement. Dancing was definitely off the table. Her shoulder was doing much better, but she was not about to chance reinjuring it. She also did not want to dance with anyone other than Emmett.

She descended the stairs in her cream-colored gown. She had a light blue ribbon around the bodice. Her parents were waiting for her in the entryway. Her mother smiled at her when she reached them.

"Are you ready?" Her mother asked.

"Do I have to go?" Bridget asked as Greg helped her put her cloak on.

"Bri, you have not been yourself since you have been back. And we get it. Your husband is injured, and you have not been able to see him or receive word about his condition. But you cannot stay cooped up in the house forever." Her father said. "Going tonight will be good for you."

Bridget shook her head but followed her family out to the coach. Someone was already inside. Her steps faltered but she continued walking. She desperately wished it was Emmett. Her heart began beating so fast, she thought it would beat out of her chest. Her head was screaming at her to not get her hopes up, that the likelihood that it was Emmett was so small. She took a deep breath before climbing into the dark interior.

"How are you this evening, Bri?" Uncle Oliver asked.

Bridget closed her eyes briefly before answering. "I would be better if I was allowed to stay home." She told him. She was so disappointed that Emmett wasn't sitting next to her.

"You will enjoy tonight. It will be good for you to be out among people." Uncle Oliver patted her hand.

She rolled her eyes and looked out the window. The only way she would enjoy tonight would be if Emmett was beside her. Bridget stared out the window until they reached the Davenport's home. Her father assisted her down and her uncle escorted her in. Bridget held her head high as they entered the ballroom. She just needed to get through a few hours and then she would ask her father to take her home.

Chapter 34

Emmett moved slowly as he lowered himself down from the coach. Milo handed him his crutches before moving to his side. "Do you think she will be happy to see you?" Milo asked with a grin.

"Just head to the address I gave you. Give John the letter and he will show you to your room." Emmett did not take his eyes from the house in front of him.

"Yes, sir." Milo climbed back into the coach.

Emmett made his way slowly inside. The surgery went well. Some of his bones were crushed and left his leg several inches shorter than it should have been. The doctors had been skeptical that he would ever walk again, but Emmett was determined to get there. At this point, he could not put any weight on the leg. Crutches were his only option to get around with ease. The pain was greatly reduced after the surgery.

Now, Emmett wanted Bridget, and nothing was going to stand in his way. He navigated the stairs, and a servant opened the door for him. The ballroom looked crowded. He could see a mass of people through the door at the end of the hall. The Davenports were known for their elaborate gatherings, and this was no different.

When he stepped into the ballroom, many of the closest people stared. He ignored them as he scanned the room. Only one person mattered. The crowd parted for him as he made his way around the perimeter. He had yet to see her.

"Lord Young, it is so good to see you." Miss Davenport moved into his path.

"Is it?" he asked, barely glancing at her before continuing to search the crowd.

She giggled and touched his arm. Emmett clenched his jaw. "I beg your pardon, but I do not like to be touched." He glared at her.

She quickly removed her hand from his arm. "I apologize, My Lord." She smiled and laughed. "I did not realize." She batted her eye lashes at him. "I guess that is one reason you do not dance."

"I do not dance because I have yet to find a partner worth my time." He corrected as he scanned the room again. He saw Lord Oliver standing in a group. To his left was a shorter woman, her face was hidden from his view.

"I have to disagree. There are…"

"Excuse me." Emmett moved around her and cut across the dance floor, not caring that he interrupted them.

People were watching him. He drew more and more of an audience the closer he got to Bridget. She did not turn around when he got close to her. He quietly rested one of his crutches against the wall and moved right behind her. He slid his hand around her waist, and she tensed.

Emmett smiled as he leaned down. "Have I told you lately how much I love you?" he whispered in her ear.

Bridget gasped as she whirled around. "Emmett."

Emmett nearly fell over with her abrupt movement. He managed to keep himself upright. A moment later, she threw her arms around his neck. He could feel her tears, and he tightened his arm around her. He buried his face in her neck and ignored the loud murmuring around them.

"What is going on here?" Mr. Davenport asked angrily as he broke through the crowd gathering around them.

Emmett leaned back and grinned down at Bridget. He kissed her, causing many to gasp in surprise. Bridget smiled against his lips. "You are going to start rumors, sir." She quirked her brow.

"I sure hope so." He kissed her again.

"Lord Young!" Mr. Davenport yelled.

Emmett sighed and straightened up. "Mr. Davenport." Lord Oliver coughed beside them.

"This kind of display is not acceptable. I do not tolerate men who take advantage of young ladies."

"Taking advantage of young ladies? I am doing nothing of the sort." He kissed Bridget's temple.

Miss Davenport moved to her father's side. She scowled at Bridget. "You are such a disgrace, Lady Bridget. Only a tramp would act in such a way."

"I would take care of how you talk about my wife." Emmett warned. "I will not stand for any level of disrespect."

"Your…wife?" Miss Davenport gasped "But…"

"I want to thank you Mr. Davenport for hosting the party where I was able to be reunited with Bridget. My doctors refused to allow any visitors during my recovery." Emmett interrupted again. He smiled down at Bridget. "Shall we head home? I was told to go directly there, but I couldn't without seeing you first."

"I would love nothing more." Bridget smiled at him. She stepped away and grabbed his other crutch that her father handed to her. He gave her a wink. "You may want this." She passed it to Emmett.

"I do not understand. You said you were not engaged." Miss Davenport sputtered.

"Emmett and I were married not long ago." Bridget shrugged. She was standing close to him as if she were seeking shelter.

Lord Mason moved to their side. "Miss Davenport, I do not believe their relationship is any of your business. But I will say this for the benefit of all here." He stepped a little in front of them. "War is hard for any couple. I wanted Lord Young and my daughter to be able to have as much time together as possible in case the worst were to happen. If nothing else, they could write to one another. Lord Oliver and I took Bridget up to the military camp where he was stationed, and they were married. Lord Young was gravely injured and has been recovering for the past month."

"I just..." Miss Davenport glared at Bridget. "I do not believe it."

"You do not have to believe it." Emmett said. "That is up to you." He bowed as much as he could. "Good evening, Mr. Davenport. And thank you Lord Mason for making sure she was here."

Emmett began moving back to the door with Bridget at his side. When they got outside, the Caverton carriage was waiting. He assisted Bridget into the carriage before placing his crutches inside and pulling himself up. He finally got up on the bench next to Bridget and sighed.

"You messaged my father but not me?" Bridget smacked his chest.

"You are back to hitting me. Is this going to happen every time you are upset with me?" Emmett couldn't help smiling. He was not at all sorry for meeting her at the ball. She looked stunning, and he loved letting society know she was his.

"You are a pain, Emmett Young." She glared at him, though her eyes shone with humor.

"And you are beautiful, Bridget Young." He cupped her face and slowly drew her closer. "Absolutely stunning. You are not allowed to look this good without me at your side."

She laughed. "You are deflecting."

Emmett's smile grew. He stopped just shy of their lips touching. "Do I need to pull you into a river again?" she scoffed and tried to pull back, but he did not let her and then he kissed her.

Bridget's hand moved to the back of Emmett's head as she kissed him back. The carriage slowed and Emmett drew back. He rested his forehead against hers. Bridget moved her hand to his cheek. "I missed you." She whispered.

"I missed you, too, sweetheart." Emmett gave her a quick kiss. "Time to go inside. Milo is probably waiting for us."

"Milo is here?" Bridget sat back in surprise.

The door to the carriage opened and Milo poked his head in. "Are you two coming in?" he laughed.

Bridget accepted Milo's help to descend from the carriage. She watched as he helped Emmett. They gave each other a nod when Milo handed Emmett his crutches. Milo hurried up the steps to open the door and she turned to go inside. She stopped when she noticed she was not at her family's home.

Emmett moved up behind her and rested his chin on her shoulder. "You didn't think I would take you to your parents' home, did you?"

Bridget turned around and put her arms around his neck. "I just didn't think about it. Now, I want to hear about the last month."

"I will gladly tell you once you are inside and we are sitting." He kissed her cheek.

Bridget walked inside and straight to the drawing room where she had seen Emmett passed out the last time she was here. She sat on the couch. Emmett moved to her side and slowly lowered himself down. Milo pushed a footstool over and helped Emmett get his leg up on it. He put his arm around her shoulders, and she willingly scooted closer to him.

"So..." Bridget glanced between Emmett and Milo.

Emmett sighed and kissed her temple. "During the surgery, they discovered a few things." He said carefully. "My leg was broken in several places. The bone was crushed in one place and was unable to be repaired."

"Okay." Bridget said slowly. "What does that mean?"

"Now that my leg is several inches shorter than it was, walking will be difficult, if I manage to get to that point." Emmett rested his head on hers.

"How is your pain though?" she laced her fingers through his.

"Manageable now that they cleaned out the crushed bone fragments."

"Good." She sighed as she leaned more against him.

"No comment on whether your husband will be able to walk again?" Milo asked in disbelief.

"I will be there every step of the way to encourage him as he recovers. But his ability to walk does not affect my views or feelings for him. I did not think I needed to say anything." She shrugged.

"How is your shoulder?" Emmett asked.

"Fine. It gets sore if I use it a lot, but overall, it is nearly back to normal."

"Hmm." Emmett ran his fingers along her arm. They sat in silence for several minutes and Bridget began to relax. Having Emmett back had taken away a lot of her stress, leaving her feeling drained. She stood and headed for the door. "Where are you going?" Emmett asked in confusion.

"I have been stressed and in a constant state of worry for over six months. I am exhausted. Goodnight, gentlemen." She walked out into the hall.

"Is she serious?" Milo laughed. "Does she even know where to go?"

"Help me up, Milo." Emmett sighed.

Bridget smiled when she saw John. "Could you please show me to my room, John?"

She followed the butler, and in no time, she stepped into a large bedroom. She thanked John before closing the door. She undid the back of her dress and laid it over a chair. She sighed when she lay down on the bed and closed her eyes. A few minutes later, the door opened and closed softly. She heard Emmett's crutches as he approached the bed.

He was moving around but she could not tell what he was doing. The covers were pulled back and Emmett carefully laid down. When he was settled, she scooted closer to him. She tensed for a second when she realized he was not wearing a shirt. Her cheeks heated.

"You know, I could have shown you where our room was." He pressed a kiss to her forehead.

"You could have." She kissed his shoulder before laying her head on his chest.

Emmett tangled his hand in her hair, and she looked up at him. His lips met hers and she smiled. "I told you this was going to be more comfortable than the cot." She laughed.

"Bri," Emmett smiled. "As long as I have you, I am comfortable." She kissed him again as she put her hand on his jaw.

*   *   *

Bridget sat down next to Emmett in their drawing room. Her parents were there for a visit. It had been a full week of having Emmett back, and she could not be happier. He and Milo spent several hours a day working on walking. He was determined and she fully supported him, but it was hard to watch sometimes.

Her father gave her a smile. "You both look happier."

"I cannot tell you how happy I am to be out of the hospital. Bri is much nicer than the doctors." Emmett smiled. Bridget elbowed him, causing him to laugh.

"We have a letter for you from the Pheonix." Her father said, handing Emmett an envelope.

"The phoenix?" Emmett took it. "I thought I was out, all things considered."

"Just read it." Her father sat back in his chair.

Emmett scanned the note before passing it to Bridget. "The Phoenix wishes me to take over this branch of the Hunters? Why? I am not of much use."

"You are of plenty of use, Emmett. We feel like you are the best choice. Mason wants to retire from the business to enjoy our grandchildren, and Oliver is courting someone and wants to not have to deal with it anymore. We will, of course, stay as silent partners in Caverton Security, but you will have full reign of the business." Her mother said.

Emmett's mouth fell open. "Mother, you realize what you are asking him, us, to do. The Hunters and Caverton Security are both very demanding."

"I may have seen a few things, Bri. You will need to trust me on this." Her mother smiled.

"You?" Emmett was still in shock. "You, are the Pheonix?"

"I am a Guardian with the Gift to see visions." Her mother explained.

"That makes sense." He muttered as he rubbed his jaw. He froze before slowly turning to Bridget. He looked between her and her mother. "Grandchildren?" He said quietly as his gaze dropped to her stomach. Bridget's eyes widened as she turned to her mother.

"Uh...well I would hope you two would give me some eventually." Her father said quickly.

"You have seen them, haven't you?" Bridget asked her mother.

"She will not tell me about them, so she isn't going to say anything to you." Her father sighed.

"I will tell you this. In the coming years, the fighting and mistrust only grow. Shifters are barely tolerated now, but soon they will be completely hunted for who they are. No one crosses the borders, Arlania becomes completely isolated. The skirmishes on the borders become full on battles. Army against army. You must make some decisions when it comes to any children you might have."

"Can you be more specific?" Emmett asked. "How many kids are we talking here? I have never thought about being a father before. Mine abandoned me and all other male role models were nonexistent until I found Mason and Oliver."

"Emmett, you will be fine." Her mother chuckled. "We must be on our way. You are invited to our house for dinner tomorrow night. The next morning, we are leaving for Caverton Manor."

Bridget stood and hugged her parents. She was still reeling from what her mother had said. Being in charge of both the family business and the Hunters was going to be a challenge. She was more than happy to help with anything she could. After walking her parents out, she returned to the drawing room. Emmett was sitting on the couch just staring.

"How are you feeling?" she asked, taking a seat next to him.

"I am freaking out a little." He turned to her.

"Running both will be difficult, but I think we can manage, especially if Milo is willing to help." She kissed his cheek.

"I was talking about the whole kids thing." His eyes were wide, and he was tense.

Bridget tried not to laugh. She knew he was feeling overwhelmed and not at all up to the task, but she knew he would be an amazing father. "Lord Young, you are worrying over nothing." She kissed him.

"Not over nothing, Bri. I am..." Bridget cut him off by pressing her lips to his. He growled but kissed her back.

"I am worried about one thing, though." Bridget sat back. Emmett raised a brow in question. "If Arlania is going to get as bad as Mother said, what are we going to do? I am a Guardian; you are a Shifter. Chances are at least one of our kids will be as well."

Emmett put his arms around her and pulled her close. "We will not tell them about us. If they Shift or are a Guardian, then we will explain everything to them. I think we should move to the Young Estate so that society does not suspect."

Bridget nodded as she laid her head on his shoulder. She had no love for the Capital. She was looking forward to seeing the estate, but she was still worried. Emmett was having to see the doctor a few times a week for his leg. "We should wait to go to the estate until we need to."

"You mean once our child is born." Emmett ran his fingers up and down her arm. Bridget nodded. He kissed the top of her head as he leaned more comfortably back. Bridget's mind was swimming. They could not have a baby right now. Emmett needed time to recover before they could leave the Capital. She gave herself a mental shake. Her mother did not say they were having a baby anytime soon. She took a calming breath in and let it out slowly.

Chapter 35

When Lord Mason asked Emmett to meet him at a village near Emmett's home, this wasn't exactly what he thought would happen. Four men were dead because of this woman. Emmett had a firm rule not to hurt a woman, but he had to beat her into unconsciousness so she couldn't hurt anyone else.

Mason and Oliver were glaring at her as she sat in chains on the rock floor. She was smirking at them. She did not seem the least bit afraid. Emmett had waited for the Cavertons to arrive before asking her questions. They had wanted to be here.

"What is your name?" Milo asked.

"I will only speak to him." She looked at Mason.

"Me? Why me?" Mason asked, crossing his arms over his chest.

"Because you have what my mother wants." She smiled at him.

"Who is your mother and what is it she thinks I have?" Mason glared at the woman.

She laughed. "Oh, no. She does not know you have it yet. I just found out that your wife is in possession of it. Mother will stop at nothing to get it. Anna will not survive. She wasn't meant to be alive to begin with."

Mason pulled back his fist, but Oliver grabbed him and pulled him back. His face was red, and he was breathing hard. Milo looked at Emmett with wide eyes. Emmett could understand his surprise. The Cavertons were not ones to lose control like this. Emmett had only seen it happen one other time when Lord Percival came to the house after he had attacked Bridget.

"You will not touch Anna." He growled.

The woman's eyes danced in delight. "Mother said the best thing about attacking the castle was the fact that Little Anna would no longer be around. She said the screams were music to her ears because one of them had to be hers."

Mason lunged again. Emmett had to help drag him out of the room. "Go to Anna." Oliver told him. "We will finish talking to her." He gestured to the closed door at Emmett's back.

"She…" Mason yelled.

"Go find Anna." Oliver cut him off.

Emmett waited until Mason disappeared around the corner before turning to Oliver. "I do not think I have ever seen him so angry before."

"You know how touchy he is about Anna and the castle." Oliver sighed. "I can't really blame him. He beats himself up for being a part of it. And if anyone was talking about my wife like that, I would be seeing red."

Emmett smiled. "I killed four men for mentioning Talon's desire to kill Bridget, and we were only friends at the time."

"You were in love with her. You just did not know it yet." Oliver laughed. "Shall we?" He nodded towards the door.

They walked back in to see Milo glaring at the woman. "What is your name?"

"I told you; I will only talk to one person." She grinned.

"You will not be talking to him. You have two choices: you can talk to us, or I will make you suffer until you do. I am not above torture." Emmett flexed his hand. "It has been a while since I have been able to beat someone."

Oliver grabbed his arm and gave him a hard look. "What are you doing?" He whispered harshly.

"We tried it your way, now it is my turn." Emmett said loud enough for the woman to hear.

Torture was not in his skill set. Emmett was hoping that the woman would be scared enough to start talking. Oliver seemed to think he was capable of torture, which would play into this.

"Are you serious?" he asked in disbelief.

"Completely." Emmett started to roll up his sleeves as he turned to the woman. Her smile was gone, and she watched him warily. "What is your name?" Emmett asked, moving to his other sleeve.

"Monica Platt." she said quickly.

"Who is your mother?" Emmett looked over at Milo. "Can you go grab my supplies out of the other room? No need to clean them." Milo smiled as he headed for the door.

"I'm talking!" Monica yelled.

Milo completely ignored her and left the room. Emmett had no idea what he would be bringing back, and he was curious to find out. They were in the basement of a butcher shop, so it could be interesting.

"Do I need to repeat my question?" Emmett asked calmly. Oliver was pacing anxiously behind him.

"My mother is Sasha Carson. She wants the amulet that I saw around Anna's neck." Monica had fear in her eyes now.

Anna had told him and Bridget about the Guardian's Amulet and the attack on the castle. Oliver and Mason had also told him about the mysterious deaths that surrounded their village and the rumors that sparked the hatred toward the Guardians.

"I have seen Sasha. You look to be older than she is." Oliver said. "I thought she was married to Lord Carson?"

"My mother is blessed to have eternal youth." Monica's eyes narrowed. "She married Lord Carson after she killed my father."

"Why would she kill your father?" Emmett asked.

"He was no longer useful. Same with Lord Carson. Men are only as good as what they can give you." Monica shrugged.

"Carson is dead?" Oliver asked in surprise.

"He helped destroy those of the castle. After that he was just…extra weight to carry around."

The door opened and Milo came in holding a bag that was covered in blood. The grin on his face made Emmett smile. Milo was having fun with this. He put the bag down at Emmett's feet before stepping back.

Emmett slowly started pulling items from the bag and laying them out on the floor. He had no idea what most of these things were used for. There was a range of different kinds of knives, saws, pliers, and scissors. Every last one of them was covered in blood.

"I am answering your questions!" Monica screamed.

"Emmett," Oliver gave him a look. "You can't…"

"I find it interesting, Ms. Platt," Emmett talked over Oliver. "That you have literally drowned, tortured, and killed dozens of people, yet you do not think the same should happen to you. I know your ability and I know the stories. One stands out the most, though. A young boy was found dead on the side of the road after he drowned."

Monica was crying now. "He had to die. The villagers were still not willing to attack the castle. We needed something to push them over the edge. The boy's death would be the final straw."

"You killed Clay?!" Oliver yelled.

"Calm down, Oliver." Emmett ran his fingers over a few of the knives before picking one up.

Oliver looked at him and his eyes widened. Monica's cries grew louder. "You said your mother did not know about Lady Anna. Does anyone else know?" Emmett asked.

He knew that the boy's death had been Oliver and Mason's turning point. It was what made them second guess the women of the castle. Emmett's concern right now was Lady Anna. If others knew what she had or that she was alive, she would be in danger again. Sasha would hunt her down. He could not allow any harm to come to his mother-in-law. It would break Bridget. It would upset his kids to lose their grandmother. It would destroy Mason and Oliver. No, he could not let that happen.

"No. No one else knows. I happened upon the information and was on my way back to Ashford to let my mother know."

"Ashford?" Emmett stood slowly.

"She married a man named Walter Barnett right after getting rid of Carson. They live near Ashford."

"Is there anything else we should know?" Emmett asked. She shook her head as her tears continued to fall. He turned to Milo. "Where did you find all this stuff?"

"The butcher has a room full of all his tools down here. Man, you freaked me out a little, and I knew you weren't going to do anything."

"What?" Oliver asked.

"Do you really think I could torture a woman?" Emmett smiled at him. "I bet you were having second thoughts about letting me marry Bri, for a few minutes."

"Maybe just a little." Oliver laughed.

Monica screamed and they turned to face her. "What are we going to do with her?" Milo asked. "She is too dangerous to move."

Pure hatred burned in her eyes as she glared at Emmett. She moved her hand and the tears she had been crying lifted into the air. They covered Emmett's nose and mouth in a thin barrier, but it was enough to cut off his source of oxygen. He tried to wipe it off, but it remained in place. He threw the knife in his hand. It imbedded in her forehead. A second later, he could breathe again.

He fell to his knees, taking in large gulping breaths. Oliver and Milo were at his side. The door opened followed by a scream. They turned to see Mason and Lady Anna. She had her hand over her mouth as she stared at Monica.

"What happened?" Mason yelled, pulling Anna to his chest, turning her away from the dead woman.

"She attempted to kill Emmett, but he managed to stop her." Milo answered.

Oliver went into a longer explanation of everything that happened from the time Mason left to the moment he came back. Anna was shaking as she knelt next to Emmett and hugged him. He returned her embrace, grateful that she was safe. No one knew about her or the amulet now.

"Are you all right, Emmett?" She asked quietly.

He kissed her cheek before sitting back. "I am now. I must admit that I did not want to let her out of this room alive. She was the only one who knew that you survived the attack on the castle, and she knew about…" he stopped talking, remembering that Milo was here now.

Lady Anna gasped, and her hand flew to her chest. Emmett knew that she always wore the amulet. "How?"

"She saw you and recognized you." Oliver said softly.

"We need to get you home and out of sight, Anna." Mason was tense. "If Emmett hadn't stopped the threat, I would have."

"We did not come this far just to turn around before getting to see Bri and our grandbabies." Anna said.

Lord Mason gave Emmett a nod before helping Anna to her feet. Milo said he would take care of the cleanup and told them all to go home. Oliver stayed behind to help. Emmett's leg was hurting by the time he reached the top of the stairs and to the ground floor. It was the middle of the night, and no one was around. He limped to the forest's edge and shifted into his falcon. He could not wait to get home to Bridget and his kids.

*　　　　　*　　　　　*

Bridget smiled as she watched Blake and Miranda playing tag in the small field near their home. The surrounding forest was thick, and the southern part of the land was rocky. It reminded her a lot of the military camp Emmett had been stationed at. On the western side were open fields. They had a large stable where Emmett loved spending time with Isaac and Blake. The three of them went riding every day.

"Father!" Miranda squealed in delight. Bridget looked in the direction her daughter was running. Emmett was walking out of the house, leaning heavily on his cane.

He had taken his first steps months before Isaac was born. He had to use a cane when walking more than across a small room and he had a prominent limp, but he was walking. Occasionally, the pain would come back, but he never let it stop him from spending time with their kids.

She smiled as she watched him scoop Miranda up into his arms. He kissed her cheek before setting her back down. Bridget stood and started walking towards him. He gave her a smile that made her suspicious.

"What are you up to?" She slid her hands up his chest and around his neck.

"I am never up to anything." He grinned.

"You are always up to something." She narrowed her eyes at him.

He kissed her. "You are being paranoid, My Love."

"And you are being a pain. What have you done now?" She laughed.

He winked at her. "Isaac! Get your brother and sister inside please." He glanced over her shoulder.

"Yes, sir." Isaac said before running off.

"I need to speak with you before we go inside." Bridget said softly.

"Is everything all right?" Emmett's eyes snapped to hers.

"Do you want us in a specific room?" Isaac asked. He was holding Blake and Miranda's hands.

"Wait for us in the library." Bridget laid her head on Emmett's shoulder and smiled as she watched her kids walk inside.

"What is going on, Bri?" Emmett asked gently.

Bridget closed her eyes briefly before taking a step back so she could see Emmett's face. Isaac had been born a year after they were married and would be turning fifteen soon. Blake was two years younger, and Miranda had just turned nine. They had lost three babies before they were born over the last six years.

The loss of their three children had been extremely hard. Emmett had been so excited to be having another baby, and then crushed when they lost them. Bridget had been heartbroken each time. She waited until after the time period passed that she had lost the others before deciding to talk with Emmett.

"Bri?"

She grabbed his hand and placed it on her slightly rounded belly. He had been gone the past several weeks on business, and her belly had popped out in that time. "We are having another baby." She said, as tears filled her eyes.

Emmett just stood there. He looked completely shocked. "But..." he cleared his throat. "I mean..." he rubbed his hand over her stomach and stopped. "How far along are you?"

"Five months. I didn't want to see you go through it again if I lost the baby. I was so scared it would happen again."

"Bridget Young." Emmett glared at her. "You should not have dealt with it on your own. If we had lost the baby, yes, I would have been upset, but we would have gotten through it together." He kissed her. "We are better together." He kissed her again. He laughed as he pulled her close. "Another baby." He said excitedly.

Bridget smiled. "You get to tell the kids."

"This is perfect." He grabbed her hand, and they started walking back to the house. "This plays well into my surprise for you." He grinned.

"And what would that be?"

"Milo is here..."

"Milo!" She laughed. "You have been keeping him busy. He never gets to come anymore."

"Your parents are also here."

Bridget stopped walking. "My parents?"

"They brought word from the Pheonix. Your father said they are staying for a few weeks. He needs some grandpa time."

Bridget laughed as they began walking again. Emmett was beyond excited that they were having another baby, and absolutely terrified that this one might not make it like the previous three. He raised Bri's hand to his lips and kissed her knuckles.

He never thought he would enjoy family life as much as he did. He lived for his kids, and he couldn't get enough of his beautiful wife. They were his reason for living, his reason for trying to make Arlania a better place to live. Anna had been right. The fighting had only gotten worse. He was truly worried about the futures of his children.

Miranda had already begun taking lessons for her debut in society. He and Bridget had talked about this extensively, any daughters they had would be taken to the Capital when they turned twenty, so they could make a good match. This far north, they were so isolated. There were so few people in this part of the country, and he wanted the best for his daughter.

Their sons could take up roles within Caverton Security. They would have the opportunity to travel and find wives. Isaac was already showing signs of being a good leader and had gone with him a few times on Hunter business. Emmett was excited to see the kind of man he grew up to be. Blake was very much like Emmett was. He loved to hunt for things and figure out riddles.

Miranda loved to dress up and hated getting dirty. She was as beautiful as her mother with his dark blue eyes and Bridget's light brown hair. He dreaded the day he was going to have to take her out in society. She was bound to draw far too much attention for his liking. He vividly remembered watching Bridget from afar.

Emmett stopped walking and looked at Bridget. What if the baby was another girl? He did not think he could handle another girl. "It has to be a boy." He stated. Bridget laughed before kissing him. "I am serious, Bridget. I do not want to have to go through a second daughter being out in society. I watched your father have to go through it with you. I will be worse."

"You, my love, will survive." Bridget started walking again as she laughed.

Epilogue

"Kyrie, we are not trying to pawn you off. If you do not find a man you wish to marry, you can come home, and we can try again next year." Bridget tried to reason with her strong-willed daughter.

"No man wants a girl like me. I am the village weirdo." Kyrie crossed her arms over her chest as she glared out of the drawing room window. "I do not wish to go."

"You can take Samantha with you." Emmett rubbed his leg. "But you are going. Isaac will be with you, and if anyone gives you any trouble, he will let them know we have no tolerance for that kind of thing."

"I am going to the stables." Kyrie headed for the door.

"You cannot keep running off to the stables and into the woods, Kyrie. You are a lady and need to start acting like one." Bridget tried to follow her, but Emmett grabbed her hand.

"She is fine for now, Bri." Emmett put his arms around her.

"She gets this from you." Bridget smacked his chest before leaning against him. "I just want her to find someone who will love her for who she is. She is so strong, and her ability to speak with animals makes her so incredibly special. But when she does it in front of others, it scares them. They do not understand, and when people do not understand something, they destroy it."

"I know, Bri." Emmett kissed her forehead. "Her lack of interest in marriage and her refusal to hear us out when we have tried to explain to her about being a Guardian, worries me. At least your mother has been able to talk to her a little about it. I wish we could go with her."

"You are in no condition to travel right now, Emmett." Bridget looked up at him in concern. "Even if you could make it to the Capital, you would not be up to going anywhere. Isaac will be able to watch her."

Emmett smiled at Bri. "She is your daughter, Bridget. There is not a single man alive that could keep her under control."

"Emmett Young!" Bridget gasped. "She is more like you than she is me."

"She has your eyes, intelligence, and is a complete handful. That is why you handed down your locket to Miranda instead of giving it to Kyrie. Kyrie would be, who knows where, by now."

"I didn't give it to her because she is so much like you. I would never just take off." Bridget scoffed.

Emmett pulled the collar of Bridget's dress down enough that he could run his finger over the scar on her right shoulder. "Right." He said before kissing her. "Kyrie will be fine. I am sending Joshua and Samantha with her. Isaac will send regular reports."

Bridget sighed. She worried for Kyrie. She was so stubborn and willful. Kyrie needed to find someone that could keep up with her and compliment her adventurous spirit. Tomorrow morning, she would be sending her baby girl out into the world, and it terrified her.

Emmett gave her a quick kiss. "I need to make sure everything is ready for tomorrow. I will see you for dinner."

Bridget walked to the window and looked out over the garden. She needed to tell Kyrie about the Guardians, but every time she tried to bring it up, Kyrie would make excuses to leave the conversation. A letter. She would write a letter and send it to Isaac to give to Kyrie on her birthday. Bridget prayed that Kyrie would find the thing that would give her purpose.

She hurried upstairs and wrote a quick letter and sealed it. She found Blake and asked him to fly it to Isaac on his way to South Pointe. Like his father, Blake was a falcon. He kissed her cheek before shifting and flying off.

Emmett ran the Hunter's from their country estate, while Isaac was the one that organized everything from their townhouse in the Capital. It was a central base. It would have made more sense to move there, but Bridget and Emmett hated the Capital. Emmett still grew restless if he was there too long. And society was not very forgiving. They wanted their kids to grow up free of the constant pressures and expectations of society.

Isaac loved the city. Miranda's husband was a police officer within the Capital, and she didn't mind the crowds. Blake loved to travel. He was constantly on the move, never staying in one place very long. He did a lot of work for the Hunter's, relaying messages and tracking down those that needed to be stopped.

Bridget worried about each of her kids. She loved them all and hated that she did not get to see them often anymore. Kyrie was her last one, and she worried about her the most. She could not help it. Not only could Kyrie speak with animals, but Bridget suspected Kyrie could see the future, like her grandmother. It had only happened once or twice. It could be a coincidence, though. Kyrie had only had the Guardian fever once, to her knowledge. Her mother also reminded her that a Guardian was only ever given one gift.

She headed into Emmett's office and saw him sitting behind his desk. He looked up as she entered. He studied her for a moment before standing and limping over to the couch. Bridget sat next to him, and he wrapped his arms around her. He kissed her temple. "Maybe we shouldn't push her to go." Bridget sighed.

"She is going. She is twenty, Bri." Emmett ran his nose along her jaw. "She needs this. She needs to get away from here and have an adventure. To get into a little trouble." Bridget turned her head and pressed her lips to his.

"A little trouble is good, right?" Bridget asked, trying to hide her smile. She remembered their conversation about everyone needing a little trouble in their lives.

"Very good." Emmett smiled before kissing her again. "It worked out for me." He murmured against her lips, causing her to laugh.

THE END

www.ingramcontent.com/pod-product-compliance
Lightning Source LLC
LaVergne TN
LVHW011946060526
838201LV00061B/4230